MAGICRAFT MASTER

BOOK THREE

MAGICRAFT MASTER

BOOK THREE

Wilbur Woods

Podium

Cover design by Xiaoraini

ISBN: 978-1-0394-7344-7

Published in 2025 by Podium Publishing
www.podiumentertainment.com

MAGICRAFT MASTER

BOOK THREE

CHAPTER 1

Leading from the Front

Logan looked down from the deck of the Ark down at the forest below. Their expedition was down there, gathering materials—namely wood, of which Simmons was in charge, happily hewing away at the heavy, red-barked trees of this jungle land. Even though the tall, bulky man was now designated a class called **[Foe Hewer]**, he still enjoyed the simple chop of wood.

Logan knew this, as he could hear his enthusiasm all the way up here.

"Anything interesting going on there?" a soft voice called from behind. Logan swiveled his wheelchair and gave Freya a wide smile. She was holding a steaming mug—most likely some herbal concoction of the Faelves.

"No, thank Numa or whatever" Logan said. "Interesting is bad. Boring is good."

Freya chuckled as she offered him the mug. "Never in a million years would have I expected to hear something like that from you of all people."

"I've changed, haven't I?" Logan said and blew on the cup. An earthy scent of roots and herbs softly wafted up to his nose.

"For the better," Freya said. "It's still annoying when you go off on your adventures and leave me behind, or do something incredibly, stupidly risky. But the old you was a lot harder to love."

"I didn't deserve you back then," Logan said.

"You're saying you do now?" Freya asked, a mischievous twinkle in her eyes.

"C'mere, you," Logan said and pulled Freya down onto the chair with him. She yelped but landed with soft grace.

After they shared a kiss, Freya leaned against Logan's forehead. "I miss you."

"I'm right here."

"I know. But you work a lot. I guess some parts of the old you, I do miss. He gave me more attention."

Logan scoffed and kissed Freya on the tip of her nose. "I had more idle time, you mean?"

"You had nothing but." Freya grinned. "But I like you better busy."

"I like myself like this too," Logan admitted and squeezed her leg. "How's everything going downstairs?"

Freya leaned into Logan and started idly brushing his black hair. "The Faelves have taken everything in stride. Every time we find more, Snoff takes them in like an enthusiastic cousin. With some help from the other, less excitable Faelves, they integrate well."

"I see," Logan said. "That's good to hear, at least. I need to have lunch with Snoff when I have the time. But I expect there's a 'but' coming here."

"But . . . the humans are a bit trickier," Freya said. "They need proper leadership."

"What's wrong?" Logan asked. "There's you, Scilla, Simmons, Kat, and Balmer. Lots of leadership to latch onto."

"They would benefit from you spending time with them."

"I'm not a leader."

"Says who?"

"Me," Logan said. "I'm a creative type. I make stuff."

"Making people do stuff isn't that far off," Freya said.

Logan gave her a tired look. He knew when his wife was trying to persuade him.

"And if I say I don't want to?"

"Great!" Freya said. "The best leaders don't."

Freya smiled and kissed Logan on the head. He brought a hand up to hers and held her there. Logan could feel the excitement, as her hand traced down from his head to her shoulder.

"How is your . . . ?" she asked, breathily.

"I'm still a cripple, Frey," Logan said and smiled sadly.

"Hmph, you're not a cripple where it counts," Freya said and her hands darted down. "I've never done it on the deck of a ship."

"Yes, you have," Logan said but didn't resist. "Southern shore of Spain, three years ago."

"That doesn't count," she said as she unbuckled his pants with deft hands. "I was as drunk as a sailor."

"Then let's make this one really count," Logan said and pulled her into a kiss.

After the two of them had untangled and straightened their clothes, Freya rolled Logan in his wheelchair into the command room, which was currently occupied by Snoff, Tumor residing in his golem, and of course the strange stone orb which housed the collective consciousness of the Groloin, a hive-mind which had escaped destruction from Levemoth by transcending physical form.

"Report," Logan commanded.

"Hey, Logan!" Snoff cried out.

Tumor nodded through his golem, but it was more of a formality, since the AI actually lived within Logan's mind.

"How good of you to join us," the Groloin Collective that called themselves "Glaan" said in a grandmotherly tone. "There is not much to report. The team is doing a good job of acquiring the resources that are needed. There have been no attacks."

"I wonder why?" Logan asked. "The enemy must know where we are."

It wasn't necessary to avoid saying the creature's name, but Logan couldn't bring himself to do it.

They were on a great battleship in the sky. The Ark was as large as the ancient evil monster itself, so it wouldn't exactly have been hard to find if one were looking for them, and the world they were on was small.

"We believe the Great Thief is preparing," Snoff said. "It knows we are not easy prey on this mighty ship, so it gathers strength. Bides its time."

"Fortunate for us," Logan said and rolled his chair next to Tumor, patting him on his massive stony side. "How are we doing on the weapons-upgrade front?"

"It is going well, as you know," Tumor said. "I have been able to harness most of the cannons into an operation-ready state. But we are short on Numa."

"Direly short," the Hivemind said. "Flying this ship is a costly business, Logan. Gathering wood and food is all well and good, but what we need is energy. You need to send people into the ruins."

"Yeah," Logan said and grimaced. "I know."

"You say you know, yet you do nothing," the Groloin said, their voice still sweet but now with a harder, more demanding edge to it. "The Groloin Collective does not share the view of the Faelves. The Devourer is not preparing. It is waiting. Waiting for us to run out of energy. There are ruins nearby. Large ones. We believe it was a great city of the First Folk, maybe even a capital. We must delve."

The prospect of such rich ruins was definitely tempting. Not only did they need Numa, but the First Folk had artificed a magical alloy that Logan called darkmetal—a magnificent piece of craftsmanship.

It's risky, though. Can we afford risks?

"If we delve into the ruins, we are locked in that area for a few days," Logan said. "We'll be sitting ducks trying to defend the people going in. If the Levemoth floods the ruins with its spawn . . ."

"That's a risk every man and woman going in will knowingly take," Freya said.

"I'm sure I'm almost done with my design for the new weapon," Logan said. "If you just wait, I can soon delve into the ruined city myself."

"We have no time to wait," the Groloin boomed. "We must acquire more Numa or we will plummet out of the sky."

"I don't want to send people into a death trap," Logan snapped. "I want to go myself."

"Trust your people," Freya said gently and walked over to squeeze his shoulder.

"Your weapon will be much easier to design if you have Numa to experiment with," the Hivemind said sagely.

It was true, of course, but Logan hated to admit it. They did need Numa or darkmetal. Preferably both.

But Logan didn't want anyone risking their lives when there was a high chance that Levemoth was simply waiting for the right time to attack.

The great calamity of a beast had been weakened by transforming Malcolm Specter into . . . something. It had apparently been against the rules of engagement, whatever the hell they were in this situation. Levemoth had been punished by the Administrators, and that gave everyone in the world a fighting chance.

I'll need to go downstairs and see my old man soon . . .

But that was not nearly as pressing as making a decision. Could he go by himself? Or at least join the expedition party? Technically, he could. But the weapon wasn't ready yet. Still, going there even with a prototype would increase the whole party's chances of survival.

[I do not like the idea of you going anywhere in your current condition.]

Logan growled at that. He hated this. Hated sitting in this stupid chair, everyone worrying about him and thinking he needed endless help and coddling. Had he not proved himself a true warrior while defending the village?

Or countless other times? Had he not squeezed out a victory time and time again in the most impossible circumstances?

They ask me to trust my crew, but they don't trust me.

Logan didn't want to send people to their deaths, because that was exactly the kind of call his father would be comfortable doing, and Logan resented that.

[The fact that you recognize that means it isn't the same. Sending people in to risk their lives because you don't care about them is very different than sending them in when you do care.]

"What do you know about it?" Logan hissed.

The golem next to him stirred but said nothing.

"Sorry," Logan said, ignoring the curious looks he got from the rest of the people in the room. They were used to hearing these half-conversations anyway. "You're right, but it's not making me feel any better."

[It isn't my duty to make you feel better. It is my duty to assist you. Now you need assistance in breaking through your inertia. Make a decision.]

Logan nodded.

"Alright. Let's send a party to acquire Numa. You have the coordinates to this ruined capital, Groloin? Snoff will make the preparations for the Faelves, Kat and Balmer will equip the humans, and Tumor, you'll help me."

"With what?" the golem asked in a deep voice.

"With the weapon design, of course," Logan said. "I want to join the expedition."

CHAPTER 2

New Creations

A few floors down below the deck and the command center, Logan was creating a masterwork. Well, it would be a masterwork once he'd finished. Now it was still equipped with woefully inadequate materials, such as wood and bone. What Logan needed was darkmetal, and lots of it. But for now, lesser materials would have to do.

Logan had *some* darkmetal—what was left from the tatters of his liquid suit, along with some bits that they had managed to salvage from the village that had been destroyed—but the Groloin were currently using it as batteries to manage the ship. Logan missed darkmetal more than booze and waking up in the afternoon.

But we managed to build a thing of beauty even without it.

Twelve feet of polished wood and hard bone. It was a mechanical suit . . . or an exoskeleton, as Tumor insisted on calling it. Right now, as it was built from archaic materials, it wasn't as strong as the liquid suit. But Logan had ambitions. If he could craft this whole hulking construct from darkmetal, it would become the ultimate weapon.

And given the right circumstances, I could mass-produce these.

The mech had long arms that ended in sharpened bone spikes that protruded from giant wooden knuckles. The bone was black and gleamed in the dimly lit room. It was taken from Levespawn and molded by Logan in accordance with Tumor's instructions.

This was a brawler type, best suited for delves into the dark ruins left by people that Levemoth had decimated. It would not be the ultimate version, which would be able to shoot pure Numa energy. It would need a crystal formation to power it. And it would be able to fly.

Logan could see it in his mind's eye: an army of flying mech-suited humans circling Levemoth and shooting it.

Of course, Logan had not forgotten the vision: the last stand of the First Folk on the shores of this continent. Levemoth had crushed a much-stronger army in mere minutes. But this time was different. They weren't using forbidden technology and corrupted Numa. Whatever corrupted Numa they did acquire, the Groloin and Freya purified. Levemoth was being kept weak. And it had gambled and weakened itself even further in the process.

If there ever was a time to take it down, it's now.

CHAPTER 3

Preparations and Negotiations

When the Ark reached the ruins, everyone immediately descended. The whole ship was powered down and taken out of operation. The engines needed time to cool, and some repairs needed to be made. The Groloin and their golems would be in charge of that, with the help of some humans with the appropriate classes.

That would leave the Ark and all of its inhabitants vulnerable, but they had a reasonably strong fighting force. Most of their best warriors would be part of the expedition, though—Kat, Balmer, even Simmons. They needed to do this fast. In and out. Get what they could, and then get back up in the air.

It would not take long for Levemoth to realize that they had descended, and it would know that it would have to have been near some ruins. The big bastard was as old as the sky, so it must know where most of the juicy loot was hidden. It would most likely come. They needed to get this operation done in three days. Tumor gave slim odds for them staying hidden past that.

Logan felt fired up as Freya helped him into the mech. His blood was pumping and a soft sheen of warm sweat was dampening his clothes. It was nervousness, but the good kind. The kind that made you more focused and alert.

"Sure you'll be alright?" Freya asked as she stepped down after strapping him into the mech's seat with leather belts.

"Of course I'll be alright," Logan said. "You worry too much."

"Because you worry none," Freya countered. "Can't you wait?"

"I can't wait to kick some Levespawn ass," Logan responded.

Freya chuckled. "Figures. Just come back in one piece."

"That's the plan," Logan said.

"You were never good with plans, love."

"I know," he said and chuckled. "But I've got Tumor for that. He says goodbye."

"Goodbye," Freya said. Then she waved them off.

Logan turned and found he could keep his balance. Well, *Tumor* could keep their balance, but that was good enough. The mech lumbered forward in groaning steps. The oil he used for the joints had been extracted from seeds. At the side of the mech's cockpit was a satchel that contained some useful tools and bone bottles of oil, if needed.

Judging from the groaning joints, it will *be.*

[It will. But not yet. We need to be sparing with it. Ideally, we'll find natural oil eventually. That would have many uses.]

"Let's keep that in mind," Logan said and grabbed the two bone sticks that operated the mech's movement. "But I need to learn to move in this thing first."

Although Tumor completely **[Possessing]** the mech and operating it that way would have been ideal, Logan wanted to be in control for now. If danger warranted it, they had agreed that Tumor would take over.

But the point was for Logan to build a mech that anyone could control. Even though Tumor could multitask beautifully, Logan doubted he would be able to individually control hundreds of mechanized suits at once.

[But I'd like to try!]

"All in good time," Logan said and laughed as he fiddled with the crude controls. Tumor had the engineering know-how to make proper mechanized battle armor, as long as it had a power source. And Numa was one hell of a power source. Obviously the material was crude. Logan had, of course, reinforced it to be as durable as hardened steel, but you could only enchant wood and bone so far. He needed darkmetal.

[You will not find enough to equip an army.]

"Maybe not. But a strike force would be a good place to start."

The mech moved disjointedly. Logan's crippled leg rested on the power pedal. It routed Numa from the unit's core to its limbs. When Logan didn't need to power it up, he could just move the leg.

Logan lumbered out of the workshop down into the cargo bay and sprinted, jumped, and maneuvered as smoothly as he could, until he finally got the hang of it. After a while, Tumor **[Possessed]** a Groloin golem and they sparred until the mech ran out of Numa.

Logan's arms ached, and sweat was dripping from his hair. The mech was crude, and so were its controls. There was only so much they could do without building circuitry. But he *could* fight. That was what mattered. He could go down and help the others.

[Your chances of surviving against larger Levespawn, such as trolls, are fairly low. I estimate a—]

"Tumor." Logan cut him off. "I know you remember what we talked about regarding you giving me battle odds."

[We talked. I didn't say I agreed.]

"Touché," Logan said, but he smiled. "You've become a real pain in the ass ever since you developed a personality."

[Now you know what I have to suffer daily.]

"Damn, Tumor," Logan said. "You have absolutely no mercy today."

[I learn from the best. Also, I ran a simulation of 1,273 instances of this conversation as it happened, in order to ascertain the snappiest response.]

"How about we focus on troubleshooting the mech, instead of gloating?" Logan suggested. He ran a hand on the polished wood chassis that formed the cockpit of the mech. Being reinforced with Numa, it could withstand a full strike from a scythe-fiend. Yes, they had captured one. It was being studied by a group of scientists. Two of them even had Scientist as a class. Logan wasn't sure how useful that was given their limited tools, but it was good to know more about the enemy.

[I can multitask, but fine. When you punch with the right gauntlet, you sometimes lose balance, which causes the mech to overextend. It isn't something a beast like a scythe-fiend or a troll can notice, but an observant foe will use it against you.]

"User error or hardware issue?"

[You can compensate with your movement, but you'll be trading power for balance. Your piloting is actually quite effective as is. Same trade-off with the mech itself: balance in exchange for power.]

"Can't we just squeeze more out of the design?"

[Like I told you before, at this point, no. The construct is as mechanically perfect as I can make it, given the parameters. If you want to improve it, you will need better materials.]

"Fine," Logan said. "Let's go get some. But first I need to do something."

After piloting the mech back to the workshop, Logan put on a clean shirt and went back to the cargo bay. This was a different section, one that Logan had been avoiding during his mech training session.

There were scant supplies here, as Logan had created something of a shrine for his father's frozen monstrous form.

"Hey, Dad," Logan said.

Ever since they had captured him, Malcolm Specter—or the Herald—had been in stasis. Two times he had been possessed by the Levemoth and he had thrashed in his chains and spouted such foul obscenities that Freya had gagged him. Snoff personally ensured that the enchantments and illusions keeping Malcolm Specter in place were reinforced daily.

Malcolm Specter was encased in a black-and-blue carapace from head to toe. His left arm had a monstrous claw used for crushing and stabbing. His face still bore a faint resemblance to his father's familiar stern features and wide jaw, but the eyes were completely alien, overtaken by Levemoth.

Logan, for his part, suspected that Levemoth checked in on him whenever he visited. Sometimes he could see the Herald's eyes moving for just a fleeting second. When he looked again, the eyes were fixed as always.

Eerie as it was, it didn't bother him. Levemoth was not living rent-free in Logan's head. That was Tumor's job.

What did bother him was the sorry state of his once-so-mighty father.

There was no solution available.

Logan had asked for Freya to commune with the Numa goddess. She had tried a bunch of spells and blessings from her class to reach out to her, wasting an unfortunate amount of Numa, but to no avail.

The Groloin Hivemind had no answers. It was reluctant to help to begin with, insisting every time Logan had brought the topic up that they ought to destroy the Herald.

The Faelves, eager as ever to help Logan, had nothing to contribute other than keeping his father imprisoned.

"Do you think the Groloin are right?" Logan asked.

[You know what I think. And frankly, it does not matter what I think. He is your father.]

"You and the Groloin are both smarter than me."

[You of all people should know that intellect is not the highest of virtues, nor the best tool.]

"That might be the best backhanded compliment I've ever received," Logan said and laughed.

[I am not saying you're stupid. I am saying you have attributes that make you . . . superior to the Groloin Hivemind and myself.]

"Saying one person is superior to another might piss people off."

[Those people are fools and not to be paid any mind. There will always be greater and lesser people than you. Well, except for two exceptions . . .]

"The two exceptions being?"

[Hm, intellect is not your forte. But that is why you have me, your ever-diligent symbiote. The two exceptions are obviously the greatest person to have ever existed and the worst person to have ever existed.]

Logan chuckled dryly and sat down on the cargo floor, clutching his knees with his arms. He looked at his father. He wished he could talk to him now, man to man. Funny how at one time, he had had all the time in the world to connect with his father, and now that he finally wanted the opportunity, he couldn't.

Life sure has a way of being damn ironic sometimes.

After a while, Logan got up. He realized his thoughts had circled back to where they always did when he sat here. And that's why this was the point at which he always got up and left. There was a solution to free his father.

It was simple, really. Just one little task.

Levemoth had to be defeated.

CHAPTER 4

New Faces

The Ark descended to the ground with a smooth thud. The cargo bay hatch opened and the strike team emerged. Eighteen members. A lot of them Logan only knew by their faces, seen while passing in the mess hall. Now they were under his leadership. They gave curious glances at his strange woodpunk mech.

"So you decided to finally get out of your tinker-cave?" Kat asked and rapped her knuckles on the side of the mech. "Cool toy."

"I liked the previous one more," Balmer said.

"Yeah, me too," Logan said. "That's why I'm inclined to call dibs on any darkmetal we find."

"You're the boss," Kat said. Then she grinned and added, "Your Highness."

"Yeah, no, that ain't happening," Logan said.

"He just takes what he wants," Kat continued, tilting her head back and placing a theatrical wrist on her forehead. "A true despot."

"Fine, fine," Logan said. "If there's enough, I'll make a new toy for you."

"I do a lot with very little," Kat said.

"That's what she said," Logan said and nudged Balmer with the elbow of the mech. He sidestepped it smoothly.

"Funny," Balmer said and blushed.

Logan let it be. Kat and Balmer were *definitely* an item, but neither of them seemed to want it to be made public. Logan suspected it had something to do with them being constantly in front-line combat.

Simmons and his band of agents simply waited stone-faced for the banter to die down. The new raiders were not sure whether to laugh or follow the veterans' stoic example. A few of them snickered and Logan smiled. It was good to relieve their tension.

"Alright, team, we move," Logan said, raising his voice. "Simmons and I will take the helm. Kat, you're on our six. Balmer, you're on scout duty."

Simmons nodded, and Kat and Balmer gave their assent. Then Logan remembered the dozen other people needing direction. He suppressed an inner sigh.

"Any leaders among you?" Logan said as he turned to the new faces.

They gave each other inquisitive looks, wordlessly deciding who should lead. There was some muttering, until one man stepped forward.

He was lean and more of the type women called cute than handsome. His dirty blond hair covered his ears and, despite looking like he could be the lead singer of a boy band, he had a serious demeanor and nodded respectfully.

"Looks like I'm chosen," he said in a soft surfer's drawl.

"Good," Logan said. "What's your name?"

"Ryan."

"What class are you?"

"I'm a [**Bard**]."

"Oh," Logan said, raising his eyebrows. "That's a Numa-using class, isn't it?"

"It is," Ryan said. "I've got some with me."

"So you. uh . . . play an instrument?"

"No, sir. I sing."

Logan nodded slowly. "Riiight. And that does what?"

"I'm still learning. I'm only Level 4. But what it mostly does is affect emotions. I can make people feel somber, happy, angry . . . stuff like that."

"Sounds dangerous."

"Nah, man," Ryan said and gave Logan an easy smile. "It's not mind control and it's more subtle. I need to sing for a while for the effects to kick in, and they're more of a suggestion than a command."

"Alright, Ryan. That sounds like a good fit for a leader. You've just been promoted to commander of this squad. Your sole purpose until we get back to the ship is to keep these other fine men and women alive. When any of you have a problem, you come to me, and we discuss it. There *will* be fighting in the ruins. Simmons and his team, Kat, Balmer, and I are going to do the main brunt of it. Your job is to keep your guys calm and collected when it happens. You'll huddle up together, stay defensive, and listen to me. Understood?"

"Yes, sir," Ryan said and gave an enthusiastic thumbs up.

"Any questions?"

"None of us have done this before," Ryan said. "But when we volunteered for this raid, I thought we would be heading into combat. What are we supposed to do if we don't fight?"

"Your job is to experience a raid, survive it, and help us carry shit out," Logan said. "I'm sure a lot of you have a combat class or adjacent, like **[Hunter]** or something. I'm sure a lot of you have done fighting before you joined the Ark. I welcome that. But I want to keep you alive, and I want you to form a bond. You guys will become a unit that is useful in the fight against the enemy. Just like Simmons and his warriors, you will become a veteran group that works together. But we'll start small."

"Oh," Ryan said. "I like your style, man. Way to see the bigger picture."

"That's my jam, Ryan."

Then, Logan turned to the people under Ryan's leadership. "I'm sorry I can't lead you all directly. There are over three thousand people on the Ark, and I have a terrible memory for names. Even worse for faces."

A few of them chuckled.

"But I do appreciate your courage. Not many men and women out of those three thousand are willing to risk their necks to benefit everyone. I *will* learn who each of you are. But first you need to show me you can become a killer fighting force. Can you do that?"

"Hell, yeah," Ryan said.

"Yeah."

"Yes, sir."

"You got it, Mr. Specter."

Logan grimaced and shook his head. "Just Logan's fine."

This is where Logan felt at home. This was simple; this was straightforward.

He walked with Simmons at his side in easy silence. They advanced slowly, for you never knew what monsters await in the dark. Former Special Agent Felix Balmer was somewhere ahead in the darkness, silent as a cat, scouting a few hundred yards ahead. Eventually they would run into said monsters.

Monsters were fine. All you needed to do was punch them and the problem went away. Leadership, on the other hand . . .

Logan glanced back. Behind him walked a line of men and women, completely unfamiliar to him. He was responsible for them, and he would have to do his best to ensure that they get out of this adventure alive.

And then there was Ryan. When he caught Logan's eye, he gave that same reassuring smile and a thumbs-up. Was this all there was to him? Or were there darker thoughts behind his bright exterior? There was always a chance of a coup, or even Levemoth's influence . . .

[You're spiraling into negative thought patterns. Would you like me to adjust serotonin production?]

"I'm fine, Tumor," Logan muttered.

In the dim blue light of the strange wiring lining the ruins left by the First Folk, they walked, the heavy footsteps of the eight-foot mech echoing in the shadows.

Even if nothing nefarious is going on, there are bound to be power struggles, disagreements, diplomacy, power plays—a goddamn jungle of leadership politics.

Logan suddenly realized why his father was the way he was.

He had to be that way to win at the game.

Something resolved itself within Logan. He suddenly felt better, lighter. The troubled thoughts passed, and Logan felt an easy focus take over his mind.

It's interesting how a single thought, a single realization can go such a long way . . .

Tumor said nothing, but Logan could sense his pride in him. That made him feel even better.

After a few checks of long-ago ransacked rooms, and a little break, Balmer returned. He spoke in quick whispers: "There is a group of Blues ahead."

"Goddamn it," Logan muttered. "How many?"

"I saw five. But they're tricky. There might be more hidden. I got out quick."

Simmons grimaced and squeezed the haft of his axe, then went back to talk to his group of warrior agents.

At least he doesn't need me holding his hand.

Logan turned and silently motioned for Ryan to get closer. The young guy jogged up enthusiastically.

"We've got Blues up ahead," Logan said.

"Blues?"

"They're corrupted Numa zombies. They used to be people, but the enemy got to them."

"Oh, yeah, they destroyed our village," Ryan whispered. "They're nasty. How many?"

"At least five."

Ryan grimaced. Then, he nodded.

Adaptable. Cool under pressure.

"What do you need me to do?" Ryan asked.

"Assemble your men into a defensive formation. Shields and spears to the front, hand axes and clubs to the sides."

"What about the noncombatants?"

Logan thought about it for a moment, tapping the polished wood of his mech. "Put them in one of the rooms we checked back there. We'll come get them once the battle is over. How are you feeling?"

Ryan swallowed and took a moment before answering. "I'm scared."

"Well, don't let your men see that," Logan said brusquely. Then he added: "Hey, man, it's a natural reaction. But don't worry. Simmons and his men, Kat, Balmer, and I are seasoned fighters. We've faced worse odds. Do your best and keep your men alive."

"Yes, sir."

Logan watched Ryan as he went away and started issuing commands to his troops. Kat came up.

"Look at you," she said.

"Yeah, yeah."

"For all the shit I give you . . . seriously," Kat said, "good stuff."

"Thanks," Logan said. "I was told I needed to step into even bigger boots."

"They're a good look on you," Kat said. Then she punched the air with her darkmetal knuckle-dusters that Logan had made back when they still had darkmetal to spare. "Come on, let's go kick some ass."

They approached as quietly as they could. Logan got to within forty feet of the Blues before they noticed. That's when he rushed in with the full power of his mech. He knocked into the first one with a shoulder, sending it flying into a dark corridor. The next one jumped at him, and he took a haymaker. The blow made Logan stagger and almost fall, but he pivoted, planted an arm down, and in the same movement swung a mech-leg that kicked the Blue in the chin.

[Skill Level Up!]
[Power Armor Fighting Level 19]

Nice. It's been a while.

There were definitely more than five. Probably ten. The zombie brutes jumped out from the shadows, and all of Logan's carefully crafted battle plans were tossed into the bin. It was an all-out brawl. Simmons swung his axe in wide arcs. Balmer darted in and out, stabbing the Blues with his rapier, and Kat laughed as she head-locked a Blue and started smashing its head.

The only part of the plan that held together was Ryan and his troops. They were huddled against the doorway they'd entered from, holding the exit with a shield wall. Over the wall, they lobbed stones and spears, and behind them all, Ryan sang.

It was a song like Logan had never heard before. And something he certainly had not expected.

Ryan was throat-singing.

It was an uncanny sound, coming from such a young boyish guy with gentle features. A guttural deep sound resonated and echoed throughout the chamber. The sounds of smashing, screaming, and grunting were all drowned out by the song.

Logan felt energized, brave, and powerful. In a word, he was inspired. Battle-inspired. He found himself grinning just like Kat as his mech's upper body did a three-sixty spin and smashed into a Blue that Balmer was distracting. It fell and struggled on the ground, bleeding from its skull. Logan held it down with a massive mech-foot while Balmer stabbed it until it stopped moving.

"Good job! Keep going!" Logan roared over to Ryan. He nodded and kept focusing.

The Blue twitched one last time beneath the mech-foot before going still. But there was no time to celebrate. From the far end of the chamber, the hulking form of another Blue burst from the shadows, its body grotesquely swollen with layers of corrupted sinew. It roared—a wet, gurgling sound that sent shivers through Logan's spine.

"Another one incoming!" Logan shouted, spinning the mech to face it.

The creature charged, closing the distance in seconds. This one was as big as a bodybuilder back on Earth.

Logan braced himself, slamming the mech's spiked fist into the creature's shoulder as it lunged. The impact sent a crackling shockwave through the chamber, the Blue staggering to the side. But it didn't fall.

Instead, it reared back and slammed a massive, clawed hand into the mech's torso, sending Logan skidding backward. Sparks flew as the wood-reinforced metal screeched under the force.

"Logan!" Kat yelled, her voice sharp. She darted forward, leaping onto the creature's back with a feral grin. Her darkmetal knuckle-dusters gleamed as she rained down punches on its head and neck, each strike cracking the corrupted flesh like brittle glass.

The Blue roared, twisting wildly to shake her off. Simmons seized the opportunity, lunging forward with his axe. He swung in a wide arc, the blade cleaving through its side with a sickening crunch. It flinched but kept limping forward, its attention still locked on Kat.

"No, you don't!!" Balmer called out, his rapier flashing as he darted in and out, targeting its legs. He managed to hamstring the creature, forcing it to stumble and slow, but its sheer size made it difficult to take down.

"Tumor, I need more power!" Logan snarled, gripping the mech's controls tightly.

[Redirecting auxiliary reserves. Be warned: sustained use at this level will burn through Numa quickly.]

"Just do it!"

The mech hummed, its limbs glowing faintly as the redirected energy surged through it. Logan charged forward, the mech's spiked fist slamming into the Blue's chest with enough force to lift it off the ground. The creature crashed onto its back, struggling to rise, but Kat was already there. She drove her fists into its head repeatedly, screaming at the big Blue as she pulverized its skull.

The Blue twitched violently before a meaty crunch made it go limp.

"Nice work!" Logan called out, his voice hoarse. But there was no time to rest. More shapes emerged from the shadows—three, no, *four* more Blues, their glowing eyes fixed hungrily on the group.

"Fall back to the defensive line!" Logan barked. "Ryan, get your people ready to cover us!"

Kat and Simmons regrouped quickly, both breathing hard but still battle-ready. Balmer joined them, his rapier already slick with ichor. The three of them flanked Logan's mech as the new wave of Blues advanced.

"Ryan, keep singing!" Logan shouted over his shoulder. He could feel the deep sounds Ryan made empower his mech, as if it was now running slightly smoother, every turn of the joysticks unnaturally precise.

The guttural resonance of Ryan's throat-singing grew louder, filling the chamber with its eerie, primal power.

Logan felt the surge of energy again, a steady pulse that pushed back his battle fatigue. Behind him, the shield wall held firm, Ryan's recruits pelting the advancing Blues with rocks and spears. One of the brutes charged ferociously at them, ripping one person's shield off. The woman holding the shield gasped and fell, but before the Blue could get on him, the rest of the new recruits let out a heroic battle cry and hacked at the brute with spear, axe, and club.

"Hell, yeah!" Logan managed to call out before turning his attention toward the enemy reinforcements.

The first of the new attackers lunged at Simmons, its claws flashing in the dim light. Simmons ducked low, his axe rising in a brutal uppercut that split the creature's torso open. Kat took the next one, sidestepping its wild swing and delivering a spinning punch that shattered its jaw. Balmer kept to the edges, his rapier striking with surgical precision, disabling limbs and cutting tendons before darting away like a shadow.

Logan focused on the largest of the group, a towering brute, clearly another athlete from the old world.

Logan met it head-on, his mech's spiked fists slamming into its chest like twin battering rams. The creature howled, swinging wildly, but Logan dodged, pivoting the mech to deliver a devastating kick to its knee. The joint buckled with a sickening crack, and the brute collapsed, still thrashing.

[That one will need a repair. Finish it!]

Logan roared, slamming the mech's fists down onto the creature's head in rapid succession. Its skull caved in with a final, wet crunch, and it stopped moving.

The chamber fell silent. Logan let out a heavy exhale, his mech whirring softly as it powered down into a lower-energy mode. The adrenaline still coursed through Logan's veins, but the immediate danger had passed. He exhaled before collecting himself.

"Everyone okay?" Logan called out, his voice echoing in the cavernous space. His mech's limbs creaked as he turned to face the group. Simmons and Kat stepped back into the soft blue light of the ruin's wiring, both looking worse for wear but unbowed.

"All good here," Kat said, wiping blood—some of it hers, most of it not— off her cheek with the back of her hand. She grinned like a feral cat. "That was fun. Let's do it again."

Simmons grunted, his axe dripping with blood. "I've had my fill, thanks."

Balmer strode over, rapier in hand, his movements deliberate, his composure solemn. Despite their victory, he looked dejected. "I guess there were more than five."

Logan couldn't hold back a smirk. "A little bit more."

"Sorry."

"Look," Logan said. "You put your ass on the line every time you go up ahead and scout for us. We expect you to bring information, not perfect information."

"Well said," Kat said and clapped Logan on the shoulder. Then she went over to Balmer, kissed him on the forehead, and hugged him fiercely.

Logan smiled at that. He got what Kat meant. Surviving another life-or-death situation was not something to take for granted.

Once Balmer had untangled himself, he continued being a sourpuss.

"I'll do better next time."

"It's cool, man," Logan said. "Don't worry, don't beat yourself up, and keep your head cool. We're still in a dungeon." Logan then clapped Balmer on the shoulder before turning away.

He surveyed the scene. The battlefield was littered with ravaged bodies, their corrupted, blue-tinged flesh twitching faintly even in death.

Logan looked back to where in the faint blue light he could see a row of faces, bloodied and eyes wide with shock and horror. Amongst them Logan spotted a blond shag of hair.

"Ryan!"

The bard emerged from his group by the shadows near the doorway, their formation still intact. The shield wall wavered as the tension eased. A few of the men dropped down on their knees and cried quietly. Most were silent. Two were wounded, neither of them badly.

Ryan stepped forward, his face pale but resolute.

"We're all here," he said, his voice steady despite the faint tremor in his hands. "No casualties."

Logan nodded approvingly. "Good work. That song of yours—damn, that was something."

Ryan chuckled, rubbing the back of his neck. "Didn't think I'd ever be throat-singing in a fight, but, uh, seemed to do the trick."

"You can drop that off your bucket list" Logan said and laughed. "Keep it up. Your team held the line, and that's what matters."

Ryan glanced back. "I think we are going to need a break."

Logan nodded. He didn't like it, but he had to agree. Most of the new recruits were in some form of shell shock. One of them, a young woman with short, messy hair, stepped forward. She was holding a bleeding arm with a broken shield still tied to it.

"Sir," she said, timidly, "what now?"

Logan motioned everyone to gather around.

"We'll take ten minutes to patch up the wounded and rest. Eat whatever rations you brought, breathe deeply, get it out of your system."

Logan was mostly addressing the new recruits, but he knew even Simmons's agents had a tough time dealing with the ferocity of the Blues.

"After that, Kat, you'll take two of Ryan's men and help them take these wounded back to the Ark."

Kat nodded. "Should we come back?"

"Absolutely," Logan said. "We'll, uh . . . Tumor, let me out of this thing."

With a hiss of releasing pressure and some struggling out of a harness securing him into the chair of the mech, Logan managed to clamber and limp out. It was undignified as all hell, but it got the job done.

Logan retrieved an **[E-grade Numa Crystal]** from his pocket and went about ripping the half-rotting clothes off the dead Blues.

"[Repair]."

[Skill Level Up!]
[Repair Level 21]

"Nice," Logan muttered. "Gained a level!"

"Good stuff," one of the agents watching him said.

What had been rotten and tattered was now a bundle of clean and smooth cloth, as if freshly made. Logan transmuted it into a massive ball of yarn. Then he tied it to the ankle of the nearest corpse.

"We'll leave you a trail," Logan said.

"Smart," Balmer said.

"Stupid," Kat said and crossed her arms. "This isn't a labyrinth. You think I won't catch up to you without training wheels?"

"I don't like taking dumb chances," Logan said. "Besides you're babysitting two newbies."

"Fine," Kat said and blew annoyedly at some of the fiery red hair dangling over her forehead.

Logan got up and glanced around the chamber. The ancient ruin stretched into darkness beyond the group, its walls covered in intricate carvings that pulsed faintly with blue light. The wiring hummed softly, the only sound beside Logan's softly churning mech.

"We move forward," Logan said. "This was just the welcoming party. If the Blues are here, it means we're on the right track. There should be Numa close by. If we find enough, I can make us seriously better equipment."

Simmons stepped up beside him, his axe resting on his shoulder. "And if there are more of them waiting for us?"

Logan met his gaze. "Then we deal with them. Same as always. Help me back up into this thing, Simmons."

Simmons nodded and proceeded to give him a hand.

Kat clapped her hands together. "Alright, let's get moving. Standing around in this creepy-ass ruin isn't doing my nerves any favors. You two, uninjured? Good. You're with me."

Logan turned back to Ryan. "Get your people ready. We're heading deeper in. Stay alert, stay together. If anyone sees anything out of place, call it in immediately."

Ryan nodded and began issuing quiet instructions to his group. Logan turned to Tumor, whose presence was a steady hum in the back of his mind.

[The wiring along the walls indicates that this area once had a significant power source, larger than the ones we have found previously. If the Numa crystal is still functioning, it will be deeper within the structure.]

"Good eye, Tumor."

[Thanks.]

"What kinds of odds do you think that gives this place of having a lot of Levespawn?

[Very high. As you know, the corruption typically concentrates around sources of Numa. Expect stronger resistance the closer we get.]

Logan sighed. "Of course."

CHAPTER 5

Ruins of the First Folk

The group moved cautiously through the ruins, the air growing colder with each step.

It was clear this was no ordinary ruin. It had vast corridors and countless rooms, more like an underground city than a building. But it was austere. It might have been a capital, but it was clearly made by war-torn people, judging by the walls, which were lined with carvings depicting scenes of battle, creation, and destruction—ancient wars fought by the First Folk against creatures that looked disturbingly similar to the Levespawn. The blue glow cast eerie shadows, making the carvings seem almost alive.

Despite their hardship, they still made time for art.

Logan's mech clunked softly with each step, the crude materials straining under the weight of its movements. He gripped the bone controls tightly, his eyes scanning the darkened corridors before them. Balmer led the way, his footsteps nearly silent as he scouted ahead. Simmons flanked Logan, his axe at the ready, while Ryan and his group followed at a cautious distance.

"This place gives me the creeps," Logan muttered. "Feels like the walls are watching us."

"Maybe they are," Simmons said grimly. "Levemoth can probably see through any of his creatures."

Logan didn't respond. Simmons was right, but he didn't want to mention it.

His focus was on the path ahead, where the corridor widened into a massive chamber. The ceiling was high and the room was round, as if this had been a town square of sorts.

The air was thick with the hum of energy, and the blue glow was brighter here, illuminating the space in an unnatural light.

The chamber was dominated by a massive structure in the center—a towering pillar of floating crystalline material that pulsed with faint blue light. This was it. The Numa crystal. A big one.

This one was *quality* work. A well-cut, well-polished, **[A-grade Numa Crystal]**.

"We hit the motherload," Logan said, his voice reverent. "Alright, team—"

A guttural roar cut him off.

From the shadows beyond the crystal, a massive figure emerged. It was easily three times the size of the Blues they had fought earlier, its hulking form covered in thick, black-and-blue hide.

Its eyes glowed blue, and its arms ended in jagged, blade-like appendages. It used one of them to charge at them like a gorilla, while it raised the other blade in the air.

Logan had never seen Levespawn like this. It was like an unholy mix between a troll and a scythe-fiend. His instincts told him to run, possibly while peeing his pants in fear. He overrode those, subvocalizing a request for help from Tumor with a neuropathic boost. Tumor complied and a powerful rush of focus and bravery flooded Logan's mind. Instead of turning tail, he charged at the beast, meeting its rush head-on.

The monster roared again, charging forward with terrifying speed. Logan moved to intercept, his mech's limbs whirring as he brought up an arm to block the creature's strike. They slammed into each other in a terrible crash. The creature roared in anger and pain, as blood seeped from its mouth. But Logan's mech took some damage too. Splinters of wood and bone filled the air as the mech's left shoulder exploded from the force of the impact.

[Critical damage. Commencing overdrive.]

The impact sent a jolt through the mech, nearly knocking Logan out of his seat.

The mech rattled at the force. Logan hit his head on the back of the cushioned seat. His mind was reeling from a slight concussion, as the massive roaring maw of jagged teeth a foot from his face bit and snapped rabidly, only the chassis of the mech's design preventing Logan from suffering a very painful death.

"ATTACK IT!" Logan screamed, shoving back with all the mech's strength. The monster staggered but recovered quickly, its blade-like arms slicing through the air with deadly precision. Logan grabbed its arms and tried to push it against a wall, but the creature held its own. The mech's legs, on the other hand, buckled.

Simmons appeared at the creature's flank, his axe carving deep gashes into its blue flesh. Balmer circled behind, his rapier flashing as he aimed for weak points. Its crotch, mainly.

But it didn't slow down. Just like the Blue brutes, this one seemed to be able to ignore pain. The monster lashed out. It removed itself from Logan's grip and, with great force, slammed its blade-arms into the ground with enough force to crack the ancient tiles. The force of the blow sent tremors through the dark corridors.

Logan seized the opportunity, lunging forward and driving the mech's spiked fist into the creature's chest. The impact sent it stumbling back. But that only made it angrier.

[We cannot keep this up, Logan. The mech is damaged. The shoulder is at 29% power, and we are bleeding Numa.]

"Keep it off-balance!" Logan shouted to his team. "Don't let it recover!"

The team pressed the attack, their strikes coordinated and relentless. Ryan's voice rose above the chaos, his throat-singing filling the chamber once again. The sound was haunting and powerful, bolstering the group's resolve.

"Take control of it, Tumor. I still have some Numa. I'll fix the mech."

[You got it.]

The mech started moving of its own accord, as Tumor used their **[Possess]** ability granted by his **[Machine Soul]** class. The mech moved with efficiency and precision, but Logan could tell the moves were predictable. He just hoped Tumor could buy them enough time.

The Levetroll roared in frustration, its movements growing more erratic as it took damage.

Logan's hands worked faster than his mind. It was all instinctive.

First, he snapped the harness off. The mech shook, and Logan did his best to balance on one-and-a-half legs.

[Logan, be careful!]

Logan climbed to the edge of the framework surrounding the mech's cockpit and placed the Numa crystal he had taken out of his pocket onto the mech's shoulder joint.

[Hold on to something.]

Logan didn't ask questions. He pinned his good leg against the cockpit and held onto the shoulder.

Tumor spun the mech's whole upper body while the legs held still, breaking free from the monster's grip and slamming it with a devastating haymaker. The creature stumbled back and Simmons jumped at it, roaring in a high jump, bringing his large axe down in a powerful cleave.

The mech clunked and sputtered. The movements became glacial.

[I need to shut it down or the energy leakage will grow exponentially.]

"**[Repair]**," Logan said. Magically, the wooden shoulder knitted itself back together. "There's still some energy in this. Where do I put it?"

[Here.]

A small shaft opened in the cockpit, under the seat.

Logan climbed back into the cockpit, strapped himself in, and dropped the half-used **[D-grade Numa Crystal]** down the shaft. Immediately, the mech sprang back into life. Tumor didn't wait. Simmons was getting overpowered. There was a nasty gash on his chest that was bleeding with every swing of his axe.

The mech crashed into the beast with breakneck speed. The monster was swept off its feet and toppled. The mech pinned it down and kept the thrashing creature in place.

"NOW!" Logan roared. "Finish it!"

The party didn't have to be told twice. All of them—including Ryan's recruits—rushed toward the creature in a tight line, all screaming and wildly attacking the creature until it finally stopped thrashing.

Logan found himself panting in the mech's cockpit, shoulders tense and heart pounding. The hulking monster had stopped twitching, but the room was still, everyone holding their breath to see if the creature was still alive.

Logan looked around to see how his crew was doing.

Ryan's recruits were huddled in a corner, trembling. This had all been a bit much for their first trial by fire. They'd fought off waves of regular Blues, giving them their first lesson in fighting a real battle. But that monstrous scythe-armed troll-thing had been a whole other story. Logan caught the eye of a young man clutching a hand axe dripping with the monster's innards and looking away, eyes wide with horror.

"Everyone, just breathe," Logan said, forcing calm into his voice. "It's down for now. Relax."

The new recruits all collapsed to the ground in response.

"Ryan," Logan said.

The young man approached. "Yes?"

"Sing something that will help everyone calm down and get back some energy. Can you do that?"

"I think so," Ryan said and nodded.

"Good," Logan said.

Ryan started a soft lullaby. It had no words, just gentle, lilting sounds, like a hymn. Logan felt his shoulders relax immediately. But he had no time to take it easy quite yet. He looked at his second-in-command.

"Simmons, you're hurt."

"Only a flesh wound," Simmons said. He gave a cough that sounded wet, but when he stepped away from the monster's fallen form, Logan could see the big man was still standing. Blood stained his shirt, and it was ripped, a gash made by one of the giant blade-arms clearly visible through the tear. Just a flesh wound, indeed. A deep one.

"That thing was huge," Balmer said softly, stepping forward. His features were unnaturally pale as he swallowed, forcing composure. "But what the hell is it?"

"Good question." Logan said. "Must be some kind of troll-cross, like troll-spawn. If the enemy spliced a scythe-fiend and a troll, and maybe even a Blue or something like that . . . makes sense it would be bigger, badder, and harder to kill."

Everyone fell into a contemplative silence at that. If Levemoth could make a lot of these things, they'd be in trouble.

The silence lingered.

That was fine. Logan wasn't feeling chatty.

He glanced at Kat's empty spot. She still hadn't returned from escorting the wounded back to the Ark. He didn't like it. But he couldn't just wait around. There was more rummaging and growling echoing outside the cavern. There were more enemies here.

[We need to act, Logan.]

"Alright," Logan said. "We need to rest here. I'll start working with this Numa crystal soon enough. Simmons, you secure the perimeter. Ryan, take your group somewhere away from this mess."

Ryan guided his recruits away from the gore. They stared at the corpse in wide-eyed silence, some wiping blood and sweat from their brows. Some of them looked at Logan, some looked at Simmons' wound, and a few stared at the mech in awe and fear. They had probably never seen fighting like that before. Hell, neither had Logan.

I do miss the Armor though . . .

[Me, too. It was an excellent design. But we have no time for reminiscing. The mech's sensors are detecting tremors. There is something large moving this way. It's still faint. I don't know how far away it is.]

Logan felt his gut clench. Another one of those monsters? They might not have the resources to handle a second giant scythe-armed troll. The mech's shoulder was still creaking, even after the makeshift repair.

"Change of plans," Logan called out. "We've got company."

Simmons limped but steadied the grip on his axe. Balmer swallowed and took a ready stance, though he was breathing like he'd just run ten miles.

There was one long, tense moment of silence. Then Logan could hear the tremors too.

A roar tore through the half-collapsed entryway. The sound was raw and angry, resonating throughout the chamber. The footsteps that followed were thunderous. And then another one of those troll-mutants finally came into view, hulking like the first but with sharp bone spines along its back, just like the scythe-fiends.

The monster wasted no time. Instead of charging Logan's group, it rushed toward Ryan's line of recruits, as if drawn to the fear wafting off them. Ryan tried to rally them, launching into that same throat-singing that had lent them courage in the earlier fight. But before the effect could help, the monster was amongst them.

Screams echoed as one recruit was sent flying in two pieces, the result of a huge scythe slicing through him. Another's spear snapped like a twig when he tried to block. The shield wall they'd formed earlier broke apart in seconds. Ryan dove to the side, narrowly avoiding a lethal swipe.

Logan cursed under his breath and shoved the mech forward, ignoring the jolt of fresh pain in his battered shoulder. The mech's stride was uneven, but it thundered across the chamber. He aimed to grab the trollspawn before it slaughtered the entire group.

Logan was too slow. Another brutal strike was slamming down on Ryan, who was scrambling out of the way in a panic.

A streak of red hair shot into the fray the next instant. Kat was back. She tackled the monster mid-strike, toppling it off balance. It only just missed Ryan.

Kat slipped her arms around its massive neck and tried to choke it, but it jerked around violently. She turned her hold into a headlock, putting all her weight on it.

"Kat!" Logan yelled, steering the mech around, trying to avoid hitting her while lining up a punch.

"Little busy," she growled, clinging to the thing's back. There was a flash of her darkmetal knuckles as she attempted to pummel its skull. A spined ridge along the back of the creature's neck lashed out, catching her in the ribs. She gave a pained scream and lost her grip.

Balmer roared. "Get off her!"

Logan was already there. He seized the monster's arm with the mech's massive wooden fingers. Tumor boosted the hydraulics, straining to keep the troll in place. With its free arm, the creature swiped downward, slicing deep into the mech's elbow joint. Sparks and splinters flew.

[The arm will give out soon. We are already at near-max capacity.]

"Just hold it!" Logan said. He flicked a switch and reached for the half-depleted Numa crystal he'd used earlier. They needed something bigger. "We're not going to brute-force this one. We're gonna blow it the hell up."

Kat lay on her side, coughing and pressing a hand to the blood seeping through her leather vest. Balmer and Simmons tried to get a shot in, but the trollspawn's frenzied thrashing made it impossible to close in safely. Meanwhile, Ryan scrambled to pull the recruits back, looking pale but steadfast.

Logan's mind raced. "Tumor, can we jettison one of the mech's arms? The one that's busy hacking?"

[We can, but it won't be functional afterward. Are you sure?]

"Yes. We need a distraction."

[Affirmative.]

Outside, the troll roared in fury and staggered, still pinned by the mech's grip. A loud crack reverberated as Tumor disengaged the left arm. In a spark of blue energy, it detached, blasting through the air, still latched to the monster's blade-limb, spinning both it and the troll in a half-circle. The troll gave a crazed shriek as it toppled sideways, losing balance.

Logan took that opportunity. He scrambled out of the mech's cockpit, awkwardly hopping on his weak leg until he was behind the machine. The leftover D-grade Numa crystal had maybe enough juice for a quick **[Repair]** spell. But that wouldn't kill this monster. They needed something bigger— something that would blow a crater into it.

He dug into the mech's storage compartment and pulled out a small water flask made of thick, bone-laced resin. Perfect for storing liquids, hopefully stable enough to hold raw Numa.

[Hurry, Logan. Its focus is shifting.]

"I'm working on it." Logan took the battered crystal and made a hobbling sprint toward the giant floating Numa crystal.

"**[Funnel]**!"

The massive crystal barely flickered as it was drained to fill the **[E-grade Numa Crystal]** in Logan's palm. He then quickly transmuted it into a cylinder form and dropped it into the flask.

To hell with worrying about corrupted Numa now.

Immediately, the giant beast turned, and for a fleeting, terrifying moment, met Logan's eyes with its rabid gaze. It started to barrel toward him.

"Logan!" Kat yelled, but she was on the ground, too wounded to do anything.

Logan pressed the flask to the massive floating crystal. He inhaled, willing the Numa to flow. The glowing essence bled from the crystal in glimmering threads that twisted into the flask. As soon as there was a sufficient amount of Numa inside, Logan chanted softly under his breath:

"Fill this Flask to the brim with unstable Numa. Make it explode into pure energy when the flask breaks on impact."

The item flashed pale blue.

[Subclass Level Up!]
[Transmutation Level 37]

"Done," he rasped, letting the fresh minty feeling wash over him as he gained another level. Now was no time to celebrate.

Tumor tackled the monster with the mech, and toppled it just in time, a mere eight feet before it reached Logan. It still attempted to scramble forward in a rage. The mech grabbed the monster's leg. Logan didn't hesitate.

The monster lurched up, wrenching free of the mech's damaged grip. It snapped the limb off, shattering it into wooden shards, then turned its burning blue eyes on Logan. In that split second, Logan saw genuine, lucid hatred there. This was no mindless beast. The monster flashed a malevolent grin.

Levemoth.

It roared and lunged. The mech, controlled by Tumor, stepped into its path. It used its shoulder to push the monster aside, preventing a direct hit on Logan but paying for it. The troll's own spined shoulder jammed into the mech's torso with a sickening crunch of wood. Sparks and azure glow sputtered from the cracked cockpit area.

Logan knew this was the moment. He threw the flask and fell on his knees. The flask struck the monster's thigh and dropped onto the ground at its feet. The monster looked at it, then grabbed it, intending to throw it back. Logan crawled the hell away as fast as he could.

"Simmons! Balmer! Clear out!" Logan yelled at the top of his lungs. "Everyone, down!"

The recruits scattered, Ryan diving for cover with them. Kat was close by, gasping with pain. Balmer surged from where he was standing to blanket her with his body. Simmons dove behind the remains of a fallen stone column.

A brief silence—then, a blast ripped through the air.

Blinding white-blue light flooded the cavern as the flask detonated. The shock wave hit like a sledgehammer, throwing dust, debris, and bits of the monster in all directions. Logan felt the surge in his bones. The mech's body shielded him from the worst of it, though a few chunks of stone struck his shoulders and back. He rolled onto his side, covering himself in the fetal position, hands over head.

For a few moments, no one spoke. The explosion had drowned out all other noises in a deafening crescendo that left ears ringing. Slowly, Logan pushed himself upright, blinking away spots from his vision. He coughed, throat raw from the swirling dust.

"Everybody alive?" he croaked.

From behind a pile of broken pillars, Simmons coughed. "Aye, I'm good."

Kat coughed loudly as well. "Saved by my knight in shining armor."

Balmer groaned in pain. "Still kicking."

Kat looked at Balmer, and her eyes widened in shock. His back was messed up.

"Someone help him!" Kat yelled. "Medic!"

One of the agents sprinted toward Balmer, getting a piece of clean cloth from his satchel.

The monster was no more. Where it had stood was a blasted crater, its charred remains giving off a nasty stink. Bone and burnt-off gore lay scattered around. The floor was blackened, and bits of the ruined mech arm were fused into the stone.

Logan forced himself to stand, leaning against the floating crystal. The blue gem was warm and comforting. He felt like he'd aged ten years in ten minutes.

And yet, I must be the one to get on my feet first and lead.

Ryan stared at the crater, slack-jawed. "That . . . was intense," he said, voice hoarse. He was trembling but alive.

Kat limped over to Logan, pressing a hand to her wounded side. Blood stained her fingers. "Nice job with that boom. Saved our asses."

He nodded laughing, short and exhausted. "I always had a flair for dramatics."

From the far side, Simmons walked over, wincing at his chest wound. He leaned against his axe for support. "I've got another flesh wound. We are going to need medical assistance. There's also . . ."

Simmons pointed and Logan followed with his eyes. Two of the recruits had been slashed up by the monster. They weren't moving. Hell, one of them was in two pieces.

"Goddamn it," Logan said.

Balmer, eyes still darting warily around, said, "We need to get out of here. That explosion might attract every monster in the ruins."

"No," Logan said, voice grim. "We stay and harvest the crystal. After that, we will have expendable Numa again and I can make us equipment and—"

"Don't be ridiculous," Kat snapped, even though her voice was shaky. "You want us to keep going?"

"She is right," Simmons said matter-of-factly. "Look at us. Almost everyone is wounded."

"I don't think we should keep going, sir," Ryan chimed in. "My group . . . they can't just keep going. Not after what happened to Samuel and Jessica . . ."

Logan looked at the two corpses and he stopped. They were right. Maybe the agents could go on. But Simmons was bleeding. So were Kat and Balmer. Logan himself was injury-free by some kind of miracle, but his mech was absolutely destroyed, nothing but stray bits remaining. He couldn't soldier through, unless he wanted to crawl.

And yet . . .

"If we leave this crystal as is, more monsters are likely to congregate. Plus, we can't keep the Ark on the ground for long or we risk Levemoth absolutely flooding us with monsters. All of you can go. I understand this has been . . . A lot. But I have to stay and make use of this Numa crystal or Samuel and Jessica died for nothing."

There was a long silence and then a lot of muttering. Kat was clearly about to say something, but Balmer grabbed her hand and shook his head.

Logan cursed to himself. He knew they were tired and hurt. Hell, he was tired too, albeit not hurt, which actually made the situation worse. But his mind was made up. It was for the good of their cause, and he needed his comrades to suck it up this time.

So he kept silent and only glared sternly at all of his allies one by one. Only Kat glared back; the others averted their eyes.

[A pragmatic decision. I approve of it.]

"Yeah . . . It's the only choice," Logan muttered under his breath. "But that sure wasn't a people-pleasing announcement."

[Your job is not to please them. It is to lead them.]

"Goddamn right. But damn, is it a shitty job sometimes."

The silence lingered. Finally, Simmons groaned and got up, leaning on his great axe.

He spoke up first. "Fine. I understand. I will stay and guard you."

Then he turned to one of his agents. "Hosenbaum, run back and get me Group Two. Also, tell Freya that we need a rescue party organized."

An agent with shaggy red hair and beard nodded and got up.

Logan was about to interject, but Simmons cut him off.

"You did well, Young Master," Simmons said, using Logan's old moniker from their old world. "You aren't the stupid brat you once were. These are hard decisions to make. I am impressed you have the guts for it. Now, let me do the rest."

Logan groaned, raised a weak thumbs-up, and slumped on his back.

Then, something strange happened. Logan wasn't crafting anything nor manipulating Numa in any way. However, he got a system message.

[Special Milestone Reached.]
[Artificer Level 10]
[Keystone Skill Acquired: Transmutate Material]

"Holy crap."

CHAPTER 6

New Gear

The rescue party came and went. It consisted of two dozen humans and half as many Faelves. They were led by a strike force of agents, Hosenbaum at the helm.

The rescue party worked efficiently, as Freya had trained them. They patched up the wounded right there with bandages, healing salves, and a bit of magic. William, the **[Alchemist]**, was with them, and Logan gave him a wave. Their primary **[Healer]**. Dr. Rosenbaum, was old and certainly not the type to delve into dungeons, so Logan wasn't surprised he wasn't there.

Additionally, a team led by Faelves came with carts filled with bars of darkmetal. Logan looked at the piles of precious metal covetously, but he knew that the ship needed fuel. Most of the Numa in the massive crystal would be used by the Groloin Hivemind.

But I'll get to play with the leftovers.

Logan couldn't wait. He knew precisely what his new skill did, whether because the Administrators had somehow imparted him with the knowledge, or it was something instinctive related to his class.

Either way, it was awesome.

Once everyone was patched up, they laid out stretchers to carry the wounded and the two dead recruits away. Kat and Balmer went too, as both of their wounds were fairly serious.

That left Logan alone with Simmons and ten of his agents.

After the echoes of the departing rescue party faded into the high shadows of the strange blue ruins, Simmons set up a guard perimeter. Since there were only two entrances into the large chamber, it was easily done with just a few men. After that was settled, Simmons came up to Logan.

"What now?"

"Now—" Logan said, pausing for dramatic effect, "—we make magic happen."

He groaned as he got up and stood next to the giant floating crystal, leaning against it.

"Bring me that splinter of my busted-up mech," Logan said to Simmons. "Actually, grab a friend and bring all of the wood, bone, and even bits of those two ugly-ass monsters here."

A few of the agents looked at each other and shrugged. Sure, everyone sort of knew what kind of abilities Logan had, but most of them had only ever witnessed the end result of his gadgets.

Frankly, I prefer it that way, but today calls for an exception. Besides, if this skill works like I think it does, then some really awesome stuff is coming.

Logan first picked up the massive ripped-off arm of one of the troll-scythe-monsters. It was still dripping with blood, and it weighed a ton, but with Simmons's help, he managed to drag it next to the crystal. Touching the arm with one hand and placing the other on the crystal, he cast a command:

"Turn the flesh and bone into steel."

[Keystone Skill Level Up!]
[Transmutate Material Level 2]

[Logan . . . This changes everything.]

"I know, right?" Logan said and grinned.

The arm glowed blue for a while, until it started turning into gleaming metal, spreading out until it enveloped the whole arm. It clunked when Logan let go of it.

"Impressive," Simmons said. "Never do that to me."

Logan's eyes went wide. "Damn . . . I didn't even consider that. Admittedly I got the ability to do this kind of alchemy just now. I'll have to try it out. Although I doubt it will work."

"Why's that?"

"Because that'd be too easy," Logan said and gave Simmons a wry smile. "And we don't do that here."

Simmons and Peterson, the muscular agent beside him, laughed.

"Right you are, sir," Peterson said.

"Just Logan."

Peterson rubbed the back of his bald head. "I'll try."

"What's next?" Simmons asked.

"That's easy," Logan said. "Tumor, give me the specs for a tactical knife. No handle, just tang."

Tumor did as requested, and Logan chanted a command to remove the exact ounces of metal from the giant metal arm. Then he transformed it into a beautiful and sharp tactical knife.

"And now for the fun part," Logan said. "[**Mass Produce**]."

[Skill Level Up!]
[Mass Produce Level 15]

The metal arm transformed into a massive pile of blades and tangs. There had to have been at least thirty of them. They clattered as they hit the ground.

"You can never have too many knives, right?" Logan said and smiled, a devilish grin on his face.

Simmons laughed. "Ain't that the truth."

"Make sure everyone who was on the expedition gets one," Logan said.

Simmons grew serious immediately. "Of course."

"Have the crafters process and finish them. I'm sure they'll love the opportunity to level-up."

"That's great," Simmons said. "How much juice does that crystal have?"

After the darkmetal batteries had drained it a bit, it was significantly dimmer than the bright blue it had been during their fight. However, it should have still had a solid amount for Logan to play with. Logan inspected the Numa crystal.

[A-grade Numa Crystal, 18%]

"Enough for me to have a look at that axe."

Simmons hesitated but handed it over. It was a dented old thing, and Logan had made a new axe head and shaft for it at least a dozen times. However, this time, since they had the Numa to spare, he would craft something special. He had learned a thing or two about molding and enchanting wood lately when working with the mech.

He first used [**Repair**] on the axe and then started placing enchantments on it.

"Make this axe light to wield. Make it hard as a diamond, and accelerate the swing on every strike."

Logan closed his eyes and felt the axe. That was about as much as a regular axe of wood handle and steel head could hold. The fact that they had steel was simply amazing, and Logan was the only person who could produce it currently.

"It's not as much as I'd like to give, but I don't think you've wielded better."

Logan offered the axe, now easily handing it over with a straight hand. Simmons took the axe and his eyes went wide.

"It's so light!"

"Take a swing with it, and smash it into the ground."

"The ground? It's stone."

"Humor me."

Simmons hesitated but did as ordered. With a grunt he smashed the axe into the floor. It cleaved a wide gash a foot deep and almost lost balance in the process.

"Goddamn," Simmons said and whistled. He started swinging the axe around, in excited wide arcs.

"Glad you like it," Logan said.

With all of the materials at hand, he enchanted his own clothes as well as Simmons' to be extra durable and to repel moisture, basically making them waterproof.

Then he made more weapons—mostly spearheads and shield bracings. He gave the spearheads a light sharpening enchantment that a regular user would barely notice. But it would make a difference.

Logan wanted to make all kinds of wild things. Scythe-rangs, blade-whips, rapiers with extending heads when used to lunge, like the one Balmer had. But after several long discussions with Tumor, he had relented.

More spearheads and shield bracings it is . . .

They were simply the most cost-effective. Spears and shields tended to be the best approach, especially with inexperienced warriors fighting in formations. A blade-whip? That was just asking for someone to lose an ear.

The unfortunate downside was that making those items was so by rote that Logan didn't even need to ask for the specs for their dimensions and weight. He knew them by heart. Which also meant, by the strange system governed by this world, that he barely gained any levels or experience.

But this is how it's gotta be.

He did, however, get some levels by using his new ability on the broken bits of the mech.

The mech itself was beyond repair, and Logan had no time to make another one here. But through his wits, he did manage to make a pretty nifty power armor.

"Turn these pieces into aluminum."

[Keystone Skill Level Up!]
[Transmutate Material Level 3]

"Turn these pieces into a fiberglass composite."

[Keystone Skill Level Up!]
[Transmutate Material Level 4]

[Logan, did I already mention this was amazing?]

Logan grinned. He started transmuting the material to the shapes suggested by Tumor and soon he had simple power armor.

It was basically enchanted sticks of composite affixed to two elastic rings that attached to Logan's chest under the armpits and his hips. The sticks were then attached to his arms and legs, and *voila!* Makeshift power armor. The sticks were also flexible to allow full movement, and they had enchantments for strength, so Logan could actually do his job as a warrior and all-around impressive leader.

"No more wheelchair for me," Logan said. "Feels good to not be limping."

"Why didn't you make one before?" Simmons asked.

"We were so strapped for resources. I used my . . . allowance on the mech."

"I'm sorry, allowance?"

"I'm in charge of operations, but the Groloin Hivemind is in charge of Numa usage. It's better that way, since it . . . they . . . whatever you want to call them, is in charge of keeping the ship in the air."

"Makes sense," Simmons said. "It just seems like a lifetime ago since I heard of you having an allowance."

"Don't I know it, Simmons," Logan said and laughed.

Then he surveyed the pile of leftover bone and steel from the partial remains of the mech and the chunk of troll-metal he'd harvested. He had big plans for them, but a quick glance at the now-nearly dimmed **[A-grade Numa**

Crystal] told him he was running low on juice. The swirling blue glow pulsed feebly, indicating it might only have a handful of transmutations left to give.

"I've got enough for a couple more goodies," he said. "Tumor, confirm?"

[We're down to less than 7%, if that. We can safely do two, maybe three major enchantments or item modifications before the crystal is spent.]

"That's what I figured," Logan said. He knelt by the meager salvage from their makeshift camp. There were splintered shield boards, broken spear shafts, and a few lumps of steel gleaned from the remains of the monster's bone plating, plus some leftover scraps from the destroyed mech.

Simmons paced around the perimeter, his new axe resting on his shoulder. A couple of his men sat in a circle, passing a water canteen and munching crumbly rations. Ryan's people had already been sent back to the Ark with the rescue party, along with Kat, Balmer, and the rest of the wounded. It was just Logan, Tumor (in his mind), and a large, half-collapsed ruin chamber guarded by Simmons' men.

Logan stretched his shoulders, ignoring the dull ache that threatened to seize him any time he rested for more than a minute.

"Alright," he announced, "I'm not gonna do anything super fancy. But I think I can cobble together better gear than you guys have now."

"Works for us," Simmons said. "They were talking among themselves earlier how they wish they had bone-plates for better coverage."

Logan nodded. Bone-plate. Standard fare. He would have loved to make Kevlar and flex his new transmutation ability, but it was costly in terms of Numa, as Tumor had noted.

But that didn't stop him from wanting to add a dash of his own spin to it. He pointed at the lumps of troll-bone and wood. "Bring those over."

Two of the soldiers dragged them to Logan. He sat next to the crystal, placed a hand on the shards, and closed his eyes. Taking a breath, he felt for the swirling essence in the crystal. Tired as he was, he still had some mental focus to manage an enchantment or two.

"I want these scraps to become a bone-plate," Logan said, voice rhythmic. Then he added the dimensions and math that Tumor fed him.

[Attribute Level Up!]
[Focus: 39]

A faint glow shimmered around the bone, crawling over every splinter. Then, one by one, the shards molded themselves into curved plate segments.

The bone fragments fused into the plates, forming sleek edges and reinforcements.

Then Logan added the enchantments.

"Flexible. Sturdy. Blood-repellent. And maybe a bit of shock absorption for when these guys get slammed." He paused. "Oh, and add in some Flame Resist, just in case."

[Attribute Level Up!]
[Efficiency: 44]

Then he used **[Mass Produce]**.

By the end of Logan's process, a neat stack of segmented breastplates lay on the floor, each with matching pauldrons, forearm guards, and shin-plates. And now the large Numa crystal was almost spent.

"Not exactly tailor-made," Logan said, "but we can strap them on the guys easily enough."

"Nice," Simmons muttered. "We'll take it." Then he motioned to the nearest guard. "Jones, put one on and tell us how it feels."

The guard—a tall, skinny fellow—tugged on the segmented chest-plate and secured the Velcro-like buckles Logan had fashioned from monster sinew. He twisted from side to side, testing the fit. Then he gave a thumbs-up.

"It's snug but comfortable, sir."

Logan let out a long breath. "That's it for major gear. I might do one last item for myself, but otherwise we're tapped out. Then we'll get the hell out of here."

Some of the guys nodded, relief evident on their faces. Even if these guys were half-boiled, they wanted back to safety.

Logan rummaged around the bits of charred monster flesh and made himself a reasonable pile.

"Alright, Tumor," Logan murmured under his breath so the others wouldn't have to be reminded that he was basically talking to himself half the time. "Think we can do something neat with this? A weapon, maybe?"

[We can, but keep it simple. We are really low on Numa. Less than 1%.]

Logan's lips pursed. "Alright, damn it. I kind of wanted a cool staff, like that monkey guy from the Chinese epic."

[That is very you, if I may say so.]

"You can say whatever the hell you want, Tumor," Logan said. "And don't you forget it."

[Then let me say this. A staff is out of the question, but how about a cane?]

Logan nodded. He wouldn't mind one, so he could walk on his bad leg without the power bracing, if need be.

Logan sat down next to the charred pile of monster and dug bones out of it. This was something simple that he didn't need Tumor for.

He pictured a cane about as tall as his waist, with a small curved handle at the top for grip. He wanted the bone to be stable enough to handle his weight but also flexible enough not to break under stress. Blue light flared briefly.

When he opened his eyes, a bone-white cane lay on the floor, glinting faintly. Logan picked it up. It was surprisingly light, almost like hollow carbon fiber. Leaning his weight on it, he found it supported him easily—at least if he wasn't decked out in hundreds of pounds of gear. He gave it a few experimental taps against the stone floor. The tile clicked softly.

"Perfect," Logan said, satisfied. "Strengthen this material to be hard as steel." He pressed the tip to the side of the crystal, and it went dim. "That should do it."

[Nice work, Logan.]

"Damn right," Logan said. He rubbed the cane handle. Then he looked up and raised his voice. "I'm calling this done. Guys, help me pack this stuff up."

In quick order, they gathered up the new gear, distributed the bone-plates among the men, and got ready to leave. Logan tapped the cane against the ground once more. "Let's head back. I've had my fill of this place."

Simmons hefted his new axe, and a couple of the men started carrying shield bracings and spearheads to one of the carts that had been left for them. Then they started filing out of the chamber. As they passed the crater where the second monster had exploded, a few of them muttered quiet prayers for the dead recruits. Logan dipped his head in a moment of silence.

Goddamn, what a battle.

The outside air, when they finally reached it after a tense journey along the winding corridors, was a breath of salvation. The sun had drifted well past noon, cutting through the jungle canopy in scattered beams. The Ark loomed in the distance, resting in a broad clearing. Even though it was on the ground for now, that massive hull stretching into the sky was a welcome sight.

Toward the Ark's ramp, a small cluster of humans and Faelves saw them coming and hurried to greet them. Logan recognized a few of the Faelves—mainly Snoff, who dashed up with an eager grin.

"You're alive!" Snoff said. "Got anything interesting?"

Logan waved the cane. "Some new gear. Tired bones. Not much else. I used up a big crystal."

Snoff nodded. Logan knew he wasn't happy about him using corrupted energy to craft, but he said nothing. "The Groloin are hooking up the final bits of that energy drain. I'd say we can be airborne by sundown."

"We'll see about that," Logan said. "But right now I need a bath, a meal, and a nap. In that order."

He half-expected to see Freya sprint up next, but she must have been busy purifying the Numa energy they were using for fuel. Making a few spearheads wouldn't give Levemoth much power, but a whole A-grade crystal's worth of Numa? Logan shuddered.

Snoff helped with loading the last of the gear while Simmons and his men walked ahead. One by one, they trudged up the Ark's loading ramp. The battered group was greeted with slaps on the back and cheers from the crew who lingered around. Even Logan found himself exchanging tired smiles and nods with them.

He made his way to the deck, leaning on his new cane, grateful he wasn't stuck in that wheelchair. He felt exhaustion tugging on every fiber of his body, but it was a victorious sort of exhaustion that kept him going, despite the fatigue. That and the new power-bracing-armor thing was keeping him upright.

Simmons plopped down next to him, letting out a ragged breath. "Y'know, I think I can appreciate an easy day now more than ever."

Logan laughed. "Never thought I'd hear that from you, tough guy."

Snoff hopped onto a crate beside them, hugging his knees. "Was it really that bad down there? If even Mr. Simmons needs a break . . ."

Logan gave a light chuckle. "Oh, you know. Just a massive abomination or two. No big deal."

Snoff's eyes went wide. "'Tis good that we have such formidable warriors as you two."

They all fell quiet then, letting a comfortable, if tired hush settle over them. The hum of the Ark's engines stirring to life in the distance might've been the best sound Logan had heard all day.

[We did good, Logan. Good job.]

"Thanks," Logan whispered back. He closed his eyes for a moment, letting the tension drain from his body.

"You okay?" Simmons asked, noticing Logan nodding off.

"Yeah," Logan said, stifling a yawn. "Just . . . real tired. I think next time I might do less adventuring and more delegating."

"I doubt it, Young Master," Simmons said, not unkindly.

Logan chuckled and made his way back into the Ark. He wanted to see Freya, and he had plans for his new ability.

CHAPTER 7

Hard Worker

Freya found Logan slumped over a table in his workshop. He was still wearing his half-patched clothes, his new bone-white cane propped against a stool. There was a thin line of drool dripping from the corner of his mouth, and he was snoring softly, head pillowed on his folded arms.

She sighed and smiled to herself. Stepping forward, she placed a hand gently on Logan's shoulder and brushed away some of his black hair sticking to his forehead. Even in sleep, his brows were knitted, as though still wrestling with some half-finished problem in the back of his mind.

"Hey," Freya whispered, "you're going to get a crick in your neck if you sleep like this."

At first, Logan didn't stir. Freya let a soft chuckle escape and tapped him again, a bit firmer. "Logan, come on."

He jerked upright with a startled gasp, blinking rapidly. His eyes darted around the room until they settled on Freya's face, and a faint smile tugged at the corner of his mouth. "Oh . . . hey," he mumbled, rubbing his eyes. "Didn't realize I dozed off."

"How long have you been here?"

He shrugged. "I don't know. I was taking a break, just sat down for a second . . ." He paused, glancing at a bunch of metal bits he'd apparently been tinkering with. "Guess I passed out."

Freya crossed her arms. "You didn't properly rest after you got back from your raid."

"We needed a few more items for the next step. Need to go back in there," Logan said. He straightened, rolling his stiff shoulders. "Couldn't sleep yet. We're short on, well, everything. But I made something."

He reached for a makeshift wooden box on the edge of the table. Carefully, he pulled the lid off, revealing five small orbs of steel-laced bone. Each was knurled for better grip.

"Think of them as mini-shock-grenades," he explained. "You press here—" He indicated a shallow imprint. "and it'll prime, then toss and watch the sparks fly. Great for crowd control."

Freya eyed them warily and prodded one with her fingertip. "You made something like this before, didn't you?"

"I've made all kinds of fun stuff by this point. Hard to keep track," Logan said, stifling a yawn. "But these are nonlethal. I don't want the new recruits blowing themselves up. Or me, for that matter."

"You're giving them grenades?"

"Have to," Logan said. "I'm not sure what's going on down there, but it's full of nasties. A lot of Blues right from the get-go, and then these . . . ogres. I need every member of the party to be useful."

He shifted his weight in the seat. "The Groloin let me have one of the darkmetal batteries to properly prepare us for delving deeper. I used most of it to **[Mass Produce]** these stun grenades and things like proper riot shields. They're real composite. Polycarbonate."

"You made plastic?" Freya asked, slightly miffed.

"Look, we can worry about the environment after we've killed the frigging giant eldritch monster that's terrorizing the village."

"Hmph," Freya said, but her furrowed forehead relaxed. "Fine."

Logan exhaled, shoulders slumping in relief. "Ah, I'm still beat, even after a nap. Hopefully that's the last batch for a while. I'm about tapped out."

Freya's gaze softened. She reached over to brush the hair from his forehead again. "Well, I'm here to drag you to bed, if you can manage standing for a moment. Maybe I'll even take you to a hot bath first."

"Mmm," Logan murmured, letting her words sink in. "A bath . . . Yeah, that'd be great. With you joining me, it's as close as heaven as I can get."

Freya offered a hand to help him up. Reclining on the stool was one thing, but it took Logan a moment to gain his balance. He let out a grunt, leaning on his new cane and Freya's shoulder.

"You sure you're okay?" Freya said. "You look like death warmed over."

"I've been better," Logan admitted with a crooked smile. "But I'll bounce back. Always do."

Freya guided him gently out the workshop door.

Outside, a faint hum of conversation drifted up the corridors. Somewhere down the hall, he could hear a couple of the Faelves giggling and speaking fast, probably looking over the new gear he'd churned out.

As they made their way to the Ark's living quarters, Freya squeezed his hand. "You did good, by the way. I've heard the people talking. You've really proven yourself."

Logan let out a weary chuckle. "I guess so. Two people died, though. Hard to call it a victory."

Freya held his gaze, warm and understanding. "It's always going to be dangerous. We needed the Numa. From what Simmons told me, you sure made lemonade," she said quietly. "Sometimes, that's the best victory we can get."

"I was never much for half-victories," Logan said. "I'm more of a glass-full kind of guy."

Freya laughed. "You're more of a down-the-pitcher-in-one-go kind of guy. I love that about you."

She led him down the hall, lifting his arm gently around her shoulders so she could support him better. As they walked, Logan's eyelids drooped with exhaustion, but he forced himself to stay upright.

"Don't worry," Freya said softly. "We're almost there."

They paused at a cabin door. Freya pushed it open, revealing a small room with a simple bed, some shelves, and a little side table. It wasn't fancy, but at that moment, it looked more inviting than any penthouse he'd ever lived in.

She guided him inside, and he more or less collapsed onto the mattress. It let out a squeak of protest, but he just sighed in relief. Freya stood over him, hands on her hips, the corners of her lips curving gently.

"You can't save the world if you can't keep yourself going," she said. "Now, close your eyes. When you're ready, I'll get you that bath."

Logan reached up for her hand, gave it a quick squeeze, then let his head loll back onto the pillow. "Alright," he whispered, more than ready to surrender to actual sleep.

Within seconds, he was out like a light. Freya brushed a light kiss against his temple, then quietly left the room, shutting the door behind her.

According to Tumor, Logan slept thirteen hours, twenty-six minutes, and eight seconds. Logan told Tumor that he need not tell him the seconds, but Tumor insisted. They left the deadlock as it was, and Logan enjoyed a long bath with Freya.

After donning a clean shirt and cotton pants, he felt like a new man. He grabbed his cane and made his way leisurely to Snoff by the Faelven quarters, where he stopped to eat. Half a dozen Faelves came with plates of delicious food, and Logan told them the details of what had happened in the ruins. That had them worried.

"'Tis strange to find new beasts, but it happens," Snoff said sagely.

"Not a good omen," one of the Faelves said. "The Great Thief has plans within plans."

"Oh yeah, that reminds me," Logan said. "There was this moment I was fighting with this ogre, and I thought I saw in its eyes a . . . look. The sort that I see sometimes when I visit my father. An alien look, full of depth, yet somehow empty and void at the same time. I think it's him."

"Our tales tell that he can take the forms of his beasts, if he so wishes," Snoff said.

"Then the Great Thief must know where we are!" a female Faelf with pink porcelain skin said.

"I know," Logan said as he took a bite of fresh bread with nut butter on top. It tasted like manna from the heavens. He hadn't realized how hungry he was. He reached for a piece of pie from a nearby plate. Snoff pushed it closer, so Logan could reach it.

"The enemy is weakened currently," Snoff said. "But he is always scheming."

"We have fuel now," Logan said. "We can make a quick escape, and it's hard to attack the ship if he uses Levespawn. If he comes himself, it's going to be a battle."

"Us Faelves, we have a theory," Snoff said. "We think these Blues are another reason why his power is sapped. They have been spawning all over. Most settlements are destroyed by them. But the strange thing is that there should be more."

Logan knew there were more. They were part of some kind of proxy war, and whatever governed the rules, had punished Levemoth. But Levemoth had an ally of its own. Some dark force even stronger than it was. If that thing gave it more power . . . who knew what could happen.

"Thanks for the meal, guys," Logan said and got up. "Will you join me up on the deck, Snoff? I need to go talk to the Groloin."

"Let us go, Logan!" Snoff said.

"Hey, what's up?" Logan said as he entered the command bridge. Behind him followed Snoff, Freya, and Simmons. Tumor immediately jumped to **[Possess]** a Groloin golem specifically left in the command room for him.

"Good day," Tumor said amicably through the golem's voice box. It was a hollow robotic sound.

In the middle of the golem was a large hovering orb of green, bronze-like in appearance. It glowed softly with intricate runes.

"Logan Specter," Glaan, the Groloin Hivemind spoke in a stern, grandmotherly tone. "We take it you have recovered from your expedition?"

"I have," Logan said and nodded. "How's our ship doing?"

"The Ark is functional. It required some minor repairs, as always."

"We finally got fuel," Logan said.

"Indeed," Glaan said. "For that, we are grateful. What do you plan on doing next?"

"I think we should delve deeper into the ruins."

"We're reluctant to agree with this, but it is good to be on the same page on something," the floating orb decreed.

"Reluctant to agree?" Logan asked, cocking an eyebrow.

"The new beast."

"Yeah, the ogre," Logan said. "Nasty business. What of it?"

"We would have preferred to study the remains," the Hivemind said, "but you opted to turn it into . . . daggers and combat boots."

"You do not approve?" he asked.

"Was that unclear?" the Groloin said.

"We need equipment to do expeditions and raids."

"So you say. But what does a few trinkets gain for us?"

"It saves us casualties," Logan said immediately. "I don't know about you, but I want my people to be well-equipped and prepared when they are risking their necks. Do you even care?"

"We care about the ultimate objective: defeating Levemoth."

"At whatever cost?"

"We are not inclined toward brutality and tyranny, if that is what you imply, Logan Specter. We even allowed you to stow your father in the cargo bay."

Logan smirked to himself. What a time to bring that up. The Groloin were shrewd, if nothing else. But he knew all of the bullshit negotiation string-pulling techniques that ever existed.

"So. you think my turning the ogres into equipment was not . . . what, *efficient*?"

"That is, indeed, what we think."

"Are you just admonishing me for the sake of it, or is there a request coming?"

"Always to the point," the Groloin said, gentler now. "We do appreciate that about you."

"I'm so happy we see eye-to-eye," Logan said and gave the floating orb his best fake smile.

"We have information we would like to share before the request."

"Be my guest," Logan said.

"When you told us that the Blues had appeared, we did not make much of it. The Devourer has many machinations, and sometimes it even manages to create new dark ideas. But for us to stumble upon one so blatantly? This was planted. The enemy was surely watching and observing how the creation fares in battle."

"He was there," Logan said. "I saw a . . . glimpse in the eyes of one of the ogres."

The Groloin Hivemind was silent for a while. Logan took the opportunity to sit down. He sighed contently.

No matter who you are, mighty or small, no one can deny the absolute delight of sitting on your ass.

"The enemy knows where we are," the Groloin said.

Logan nodded.

"Should we leave?" Snoff asked.

The Hivemind's orb stirred. "The enemy has a global [**Teleport**] ability. Even in its weakened state, it should have attempted an attack already. Especially so when most of our strongest individuals were in the ruins. Yet it did not."

"Why?" Freya asked.

"It has some sort of plan," Logan said. "A trap, maybe?"

"Possibly," the Hivemind said. "Did the enemy make it clear it was watching you?"

"I don't know," Logan said. "It was subtle."

"Tumor?" the Groloin asked, in a notably friendlier tone than it took with Logan. "What is your assessment?"

Tumor's golem spoke. "I replayed the memory of Logan noticing it. I compared it to the three times Logan noticed a strange fleeting look in his father's eyes recently. It was the same."

"And have you drawn any conclusion?"

"The enemy was attempting to be covert."

"That's good," Logan said. "It means part of its plans was us not having this conversation."

"What does it want?" Freya asked. "Is it trying to lure us in further?"

"If there are more of those monsters there, why not just overwhelm us the first chance they had?" Logan muttered.

"Why kill a sheep when you can get the flock?" Simmons said. "Maybe it is waiting for us to commit to a real raid and then kill a hundred of us at once."

"If that's the plan," Logan asked, rubbing his chin, "why not just attack the Ark?"

"It knows we can lift off and battle with it in the sky."

"So, it's a trap," Logan said.

"These are just some random ruins, aren't they?" Freya asked. "Why choose this place?"

"We chose it," the Groloin said, "because it was the last known stronghold of the First Folk."

"So that means two things," Logan said. "It's the place with the most Numa available."

"And the other thing?" Simmons asked.

Snoff answered in a solemn tone: "It is also the most corrupt place on this planet."

"Yeah," Logan said. "Levemoth probably has the place crawling with monsters from floor to ceiling."

"High risk, high reward," Simmons said. "We should not take that chance. We have fuel. Let's find an easier mark."

"We agree," the Groloin said. "As much as we wanted to study these new creatures and obtain more Numa, it seems foolish to walk into a trap."

"Levemoth must be seriously underestimating us," Freya said.

"Maybe . . ." Logan said, steepling his fingers under his chin. "But there's something off about this. A missing piece."

"What could it be?" Freya asked.

"I don't know yet. Maybe it's—"

In that moment Kat and Balmer burst in, both of their eyes wide and their breath shallow. They had sprinted here. "Guys. You need to come outside and see this."

CHAPTER 8

Metamorphosis

W hat is it?" Logan asked, a knot forming in his gut.

"Just come," Balmer said, voice wavering.

So they followed, exchanging wary glances along the way. The corridor was a narrow hallway lit by orbs of Numa-lamps that glowed with a soft blue light. Kat led them up a short flight of stairs, straight to the outer deck. As soon as the old bulkhead door swung open, a wave of hot, humid jungle air hit Logan in the face.

He stepped forward—cane in one hand, Freya at his side. The midday sun hung high in a brassy sky, but that wasn't what drew everyone's gaze. Off in the horizon was Levemoth, dominating the clouds with its impossible size.

A ring of swirling black and blue motley energy wrapped around it. Logan had seen Levemoth several times before—from a distance, or in warped visions—and each time it seemed bigger than logic allowed. But now it was cocooned entirely in seething darkness. The dark cloud that usually just surrounded its underbelly, as if protecting it, was now fully enveloping the unholy monster.

The faint silhouette of its mass, hunched and reptilian, quivered inside the swirling vortex of thunderclouds. Cracks of lightning skittered across the swirling thick mass of it, and it seemed like the thundercloud was *thickening*. Like smoke trapped in a glass.

"Holy mother . . ." Simmons breathed.

"Is it . . . locked in place?" Freya whispered.

"At least it's not attacking," Kat said, her voice tense. "But you can feel the threat. I mean, look at that."

Logan's jaw tightened. He felt Tumor's presence intensify in the back of his head, like a coiled spring. The AI didn't say anything, but the force of its attention on the creature was palpable.

"Look at the sky," Tumor voiced through the golem.

Above the swirling cocoon, the sky had turned a sickly color, almost like oil slicking on water, black and blue. And the entire horizon in that direction carried a subtle weight to it, as if space itself had been turned into something heavy and oppressive.

Snoff let out a shaky exhalation. "What is this? Our lore mentions no such event. 'Tis forbidden to speak the name of the Great Thief's dark master, but . . ."

"You know of that?" Logan asked.

Snoff only nodded, his eyes glued to the horror in the sky.

Logan felt Freya's hand on his arm. She was trembling just enough for him to sense. He squeezed her fingers gently in return.

"What is it doing?" Logan muttered aloud. "It's like it's . . . gathering power?"

"In other words," Balmer said, "it's going to come out of that thing even stronger?"

Snoff nodded slowly. "Yes. If this is indeed the dark master's blessing, the Great Thief is gestating, so to speak. When it emerges from that cocoon of smoke, it will be—"

"Stronger than ever," Logan finished, his voice grim. "We need to gather everyone right now."

They hurried back inside. A hush of dread followed them down the corridor. Even the clank of Logan's cane felt ominously loud in the still air. By the time they reached the command bridge again, the Groloin Hivemind's floating orb was swirling wildly.

"Groloin," Logan said. "Are you seeing what we're seeing?"

"Yes." Glaan's grandmotherly voice was laced with tension. "Levemoth is entering a metamorphosis stage. We have rarely witnessed this. Only once in our ancient records, before it destroyed the First Folk. It is . . . fueling."

"Fueling for what?" Freya asked, though the answer was obvious.

"For annihilation," the Hivemind said plainly.

A cold heaviness settled on the entire room. Logan remembered the vision he had seen: Levemoth surging with energy, destroying the entire army of an advanced civilization.

Snoff's ears drooped. He was visibly shaking, but he swallowed his fear and spoke up. "What is our timetable?"

"Unknown," the Groloin said. "Could be days. Most likely not weeks."

Logan let out a sharp breath. "So we're short on options and short on time." He turned to the Hivemind. "We need to delve deeper into that ruin and gather enough Numa to power a real offensive. Our best chance is shooting Levemoth out of the sky with every cannon, every energy weapon, everything we have. Right?"

"Do you think that is going to be enough?" Freya asked, her striking blue eyes full of worry.

"What other choice do we have?" Simmons said gruffly.

"Yes. We concur," the Groloin said. "It is a slim hope, but it is our only one currently."

"Then it's settled," Logan said, voice hardening as if to compensate for the tremor running through his core. "We need to throw a Hail Mary. We delve deeper. No half measures."

Kat shot him a glance. "I'm up for it, but are we sure we want to land the ship again? The Ark's safer in the air, yeah?"

"Flying burns a lot of Numa we cannot spare," the Groloin said. "We shall make sure the Ark is ready to ascend within a five-minute window, but we have to keep the ship on the ground for now."

"And we don't have time," Logan said. "We have to land, gather as much resources as we can, and make something of it."

"Agreed," Balmer said, nodding grimly, "We need to find a water source and organize the people."

Logan looked over to Freya. She brushed a loose strand of hair behind her ear and gave him a tiny nod.

"Alright, that's what we're doing, then," Logan said, slapping his cane lightly against the floor. "We land. We find water. We delve. We gather enough Numa to mount a real assault. And we do it before that giant bastard breaks out of its shell."

Simmons' face was grim but resolute. "We'll have to pick a location that's not too compromised. Someplace close to the ruins, but not directly on top of them. The bigger the perimeter we can set up, the better."

The Groloin orb flickered. "The compound must be built around the ship and almost directly near the entrance. The golems will carry the water if the source is too far away. The ship must be protected as well as its crew."

"Do you think there'll be attacks?" Logan asked.

"Almost certainly," the Groloin said.

Logan tapped a finger on the command table, wrestling with a dozen concerns. "We do it, then. Tumor, draw up a complete plan for the most efficient base structure, including personnel. Snoff, gather the Faelves. Simmons, rally the humans. You'll be in charge of the camp. I want a complete ground team, but don't strip the Ark of defenders. If Levemoth tries something, we can't be caught with no countermeasures. Rotating teams, ruins, rest, guard."

Everyone in the command room nodded. The air buzzed with a new, frantic sense of purpose. Freya gave him a look that said she was proud but also terrified. Logan swallowed, forcing a half-smile back at her.

Before the group dispersed, Balmer asked, "When do we launch the next delve?"

"As soon as we can," Logan said. "Get prepared. Kat and Balmer, you're responsible for getting the first expedition ready. Gear, men, supplies. Use all the shit I've made. They're in the workshop area."

"We're on it," Balmer said.

"And get Ryan to recruit twenty good men in addition to his twel—ten . . ."

Kat gave a curt nod.

"Dismissed," Logan said, and let out a heavy exhale as everyone started going off to fulfill their tasks.

The Groloin orb hovered in place, humming faintly.

"We are impressed, Logan Specter. You are swift and decisive."

"We don't have time for anything else."

"Indeed," the Groloin said. "Despite your numerous flaws, you are what we need you to be when it counts."

"Eh, thanks," Logan said.

The Groloin spoke no more.

In that silence, Logan's mind raced with the gravity of their decision. They were about to commit to a major ground operation at the same time Levemoth was receiving a cosmic steroid boost from some dark eldritch god. If this plan worked, they'd come out ready to fight. If it failed, well . . . everyone would probably die. And even if they managed to muster an attack, it still might not be enough, and, well . . . everyone would probably die.

Depressing.

Still, the choice was made.

A short while later, the Ark banked left with a deep thrumming in its hull. Logan stood on a walkway overlooking the flight deck, leaning on the railing. Tumor had gone through the camp layout and Logan was reviewing it in his mind. It was a nice, warm day with a soft wind to ease the heat.

But Logan couldn't enjoy it without looking up at the sky every ten seconds. There it loomed, gargantuan and ominous. Their potential doom.

Behind him, a handful of Faelves bustled with cables and yard arms, preparing to anchor the ship once they touched down. Some humans rushed by with crates, arms full of gear. Others carried freshly crafted weapons or bone plates Logan had conjured out of monster bits. For all the tension in the air, there was a sense of determined camaraderie that reminded him of old times.

Freya joined him by the railing. "We almost have all the gear out of the cargo bay."

"Good," Logan said. He glanced sideways at her. "How are you feeling, by the way?"

Freya exhaled. "Scared. But I figure that's normal."

"Yeah," Logan said. "Almost comforting at this point."

She gave him a slight bump with her shoulder. "What about you?"

"I'm beyond scared. I'm . . . I don't know. Kinda resigned to the madness of it. But we have to do it."

Snoff's voice came from somewhere below them, cheerfully calling orders to the Faelves, who laughed and skipped as they worked. How the little porcelain people managed to stay so positive, was beyond Logan. But it inspired him.

Meanwhile, Simmons barked out instructions to a handful of humans who were stringing up a perimeter fence made of spiked metal and netting. Logan wondered if he should have made more. The plan was to fortify an immediate radius around the Ark so they wouldn't be ambushed in their sleep.

By sunset, they had a rough fortress set up around the landed Ark. Groloin golems roamed the perimeter, scanning for signs of infiltration. A few Faelves patrolled in pairs, tiny slingshots at the ready, while the humans lit fires and readied small ballista stands, that Logan had enchanted with self-loading, penetrative power along with durability. They had also mounted two small energy cannons that the Groloin had provided. If any Levespawn popped up, they wouldn't catch them unprepared.

Logan, feeling an ache in his shoulders, wandered away from the hustle and bustle. His new cane clicked lightly on the dirt. Freya had gone off to help the medics prepare for possible casualties. She was in charge of the resting and healing facilities. Tumor remained silent in his mind, presumably busy parsing hundreds of calculations about tomorrow's delve.

Logan found a quiet spot by the new water intake pipe the [**Engineers**] had rigged. A small pond was forming where the river was diverted, trickling quietly, and the taste of fresh air was sweet. The silhouette of the Ark's massive hull towered overhead.

Our protector. It almost feels peaceful under it.

Logan took a seat on a small crate, letting himself breathe. For a moment, he considered going to check on the new recruits or maybe seeing how Snoff was handling the Faelves. But, for once, he allowed himself five minutes of unoccupied quiet.

I should build something for the delve. But if the ogres can smash my mechs to bits so easily, it's not worth the effort . . .

To his surprise, Kat came sauntering over, still sporting bandages around her ribs. She didn't look too pleased about them, but she was on her feet, which was more than Logan had expected so soon.

"Hey," Kat said, placing her hands on her hips. "You're not going off alone again, are you?"

"Nah, just enjoying a break," Logan said. "Did the [**Healers**] tell you to walk around so soon?"

She shrugged. "They told me I shouldn't jump around. Doesn't mean I can't stroll."

"Fair enough."

Kat eyed him for a second. "We ready? Going tomorrow?"

"Most likely the day after. Tomorrow will be busy. More gear to build. More rest." He paused, staring at the dark shapes of the forest in the distance. "Will we be ready the day after? No. We go anyway."

Kat swallowed. "I think you're a good leader, you know. Even if you're kind of a weirdo."

Logan raised an eyebrow. "Say that again. Sounds suspiciously like a compliment hidden in an insult."

"You heard me," Kat said, but she smiled. "We all see the hours you put in, the half-crazy contraptions you throw together. And . . . we trust you."

Logan felt a warmth spread through his chest that had nothing to do with the muggy evening air. "Thanks, Kat. You holding up okay? Heard you got banged up pretty bad."

She rolled her shoulder, wincing. "Nothing I'm not used to. The scratch was light. Balmer took the blow from the explosion. They used Numa to fix him up."

"How's he?"

"Balmer? More worried about me than himself. Fussing over me like an old nanny."

He chuckled. "Good to hear. And you two are . . . still a secret, I guess?"

"Mm," she said, lips compressed. "No point in a secret if you keep bringing it up, Boss."

"Touché." Logan found himself smiling as Kat turned and leisurely walked off toward the perimeter, giving orders to some younger recruits along her way.

The momentary levity lightened the knot in his gut. His cane tapped lightly against the crate as he stood.

Enough me-time.

He needed to see how the water intake was coming along, then check if Tumor or the Groloin wanted any last-minute input for tomorrow.

Nightfall brought an uneasy silence over their ground camp. Patrols exchanged glances as they passed in the dim torchlight. The moon hung low, partially obscured by dark drifting clouds. In the distance, an occasional glimmer of that vile black-and-blue swirl around Levemoth stained the sky like a nasty wound. At times, eerie sounds like distant whale calls reached them on the wind, but no one could tell for sure if they were tricks of the atmosphere or something else.

Logan ended up in a shared tent near the Ark's landing gear, rummaging through some leftover supplies. He found a giant fang in the pile. It was from one of the water snakes. Rarer kind of Levespawn, those.

With a bit of transmutation, it might make a decent piece of gear for the delve—maybe a sword for Simmons as a secondary weapon, he thought. *That guy was sure to break another axe.*

Freya crept in. She pulled the tent flap shut behind her, stifling the lantern light with a cloth so they'd have some semblance of privacy. She sank onto an empty footlocker, letting out a long sigh.

"How's the triage station?" Logan asked.

"Quiet," she responded, massaging her temples. "Minimal injuries from the setup. Mostly sprains, one broken wrist. We didn't want to spend Numa to repair it, since the injured party, well, she's not a fighter . . ."

Freya shook her head.

"And you feel shitty about it?" Logan said softly.

Freya nodded.

"C'mere, you fool," Logan said and dragged Freya by her arm to his lap. "You did right."

"These are the kind of decisions you make and your father used to," Freya said. "I don't have the stomach for it."

"Hang in there."

"I know," Freya said and leaned against his chest. "I just wanted to bitch about it."

"I'm here for it," Logan said.

She giggled.

They sat silently for a while and then she continued. "I'm worried about tomorrow, though. Some of the new recruits are fresh kids. They have no idea—"

"Yeah, I know," Logan said softly. "But we need the bodies. We can't handle those ruins alone. Not after what we saw on the upper floors."

Freya gave him a sad look. "I hate that we can't coddle them, but that's the reality. The experienced combatants are spread thin as it is." She looked down. "I just wish I could keep them all safe."

Logan placed a hand on her knee. "I get it," he said quietly. "I hate losing people too. But we have to gear them up and trust they won't do anything too reckless. Ryan's a good leader."

Freya nodded sadly. Then she drummed her fingertips on Logan's chest. "So, are you going to turn in for the night or do you plan on pulling another all-nighter making weird grenades and bone gear?"

He let out a soft chuckle. "Tempting. But no. I promised you I'd pace myself. We've got to be sharp tomorrow, and I can't do that if I'm running on fumes."

"Tumor approves," she teased lightly.

"That is true," the mechanical sound of Tumor's golem came from outside the tent. "I keep telling him that his sleep deprivation is currently robbing him 22.815 percent processing power, and subsequently, me too."

"And I keep telling you to round it up to twenty-three," Logan called back.

"I'm afraid I cannot do that, Hal."

Freya and Logan laughed.

"Good one," Freya called out. "A little creepy, but I like that you're making jokes now."

"I like it too," Tumor said. "Good night, Freya."

"Night."

Freya leaned in closer and placed her hand on the side of Logan's cheek, thumb softly tracing the faint lines of exhaustion under his eye. "Come on, let's at least lie down for a couple hours."

He nodded, leaning for just a second into her touch. He had done everything he could today, and that was a good feeling. Guards were posted, golems patrolled. The camp was set up.

Freya shifted to the side, making room on the simple cot. Logan hung his cane on a hook hammered into the tent pole. He paused, letting the weight of the day roll off his shoulders.

"Alright," he muttered, lying back. It wasn't comfortable, but Freya curled up close, sharing warmth and a faint sense of comfort in this dark world. "Tonight, rest. Tomorrow, work."

Freya rested her head against his chest. "Tomorrow," she echoed softly.

They listened to the faint creaking of the Ark's frame in the breeze, the occasional clank of metal from the perimeter, the whisper of distant water. And in that hush, Logan had one last thought before drifting off:

We go down into the depths as soon as we can. We gather enough power. Then we blow that giant bastard out of the sky.

No half measures.

CHAPTER 9

Making Rounds

Logan woke up refreshed. He hadn't slept long but hadn't needed to after the previous thirteen hours he'd gotten. He attempted to spring out of bed, ready to tackle his objectives.

Freya wasn't having it, but Logan managed to gently wrestle out of her loving embrace.

"Noooooo," she muttered.

"You can stay," Logan said as he put on a shirt and kissed her on the forehead.

"But couples that get up together, stay together."

"You think I'm going to find someone better down in the ruins?" Logan said and quirked an eyebrow. "A nice troll, perhaps?"

"You never know," Freya said and sat up, looking at Logan like a particularly annoying mosquito. "Besides, you and Kat hit it off annoyingly well."

"I love it when you're jealous."

"I'm not!"

"But you did mention it," Logan said and smirked.

"Shut up," Freya said and threw a pillow at him.

Logan dodged and chuckled as he struggled to get his pants on.

"Did you ever think about it?"

Logan gave her a look. "You're still on Kat?"

Freya gave a little nod.

"Where is this coming from?"

"You just . . . I don't know. You're both fighters, you go on these missions together."

"You know she's with Balmer, right?"

"I know," Freya said and blew some hair out of her face. "But you still haven't answered. Did you ever think about it?"

Logan laughed. "Are you crazy? She's a goddamn battle axe. Snoff's more feminine than her."

Freya snorted.

"You're so goddamn cute," Logan said. "I love you. I'll go work on some things. Let's have breakfast together when you're fully out of bed."

Logan got up, kissed her goodbye, and limped out of the tent.

Outside, Logan was still smirking to himself. The early morning sky was a light gray, the sun barely peeking over the tree line. Logan made a point of *not* looking at the enemy looming in the sky.

While others in the camp were shuffling around in a half-asleep daze, Logan felt awake and fired up. He gave a quick nod of greeting to a couple of the perimeter guards as he passed. They looked hungry and tired.

I'll tell Snoff when I see him to get these guys some snacks.

He had things to do. And he had an idea—a big one—that had been buzzing in his head since they first set up this fortress.

An Ironsuit.

Well, not exactly. It would be fused from wood, metal, bone—anything Logan could conjure into a more-advanced composite. Tumor had all kinds of ideas, throwing around long words like elastomeric components and carbon nanotubes. Logan let him prattle on.

Once Tumor was done, they had a clear plan.

It would essentially be a big exoskeleton that fit snugly to his body. Basically something very similar he had had with the darkmetal Armor but of lesser materials.

He stepped around the Ark's towering hull, passing crates and gear, until he reached what had quickly become his "mobile workshop". It was just a large canvas awning with tables loaded with half-finished equipment, lumps of bone, coils of cleaned tendon, and little jars of resin. The smell was funky— metal dust, wood shavings, and that unique reek of rotting monster flesh waiting to be alchemized into something else.

A couple of human [**Engineers**] were by the tables, rummaging for pieces for their own projects. They gave Logan respectful nods as he approached.

"Morning, Boss."

"Morning," Logan echoed. "You guys can carry on. I need some space in the corner. No one come near me for the next hour, if you value your eyebrows."

The engineers exchanged knowing smiles and quickly moved to another bench.

Logan rolled his neck. "Alright, let's do this."

[We have all the materials needed. You should start with the Phase One blueprint. And do not forget to anchor the joints properly.]

"Right, right." Logan flexed his hands, looking at the floating hologram of Phase One blueprint which Tumor was projecting by tricking his mind. "Let's see . . . We need a chest piece that can lock to the shoulders—an integrated helmet or separate? Separate might be easier to repair if it gets bashed in . . ."

[Separate, I agree. Make it full-plate, and then enchant see-through capabilities.]

"Brilliant," Logan said, impressed.

Logan rummaged around, grabbing pieces of wood that Simmons and his resource crew had chopped for him. He transmuted them into aluminum. He also transmuted lumps of monster bones into a high-carbon alloy, hard enough to resist an ogre's claws—he hoped. He then turned a lump of clay into titanium to strengthen the joints.

He plopped all of the materials onto the table in organized piles. Then he took a deep breath, placing a hand on the swirling lumps.

Then Logan plucked up a purified Numa crystal and went to town with transmuting the material, shaping it to his will.

A flicker of blue light rippled around his fingers as the lumps shuddered, blending together into a large, flattened sheet. He shaped it with careful motions, forcing this newly created composite to form narrow plates that would overlap like scales. It took a toll—he felt a small headache pecking at the back of his skull—but kept going.

[Subclass Level Up!]
[Transmutation Level 38]

Bit by bit, the plates melded together into a chest piece. He outlined the collar area to ensure he could slip his head in without dislocating a shoulder. Then the back flared slightly where he planned to attach a battery or mini-reservoir of Numa.

It took him a good half-hour, sweat beading on his forehead, to get the chest piece shaped. He ended up with something sleek, reminiscent of the old ballistic vests but glinting with a metallic sheen in the morning sun.

[Are you sure about the shape of the gorget? It is thicker than in the blueprint.]
Logan frowned at the portion around the neck. "Better safe than sorry. I'd like to keep my throat not ripped out by ogre teeth."
[Understandable. Then proceed with the arms.]
"Yeah." He grabbed more lumps of the composite. "I'll do these ballistic-style bracers with an internal exoskeleton. Maybe a hidden mechanism so I can punch with an energy shock, if needed?"
[Creative. But that will require a capacity for Numa infusion.]
Logan nodded. "We have smaller crystals. I can slot them into the gauntlets. That'll let me channel a short burst of energy."
[You might also consider the rocket-fist concept we tried last time . . . or at least a retractable spike for close combat, akin to a scythe.]
Logan grinned. "Keep it simpler, or I'll never finish by noon."

Placing one hand on the lumps, the other on a small pile of monster teeth, he chanted and transformed more materials.

Slivers glowed into shape, forming curved bracers that locked around the forearms and hinged at the elbows. The interior had a mesh of hardened sinew, giving it a bit of flex. On the outside, steel-laced bone formed ridges that sparked faintly with residual Numa.

[Attribute Level Up!]
[Durability: 31]

He put them on. A snug fit—almost too snug. He twisted his wrists, hearing small clicks of the overlapping plates. "Perfect," he muttered. Then he grabbed the tooth pile. "Now, for the fists. I want short spikes on the knuckles. Retractable, if possible. Something that can pierce an ogre's hide if I punch it, but not too big or I'll get stuck in it."
[Another D-grader spent, I estimate.]
Logan sighed. "Worth it."
Time flew by in a flurry of transmutation, enchantments, curses, and sweat. After finishing the arms, he repeated a similar process for the legs: a sealed greave around each shin, with a hinge for the knee and a flexible material for the back of the thigh. He sacrificed a few extra lumps of metal to reinforce the ankles. Especially for his bad leg.
Finally, he tackled the helmet. Logan went for the full plate. Only two small vertical slits served as a sort of "breathing vent" on the front, along with a modulator through which Logan could project his voice loudly in the heat of battle.

After a final wave of transmutation and a bit of trembling from the left-over lumps, the helmet formed in his hands. He turned it over and found it appropriately light. The inside had a small cushion. He grinned, satisfied.

He tried the entire ensemble on, piece by piece. First, the chest plate strapped around his torso with heavy buckles made of Levespawn bone, then the leggings, the gauntlets, and the partial helmet. The weight settled evenly across his frame, thanks to Tumor's suggestions for distributing mass.

When it was done, he exhaled. "Now we test the range of motion."

He rolled his shoulders, pivoted on one foot, and swung a mock punch. The suit responded, moving fluidly. It felt like wearing a bigger, heavier version of a wetsuit, though it squeaked where plates overlapped.

"You know, it's not half-bad," Logan murmured to no one in particular. "Tumor, how's it from your perspective?"

[I would say it has 93% synergy with your current physical constraints. If we incorporate a knee brace or partial exoskeletal brace, your limp might vanish while wearing this.]

Logan nodded, eyes bright. "That's the next step." Experimentally, he hopped on one leg, then the other. The exosuit's reinforced joints supported him nicely. He still felt slight twinges in his bum leg, but it was a massive improvement.

Then came the finishing touch: a reservoir for Numa. He'd made a slot in the back near the shoulder blades, large enough for an **[E-grade Numa Crystal]**—nothing too fancy. He slid one in and gave Tumor a nudge. The AI used his **[Possess]** ability to control the flow of Numa. The suit gave a faint hum in response and glowed subtly around the bracers and the chest plate.

Logan raised his arms, and three retractable spikes flashed out from the knuckles in response. "Awesome."

[We should keep it its usage to a minimum outside of actual combat, as the crystal is not large.]

"Sure, sure," Logan said. But his grin didn't fade. He'd finally built something that felt properly personal. The Iron Man jokes in his head practically wrote themselves.

He spent another hour fine-tuning enchantments, triple-checking the buckles, and rigging up a small wrist launcher for "gun-adjacent" things. They had tested it. Guns still weren't possible. What a dumb restriction when fighting against a goddamn eldritch god.

But he was happy with the wrist launcher, as that one took some creativity. He borrowed design principles from a repeating crossbow, replacing the bow with a compressed coil of sinew and a sliver of metal that snapped forward when triggered. Fuel it with a short burst of Numa, and you got a small spike-shot at close range. Not exactly a bullet, but for a last-resort scenario, it might do.

I miss the Tumor-controlled bullets from the Armor.

[Me too. Piloting that thing was fun.]

Finally, Logan stowed the new suit on a stand he'd cobbled together out of scrap wood. Two helpers came over, gawking at the bizarrely sleek set of armor that was half-knight, half-modern-body-gear. Logan let them stare but urged them away when they asked if they could try it on.

"Custom-fitted," he told them. "Wouldn't move right on you. Not to mention I'd be real ticked off if you messed up my brand-new creation."

They nodded but kept their reverent stares on the piece of armor.

When Logan went out to see how Ryan was doing, the sun was higher, warming the clearing around the Ark. The fortress bustled with movement. Faelves swapped night shifts with morning watchers, humans carried fresh ration crates from somewhere near the river, and a few Groloin golems stomped about, scanning the perimeter with mechanical vigilance.

He spotted Ryan standing near a row of recruits. They all wore simple chest and arm plates that Logan had produced in bulk. Some carried short spears or small crossbows.

Ryan himself, clad in a slightly more ornate chest piece (Logan had put an extra flourish on it, just because the kid was a Bard), was going down the line, giving them instructions.

Logan limped up, letting his cane tap to get their attention. At once, the group fell silent.

"Boss," Ryan said. He seemed calmer now than the last time Logan had seen him in the heat of a fight. "We've been drilling for about an hour. Formation, basic maneuvers, that sort of thing."

Logan gave them a once-over. They looked shaky but determined. Some still had uncertain eyes, but at least they clutched their weapons with something like confidence.

"Good," Logan said. "How do they feel?"

Ryan glanced at his men and women. "Still scared, obviously. But the gear is a morale boost. Those small crossbows are a hit. We tested them on a log, and the bolts went in about three inches. That's pretty good for their size."

"Yeah, well, keep in mind they're not unstoppable. If you run into a heavy brute, you might need multiple hits or a direct weak spot. Aim for the eyes."

Ryan nodded. "Sure."

One of the recruits, a freckled young woman with blonde, braided hair, asked, "Is it true we're going into a deeper part of the ruin, sir? Past the spot where you found the trolls?"

Logan met her gaze. He saw fear there but also a spark of readiness. "Yes, we are. Listen, it's not easy. That place could be crawling with nasty surprises. Stick to Ryan, keep your heads, rely on your training." He paused, then softened his tone. "We'll try to keep casualties to zero. But if we want to stop Levemoth, we need that Numa. Understood?"

A few of them nodded uncertainly. One or two said, "Yes, sir." Ryan gave them a reassuring grin, though Logan could tell the bard was also feeling the sting of reality.

Logan clapped Ryan on the shoulder. "Carry on. Keep them at it, but don't wear them out before the real fight."

"Got it," Ryan said, returning to his drill.

Logan moved on, searching for Simmons. It didn't take long to find the tall, broad-shouldered man standing by the perimeter gate, overseeing a few of the non-warriors stacking crude barbed fences. His newly enchanted axe gleamed on his back, a proud testament to Logan's handiwork.

"Simmons," Logan greeted.

Simmons turned around and gave a slight tilt of his head. "Young Master."

"Do you think it's time to drop the 'master' thing?"

Simmons snorted. "I'll try. Anyway, you want a report?"

"Anything happen last night? Suspicious movement inside or outside the perimeter?"

"Nothing major. A few random critters sniffing around. Golems scared them off. We had a small group of Blues pop up near the southern edge around midnight, but they only lingered for a minute or so, smelled us, then slunk off. Didn't even push the fort. Probably scouts."

Logan frowned. "Eh, that's disconcerting in its own way. I hate it when they think and plan. But better than a big fight, I guess."

"Exactly. We left them alone, they left us alone. Could be the calm before the storm."

"Definitely that," Logan said. "Keep me posted if anything else stirs."

"Will do."

After Simmons, Logan made his way toward a makeshift dining area near the Ark's starboard side. A bunch of crates were arranged into benches, and some resourceful Faelves had thrown up a tarpaulin overhead. Waves of morning chatter and a smell of some savory food drifted out to him. His stomach rumbled, reminding him he hadn't eaten yet.

He spotted Freya waving at him from a crude wooden table, Snoff seated beside her. Perfect timing.

Logan flopped down on a crate with a tired sigh, cane clattering at his side. "Morning, Snoff."

"Morning indeed," Snoff said brightly. "Freya told me you were busy on some big project?"

Logan tapped his chest. "Iron suit. Or well, you know, composite suit. I want an edge when we go in."

Freya slid a wooden bowl toward him, steaming with thick porridge. She'd also set out a small plate of dried fruits and what looked like spiced nuts. "Eat."

"Yes, ma'am," Logan said. He took a big spoonful of porridge. It tasted of sweet roots and something tangy. Not bad at all. As he chewed, he glanced at Snoff. "Are the Faelves set? Will you join the support crew?"

Snoff nodded, nibbling on a chunk of dried mango. "We will send a team of eight. We can muster more, but not all of us are adept at these dark corridors. Eight is enough. The rest will help defend the Ark or gather additional resources."

"Thanks. We'll take all the help we can get."

The three of them ate quietly for a moment. Freya reached over to top off Logan's bowl with an extra ladle. He stirred it absently, his mind already racing with tomorrow's plan. They'd go into deeper levels. Possibly face more ogres or worse. But with the new exosuit and the new gear, maybe they could push further, gather bigger crystal fragments.

Snoff broke the lull, clearing his throat. "Any updates on the sky? The cocoon?"

Logan's face darkened. "No. Tumor says it's stable so far. Like it's building up strength. Could be a day, could be a week. But that's not a reason for us to slack off. If we have two days, we'd better make the most of them."

Freya swirled a spoon in her bowl. "We can do it," she said softly, as though reassuring herself. "We have a plan, we have gear, we have people. It's just . . . new territory."

Logan reached out and gave her hand a squeeze. "We'll figure it out. One step at a time."

Snoff gave a small laugh, though it carried a hint of nerves. "Indeed, one step. Then, hopefully many steps more."

They went back to their meal, each lost in their own worries. Around them, the hum of the fortress continued: metal clanging, voices shouting orders, occasional bursts of nervous laughter. Overhead, that ugly swirl of black and blue on the horizon loomed, a silent threat.

But inside that small circle, there was at least a sense of determination—and for Logan, that was enough to keep hope alive. He slurped the rest of the porridge gratefully, ignoring the anxiety twisting in his gut. Because he knew, no matter how ready they felt, it was never going to be easy.

Why can't it ever be easy?

Still, they'd built their fortress, forged their weapons, and tomorrow they would plunge back into the depths. If fate was kind, they'd emerge victorious. If not . . . well, Levemoth's spawn was sure to finish off whomever survived.

Logan put down his spoon. "Alright, I think I've had enough rest. Snoff, get your men briefed. We leave at dawn, or maybe earlier if we can't sleep. Freya, I want you to do your final checks on medical supplies. I'll handle the last few touches on the suit. Then we go."

Freya inhaled and nodded. "Yup."

Snoff smiled. "We shall. Good luck to us all."

They rose and parted, each heading off to tie their own loose ends. And with the sun climbing steadily in the sky, Logan peeled away to prepare for the greatest challenge yet—both confident and utterly petrified at the same time.

CHAPTER 10

Finishing Up Work

Logan made his way back through the busy fortress camp, the morning sun now fully rising behind him. Already, the Ark's hull cast a long shadow over the makeshift camp. It gave some slight relief from the jungle heat, though there was no escape from the humidity of the planet.

Jungle climate gets old after a while . . .

People he passed gave him brisk nods—some out of respect, some out of nerves for tomorrow's delve. Logan offered polite smiles but kept his stride purposeful. He had a suit to refine.

He ducked under the large canvas awning that served as his workshop. The Groloin golems had carried most of his gear outside.

Piled near the center was the almost-complete exosuit: chest piece, gauntlets, greaves, the full plate helm. The very sight of it gave him a swell of pride. It was a rough beauty, composite plates shaped expertly around Logan's proportions, as was Tumor's wont—an odd fusion of old-world armor and advanced tech, yet it was his design through and through.

Each part had been tested, but not under real-world conditions—meaning an ogre could, in theory, tear right through it if Logan messed up. He had some basic enchantments that would prevent the worst damage, but . . .

But what I really need is darkmetal that can hold Numa.

[The knees remain a point of concern. They might fail under extreme torque. Especially on the side of your weak leg.]

"I'll brace them," Logan said. He hoisted one greave, patted the side, and rummaged through his things for a spool of braided tendon. He looped the sinew around the knee joint, binding it securely, transmuted it into aluminum, gave it a light elasticity augment, then brushed on a light film of resin.

"That should help keep it from twisting too far."

[Agreeable. Considering the forces we can generate, it might loosen in an intense fight.]

"We'll see. What we need now is firepower."

Next, Logan plucked a fist-sized Numa crystal from a pouch on his belt—**[E-grade]** but enough to give the armor's internal lines a bit of juice. He sucked in a breath, placed the crystal against the chest-plate slot, and whispered an incantation.

Energy trickled in from the blue glowing gemstone, threading the composite plates with a faint blue hue. Strength enchantment, speed enchantment, and at-will explosive drive, which was not much given that he was using an E-grader, but enough to get him out of a jam or a deadlock with an ogre.

[Subclass Level Up!]
[Enchantment Level 42]

"Alright, Tumor," Logan said, smiling to himself at the quality of his work, "let's test this baby."

He slid the chest plate on carefully, letting it clamp around his torso. The posterior slot for the crystal locked into place with a mechanical clack. A warm hum tickled the skin between his shoulder blades, signaling the suit was powered.

[The measurements are as they should be, Logan. They always are.]

"I know." Logan said and rolled his shoulders. The front plate didn't pinch. Good. He bent each arm slowly to shoulder height, flexed his elbows, and cracked his knuckles. Next came a few lateral twists of the waist. The suit moved with him, only occasionally squeaking where plates overlapped. With a grunt, he crouched and tested the knees. They held.

"But it's one thing to make sure. It's our life we're dealing with here."

[I agree. But I cannot help but feel miffed at the requirement to test my obviously perfect work.]

Logan chuckled. "I could always mess up the transmutation."

[That has not happened in a while. For all your chaotic nature, you are quite meticulous when crafting.]

"It's necessary."

[Agreed.]

Logan looked for the half-visor helm and finally spotted it leaning against a crate. Thick composite ridges above the brow gave it a frowning, predatory look.

Logan fitted it over his head, adjusted the padded interior, and flipped the visor down. It clicked in place. The jaw part of the helmet was a protruding maw, promising menace. It was also the sturdiest part of the armor, having only two enchantments, including a small voice-enchantment, that let Logan speak loudly through the helmet at will. After that it was all about fortification and defense. His jaw was a goddamn wall.

The visor was also reinforced, but it was still missing one enchantment, for right now Logan couldn't see anything.

He plucked an **[F-grade Numa Crystal]** from his pocket and enchanted the visor with a see-through enchantment and night vision.

"Nice, it works perfectly." He raised both gauntleted fists and let out a soft exhale. "This is good." He popped the visor up. "It's damn good, Tumor. Still not unstoppable, but I haven't felt this prepared in a while."

[Do you want to add the wrist-launcher you designed?]

"Almost forgot," Logan muttered. The makeshift "Wrist Puncher" lay on the table—a small metal cradle with a spring mechanism and spool for reloading spikes. He clamped it onto his right gauntlet, double-checking its fit. "All right, let's see." He pressed the release lever; there was a soft hiss and the cradle jerked forward an inch, snapping back. "Seems functional. Good for a quick surprise shot, if nothing else."

He paced the workshop tent, taking wide steps and cautious half-pivots, even hopping once or twice, ignoring a faint pinch in his bad leg. The greaves supported him well, and Logan reveled in the free movement and extra power.

Now I can actually lead from the front.

Satisfied, he peeled off the armor piece by piece. Each segment went onto a rough wooden stand he'd built specifically for it. He'd let it air out, because wearing it for hours straight in the heat was a recipe for dehydration. Tomorrow—or whenever they actually launched into the deeper levels—he'd be ready to snap this on in minutes.

[That completes your personal gear. Unless you want to incorporate an integrated jetpack.]

"I wish," Logan said, shaking his head. "Flying's a daydream until we find a lot of Numa. I'd love it, but we have to be realistic. We might need that energy for other weapons."

[Pragmatic as always, Logan.]

He almost laughed at that. Tumor was getting decent at compliments.

Finally, Logan sat on a bench, letting out a deep sigh. The excitement of finishing the suit was giving way to the weight of it all again.

He carefully relabeled the small bin of leftover materials: lumps of bone, a few metal scraps, chips and pieces of wood, some half-empty tubes of resin. Not enough to make anything large, but maybe they could do last-minute repairs or modifications, if needed.

"Alright," Logan said aloud, forcing a smile. He wiped sweat off his forehead with the back of his hand. "Suit complete."

He thought for a split second about testing it against a real threat, maybe offering Simmons a chance to whack him with a training club just to see how it held up. But he didn't want to risk denting this brand-new baby. He'd rely on Tumor's calculations, and the fact that he'd poured his best enchantments into it.

With a final, affectionate pat on the chest plate, he rose from the bench. The sun had climbed higher, and from the workshop's open flap, he saw a bustle of activity in the camp. Sentries were sitting and watching in watchtowers made of boxes. Recruits were practicing thrusts with their spears by the dozen in rows led by Ryan. A couple of golems were stomping by, each carrying crates of rations. The day was moving along, and tonight, they'd be sleeping with one eye open before plunging into those ruins at dawn.

Logan unclasped his cane from where he'd propped it, tested his leg with a half-step, and found he had just enough energy left in him for a few more errands. He wasn't sure if finishing the suit should feel like relief or just the calm before a much-bigger storm. Probably both.

He took a moment to appreciate the exosuit's imposing silhouette on the stand—half-monstrous, half-majestic. This was either going to save his life or, at worst, let him go down swinging. That had to be enough.

"Tomorrow," Logan said to the empty air, "we see if this thing does the trick."

CHAPTER 11

Night Raid

Logan jolted awake to the sound of frantic shouting and the pounding of boots.

Instinct shoved him upright, heart hammering. Darkness. Not complete. There was a faint glow from the campfires flickering through the thin canvas walls. But the noise, the screams, the clang of steel told him something was wrong.

He scrambled to his feet, nearly tripping over the cot. Freya stirred, eyes snapping open. "What's happening?"

"An attack" Logan whispered. "Stay inside."

The world beyond their tent exploded in a chorus of shouts, inhuman shrieks, and clashing metal. Logan fumbled for his cane and made his way to the tent flap.

She caught his arm. "You sure?"

"Yes," he said, voice edged with tension. "I can't be out there fighting and worrying about you."

She gave him a curt nod. "Just . . . be careful."

Logan bolted out into the open. All his hopes for a quiet night vanished. The makeshift fortress was in chaos.

Portions of the perimeter wall were on fire or under siege by a mass of moving figures. He saw silhouettes of Blues clinging to the crude barricades, scuttling across them like oversized insects. Their glowing blue eyes flashed through the flames. Off to the left, deep ogre roars split the air. He could see at least one hulking shape tearing down a portion of spiked fencing, ignoring the barbs embedded in its flesh.

Shit. They didn't waste any time.

Logan sprint-limped across the muddy ground toward his workshop. A couple of the recruits streaked by him in the opposite direction, half-dressed, and eyes wide. Some carried spears; some only carried terrified expressions.

"Hey!" Logan shouted at them. "Circle up in front! Support Ryan's position!"

They hesitated before recognizing him, giving him panicked nods, and rushing off. *Good enough*, he thought grimly.

He slammed into the workshop tent. A corner of the canvas had collapsed, probably from someone brushing too close in the scramble, but the armor stand was still upright—his exosuit beckoned in the moon-tinged gloom. Turmoil raged outside, but Logan forced himself to calm down. *Gotta get geared up.*

"Tumor, help me suit up," he hissed under his breath. "I can't see shit."

[On it.]

He tore open the front plating and chucked it over his torso, letting Tumor guide his hands to the right buckles. Gauntlets slid on next, greaves were clamped around his legs, and then the final step: the half-visor helm, which he slammed down onto his head with a click. Next, he grabbed two spare Numa crystals from the table, which were subsequently shoved into a chest slot and a small pocket on his hip.

His body felt heavier, but the exosuit's carefully balanced supports made it manageable. He flexed once, hearing the whir of sinew and composite. Then, adrenaline coursing through him, he stalked out into the madness.

Then he picked up his staff. It was long and with a heavy jagged head, almost making it a mace. It would have been completely unwieldy for a normal human, barring someone like Simmons, but with the suit's power, Logan gave it a smooth test spin.

"Let's go."

The night was a battlefield. A shriek to his right made him twist: a cluster of Blues was lunging for a group of young recruits. One of them, the girl with braids, jabbed her spear blindly. She gave a battle cry fueled with rage and fear. Her green eyes flashed, her hair whipped in the air, and her spear struck true.

She managed to wound a Blue in the shoulder, but it hissed and swiped the weapon aside, ignoring the pain. Another Blue sprang forward, mouth gaping wide with a snarl.

Logan threw himself between the recruits and the creatures, staff raised. The suit gave a low hydraulic whine, and he slammed his weapon right into the leading Blue's head. The monster's head exploded, the impact slamming it onto the ground. Due to the unholy nature of the Blues, it kept moving, but two agents from Simmons' team came and finished it off with spear and club.

"Fall back behind the barricade!" Logan snapped at the recruits. His voice boomed through the voice modulator. "Hold your line with Ryan!"

The recruits stumbled, half-yelled a "Yes, sir!" and retreated. Logan pressed forward before the Blues could regroup. He fired the built-in wrist launcher at the nearest one, sending a fusillade of sharp metal spikes whizzing toward the enemy.

A short spike lodged in its throat, turning its roar into a gargle. Still, it ignored the pain and rushed forward, although slower than the others.

The other two Blues hissed in anger, rushing at him from both sides. Logan pivoted, good leg taking the brunt, then snapped the left Blue with a staff jab, following it up with a swift elbow to the right one. The exosuit took the burden, letting him strike far harder than normal. Both Blues staggered, letting him stomp on the second one's spine with a mechanical crunch.

That felt goooood.

The other two attacked, clawing and kicking, but Logan danced away. Arrows flew in the air and hit the Blues. That gave Logan enough time to push them to the ground with a vertical staff strike. He held them down as the recruits finished them off, with Ryan's deep throat-singing ringing eerily through the chaos.

Then, a roar from across the camp pulled his attention. Beyond the roaring flames of a collapsed watchtower, an ogre hammered at the barricades, thick arms bulging with black-and-blue motley. Logan could see a row of defenders jabbing it with spears, but the blows seemed to only irritate the monster. It swatted at them, sending two flying. One landed on his neck and did not move nor scream.

Another ogre lurked behind it, bellowing and swatting away any unfortunate soul who came too close.

Crap.

"Simmons must be that way," Logan muttered. He pivoted, barking orders at anyone who would listen as he jog-limped through the swirling chaos. Then he yelled, activating his suit's voice modulator. "Group up! Stick together! Don't let them single you out! Archers, take high ground wherever you can—aim for the bigger ones first!"

He caught sight of Ryan, standing on a stack of crates, voice raised in that eerie throat-singing. The Bard's soundwaves reverberated, giving the defenders a confidence boost. Some Blues hesitated, as if the low hum disoriented them. Ryan must have gained a level. *Good.* The bard was holding his own, a short sword in hand, while two recruits guarded his flanks.

No need for instruction here.

[Logan, dodge.]

Logan listened to Tumor and followed his instincts, stepping backwards.

A fist slammed into the ground inches from Logan's feet. He scrambled backward, cursing. An ogre, snarling with blood in its mouth, loomed overhead. Its eyes glowed an unholy blue. Drool dripped from its open maw. Bits of barbed wire were still stuck in its shoulders from the fence. That had only enraged it more.

Huh. This one has normal hands.

The beast swung again. Logan raised both arms, holding his staff. The blow crashed into it, driving him to his knees. Pain flared up his spine, but the exosuit and the staff held. He used the momentum to roll aside just as it tried to stomp on him. The ground shook from the impact.

"Tumor, we've got a big one here!"

[I will overload the left gauntlet. You might break the bracer, but it'll give you a powerful strike.]

Without hesitation, Logan sensed a funneled surge of Numa from the back slotting into his gauntlet. It sparkled with a vivid blue glow. The ogre roared, raising its giant fists. Logan hopped to his feet, ignoring the scream of protest in his bad leg, and charged.

He ducked under the ogre's next swing and drove his staff into its gut. A thunderclap of energy erupted as the crackle on his gauntlet launched a current through the staff. The ogre's abdomen crumpled under the force, sending it reeling backward with a roar of agony. Its massive body crashed to the ground, thrashing in pain.

Logan pounced on the opening. He darted next to it and started smashing its head in with the heavy end of the staff, ignoring the warm spray of vile fluid. With a final, gurgling wheeze, the ogre went still.

At least these don't keep going like the Blues . . .

He sucked in a breath, chest heaving. The left gauntlet sparked, tendrils of smoke curling from its edges. The overcharge had damaged it. But it would still serviceable, hopefully.

A loud crash nearby signaled another part of the fort's fence going down. Logan swiveled, scanning for Simmons. That's when he spotted him—and, sure enough, the warrior was locked in a savage melee with an ogre. The new short sword gleamed in one hand, his trusty axe in the other. The monster advanced, swinging a gnarly wooden club that looked more like a tree trunk.

No, wait . . . that is *a tree trunk.*

Simmons parried once, but the second blow knocked him flat onto the ground with a grunt.

"Nope," Logan hissed. He sprinted to them, vaulting over a toppled crate. He landed at the ogre's flank. It towered at least two feet taller than the one he'd just killed, with giant bone spines jutting along its arms.

The creature raised its massive club to pulp Simmons. Logan crouched, prompting Tumor to route power to his legs and hips. The exosuit hummed, giving him a load of extra force.

Logan went right for the groin.

The staff connected, and he felt a satisfying crunch. The ogre roared in pain, staggering sideways. Simmons, seizing the chance, rolled to his feet, letting out a battle cry. He buried his axe blade into the thing's calf, nearly severing the whole damn leg.

The ogre's leg buckled. It howled at the sky. Logan took a running leap, tossing his staff and hooking an elbow around its thick arm, using the leverage to scramble onto its shoulders. The beast thrashed, but the composite armor shielded Logan from the worst of the jostling and unbalanced punches.

Once secure, he jammed his gauntlet straight into the ogre's temple, channeling a flicker of Numa. The extendable spikes pierced the ogre's head and its eyes rolled back. It toppled forward, half-crushing a small stack of crates as it fell. Disoriented, it roared and thrashed about, breaking the crates and sending splinters flying.

Simmons cleaved into the beast with a massive overhead swing of his axe. The blade sunk and lodged into the chest of the ogre, and it stopped moving.

Simmons wiped sweat from his brow, chest heaving. "Thanks, Boss," he managed, voice raw.

Logan clapped him on the shoulder plate. "No problem. Gather your men together and take them deeper into the camp. Let's keep a tight perimeter."

Simmons nodded and picked up his sword. "I will go defend the north side. I saw Blues hopping the fence. Some are funneling in from behind. We're barely containing them."

"Alright," Logan said. "I'll finish off the stragglers here. You push north."

Simmons nodded, barking orders at a handful of warriors who ran up to them. Blood dripped from their armor, but they looked fired up, not frightened.

Logan dashed northwards, weaving through tents and supply crates. He noticed occasional pockets of defenders fighting tooth and nail, some unleashing volleys of Logan's crossbow bolts at the Blues.

He spotted Ryan's recruits working in a tight phalanx—shields overlapping, short pikes stabbing through the gaps. Blues bunched up in front, then Ryan's group threw in a stun grenade. A chunk of the Blues collapsed on their knees and the phalanx attacked them with great fear and anger.

Encouraged by the sight, Logan propelled himself forward. Another roar from the northern fence. This time, multiple ogres battered it, tearing wide breach points. In the flickering torchlight, Logan saw at least three massive silhouettes, with some smaller shapes crawling around them. The clash of steel, the screams of pain and anger . . . it made the hair on the back of his neck stand up.

Behind the line of defenders, Kat and Balmer appeared. Kat grinned fiercely when she spotted Logan coming. She was battered and bloodied but still wearing those signature knuckles, one of which was caked in gore. Balmer clutched his rapier with a tight expression, scanning for weaknesses.

"Logan!" Kat called. "We've got at least three ogres up front. Don't think the crossbows are gonna cut it at this range."

"Then, we go up close," Logan growled, feeling the exosuit's plates dig into his shoulders. "I'll lead the charge. Kat, flank left, Balmer, flank right. Keep the small ones off me if you can."

They readied themselves. The ring of defenders parted, letting Logan through. He gave a sharp nod. Then he sprinted straight at the closest ogre, visor down, heart pumping.

It swung a tree trunk sideways. Logan ducked, letting it crush a barricade behind him, and smashed his staff into its ribs. It stumbled, roaring in pain. Kat came in low, hooking her knuckles into its ankles, nearly toppling it. A second ogre rushed at them from the side, but Balmer intercepted, darting around with rapier strikes, distracting it as his men hurled spears at its flank.

The first ogre, wounded but enraged, whipped around and tried to backhand Logan. He blocked with his bracers, wincing at the force. Sparks flew from the damaged left gauntlet. *Time to finish this.* He gathered the last bit of Numa from his hip reservoir, letting it flow into his right gauntlet, then clobbered the ogre with a spiked uppercut under its jaw. Its skull jerked back with a sickening crack. It wobbled for a half-second, then collapsed on its back.

[Skill Level Up!]
[Power Armor Fighting Level 19]

A savage cheer rose from the defenders behind them. Logan didn't even pause to revel in it. Instead, he turned, panting, as the second ogre struggled under a barrage of quick stabs from Balmer and a ring of spear-wielding Faelves who were trembling with fear.

The monster swung blindly, but Kat ducked beneath its wild arm, hammering a flurry of punches into its gut, and Balmer drove his rapier through the juncture at its throat. The beast gave a final wet gurgle before dropping to the ground like a felled tree.

Across the breadth of the camp, more shouts echoed. Logan saw pockets of Blues fleeing. Some of them slinked away into the darkness, leaving behind carnage. A handful of defenders chased them, hurling crossbow bolts and spears at them and cheering. A dull boom rang out near the southern side—someone must have thrown another stun bomb. The brief flash lit the sky, accompanied by a chorus of pained shrieks. Then, silence. Or, at least, something close to it.

They're fleeing. Just like Simmons said they did when their scouts were spotted.

[This attack was too organized to be random.]

"It sure was," Logan said. "And I don't like it."

Logan stood there, chest heaving, armor plates cracked and smoking in places. Sweat drenched his brow under the visor. He looked around, seeing pockets of wounded defenders but no fresh wave of attackers. For the moment, it seemed the main threat was broken.

"Alright!" he roared, flipping the visor up. "Medic teams, get in here! Kat, Balmer, start a headcount. Make sure the perimeter is sealed again. Everyone else, check for wounded or stragglers—Simmons, go after them, but don't chase them too far!"

There was no shortage of chaos, but the defenders rallied. One by one, small squads took up posts at the battered barricades, largely breathless but determined. The stench of ogre blood and burnt wood hung in the air, a testament to the night's violence.

Logan let out a shaky breath. Tumor told him that the Numa crystals were depleted. The left gauntlet was half-fried. But the camp still stood. They'd survived a savage assault.

[We sustained moderate damage. But so far, the exosuit is intact enough. The first test is a success. It will need some basic maintenance, and we need more Numa.]

"Let's hope we don't need it too soon," Logan muttered. "At least not tonight."

Logan scanned the cooling-down battlefield, helping a wounded recruit to her feet, and barking instructions to a couple of shell-shocked men. Through the haze of smoke and flickering fires, he spotted Ryan in the distance, leaning on a spear and clutching his side but mercifully still alive. Simmons vanished into the woods with a group of his agents. Freya emerged from her triage area, hurrying over with bandages at the ready.

"You hurt?" she asked, rushing over to Logan.

Logan shook his head. "I'm fine."

"Thank the Goddess," she said, and a trickle of tears glimmered in her eyes as she rushed over to him and kissed him. He answered in earnest.

Once they had unentangled themselves, Logan told her to return to the wounded and promised to come see her soon. She nodded and left.

Exhaustion weighed on Logan's limbs, but victory coursed through him. They had done it. He felt a fierce grin tug at his lips.

But looking at the mangled bodies and bleeding recruits, Logan realized they had paid heavily for survival tonight.

[Casualties were going to be inevitable.]

"We'll avenge them."

Whatever Levemoth was planning, it had just sent them an ugly preview. They'd withstood tonight's ambush, but tomorrow, or the next day, they'd have to venture into those dark ruins anyway. Because if attacking them at night was this easy, Levemoth might do so again, stronger each time.

And next time, our forces will be split.

And in the blood-soaked, flame-lit night, the battered defenders steeled themselves for whatever dawn would bring. They were bruised and shaken but not broken.

"At least people leveled up a bunch tonight," Logan said. "I feel that by the end of this, we will be whittled down to a gleaming blade of hard warriors. Levemoth had better goddamn watch out."

CHAPTER 12

Wounds and Splinters

By the time morning came, the fires had been reduced to scattered embers. The camp was busted—splintered barricades, scattered debris, and the scent of blood lingering in the damp earth. Logan stood near what used to be a crisp, wheat-colored tent, now torn half to shreds, with dark stains spattering the canvas. A fresh band of recruits, who looked like they'd aged a year overnight, knelt beside the fallen, covering the bodies with spare blankets.

Logan clenched a fist, pushing away the emotions. Now was not the time.

Freya stepped up quietly next to him. She'd been tending the wounded all night, eyes bleary but resolute. "It's worse than I thought," she murmured, closing her eyes.

Logan gave a tiny nod. "Casualties?" he asked.

"At least two dozen dead," she said softly. "Another forty wounded. Some lightly, some . . . not so lightly."

Logan exhaled. Out of around six hundred fighters, that was acceptable. But it had just been a single attack.

Even with the improved defenses, real battle was messy.

"We need to bury them," Freya said, gesturing at the blanketed corpses. "We can't leave them out in this heat."

"No," Logan said curtly. "They'll get dug up and turned into Blues."

A few of the mourning recruits looked up at Logan, and Logan met their gazes one by one. There was defiance and anger in those eyes.

Logan didn't budge. "Would you guys rather burn your friends or fight them tonight? Huh?"

One of the women on her knees burst into tears. The rest averted their eyes.

Logan's gaze bore into Freya, waiting for an answer.

Freya answered stiffly but earnestly. "We'll see it done."

Logan turned, eyes scanning the camp. A few golems from the Groloin Hivemind lumbered about, assisting in cleanup. One used a pincer-like arm to lift an ogre's huge severed limb, depositing it on a makeshift pyre. The Faelves had begun a solemn ritual for the dead, chanting in soft voices. They had already gathered their dead in a pile. There were not many, since most Faelves didn't fight. Still, even seeing four child-formed Faelves with sickly pale porcelain skin made Logan sick.

No time for that.

Somewhere on the other side of the camp, Ryan's recruits were collecting the last bits of scattered gear from last night's skirmish. Everyone looked exhausted.

They need sleep. But it's in short supply.

Logan spotted Simmons helping pile wreckage into a corner. The man's face was set in a stern frown, a fresh gash on his arm bound crudely with a cloth. They had some spare Numa for the **[Healers]** to use on the severely wounded. Everyone else with light injuries would just have to wait.

We will need a healer with us on the delve.

Kat and Balmer walked through the ruins of the fence, quietly taking stock of what sections needed immediate repair.

"Time to get on it," Logan said to Freya, gently this time. "I'm going to walk the perimeter, see who needs me."

She nodded. "I'll get Ryan to give me some men to help carry the dead."

"Ask if the Faelves are alright with one big pile," Logan said, then hesitantly added. "I know it's not the most . . . reverent, but we are short on time and energy. Any efficiency helps."

"I understand," Freya said quietly.

Logan set off, stepping over soft mud, pools of blood, and splinters. As he passed people, he gave them stiff nods. Some tried to mumble greetings or half-smiles of gratitude. Others only stared dully at the horizon, eyes still glazed with shock.

Near the northern breach, where the heaviest fighting had raged, Logan found Snoff directing a team of Faelves. They were setting up new wooden stakes. Snoff's face was tight, his usual cheer gone. But he still offered Logan a wave.

"We'll get it shored up by midday," Snoff said, voice grave. "Though, next time, we might not be so lucky."

Logan glanced at the remains of a torn ogre corpse splayed across the ground. "I know. Any idea how many more of these things might be out there?"

Snoff gave a small shrug. "No clue. A lot, I wager. Regrouping or waiting for an order from the Great Thief."

Logan followed Snoff's gaze. Beyond the tree line, you could just see a hint of that swirling black-and-blue mass in the far distance, blotting out the dawn's colors. *Levemoth.* No one needed to name it. The sight of it alone soured Logan's stomach.

"We are going to need more Faelves in the defense, Snoff."

The Faelf were quiet for a while, considering an answer. After a moment, he spoke.

"We are not fighters, Logan."

"I know that," Logan said impatiently. "But thirty of my best will be going to the ruins with me, along with a sizable support crew. What happens to our defenses here without them?"

"They will snap like a dry twig in a storm," Snoff said.

"I know I ask for a lot," Logan said. "But we are stretched too thin."

"I understand," Snoff said in that same tone Freya had used.

Logan cursed under his breath. How many times did he need to hear those reluctant words?

"We have our own magic," Snoff said. "We can create illusions, distractions, smoke and mirrors, even traps. But we are no match for an ogre."

"I know," Logan said. "Do what you can. Use every trick in the bag."

"I will do it, Logan. Even though this will cost the lives of many of my friends, I understand."

Logan thanked Snoff and moved on. The exosuit felt heavier with each step—partly from last night's damage, partly from the weight of everything. Tumor's presence came up in his head, silent for the moment but poised to say something. In the end, he remained silent, and Logan was thankful for it.

Halfway through the battered camp, Logan heard a sobbing sound. He spotted the girl with braids from the night before. She was hunched beside a torn-up patch of ground, wrapping a shattered spear in cloth. He recognized it as the weapon of one of her friends. Her shoulders shook, though she made no noise beyond hitched breaths.

Logan approached, mindful of her grief. He laid a gentle hand on her arm. "I'm sorry," he said quietly.

She nodded, not looking at him. A moment later, she rose to her feet, took a shaky breath, and cleared her throat. "I . . . we have duties. The others—"

"What's your name?" Logan asked.

She hesitated. Such a fierce battle-maiden last night. Now, a shy young girl.

"Elise."

"You're free to rest, Elise," Logan offered.

She shook her head fiercely. "No. I need to do something. But thank you, sir. Thank you for that, and . . . for saving my life last night, I—"

Her face scrunched up and she struggled to hold back tears.

He gave her shoulder a squeeze, then let her go. There was nothing to say. She hurried off into the bustle, cloth-wrapped spear in hand.

A heaviness built in Logan's chest. This glimpse of raw loss made him want to rage, to meet Levemoth face-to-face and let it all out. But that was just frustration. Right now, they had to be smart. Last night was a warning—or maybe just the start of a longer barrage.

He trudged back toward the Ark, feeling a prickle at his senses. For a heartbeat, he almost heard it—a deep, distant thrum tugging at his consciousness. The sky seemed darker, as though something out there was flexing its power. A chill raced down his spine.

[I felt it too. It's Levemoth.]

Logan's fists clenched. "Great. Guess we're not out of the woods yet."

[The clock is ticking, Logan.]

Logan exhaled slowly, forcing himself to stay calm. He resisted the morbid urge to look at the sky. He knew what he would see. An ancient monster overshadowing every living thing beneath that corrupted sky.

"All the more reason to hurry."

He found a group of humans and Faelves near the cargo bay ramp of the Ark. Simmons was there, along with Kat, Balmer, Ryan, and a handful of others. They were stacked around a makeshift table with a half-burned map pinned down by daggers, designed by the one and only **[Cartographer]** in their midst. The map was an accurate depiction of the camp and its surroundings. When they saw Logan approaching, they straightened, faces grim.

"Gather 'round," Logan said with grim humor, removing his helm and tucking it under an arm.

Simmons folded his arms. "We lost some good people," he said, voice tight. "And it won't be the last of it. Last night proved that they can hit us any time they want."

"How many did you manage to chase down after the attack?" Logan asked.

"Two dozen Blues, one ogre," Simmons said. "Not enough."

"Let's hope it'll buy us a few days," Logan said. "Ryan, what do you have for me?"

Balmer nodded. "The soldiers are on edge. We can't keep them at full alert around the clock. We need rest."

Kat jabbed a thumb behind her. "We're low on equipment too. We lost fifty spears and shields. The crossbow ammo's half-gone. Not to mention your exosuit looks pretty beat up."

Logan grimaced. "I'll do some quick repairs. But time's short, and I can't spend all day forging new gear."

Ryan ran a hand through his disheveled hair. "Are we still going down to the ruins? Or do we hold here?"

The question hung in the air. A few of the defenders working nearby paused, obviously straining to listen.

Logan stepped closer to the table, leaning against it for emphasis. "We don't have a choice. If we stay holed up, Levemoth will keep sending attacks until we're whittled away. And then what? We need to get on the offense."

Simmons let out a grunt that gestured agreement. "Then, we proceed. But we have to do it carefully. We can't take the entire camp. We need a skeleton crew to keep the walls defended."

"Exactly," Logan said. "We'll select a strike team of thirty men. Enough to handle the dungeon's deeper floors. Along with a support crew, so we don't have to keep rotating men and gear."

"Solid plan."

"Kat, you're on that team. Balmer too," Logan said. "Ryan, I want you— you and, say, twenty of your best men and women. The rest stay here under Simmons."

Ryan swallowed but nodded. "Got it."

"Balmer, scrounge up any leftover Numa shards and banged-up equipment. We'll need whatever we can get to power my exosuit, plus the repairs for broken gear. Simmons, give me five of your agents. They get priority on the freshest gear. Then, get some food in them. We head out at first light tomorrow."

Simmons nodded. "It will be done."

Logan's eyes swept the group. "That's about all the time we can afford, given the Big Bad in the sky. Any questions?"

None answered. They all bore the same grim expressions.

"Good," Logan said. "Then let's do it. Go."

They scattered, each to their task. A hush settled after they left, as if the camp itself was holding its breath.

Logan spent the next hours tending to what he could. First, he swung by the triage tents to check on Freya. She was buried in the wounded, sleeves rolled up and hands gloved in dried blood. She paused long enough to meet his gaze, offering a sad smile.

"Some we can save. A lot of them need Numa intervention. We're short on crystals, so we have to make shitty choices," she said, her eyes blazing with weary resolve.

He nodded. "Use all you can. We can't let them die if it's preventable."

She gave him a quick squeeze on the arm. "We're doing our best."

"Thanks," he murmured, forcing out a reassuring nod before ducking back into the chaos.

He headed for his workshop tent to see what could be salvaged. The exosuit needed a fresh gauntlet. *Maybe reinforce the left arm with another composite layer.* The staff, battered from ogre skulls, needed a reforged head. So. he propped them on the bench, rummaging for scraps of sinew and leftover metal shards.

[We won't have time for major fixes.]

Logan grimaced. "I know. Just enough to keep it from falling apart mid-fight. That's all we need until we find another power source."

[Understood.]

He worked quickly, hands moving with mechanical precision as he smoothed out dents and fused fractured plates with **[Transmutation]**.

Sweat poured down his back. The sun rose higher, lending a sticky heat to the air. From behind the tent walls, the clamoring kept up with the hammering of nails, the moans of the injured, and barked orders. And overlaying it all was that feeling wrongness being projected by Levemoth's pulsing cocoon up in the sky.

By the afternoon, the exosuit was passable. Logan tested the left gauntlet by punching a wooden post. It held, though it groaned. The staff was heavier now thanks to a recrafted head, which would increase the damage to ogre skulls. Tumor gave him the relevant statistics from an analysis of last night, and Logan had no reason to complain.

Before dark, Logan convened once more with Simmons, Kat, Balmer, Ryan, Snoff, and a couple of others, ironing out final assignments—who'd be responsible for what. There was a lot to consider. Defense, scouting, logistics. Simmons would be his second-in-command. And there was the Groloin Hivemind, of course, but they were a passive decision-maker at best.

"Remember," Logan said, voice low, "they'll likely send more attackers. But when we can claim deeper crystals, we will send some back up. You have to keep fighting long enough. That's the goal."

Simmons uncharacteristically clapped him on the back, but it felt right to Logan. Enough misery together had built true camaraderie. "Then. we'll do it. Just don't let us get overrun."

Logan gave him a faint grin. "It's not like we're going to be having a picnic down there ourselves."

Simmons laughed. It was a little forced, but any kind of shitty gallows humor helped at this point.

Finally, long after the sun had dipped below the horizon, the camp settled into a tense hush. People tried to rest. Guards kept vigil on the newly repaired barricades. Torchlight flickered, casting dancing shadows across the battered ground. Overhead, a swirl of roiling clouds promised the possibility of a storm. Or maybe it was Levemoth.

Logan hobbled to his small corner of the camp, where Freya stood, arms folded. She offered no words, just a weary half-smile. Together, they eased into a makeshift tent, battered from the prior night's chaos. Logan placed his staff on the floor next to the exosuit.

They both silently acknowledged the same fear: that this night might bring another savage attack, or that tomorrow's delve could be the real end of it all. But neither said it. Instead, Freya gently guided Logan to lie down, placed a palm on his chest, and lowered her head to his.

"Short rest," she whispered. "We take it where we can."

He wrapped an arm around her, feeling the tension in her muscles, the unrelenting worry in her eyes. "We'll survive," he muttered, more hope than fact. "We have to."

She nodded, lips pressing together in a silent vow. Then they both closed their eyes, pressing back the dread for a few hours. Above them, the Ark's silhouette rose like a sleeping giant, while the foul swirl of Levemoth's cocoon roiled in the distance, all of it a reminder that time was not on their side.

Despite their exhaustion, their hands and lips moved in silent agreement to more intimate and intimate places. Both of them knew they might not see each other after tonight.

CHAPTER 13

Second Attempt

Logan's boots echoed softly on dry stone. The narrow corridor ahead was lit only by the faint light of a handful of magical flashlights that Logan had made, each carried by one of his people. Behind him, a dozen more figures trod carefully, weapons at the ready, breaths echoing in that stale, restlessly quiet air.

They'd entered the ruins an hour ago. The first steps down the massive stone ramp were familiar—this was the same path they'd cleared earlier. A few chipped corners and cracks where they'd battled Blues last time remained in evidence. It was a reminder that this place was dangerous.

No one spoke much. Conversation was kept to a minimum: short gestures, soft confirmations, occasional whispers. Every so often, Balmer crept ahead, stealthing quick and light like a cat made of shadows. Sometimes Logan envied his easy movement. Dressed in light leathers with a rapier on his belt, Felix Balmer moved like a ghost.

At least for now all the pressure is on him. That's a nice change of pace.

[You are still in charge the minute something goes wrong.]

"Don't remind me," Logan muttered.

The corridor curved, and they had to cross a narrow bridge. It was made from solid stone, was slightly crumbled, and had no safety railing—clearly intended for defense. Logan jumped over it with a Numa-powered leap, not wanting to stress the structure with the weight of his suit.

After hesitation and negotiating, the rest of the group followed, and they all went forward. They passed a long corridor which led into a domed chamber they'd all recognized from the previous run. The drained Numa crystal floated alone in the center of the massive room. Artistic carvings lined the walls, faded by time. There were dozens upon dozens of empty rooms carved in stone. They had to have been houses for the First Folk.

Ryan stepped up to Logan's side. His flashlight revealed a way forward deeper into the darkness. Anything could happen from this point onwards.

Ryan said, in a near whisper, "We still heading through that tunnel?"

Logan nodded. "We are. Balmer and you go first. Then the rest of the group. Keep it tight."

Balmer, who was listening close by, nodded. He slid forward silently, picking his way carefully over toppled stones and the remnants of a broken doorway.

Behind them, the rest of the team inched along: Kat with her knuckle-daggers strapped across her waist, a few of Ryan's recruits carrying short crossbows, as well as a few agents that Simmons had graciously given them.

Eventually, they reached a wide corridor with tall, arched ceilings. As if by chance, Logan's flashlight pointed in the right direction and he saw it. A button. A small one, made of plastic, for a cheap office shirt.

Blues . . .

Kat glanced around, knuckles flexing. "It's too quiet," she muttered.

Logan agreed silently. He'd almost rather they face some minor resistance, just to dispel the tension. But better no fight than a savage ambush, he reasoned. He led them onward.

Ahead, Balmer paused, kneeling by the threshold to examine footprints. He traced the dusty floor with two fingers, squinting at the hue of the debris there. Then he turned back to Logan. "Nothing fresh. These scuffs look old."

"Alright," Logan replied softly, "let's move on."

Balmer waved them over to the far side of the room, where an ornate archway stood half-buried in rubble. It was large enough for them to crawl through one by one, but it would take time. Balmer went first and after a moment he whispered from the other side.

"All clear."

Logan clambered through, his suit proving to be a bit cumbersome for the first time. It wasn't designed for crawling. Despite the high-end material and numerous enchantments, it was stiff.

With the darkmetal Armor I would have had no problem at all . . .

The passage on the other side stretched forward in a slight decline, its walls carved with faint designs—swirling lines, maybe symbolic or decorative. Some looked not fully finished, as if the makers had abandoned the corridor mid-chisel.

They walked, footfalls echoing. Occasionally, water dripped from cracks above, forming little rivulets. Twice Logan ordered them to drink up and fill their flasks from the little streams. They went deeper. The temperature dropped noticeably. Logan felt a chill on his cheeks, despite the layers of the exosuit.

As they went on, they paused every so often at side alcoves or branching corridors that turned out to be dead ends. Balmer scouted carefully, tapping the floor with the heel of his boot to detect traps. None appeared. No holes, no hidden spikes. Some rooms were empty, dusty storage spaces, their contents long decayed. The only thing out of place was a pervasive silence that pressed on Logan's ears.

One of Ryan's recruits whispered, "Feels like a tomb."

Logan agreed silently. Even the distant hum of wind didn't reach here. It was an oppressive quiet, like the ruin itself was holding its breath, waiting for them to cross a line they shouldn't.

They proceeded with methodical caution. For every twenty or thirty paces, they paused, listened, and sniffed the air. No rotting stench, no growls.

Kat, near the front, muttered at one point, "Wouldn't mind a couple of Blues about now. At least that'd give me a reason to punch something."

Logan shot her a reproving glance. "Shh."

They pressed on. After what felt like a mile of winding galleries and partially collapsed side chambers, they reached a set of wide stairs that descended deeper into the ruin. The steps were worn smooth, the architecture shifting style here—more blocky, less ornate. Balmer told them to halt at the top, where they were able to scan the gloom below.

Logan sidled up. "Check it out?"

Balmer nodded. "I'll go first."

A minute later, Balmer's voice floated back up, hushed but clear:

"Mostly empty. Some old pillars. No movement."

They descended in a careful file. At the bottom, a spacious hall spread out, maybe a hundred feet across, dotted with stone supports. Chiseled murals along the walls depicted strange, swirling shapes—images once painted but now flaking away. Kat took a brief moment to run her knuckles over a portion that showed what might have been a giant whale-serpent with its bottom half covered by a thundercloud, devouring a sun. Or maybe it was just some idle doodle. Hard to interpret in the dark.

"Anyone see anything?" Logan asked softly.

They all peered ahead. Nothing moved. Another recruit leaned forward, shining a flashlight. The corner in question contained a cluster of lumps and debris. Balmer advanced warily, rapier held in one hand, the other closed in a stressed fist.

Then he crouched and prodded the lumps with his blade. A dull clank answered.

"Metal," Balmer whispered. "And . . . bone?"

Logan came over, stepping carefully. He looked downwards, squinting, and saw what looked like a scattering of dull black lumps of iron or maybe slag. But once he picked up a piece and turned it in the lantern light, he recognized the glint of darkmetal, the same near-obsidian sheen shot through with faint grooves. His heart started thumping in elation.

"Darkmetal." He breathed. "And it looks there's some decayed skeleton just over there . . ." Hard to say. The bones were fused to the floor, as if they'd melted.

Kat stepped around them, careful not to touch anything, her brow furrowed. "You think it was storing darkmetal? Or the occupant died here?"

Logan shrugged. "No idea, but I'm not complaining. We can use it." He held the piece up, letting the faint Numa-lamps catch its gleam. Even a small chunk of darkmetal was beyond valuable. Logan's mind was spinning with possibilities. "Gather it. Be careful to not miss so much as a speck!"

The recruits took a few moments to collect them, stowing them in thick pouches. Meanwhile, Logan scanned the ceiling, looking for any hazardous structural cracks. Nothing. Just a swirl of dust and silence. He let out a small sigh of relief, as if the place was granting them a peaceful passage for once.

They moved on, finding a side corridor that eventually looped back to the main hall. Another dead end, though one with interesting runic etchings on the walls—some repeated pattern like a serpent devouring its own tail. The Faelves paused to examine it, but none could decipher its meaning.

Time stretched. The entire expedition advanced in increments, Balmer scouting thirty yards ahead, the rest following. Ryan kept a hand on his sword hilt, face tense but determined. The Faelves stuck close, occasionally using small illusions to light corners or test for illusions laid by enemies. Each corridor echoed with their subdued footsteps, seemingly deeper than the labyrinth warranted.

Logan wanted to stop. The troops needed rest, and he wanted to use the darkmetal. Although with as little Numa as they had, he couldn't unleash its full potential.

Always something, isn't there?

Eventually, the path sloped down even further, leading to a cluster of smaller rooms with weird hexagonal doorways cut into the rock. Each door led to a chamber of nearly identical layout: a half-collapsed pedestal in the center, ringed by arcs of stone. On each of those pedestals, they discovered, a faintly glowing Numa crystal floated. Not large—maybe the size of a child's head.

D-graders. Six of them. Enough to siphon for immediate use.

Ryan gave Logan a hopeful glance. "We taking these?"

"Absolutely," Logan said. "Careful, though."

Logan carefully pried the crystal free from the pedestal. Whatever force was keeping it afloat resisted when he pulled but eventually relented.

Logan weighed it in his palm, feeling the hum of raw energy. He checked it.

[D-grade Numa Crystal, 100%]

With six of them, combined with the darkmetal, he could make magic happen.

Kat exhaled, a little of the tension leaving her posture. "Finally, something good we can bring back."

"Right," Balmer said softly, gaze flicking around. "Still no sign of any threats, though. You'd think something would be guarding this place."

They all felt it. The deeper they explored, the more uneasy they grew with the absolute stillness. But for now, that was a boon.

Logan collected each of the crystals from all of the pedestals. He was worried something might happen after removing the last one—but nothing did. He put the crystals in one of their carts, and they carried on. Now they just needed a place to rest.

They pressed on, exploring a few more identical side rooms—all of them empty. Logan could hear some ragged breathing and when he looked back, he saw tired faces.

"How's everyone holding up?" Logan asked quietly. "We can push ahead another couple of hours or head back to camp now. I want at least a good sense of what lies below."

Kat shrugged. "I'm good to keep going, but some of these recruits look frazzled." Indeed, a few of Ryan's newer folks were avoiding Logan's gaze.

"We will rest at the first defendable place we find," Logan decided.

Balmer adjusted his rapier. "All right, I'll keep scouting."

They continued. The corridor here was narrower, funneling them into single-file. The walls pressed close, carved with that same swirling motif. In the flickering light of their lamps, the patterns almost seemed to move. A trick of the eyes, perhaps.

Eventually, they reached a spot where the corridor opened again into a small antechamber. The floor was littered with rubble. A single door stood on the far side, but it was heavily cracked, sealed by time. Balmer tested it gently, but it barely budged. Trying to open it would take serious force—likely an explosion or heavy machinery.

Logan grunted. "We'll mark it. Let's not waste the day blowing open any sealed rooms yet. We've got no guarantee it leads anywhere vital."

Balmer nodded, pulled out a small stub of chalk, and drew a quick sign on the stone: a circle with a slash, indicating "sealed passage."

Then they backtracked, carefully retracing their steps. Each footstep echoed in the same eerie way. Occasionally, a distant drip of water broke the hush. They circled through a side corridor they hadn't fully examined yet—just to be thorough—and found nothing but a collapsed wall and more half-etched murals.

Kat let out an exasperated grunt at one point. "Does this place go on forever?"

Ryan gave a faint smile. "If it does, we'll map it eventually. For now, I'd rather a giant sign that says 'Treasure this way.'"

"All the same," Balmer said quietly, "I'll take empty corridors over a pack of ogres."

No one argued.

Finally they found a large-enough room to house all of their forty or so people, with space for most of them to lie down and take a power nap. The room was large, like a mess hall, easily fitting two hundred people. It had one entrance at which Logan immediately set up a watch. Then he hustled around, making sure everything was just so before he sat down and sighed.

Kat fell in step beside Logan, voice still hushed. "So, we found a few lumps of darkmetal and some Numa to boot. Not a bad haul, all things considered."

Logan nodded. "It's a start. Could do a lot with that darkmetal in the short term, maybe patch the exosuit better or craft some new weapons. I'll need to think while we rest."

Ryan overheard and gave a small smile. "Might not be a big fortune, but we'll take it as a victory. No losses, no injuries."

"Agreed," Logan said, shoulders loosening. "I've got some wild ideas for the darkmetal. Too bad we don't have more . . ."

"If there was a goddamn mountain of it, it still wouldn't satisfy you," Kat said and smirked.

"What can I say?" Logan said. "I am a man of big appetites."

"I know . . ." Kat said and smiled like a cat. "Me and Freya talk."

Logan sputtered out the water he'd been drinking, and Balmer laughed, clapping him on the shoulder.

"Nice to be on this side of the table for a change," he said to Logan as he chuckled.

CHAPTER 14

Upgrades

After Logan had rested his eyes for fifteen minutes, just breathing and lying down, letting Tumor optimize his brain chemistry, he felt relaxed again. Even though nothing had happened so far, it was nerve-wracking to be responsible for so many lives.

I think I'm ready, though.

[I think so, too.]

Logan surveyed their little resting place. Most people were resting as well. Some were chatting in a corner or just keeping to themselves, stress visible on their faces. Nothing was out of place, though, and that was good.

"Tumor," he said quietly, though in the silence it sounded louder than intended, "I want a headcount of our resources."

[We have enough rations for another two days. Water for three, if we don't mind more trickles. Bandages and other medical supplies haven't been used, so we are still good on that. Everyone is slightly fatigued, but even the ones with weaker constitutions can still go on. As for the darkmetal, we have twenty ounces of it.]

"No decimals?"

[The mood is not right.]

Logan chuckled and started rummaging through one of the pouches strapped at his side. Sure enough, the lumps of darkmetal seemed to weigh around that. It wasn't a lot but definitely enough to do something interesting.

"Good enough," Logan said. "Better than nothing."

He took a glance around to ensure the others were settling in okay. Ryan was distributing dried meat, nuts, and water. One of his recruits was munching on a hard biscuit made by the Faelves, eyes flicking from the group to the entrance.

Settling deeper, Logan pulled the lumps of darkmetal onto a rag and set them on the ground in front of him. Gently, he began running a hand across them, feeling them out, letting his thoughts flow freely to find something creative.

"I'm open to suggestions, Tumor," Logan said under his breath. "What's the best use of this? A new plating? Another staff head? Or . . .?"

[We need more firepower. Ogres are savage. The quicker we can cut them down, the fewer hits they land on us. A heavier offensive approach might serve better than extra armor right now. Because if you can put them down fast, they won't get the chance to hit you at all.]

Logan nodded slowly. "I was thinking the same. Best defense is a good offense. Half the time, I'm slogging away with big hits that only wound them. If we want them gone quick, I need something that hits like a chunk of lead to the face."

[Exactly. We could shape it into a wrist attachment. That way, we can also fit it for defensive purposes.]

Logan rubbed his jaw, eyes locked on the lumps of black metal. "Great minds think alike! We are obviously going for the same ideas we used with the Armor. We'll make it liquid and have you control it. That will give us a lot of options."

[Quite so. We can link it via the exosuit's left bracer. That way it'll be easy to use as a swordlike blade or a shield, or even use it to fling a small projectile.]

"No bullets this time, sadly. We don't have the budget for it. But maybe something that's adjacent to projectiles . . ."

Logan glanced at the corridor. Everyone else was preoccupied, so he arranged the Numa crystals and darkmetal onto a cloth in front of him. He felt like he was ready to work, excitement building in him with the opportunity to use darkmetal again.

"Alright, let's do this quietly," he said to Tumor. He then lifted his gaze at the sound of Kat approaching with an easy gait. She looked at the arrangement in front of Logan and raised a brow. "Strange picnic you've got there. What are you up to? Something for me?"

Logan scowled. "Don't you even. You and Balmer already have darkmetal toys."

"Tsk, such a selfish and greedy leader," Kat said.

Logan gave her a tired look.

She smirked and left him to concentrate.

Logan closed his eyes, letting out a measured breath. He placed both hands over the lumps of darkmetal. Beneath his palms, he felt the cool, slightly slick texture of the substance. Logan had to savor the moment and just admire the darkmetal for a moment. This was no normal metal that had existed on Earth. It had an almost hypnotic dark sheen, like obsidian that drank up the faint light from the flashlights set around the room.

"Alright, time to make you into a thing of beauty," he murmured, once Tumor was finished with his calculations and had shown Logan a floating hologram of the shapes and told him the measurements. It was a simple, thin shape, like an extra plate to attach to the right forearm of the suit.

A faint glow shimmered around his hand. The other was holding a Numa crystal. The lumps shuddered, merging together. Slowly, the metal softened like molten wax under a flame. The metal worked with him *easily*. Even though he was only doing some basic transmutation, combining the materials and morphing them, the material was very responsive. Whereas things like wood, bone, and stone were dead, it was almost like darkmetal cooperated with him.

Beads of sweat formed on Logan's brow. He pictured the lines and the shape and chanted the measurements just as Tumor said them.

Gradually, the darkmetal formed a sheet of metal, thick as cardboard.

"You're doing okay?" Kat whispered from a few feet away, eyeing the spectacle.

Logan only nodded, too focused to speak.

[Now, mold it around the forearm armor.]

Logan noticed the suit was pretty beaten up, so he spared some of the Numa to use **[Repair]** on it.

[Skill Level Up!]
[Repair Level 22]

Then, Logan carefully positioned his arm forward. He placed the sheet of darkmetal on it and transmuted it to wrap around the forearm, forming a broad cuff.

"Perfect," he muttered. "Now's the time to enchant it."

Logan gave the darkmetal attachment a liquefaction enchantment. Then he poured everything into strengthening the material. He used a total of four of the D-graders. That would allow the darkmetal to remain hard and solid even when stretched thin.

[Attribute Level Up!]
[Control: 40]

Logan would have used more, but the darkmetal couldn't take any more. So, he used one crystal to **[Repair]** various equipment that had been second-rate, and gave one crystal to the medical team.

Then, Logan tested the new device. With a soft exhalation, he sent a mental prompt to Tumor, who responded immediately by controlling the metal. The cuff rippled, then extended a smooth black blade five inches outward from his forearm. Another subvocalization to Tumor made it retract, smoothing itself into a sleek band.

Kat, who'd been watching from a few feet away, gave a low whistle. "That's pretty sick."

Ryan, munching on a piece of dried fruit, came over, too. "So, does it just, like, become a sword?"

"Or a shield. Or anything I can think of."

"Very creative," Ryan said. "Gives you lots of options."

"Yeah . . . You'd think so before you realize how little time you actually have to think in fights."

"I know, right?" Ryan said and shook his head. "In stories, fighters always seem to have all these options. But in reality, fights happen in seconds."

"So far, you're doing good."

"Well, I am alive, aren't I? But I'm in the backline, just singing."

"Keep doing that," Logan said.

"So . . ." Balmer came up to them. "We moving?"

Logan nodded. "I'll be efficient."

He looked around at the group. Some were dozing lightly, others eating. The agents Simmons had given him were keeping watch by the door.

Ryan, who had strolled off earlier, returned, holding a small piece of polished wood. That was odd to see in a dungeon. The First Folk preferred stone. "Hey," he said softly, "we found some random scraps of . . . I think it was a statue pedestal. It's not rotten. Might be good for carving. Or whatever you do."

Logan quirked a brow, glancing at the wood, then at Ryan. "Why do you need that?"

Ryan smiled embarrassedly. "I leveled up and got a skill, **[Accompaniment]**. It tells me my effects are much stronger when I sing and play. Figured you could make me an instrument."

Kat snorted from her seat. "He's a Bard, remember? He wants to do musicals in the middle of a ruin."

Ryan shot her a mock glare, then turned a hopeful gaze on Logan. "But we do have some leftover Numa, right? I was thinking maybe a small lute or something. If it's not too much to ask."

Logan considered that. He had just given away the leftovers from their loot, but he had some of his own to spare. Ryan's voice had definitely played a big part in keeping morale high, disorienting the Blues around them. If his effects could even become stronger, an instrument could tip the scale and make hard fights more manageable.

He gave a small nod. "All right, sure. We do need that advantage, and your singing definitely shakes up our enemies." He motioned for the piece of wood. "Give me that."

Ryan's tired face lit up with gratitude. "Thank you! I promise I won't stand in the middle of a fight strumming away like an idiot."

"Just don't break it over your knee in a fit of musical inspiration," Kat teased.

Logan pushed off the pillar and flexed his shoulders, ignoring the dull ache. Hanging around in armor sucked.

Logan took the battered piece of pedestal from Ryan, turning it over in his hands. It was about a foot long, wide as a forearm, and the grain was still solid—some type of ancient hardwood. How it had survived the test of time was beyond Logan. Tumor had some suggestions, but Logan wasn't interested right now.

"Can you give me the specs on a lute?"

[That's not something that's in my database, actually. But I can extrapolate. Give me a minute.]

"You got it," Logan said.

He waited, letting Tumor do whatever Tumor did best: run simulations, crunch variables, engineer blueprints. Finally, a floating image of a lute appeared in Logan's vision.

Logan plucked an **[E-grade Numa Crystal]** from his pocket and went to work on the piece of wood.

The wood twitched, faint lines of blue dancing along its surface. He coaxed the shape outward, smoothing the edges, and hollowing the inner section a bit.

After several minutes, the piece began to resemble a lute with a short neck, minus strings. The back curved slightly; the front was flatter. A small hollow chamber inside would amplify the sound. Next came the trickier part:

forging or crafting strings. They had no catgut or standard wire on them. However, Logan rummaged through a small supply pouch and found a coil of monster sinew. He was considering transmuting the material before Ryan interjected.

"Perfect! Let me put them on."

Logan only nodded and gave him the pieces of string. They wouldn't be perfect, but Logan had no idea how much the quality of the instrument would affect the spells. He was sure the lute was fine.

Ryan beamed. "Thank you! I'll get right on tuning it."

He went away happily, occasionally stringing out a sound from his new toy.

Kat raised an eyebrow at his back. "Huh. Not bad."

Logan grinned. "We'll see how it holds up. It was a big morale boost for him for very little Numa."

Ryan plucked a string experimentally in the background. A soft, warm note rang out, lingering longer than it should have.

Balmer glanced over at him, leaning against a wall. "That's . . . soothing," he remarked.

Ryan took a slow inhalation, pressed his fingertips to the makeshift fretboard, and strummed a simple chord progression. The notes rolled softly through the ancient chamber. It wasn't loud, but it carried a beautiful vibrance.

"Nice," Kat said. Even she seemed impressed.

Logan smiled, satisfied, and nodded firmly. "Good stuff, Tumor."

[My pleasure.]

They let another half-hour pass in quiet rest. Ryan tested the new lute in near-silence, strumming out gentle melodies that soothed the crew. Kat did a final pass on her knuckle-daggers, polishing the gleaming metal. Balmer dozed with his head on his arms, though he jerked awake every so often to recheck the corridor. The recruits maintained their watch, though their eyelids drooped from time to time. It had been a long day.

But we have to keep going. We don't even know how much time we have.

Logan ate a bit of dried jerky and forced down some stale water, ignoring the throbbing in his leg. The mental drain of crafting items was one thing, but leading was what really sapped his energy. He leaned against the stone wall and closed his eyes. The wall was cold, but it was better than standing.

[You should have slept a little.]

"I'll manage," Logan murmured, glancing at the door illusions. "We'll keep pushing forward soon."

[Alright. But don't overextend yourself, or you'll collapse mid-swing next time you fight.]

"Worrywart."

The silence of the ruins pressed around them, broken only by the occasional drip of water or the faint chords from Ryan's lute. For now, at least, they had a safe bubble in this underground labyrinth.

At length, Kat rose and stretched. She swept her gaze over the group. "So, folks, are we moving or what? I don't fancy sleeping here all night. There could be Blues creeping around."

Logan slowly got to his feet. A bout of dizziness made him pause, so he steadied himself on the staff. The new darkmetal cuff glinted on his left wrist. He gave it a testing flex—still good. "Yeah," he said, voice subdued. "We move for an hour or so, see if there's a path further down. Then we find a safer place to hunker down for the night."

Ryan's recruits sprang to motion, packing up what little they had brought. Kat checked her weapons again, motioning for Balmer to lead. He pulled out his rapier.

Balmer yawned, nodded, and rolled his shoulders. "Alright, I'll take point again—just gimme half a minute to collect my wits."

Ryan slung the newly crafted lute over his shoulder, using a small, improvised strap. He offered Logan a grateful tilt of his head that spoke louder than words. Soon enough they'd see if this instrument lived up to the hope they'd pinned on it.

Logan gulped down his last mouthful of water, then took position behind Balmer. "Line up," he said softly. "Same formation. Move on my signal."

A quiet ripple of affirmation passed through the group. Everyone was tired, but at least there was a bit of renewed morale. They had had a little rest and now had a new tool for Ryan, along with the knowledge that they could push a bit deeper without collapsing from exhaustion.

At Logan's signal, Balmer eased out of the chamber's sole exit. The corridor looked the same as before: still dusty, still illuminated by an eerie blue light by the wiring in the ceiling.

Where they had been relaxed a minute ago, now the group grew tense. Logan could hear Ryan close by, humming a subdued melody under his breath—maybe to keep the recruits focused—and Logan felt that faint chord of unity in the group.

One step at a time, they delved once more into the unknown corridors, the familiar silence about them. They moved as a single careful creature, each footfall a whisper against centuries-old debris.

Logan was sure they might face monsters soon—ogres, Blues, or something new. But for now, they had something approaching confidence. Logan glanced at the darkmetal wrist attachment for the umpteenth time.

I can't wait to test this out on an ogre.

As Logan strode along, staff in one hand, new metallic cuff on the other, he cast a quick, sidelong glance at Ryan's lute. Logan wondered how effective their Bard would be now.

I'm sure we'll find out sooner than I hope.

CHAPTER 15

Pushing Deeper

They pressed on through the winding passages of the ruins, single file, flashlights bobbing in the gloom. The shadows on the chipped walls made odd silhouettes—looming shapes that seemed to watch their steps. Water dripped intermittently from cracks in the darkness, a steady reminder of how far belowground they'd ventured.

Logan once again told them to drink up and fill their water flasks.

Balmer took point again. His class, [**Phantom**], thrived in the darkness; he slipped around corners, scanning for traps or stray Blues, rapier at the ready, eyes flicking warily over the floor.

Logan was walking fifty paces behind him, exosuit humming faintly with each shift of his weight. He still moved with a slight limp, but the braced knee kept him steady.

Ryan's recruits followed, carrying a crossbow or shield and spear, eyes wide and alert. Ryan himself walked near the back, the newly minted lute slung across his torso. He occasionally strummed a few notes and hummed rhythmically. The subtle chords vibrated in the stale air, giving everyone a sense of calm, or at least a distraction from the gloom.

After the break they'd taken, Logan felt sharper, as well as curious. He occasionally paused to note symbols carved into the walls. Most were worn to near illegibility, but a few patterns repeated—spirals or serpentine coils. They'd encountered them deeper in, but nowhere near as frequently as here. Could've been ceremonial or merely decorative, but either way, he kept track. He never knew which odd detail might prove crucial.

I don't understand shit, but maybe Tumor can learn patterns here.

[I don't have much to work with, but I'll delegate a sub-mind just in case.]

Eventually, they came to a fork in the road, the corridor diverging in two directions. Balmer crouched to study the ground with a flashlight, checking for footprints or tracks. After a prolonged moment, he murmured, "Left seems more traveled. Dust's not as thick."

Logan weighed the options, exchanging a look with Ryan and Kat. "Blues."

Balmer nodded. He eased into the left corridor, rapier pointed forward, free hand guiding the flashlight. The rest bunched up slightly into tighter formation.

Ryan's recruits, looking a bit tense, scanned the walls. Kat's brow furrowed; she always looked half-disappointed when they didn't run into trouble. Logan glanced at Balmer. He seemed sweaty and tense.

How do these two make it work?

They went a short way, the tunnel slanting downward a few degrees. The air here smelled faintly musty, tinged with an unpleasant metallic undertone. Logan recognized that scent. It reminded him of dried blood. He squeezed the staff in his hand.

Then, a quiet hiss echoed from somewhere ahead, resonating off the stone. Everyone froze. Balmer held up a fist to indicate they should all stop in their tracks. The recruits lifted their crossbows. Logan inhaled as quietly as possible and nodded for Balmer to scout a step further.

Out of the gloom, shapes emerged—hunched silhouettes slinking down the corridor. A blue glow from their eyes gave them away: Blues. Maybe half a dozen.

Their mouths hung open in silent snarls as they approached. Behind them, a larger form lurked, stooped under the corridor's low ceiling. It shuffled, dragging something heavy, and breathing in ragged bursts. A single, monstrous grunt echoed. Logan's heart sank. That was an ogre.

Balmer darted back, pressing himself against the wall, rapier trembling with readiness. In a hush, Logan signaled. "We hold position. Ryan, be ready with that lute. Keep your men in a tight formation. Kat, sidestep and flank them. I'll see if I can pin down that ogre."

They repositioned swiftly, stepping behind a partial alcove formed by a collapsed pillar, forming a semicircle. The corridor was tight enough that the Blues wouldn't be able to swarm them easily, but the ogre's raw power was a threat. Once it saw them, the fight would ignite.

"Can they see us?" Kat asked. "They're coming this way."

"Yeah, they've been acting weird lately . . ." Logan muttered. "I think it's because they're under the enemy's direct control."

Ryan flicked his gaze to Logan. "On your mark," he whispered, slipping the lute off his shoulder, one hand on the neck, the other brushing the strings.

Logan took a calming breath. "Now."

Ryan raked his fingers across the strings, unleashing a chord that rang out in the confined space like a clarion call.

Immediately, the corridor reverberated with a layered tone that pulsed through the ear. Logan felt it stirring in his chest, a not-quite-painful vibration that sharpened his senses. The recruits visibly straightened, crossbow arms set firm. Kat grinned, shoulders rolling loose, ready for a brawl.

The Blues hissed and snarled at the sudden noise, staggering. A few slapped both hands over their ears, as though the chord physically hurt them. Another snarled and sprang forward, loping on all fours at them like a gorilla. A recruit fired a crossbow bolt, striking it in the shoulder. The creature stumbled but didn't go down. Instead, it let out a horrible shout, alerting the rest of the enemy, and they all screamed angrily in a discordant chorus. Two more Blues flanked it, shrieking with feral intensity.

Balmer lunged first, rapier tip slicing a quick line across one Blue's throat. It gurgled and tried to swing at Balmer, but he sidestepped. Another recruit loosed a second bolt that clipped the monster's knee, sending it tumbling. Kat jumped into the fray, teeth bared in a fierce grin, slamming her knuckle-daggers into another Blue's chest, punching repeatedly until another one came and tried to take a swipe at her. She blocked, counter-punched, and took distance.

Then, the ogre stepped into the lamplight, a hulking shape with low-hanging arms, shaped like clubs with no fingers, while its shoulders brushed the corridor's upper arch. Logan's stomach clenched. One blow from that thing could break bones. But this time, he was prepared.

He glanced down at his forearm. The darkmetal band, shaped like a bracer, glinted in the dim, blue light. He felt Tumor was ready at the first syllable of instruction. The brute started charging. Logan wanted to end the fight quickly, before any of the recruits could get hurt. He searched for an idea in the split second he had. Then, with a rush of adrenaline, he flung out his left arm.

"Bind that brute," he hissed. "Tripwire."

The metal shot forward in thin, black wires, like a dozen writhing snakes made of molten steel. They whipped around the ogre's torso and arms, coiling tight with surprising speed. The creature jerked back with a startled bellow, confusion flickering in its ugly eyes. Then at Logan's mental command, Tumor routed Numa from the armor through the lines. In that moment, Logan transmuted the pure Numa into electricity. Sparks danced along each tendril, zapping the ogre's flesh in short bursts of crackling energy.

[Keystone Skill Level Up!]
[Transmutate Material Level 5]

The beast roared in pain. Bracing its tree-trunk legs, it strained to yank free, but the wires dug into its hide, each surge of electricity undermining its strength. This wasn't an immobilize that would last forever—already the ogre was thrashing mightily, thick arms bulging with sinew. But for now, it was pinned at the corridor's center, a big target for the rest of the party.

"Open fire!" Logan barked.

Ryan's recruits unleashed a volley of crossbow bolts. They sank into the ogre's chest and arms. Some stuck fast, others glanced off of its tough hide. Kat circled around on the left, narrowly avoiding a flailing leg. She hammered a dagger punch into the beast's calf, carving a deep wound into it. Balmer darted in, rapier flashing, trying to sever an artery in the ogre's thigh. The monster howled, seizing one wire, trying to tear it free, but the electric arcs flared again, making it reel.

Meanwhile, the Blues screeched, some attempting to intercept. Two recruits worked together to keep them at bay, each letting off crossbow bolts in unison. One Blue managed to get close, swiping at a recruit's arm with blackened claws. Ryan strummed another chord, this one a piercing note that reverberated with an almost-psychic impact. The Blue reeled, giving the recruit enough time to jam a spear through its eye socket as he screamed in fury and fear.

Logan gritted his teeth, pouring focus into that roiling loop of darkmetal wires. Each second he held the ogre, the more Numa he burned. But oh, boy, was it satisfying to zap this bastard.

Logan could sense Tumor calculating how much power was left in their crystals. They had enough for a short burst. Probably.

Time to finish it.

"Someone get a clean strike on the damn thing!" Logan roared, sweat trickling down his temple.

Kat responded first. She locked eyes with Balmer, gave a short nod, then lunged for the ogre's flank. Balmer feinted from the front, jabbing a shallow rapier thrust that drew the ogre's attention. The beast tried to swing a meaty arm, but the wires held firm, crackling with renewed arcs. Kat slid underneath that arm, slashing at the ogre's exposed side and hooking a dagger under its ribs.

The blow must have caught something critical. The ogre bellowed in raw agony, collapsing sideways to a knee. The recruits, emboldened, rushed forward. One slammed a spear into its back, another hacked at its neck with a battered hand axe. Balmer stabbed the rapier upward into the creature's throat. Blue-black blood poured out in a sickening fire hose of a surge, painting the corridor floor, along with everyone in the vicinity.

Damn, that smell stings the eyes.

Logan felt the tension on his wires suddenly slacken. The ogre sort of slumped, roaring one last time before it went limp on the ground. Foul stench wafted in a miasma around them.

The two remaining Blues looked at the ogre and immediately ran off into the darkness.

"Don't chase them!" Logan commanded.

Kat looked at him and hesitated but eventually nodded.

Logan prompted Tumor, making the darkmetal wires slither back toward his bracer. They re-coalesced into a single black cuff around his forearm.

He staggered back, panting. The exosuit's hip reservoir flickered emptily—he'd used a chunk of their stored Numa to keep that trap going. But it had worked. They'd taken the ogre down in less than half-a-minute. That was a major improvement from before.

Kat, blood splattered across her face, exhaled in triumph. "Hell, yeah. That's how you do it."

Balmer checked the ogre's body carefully, making sure it was well and truly dead. The corridor was littered with twisted bodies now. But the party looked mostly okay—some scratches, exhaustion etched on their faces, yet no major wounds.

Ryan lowered the lute from his chest, letting the lingering chord fade. His eyes danced with relief. "Are we done?" he asked, voice a bit raw from the tension.

"Yeah," Logan muttered. "For now, anyway."

Everyone took a quick moment to catch their breath. One of the recruits peered at the ogre's corpse warily, as if expecting it to twitch. Most of them sagged in relief and clapped each other on the back. None of them cried or were shocked.

That was an improvement. Ryan's good.

Kat let out a harsh chuckle under her breath. "Nice trick you had there, Boss. That thing went down fast. Whole lot easier when you can keep it from swinging for even a few seconds."

Ryan's recruits nodded. One of them, a young man with a shaved head, grinned. "That singing helped too. I swear I felt, like, braver."

Ryan shrugged modestly, plucking a quiet chord again. "It's half-skill, half-magic. But as long as it helps, I'll keep playing."

Logan turned a slow circle, staff in a loose grip. He listened for any more distant shrieks or steps. Nothing. The corridor was quiet, save for their panting. He scanned the blocky walls, noticing that beyond the fight scene, there seemed to be a partially open door on the right side. Light—faint, bluish—glimmered from inside.

A surge of curiosity tugged at him. "Hey, check that out."

Balmer, breathing heavily, scouted forward. He peered around the door's corner, rapier extended. After a tense moment, he motioned them over. "I see something glowing in here."

Logan joined him. The doorway led into a small chamber, maybe thirty feet square, with a fractured mosaic on the floor. It design was now mostly defaced either by time or deliberate damage, but jagged lines of color hinted that it had once depicted swirling runes. Off to the corner was a broken pedestal of carved stone. Beside it, a luminescent crystal about the size of a man's head pulsed with a gentle, azure glow. It had clearly fallen off the pedestal at some point in the past.

Kat whistled low. "That's a big chunk."

Ryan moved closer, eyes reflecting the glow. "Is it safe to grab?"

Kat scoffed. "Why wouldn't it be?"

"I don't know," Ryan muttered. "I'm new at this."

Logan stepped carefully into the room, staff raised. He scanned for obvious traps, such as pressure plates or hidden lines in the mosaic. The place looked neglected, with layers of dust and no footprints indicating Blues or ogres rummaging inside.

Were they coming for this?

Logan nodded. "Balmer, watch the door. Everyone else, keep an eye out."

Logan crouched and carefully lifted the crystal off of its resting place. Logan checked it. **[C-Grade Numa Crystal, 28%]**. "I think we just found ourselves a half-decent power core."

The party gave a subdued cheer. One of Ryan's recruits pumped a fist. Another whispered, "Now, that's a haul."

"It's not full," Logan said over his shoulder. "But it's a lot of Numa."

Ryan grinned at Logan. "That'll keep your suit juiced up for days, right?"

Logan nodded, but that was a discussion for when they'd reached safer ground. For now, they had to get out of the corridor with this crystal in tow.

Logan looked over his shoulder again. "Let's hold here for just a minute, see if anything else is in the corners."

Kat and Balmer did a quick circuit around the small chamber. There was nothing remarkable—just a few broken pottery shards in one corner and a collapsed portion of the mosaic in another. Logan shrugged.

The rest of the recruits hovered near the door, scanning the corridor where they'd just fought. So far, no sign of more Blues.

Kat glared at the corridor. "I think we should move."

Logan nodded. "Agreed. Everyone, form up."

He slipped the crystal into a cloth bag, then carefully placed it in one of the carts they had brought. The blue glow shone through the fabric.

Another chunk of Numa—this one bigger than anything they'd found in days. Enough to craft new bombs or upgrade the exosuit or heal half the wounded. It was a lot of Numa, and Logan was feeling happy. But immediately, another thought tackled him.

This is just a drop in the ocean of what we need against Levemoth.

Logan pushed the thought away. Kat looked at him quizzically, but Logan only shook his head. He wouldn't mention it. Couldn't mention it. He was burdened by worry. He needed his troops to have high morale.

"Lead on, Balmer," he said quietly.

The scout moved out into the corridor again, stepping around the half-eviscerated ogre. The rest followed, carefully picking their way among the scattered bodies of Blues. Kat took the lead in checking for any that might still be twitching; she delivered a few final stabs to heads that looked suspiciously intact. Nothing moved. She turned to grin at Logan.

The corridor stretched onward in two directions from the combat site, but the path they'd followed presumably led here. They had what they needed, and odds were good that beyond these corridors lay more labyrinthine tunnels. That might be worthwhile to explore another day. For now, they had something valuable. And Logan sensed that pushing deeper in their current state—drained from the fight, short on rest—could be suicidal.

He turned to the group, voice low. "We need to figure out if we're heading back or if we push further. This chunk's too precious to lose."

Kat looked around. "I vote we head back. We don't even know if these corridors loop around, but we already have a prime find. Let's not get greedy."

Ryan's recruits murmured agreement. A couple of them looked relieved at the suggestion. The Faelves said nothing, but it was clear from their wide eyes that the idea of venturing deeper didn't thrill them.

Balmer gave a slow half-shrug. "There could be more treasure ahead, but we're battered, and if we run into a large group with ogres, it might just do us in."

Logan flexed his battered staff in one hand. The fight had gone well, but it had also cost him a good chunk of the exosuit's energy. Not to mention, he could feel that heavy fatigue creeping back. He sighed. "Alright, we'll track our route carefully on the way out so we can come back better prepared. Let's regroup in that larger chamber we passed, then figure out how to head up."

No one argued. With a sense of collective caution, they stepped away from the carnage, heading down the corridor. The flashlights danced over the old walls, shadows flickering. Ryan kept a hand on the lute's strings, periodically plucking a tension-easing chord. Whether it was for them or due to the possibility of more foes, Logan wasn't sure, but he didn't mind.

The quiet tension landed on them again, but this time it was different.

Now they had a trophy—a large B-grader that glowed in the cart, in addition to the darkmetal they'd scored earlier.

The group stayed in a tight formation, adrenaline still buzzing. He'd let them rest once they found a more defensible area, maybe back in that rectangular hall with columns. Then, eventually, they'd make their ascent.

For all the danger of these ruins, the battles, the tension, it felt damn good to walk away with a real advantage. Logan tested the new bracer one more time in mid-step, feeling the darkmetal shift in response.

[Don't be wasteful.]

"Come on, I just want us to be ready for action."

[You know I will always be.]

"I know. But humans are insecure, silly things."

[And yet so extraordinary.]

"That we are," Logan muttered.

They were still short on time. They were still under the threat of calamity. But they had won.

The corridor's gloom swallowed their footsteps as they marched on, leaving the lifeless bodies and the oppressive hush behind. Slowly they started moving upwards, still checking corridors for loot, but eventually they would get back to the camp.

Back to Freya.

The day had been long. But by the looks the others flashed him, he could tell they all believed it was worth it.

Worth it to stand a chance.

Worth it to live another day.

They pressed forward, exhaling as one, the newly won crystal's glow bobbing faintly on the cart.

CHAPTER 16

Old Acquaintances

They regrouped and stopped in an enclosed alcove they found near the main hallway. They were *tired*.

The party was battered from the recent encounters, but they were intact, and at least morale was still high.

Ryan's recruits grouped near him, crossbows set aside for a moment's rest, and Logan could see their pained expressions. Half of them had some minor injuries from the fights, and everyone was fatigued. Kat and Balmer kept watch near the corridor's mouth, listening intently for any scuttling footsteps that might signal another wave of Blues or worse.

Logan walked up to their support crew and found William.

"Hey, man," Logan said.

The young **[Alchemist]** perked up and smiled at Logan. "How are you, Boss?"

"A little beat up," Logan admitted. "But I'm in power armor. The rest of my fighters . . . Well, they're on their last legs."

"I can see that," William said. "Is there anything I can do?"

"I was hoping you could," Logan said. "I gave you guys a Numa crystal, and I figured it'd be a good idea to use it. Could you make some sort of energy drink?"

"An energy drink? You mean like—"

"Not like on Earth. More like a stamina potion or something that can keep our guys going."

"Oh!" William said and flashed an apologetic smile. "I've never done that before. I don't have a recipe for anything similar in my class abilities."

"Eh?" Logan raised a quizzical eyebrow. "I don't have jackshit on my class abilities. I just make stuff up on the fly."

"Wait, you can do that?"

"Have you tried?"

"Well . . ." William shifted uncomfortably, glancing sideways. "Not really."

Logan sighed and forced a smile on his face. "Time to learn something new."

William chuckled nervously, and Logan shooed him off to make a potion. In the meantime, he picked up a few rocks and transmuted them into a cauldron with the volume of a few coffeepots. He dragged the stone cauldron to where William was laying out his equipment.

The E-grader he held had still some power left. Not much but enough for something small. Logan weighed the little rock of a magic battery on his hand.

"You're burning through these, like you're some prodigal son of a billionaire," Kat said and smiled as she approached.

Logan gave her a thin smile. "Crazy, right? I never learned to be moderate."

"Yeah, I won't lie, though. It's pretty hot," she said but then flashed an affectionate look at Balmer. "But the truth is, I like moderate."

"Something for everyone, right?" Logan said, thinking of Freya. "I like moderate, too."

"Nothing moderate about Freya," Kat said. "She is awesome."

"She sure is," Logan said. "I want to show her that more often . . . It's just that lately I've been . . . preoccupied."

"Like trying to save humanity from utter destruction? I'm sure you'll get a pass for now."

Logan chuckled dryly at that. "I hope so. I'll make up for it."

"I'll make sure that you do if we get out of this alive," Kat said and punched him lightly on the shoulder plate.

She left Logan alone and he resumed staring at the Numa crystal. Since he could only make something small out of it . . .

Logan shrugged, then looked over his shoulder at Ryan and his recruits. "Hey, Ryan—bring me your three best shots. I've got something for them."

Ryan lifted his gaze, lute slung across his shoulder, and beckoned three of his crossbow-wielding recruits over. They gathered around Logan with timid expressions. One was the young man with a shaved head, who had earlier commented on Ryan's singing. Another was a tall woman, eyes fierce in an otherwise tired face. The last was a stocky fellow with sandy hair who'd proven a decent shot in previous scuffles.

Logan reached for the small stash of leftover crossbow bolts. A little over a dozen, all told, fletched with simple feathers. "You've seen how tough some of these monsters can be," he said quietly. "A standard bolt might not break an ogre's hide, or if it does, won't go deep enough. So, I'll give a few of these a little extra punch."

Then he pressed the half-drained Numa crystal against the tips of four or five bolts each—a simple penetration enchantment and a guiding enchantment, which was basically aim-assist magic. Faint arcs of bluish energy sparked and got sucked into the tips of the crossbow bolts. He proceeded to do the same to all of the bolts and found the crystal had gone completely dim.

"Feel free to use them liberally. It didn't cost much," Logan said. "If it saves a life or even an injury, it will have been 100 percent worth it. Extra penetration and guiding aim. Four for each of you. Decide amongst yourselves who gets the extra two once you've spent the initial four."

The recruits thanked him with hushed gratitude. They each accepted a short bundle of the newly empowered bolts, securing them carefully in leather quivers. Ryan watched with approval. Even if it wasn't a giant upgrade, it was something.

Logan walked away and Tumor stirred.

[Look at you taking on a leadership role.]

"Yeah, yeah," Logan said. "I still don't like it."

[Good leaders never do. But someone has to do it.]

William had managed to concoct his energy drink, and everyone was given a cup of it. When Logan swallowed the first mouthful it was like a lightning bolt had struck directly through his spine.

"Holy shit, William!" Kat exclaimed. "What the hell did you put in this?"

William had also drunk a cup and was visibly shaking.

"It's pretty good, isn't it? Maybe I'll have another cup . . ."

"How about you leave some for the fighters?" Logan said and shared a smile with Kat.

After all of the recruits had their brains jumpstarted into gear, they were readier than ever to explore the leftover parts of the ruined city while they made their way back to the camp.

They set out again, with Balmer leading. The corridors twisted in slow arcs, sometimes doubling back. Attempts to map it were muddled by confusion, but Logan was fairly sure they were making their way back toward the surface. He could taste it in the air and the stream of water they found.

Things got tense when they heard skittering up ahead. Balmer halted, rapier tight in his fist. The group bunched together, crossbows raised. But the scurrying turned out to be nothing but rats. They squeaked and fled at the first sign of humans, vanishing through a crack in the wall. A mild relief, if also unnerving.

Soon after, they arrived at a narrow passage with carved reliefs along the walls—some ancient script swirling in half-circles. The floor sloped upwards, but they hadn't been here before.

Kat wrinkled her nose. "This place seems endless. Are we going in circles?"

Logan shook his head. "It's a big city."

Balmer advanced, footsteps nearly silent. Suddenly, a shrill cry rang out from somewhere ahead, answered by a second. The corridor narrowed, forming a choke point. Two tall, gangly silhouettes lurched into the lamplight—a pair of Blues, but unlike the hunched brutes they'd fought before, these looked elongated, limbs spindly and half-crawling on the walls, moving in disturbing, disjointed lurches. Their black-tipped claws clicked against the stone as they dragged them behind them, and their eyes glowed with an evil blue as dull slime dripped from their jaws.

"What the—"

"Positions!" Logan snapped. In a heartbeat, the recruits formed a firing line across the corridor, crossbows lifted. Kat and Balmer took either edge, near the walls, while Logan planted his staff in front.

One of the skinny Blues let out a gargling hiss, skittering sideways along the wall as though gravity hardly mattered. The other lunged. Ryan's recruits fired. Two bolts thudded into the first one's torso. Another bolt missed, glancing off stone and vanishing into the darkness. The long-armed Blue twisted and howled, then leaped forward.

Logan pivoted, pressing a mental command to the bracer. The dark-metal liquefied, forming a short, curved blade at his wrist. He slashed at the Blue mid-lunge, cutting deep across its chest. A spray of blackish fluid spattered the corridor floor. The beast shrieked, flailing. Kat seized the chance, driving a knuckle-blow into its spine. It collapsed in a writhing heap.

The second Blue crawled overhead, clinging to the ceiling with sharp claws scraping stone. Balmer lunged with his rapier, but the creature jerked out of the way, silently launching itself at one of Ryan's recruits.

The young man barely dodged, stumbling back. Another recruit fired a glowing blue bolt, which hit the Blue's flank, sinking deep into the flesh.

Nice. One of the enchanted ones.

The monster shrieked and Balmer followed up, rapier slicing through the creature's side, pinning it to a wall. It thrashed and shrieked, but in seconds, the recruits were on it and had hacked it to pieces.

Ryan's lute strummed a low chord that made the recruits shiver slightly. It was a half-baked illusion meant to confuse any additional foes. None were startled out of the shadows, though. The corridor was silent again, save for ragged breathing. The roof-crawling Blue was dead, but the one they had struck down first, twitched and attempted to lurch and crawl its way to escape in the shadows, but Logan pinned it with his staff, crushing its spine. It shrieked. He knelt and cut its throat with his darkmetal blade.

"Just one thing after another," Kat muttered, shaking out her wrists. "They can spider-climb now?"

"I thought you'd be excited to be facing a new type of enemy," Logan said.

"Hell, no," Kat spat and shivered. "Those things were *creepy*. I never want to see them again."

Balmer flicked gore off his rapier. "Better these two than a swarm."

Logan exhaled. "Keep an eye out for more. Let's not get ambushed from above."

The group reformed, stepping gingerly around the twisted corpses. A few crossbow bolts were retrieved where possible; any bent or broken ones got discarded.

They advanced again, deeper along the corridor as it curved gently to the left. The architecture changed: stone pillars thicker, walls lined with that strange script, more streaks of blue mold.

Much of the journey took place in tense quiet as they carefully listened and kept scanning overhead. Eventually, they passed a squat, partially caved-in archway with language in the runes of the First Folk etched around it. Perhaps a collapsed side chamber. Logan peeked in using the night vision from his helmet and deemed the route a dead end.

Eventually, they emerged into a wide antechamber—the corridor opened abruptly, revealing a dome-like ceiling supported by multiple pillars. The space was vast enough that their flashlights didn't fully light up the perimeter. A chill breeze, or so it felt, rustled the hair on Logan's neck, carrying a faint odor of rot and something else foul.

Something's wrong.

[Yes. I can feel it, too.]

Ryan inhaled sharply. "Wow. This is big."

Kat aimed her lamp at the nearest wall. Sticky, mucus-like strands dripped from the stone. Some were black, some tinged with a sickly blue. They pulsed gently, as though something in them was alive. Everyone's stomach churned at the sight.

"What the actual—"

"Levemoth's corruption," Logan said quietly.

He swallowed and took a step further in, staff clutched tight. The pools of oily substance reflected the light of their flashlights as they passed pillars of strange, corrupted flesh.

The center of the chamber opened into a dais or platform, half-encased in that pulsating goop. A faint hum echoed from it, as if filling the air with a slow, methodical heartbeat. Or at least, that was how it sounded in Logan's ears.

Kat hissed under her breath. "Are we sure we want to be here?"

"I vote we set this place on fire and leave," Balmer whispered.

Logan shook his head. "I don't like it, either. But I want a further look around."

They split into smaller groups: Ryan and two recruits circled left, Kat and Balmer right. The distant corners of the dome were lost in thick shadows, so Logan advanced slowly, staff extended, lamp bobbing.

As he approached the central dais, the floor gave way to what looked like a shallow pit, clogged with oily black-and-blue goo. Tendrils of it crawled up the dais' edges, congealing into a glistening mass. In the middle stood . . . *something*.

The shape had vague humanoid features, and Logan thought he saw a head, but the lines were too covered by that black-blue mucus to tell. Some part of it was chitin, some part of it pulsating flesh. A blasphemy of shape, part humanoid, part beast, mostly a shapeless cyst.

"Gods," Logan muttered. "Is that thing . . . alive?"

The pulsating growth stirred. A single eye—sealed beneath eyelids caked with black slime—suddenly flicked open, revealing a depthless gaze. It seemed confused, looking around. Logan froze, staff clutched tight, chest hammering with alarm.

Kat and Balmer converged from the other side. Kat's eyes widened. "What in the goddamn hell is that thing?"

The creature let out a shuddering rasp, almost like a gargle of breath. The entire dais trembled once, as if acknowledging the presence of the intruders.

Logan took a half-step closer, ignoring the protest in his mind that screamed to run. He forced himself to look into the thing's face. Then he recognized something in that half-lidded eye: an intelligence that transcended simple monstrosity. A depthless malevolence.

Levemoth.

Logan's heart seized up. The eye glowed an intense azure-black swirl, full of cruel purpose.

Then, an alien voice reverberated in the chamber and Logan was not sure if others could hear it or not—a terrible whisper that attacked him from multiple angles. Tumor grounded him and he withstood the tremendous psychic pressure.

"I see you . . . Logan Specter."

CHAPTER 17

A Little Conversation

You," Logan growled, eyes locked on the abomination before him. The twisted growth towered in the center of the chamber, half-submerged in that vile black-blue mucus that looked like thick oil. Each drip seemed to echo in the suffocating silence, punctuating the tension.

"**I,**" came the resonant, alien voice. A fleck of slippery fluid dribbled off the creature's elongated chin, landing with an audible plop. "**Like the simple beasts you are, you fell into the most basic of traps.**"

Logan refused to betray any fear, though the stench of rot coming off the slime made his stomach churn. In the periphery, Ryan and the others kept their distance, crossbows lowered but ready.

Balmer hovered protectively near Logan's flank, rapier twitching to strike at the first sign of hostility. Kat, jaw clenched, stood off to the other side, knuckle-daggers gleaming in the foul lamplight.

"**Too much of a crowd this time,**" Levemoth said, and suddenly in a blink, Logan was enveloped in total darkness, where only the pulsing cyst and he remained.

"What is this?" Logan demanded. He forced a mocking edge into his tone, despite his mounting distress.

"**A simple pleasure for me,**" the creature said, voice low and ominous. Some inner light lit its single visible eye, a luminous swirl of black and azure.

A creeping sensation crawled over Logan. A presence, so cold, alien, and hostile that it made him shudder. It started to envelop him, until he could not move. It started constricting, and Logan gasped in pain.

Logan set his jaw. Had he messed up?

He pushed back against it with his mind and found that the presence noticed. It attacked immediately.

There was a flash of pain, but immediately the hostile presence recoiled. Something had psychically slapped it away.

Logan could sense another force overhead—distant, yet watchful, like an unseen guardian. The Administrators, he realized—the alien watchers who had enforced certain rules upon this world. That sense of them sharpened Logan's courage. Levemoth might fill this chamber with an oppressive aura, but his wasn't the only power in play.

You have to play nice, don't you?

"Are you going to attempt to break my mind?" Logan asked, voice cutting.

"**Alas**," Levemoth's voice rumbled, vibrations rolling through the chamber, "**the circumstances are not ideal. You know I cannot do that easily because of that pesky bug inside you.**"

Logan's lips curled in a faint grin. "Tumor says hi."

"**Tumor? What an amusing name.**"

Logan tightened his grip on his staff. "What are you doing in the sky?"

A ripple of laughter answered him, low and unpleasant, bouncing off the darkness. Levemoth took his time in answering. "**Preparing a spectacle.**"

"Got tired of fighting us fair?" Logan retorted. Flecks of sticky spittle clung to the creature's mouth. Logan stared at them with morbid curiosity, just waiting for them to drip off.

"**Fighting? Fair?**" Again, that rumble of amusement, the lethargic answers. "**Gods do not fight insects. We squash them when they become a noticeable pest.**"

"Oh . . ." Logan said, rolling his shoulders languidly, trying not to show how the statement had chilled his blood. "I didn't realize you were losing sleep over us poor little insects."

A soft, menacing hiss. "**Do not get cocky. You have managed to stumble from one lucky encounter to another.**"

"How many times does it need to happen, before you stop calling it luck?" Logan said and smirked.

"**It matters no longer,**" Levemoth growled, and the deep alien voice reverberated throughout the darkness, filling it. "**I have made sure you run out of luck.**"

"Yeah, yeah," Logan drawled, letting his exhaustion color his sarcasm. "Heard it all before. Tell me this, Levemoth. What's inside these ruins that you don't want us to find?"

The growth pulsed, and the twisted blasphemy of a mouth curled. "**You are the ones who chose this place.**"

"What a wild coincidence that you were here waiting for us," Logan said, eyebrows knitting in faux-confusion.

"You presume much to think you can understand my mind," came the retort, each word dripping with scorn. And dribble. Way too much dribble.

Logan narrowed his gaze. "For all your huff and puff, you're a terrible liar."

"Do not think you can read me."

A flash of dark satisfaction surged through Logan. *Defensive. Just a tad.* "Why did you plant your cool new toys here? And when we defeated them, you pressed an emergency button. You're scared."

A terrible roar exploded from the cyst, its mouth twisting impossibly. **"YOU DARE THINK I PAY HEED TO THE INSIPID NOISE OF AN INSECT?!"**

The chamber shook. Plasma-like arcs of black lightning crackled across the darkness, and Logan experienced a crushing psychic assault. He fell to his knees, staff clattering on the damp stone, teeth clenched as a splicing headache tore through his skull. Strange shapes and colors swam behind his eyes—bizarre illusions that threatened to consume his mind.

But something else rose to meet the onslaught: the Administrators' presence. They flared within Logan's consciousness, unseen watchers applying intangible wards. The swirling madness recoiled, as if stung. The searing pain in his head dulled, leaving Logan shuddering but conscious. He was reeling, left weak and disoriented.

Tumor pounced immediately, releasing a chemical cocktail into Logan's brain.

[Control your breath. Breathe. In. Out. Relax.]

"Thanks," Logan muttered. After some focused breathing, he regained himself.

He slowly stood, ignoring the tremor in his limbs. The rest of the group watched in horror—none of them had experienced the brunt of that mental blow, but the wave of fear was palpable. He steeled himself, forcing his gaze back to the abomination's single eye. It didn't blink, staring at Logan with a deep, alien intensity.

"You will not break me," Logan said in a low, ragged voice. "We will find what's in here, and we will destroy you."

Levemoth hissed out something akin to laughter, a chilling rumble. **"What can an insect like you do where several civilizations before yourself failed?"**

"You've never been this weak before," Logan spat out. His breath was still uneven.

A pause. **"I have never had this puny a foe, either."**

"Sounds like I'm not the only one who's been getting lucky," Logan said. A half-smirk played at his lips.

"You are an insolent little brat. Once all this is over, and I bring calamity raining down, I hope you survive. That way, I can have you all for myself. I will take my sweet time breaking you . . ." Each word coated the air like poison. Logan could feel Levemoth infusing his terrible presence into these words.

"You think you're the first big, scary, powerful jackass I've dealt with?" Logan asked, giving a wry shrug, pushing away his fear. "Excellent case of posturing."

"I do not posture. I do not make threats." The cyst shuddered in rage. **"I DEVOUR WORLDS!"**

Darkness flickered like a negative flash in Logan's vision. Monstrous shapes overlapped—fleeting images of apocalyptic horrors. Logan cried out, glimpsing hellish landscapes. Then, just as swiftly, the Administrators' presence rose again, neatly snuffing out the illusions. The chamber's stone outlines returned, and the abomination's eye glistened with frustration.

Logan, regaining some composure, flipped the cyst a rude gesture. "Devour this."

"Very well, Logan Specter," Levemoth hissed, saliva dripping from parted lips. **"Search. Search away. But each minute you spend here, I will grow stronger."**

A flicker of perplexity danced in Logan's eyes. That statement dripped with a smugness that didn't fully make sense. For a long moment, the abomination watched him, silent tendrils of black mucus twitching along the walls. Was it stalling for time?

Levemoth's voice returned, sliding like venom into his ears. **"I might not be able to break you. We shall see . . . Once I am strong enough to fend off those . . . Watchers, I shall have you, and we will see if your mind can handle my vastness. You are strong, I will admit. Your father, however . . . Ah, he was a delight to subdue. If only you were more like him . . ."**

Logan's gut twisted at the mention of his father, lips thinning. He refused to let his pain show. But there was a subtle tension in Levemoth's words, a strange undercurrent.

Something's off.

Then, like a bolt of clarity, the realization struck.

Levemoth was buying time.

[Oh. Damn, you're right. Why didn't I think of that?]

At least you're good at tinkering with stuff.

[I am excellent *at that, thank you very much.]*

Logan shot a glare into the darkness beyond Levemoth, addressing the intangible presence overhead. "Oi, administrators, I think I'm done with him! Get me out."

It was as if a black veil had been yanked aside. The darkness receded in an instantaneous blink, bringing Logan back into the room with his comrades. The cyst remained in the center of the room. The abomination's fat-lipped grin remained. Its eye was fixed on Logan.

"So soon? Well, maybe you are not as stupid as your father. Rush along, Logan Specter. Run and put out the fires . . ."

The threat in that voice promised more battles, more torment. Logan felt anger surging in his chest. That damn bastard was way too smug. Something bad was waiting for them at the camp.

"Follow me," Logan snapped at his people, staff pointing back the way they'd come. "Back to the camp—double speed!"

Even Kat nodded firmly. Balmer ushered Ryan and the recruits into a swift formation. They obeyed with haste. There had been something in Logan's tone that had been absolute and requiring an instant reaction. No time was wasted.

The distant shadows of the chamber seemed to watch, malignant and hungry.

As Logan turned away, he felt Levemoth's eye burn on his back. The abomination let out that same, low chuckle, and the chamber trembled once more beneath them. Logan didn't look back. He only gritted his teeth, leading the group onward, heart pounding in anger and fear.

They had gleaned vital information as well as experienced Levemoth's direct presence. Though they'd survived the mental assault, Logan knew a larger catastrophe loomed. The words, **"I will grow stronger,"** echoed in his mind. Whatever the next step turned out to be, Levemoth was confident that time was on its side.

But Logan and his companions weren't planning to let Levemoth gain any more ground. He'd face his dread head-on, as always. Pushing deeper might uncover more secrets and more nightmares. For now, though, they had to run before the trap fully sprung.

Before Logan left, he was momentarily overtaken by anger. He spun and smashed the growth with his staff. The ugly mouth curled into a sneer before it collapsed into pus and bits. The eye still stared at Logan with livid cruelty, but at least Levemoth wasn't laughing anymore.

Logan shook the mess off his staff and turned. "I'll go ahead. Balmer, you're in charge. See you at the camp."

And with that, he boosted off, prompting Tumor to increase the power of his suit's legs.

CHAPTER 18

Rush to Battle

Logan tore through the corridors in his exosuit, each booming stride cracking ancient stones underfoot. Dust plumed around him, billowing in his wake.

Faster, Tumor.

[It is not energy-efficient. You need to conserve Numa for a potential battle.]

"Tsk," Logan spat out, frustrated. "Fine."

The rafters overhead blurred as he sprinted past the room with the drained Numa crystal—the same chamber where he and his group had once battled a swarm of ogres. He remembered killing their first ogre in here not so long ago. Now, the place was silent, littered with crusted bloodstains and debris. No time to linger.

He vaulted a broken divider in a single leap, power-suit servos whining, then hit the ground running. A small stone bridge loomed ahead, bridging a treacherous gap that had taken some of the more-timid recruits a while to cross.

Without breaking stride, Logan coiled his muscles and hurled himself across it. He landed on the other side with a crash, bits of stone and mortar shearing off under the weight of his power armor.

[Skill Level Up!]
[Power Armor Fighting Level 20]

Through the final stretch of corridor, a smear of pale natural light beckoned him. He picked up speed. Tumor's voice pinged sporadically inside his head, painting a conceptual map, telling him where to turn or cautioning him about structural hazards.

Logan tuned most of it out. He trusted his instincts. He knew when he needed to rely on them. This was definitely one of those times.

Besides, the high-pitched ring of metal, chorused by screams of pain told him everything he needed to know. Chaos raged outside, and he had to get there *now*. Freya was there.

[Another attack.]

"Maybe," Logan said between breaths. "But there's something more, I can feel it."

[How can you know?]

"I just do," Logan growled. "It's a human thing."

He burst from the ruins, emerging in an explosion of grit and sweat into the ruined camp. The horrible sight stole his breath for half a beat.

Where once a battered but orderly camp had stood, now there was carnage: tents shredded to rags, smoldering embers strewn across the ground, long fingers of flame licking supply crates and tent support beams. Corpses lay sprawled in unnatural positions, and scattered lumps of flesh indicated partial devouring. Too many corpses.

The noises of battle hammered at Logan's senses. Overhead, an early sun bled through a haze of black smoke. The foul stink of burning gore choked the air.

Logan could see a ring of battered defenders, their disarray telling him they'd been caught off-guard. Spears formed a shaky perimeter, keeping a cluster of Blues from overrunning the entire camp in one savage sweep.

Logan glimpsed at least two dozen fatalities lying in the mud: some men, some women—maybe more. And another dozen Faelves.

The poor little ones never stood a chance . . .

To his right, a trio of Blues pinned a single soldier against a toppled crate, gnashing at his raised shield. Blood spattered. The soldier's scream was harrowing. It was cut short with a gruesome *crunch*.

But the centerpiece of the chaos was near the center of camp, where two figures clashed in a brutal dance of blades.

Simmons—grim-faced, a gash dripping blood from one shoulder—faced off against the Herald, formerly known as Malcolm Specter, Logan's father, or at least what remained of him, somehow turned into something even more monstrous than before.

The figure stood tall but was no longer clad in a streamlined carapace of motley black and blue. Now it looked like he had a pustulant, pulsing infection covering most of the Herald's large frame, whatever was left remaining a brutal jagged carapace. His left arm was the same as before—a monstrous pincer, chitinous and sharp. He hammered and stabbed it at Simmons, who was barely managing to deflect it with his axe.

Logan's eyes widened. Simmons was holding his own by pure skill, but the Herald had superhuman strength, each of his blows forcing Simmons backwards. If the pace continued, Simmons wouldn't last long.

As Logan processed all of this in an instant, he knew he had to choose. The Blues rampaged, ripping through the camp like feral animals, but there were only around ten of them. They were unbelievably savage, but the line of defenders might be able to hold them if they had even a little help. And that gave Logan just enough mental space to realize there was an ogre, too—lurking to the far left, thrashing at pinned recruits, scattering their formation. He heard the deep roar and saw tall silhouettes flailing in the wavy heat haze.

He had to act.

Logan slammed forward, staff raised high. The first Blue didn't even see him coming. He smashed its skull with a savage overhead blow of his staff, cracking it like an egg. Bone, thick black gore, and a rancid stench exploded in a sickening shower. The creature collapsed instantly, body twitching.

"You two," he snapped at the nearest pair of agents, who stood panting behind battered shields, "go help Simmons."

"Yes, sir!" they barked and sprinted off, weaving through the carnage to close in on the Herald's flank.

Logan pivoted, senses screaming. A second Blue lunged from behind a shattered wagon, swiping at him with jagged claws. He dodged on reflex.

The nails scraped across his exosuit's torso plate, sending sparks airborne. He responded with a vicious elbow strike, Tumor making the darkmetal module liquefy and form a savage spike. The metal plowed through the Blue's eye socket, goring it in one vicious thrust.

For a split second, the Blue hung there, pinned like some macabre doll. Then Logan felt the darkmetal pulse. Thin spines erupted outward from the initial spike, shattering the Blue's skull from inside. A wet gurgle was all it managed before it slid off the darkmetal and collapsed, limbs spasming.

Logan had no time to dwell on the horror. He glimpsed a soldier screaming for help a few yards away—pinned by yet another monstrous shape. He dashed over, staff raised. The soldier was an older man, face contorted in terror, fighting a female Blue in tattered rags who hissed and tore at his armor straps.

Before Logan could strike, a crossbow bolt whizzed in from the side, burying itself in the creature's spine. The Blue shrieked, arching its body. That gave Logan the opening he needed. He lunged, staff tip crashing down into its midsection with a meaty crunch. The Blue curled inward and died with a final hiss.

A grunt behind him made Logan whirl. Another recruit—someone he faintly recognized from a prior skirmish—was wrestling with a Blue that had latched onto his shoulder, biting through the gap of his armor. The poor recruit's face twisted in agony as blood sprayed across his collar. Logan hurled the staff like a spear, striking the Blue in the ribs with enough force to snap bones, dislodging it from the recruit. The creature flopped over in the dirt, shrieking. Logan kicked it across the jaw, then stooped to yank the staff free. Another blow, crushing its chest, and silence replaced the shrieks.

Logan shouted through his suit's voice amplifier. "Regroup! Stick together. Converge around the agents!"

He took a step back, scanning the battlefield. Already, the presence of a single exosuit had helped tip the scale against the Blues. The battered line of defenders reformed. Spears jabbed and crossbow bolts flew. The once-deadly horde of Blues shrank rapidly, either slain or bleeding out. A few tried scrambling away, only to be run down by angry agents.

That left the ogre. Logan's eyes snapped to the creature. Looming above them almost nine feet tall, its arms forming into terrible sharp and long hooks, like giant sickles. On the ground near it lay three corpses split open.

"Here we go," Logan muttered, chest heaving. Another wave of adrenaline flared. He had only so much Numa left after that last bracer spike, but it would have to do.

The ogre swung its hooks. One man, not quick enough, took the blow square in the chest, and he was ripped open. He soared through the air, colliding with a battered tent frame. Another agent lunged forward with a spear, trying to stab the ogre's flank. The spear snapped on impact, the ogre's hide too thick. The creature swung at him, but the agent slipped away and threw a stun grenade in his wake which disoriented the ogre for a flash of a moment.

[We have enough Numa for a short restraining hold or a lethal blow but not both. Decide quickly.]

Logan clenched his staff tight. "We'll hold it first. Then I'll coordinate a group strike."

[Understood.]

Logan began sprinting. The exosuit's servo motors whined as he closed the distance in seconds. The stunned ogre sensed him too late, turning with a snarl. Logan channeled the darkmetal module again. Streams of pitch-black metal shot from his wrist, coiling around the ogre's ankles. The creature roared, stumbling. He poured a spark of Numa into the lines, electricity dancing over them.

The ogre convulsed in shock, hook arms flailing violently. One blow glanced off Logan's side, sending him skidding in the mud. Pain flared, but the exosuit took no more damage than a scratch. The darkmetal wires loosened momentarily, but Logan snarled and forced them to tighten. He yanked and pulled as hard as he could, and the ogre toppled.

"Now!" he shouted to the agents. "Hit it hard!"

Three or four battered soldiers rushed forward, brandishing axes, swords—whatever they had left. Even two brave Faelves flew at the ogre's face, blasting it with illusions, confusing it briefly. Enough for a blade to sink into its exposed side. Then another. One soldier hammered the creature's ribs with a morningstar.

Logan weathered each shock of impact channeled through the wires as the ogre flailed in agony. One more well-placed blow to the chest. Another savage hack at the neck. Blood spurted, painting the ground and the fighting recruits black.

With a final roar, the ogre toppled. The ground tremored under its massive weight. Logan let out a ragged breath, releasing the darkmetal. It slithered back into the bracer.

He took stock for half a second: despite battered weapons, the line of defenders was winning. The Blues had been nearly wiped out. The ogre lay still, besides a twitch in one massive leg that soon stopped. On the other side of the field, maybe one or two final straggler Blues tried to retreat, only to be taken down by an angry thrust of spears.

"You—" Logan pointed at the agent. "—take command of these people. Get unbattered weapons from the field armory, and rejoin the fight."

The agent nodded crisply and started issuing commands, calling people over to him.

Logan turned. Now it was just the Herald. Malcolm Specter.

A hundred paces away, Simmons and the Herald continued their brutal exchange, though the two agents Logan had sent over were trying to help. One agent tried to land a broadside slash on the Herald's mutated arm. The Herald seemed to sense the approach—he whirled, chitinous pincer flashing. The agent's sword shattered on impact. With monstrous speed, the Herald raked its pincer across the agent's torso.

Logan heard the sound of wet ripping even from where he stood. The agent spasmed, blood spraying from a diagonal slash, then collapsed face-first. Gone in a heartbeat.

Simmons roared in defiance. He surged forward, swinging his massive axe at the Herald's neck. But the Herald pivoted, parrying with a forearm twisted and reinforced by black chitin. Sparks flew. With his free hand—an arm still somewhat human but unnaturally strong—he delivered a savage punch that hammered Simmons's breastplate. Metal groaned and dented. The man staggered back, holding his chest.

The second agent tried to circle from behind, but the Herald whipped around again—almost impossibly fast—and drove his mutated arm straight through the agent's chest. The blow pinned the poor soul to the ground. Blood gushed, the agent's eyes rolling back. A single, choking gasp, and he was dead.

Logan's heart thundered. He started sprinting. "Simmons!" he shouted, pushing through a cluster of half-dazed soldiers.

Simmons, breathing ragged, swung once more at the Herald with the last of his strength. The Herald battered the sword aside, sending it spinning out of Simmons' grasp. Then he lunged, that pincer arm scissoring wide, intent on snipping Simmons in half at the waist.

Logan moved on instinct. He lunged the final yards, staff interposed. He slammed it between the pincer's blades and triggered a tiny burst of Numa powering the suit to give it more torque. The carapace cracked on the edges, and the Herald snarled in surprise, a flicker of fury twisting his monstrous face.

Simmons stumbled back, clutching his wounded side, blood thick under his gauntlet. The man's eyes were wide, a mixture of relief and horror.

Logan forced the Herald's pincer upward. The half-chitinous monstrosity resisted, but Logan had the exosuit fueling his push. Metal servos whined as he shoved the pincer aside, muscles burning. The Herald responded by lashing out with his other hand, nails elongating into knife-like protrusions. Logan dove under them, rolling in the mud. He sprang up, staff raised, dark-metal swirling around his wrist.

That's a new trick.

For a tense moment, father and son locked eyes. The Herald's expression revealed no familial warmth—only bottomless contempt.

Not like there was warmth when he wasn't a literal monster.

One foolish soldier tried to rush in from the flank, but the Herald moved with uncanny speed, spinning his entire torso. His human hand backhanded the recruit across the face, snapping the man's neck in one savage blow. He dropped like a stone.

Logan's jaw clenched. Now it was just him—Simmons was too hurt to fight, and the rest of the campsite were locked in their own battles or too wounded to move.

The Herald stared him down intently and snapped his pincer for emphasis. The pustulant black-and-blue mass at his side pulsed, as if gathering energy.

Then, with maddening calm, the Herald lifted his gaze to Logan, cruel amusement burning in those half-dead eyes. He spoke with a voice that layered Malcolm's old baritone under a cold, alien sneer:

"I see you."

He advanced, scraping the pincer against the ground, carving a shallow groove in the dirt. Behind him, the sounds of battle continued—the moans of the wounded, the final shrieks of a cornered Blue, the snap of a battered tent. But for Logan, in this moment, the entire world focused on that twisted figure who used to be his father.

The Herald raised his pincer arm, letting dripping gore patter on the muddy ground. He regarded Logan for a moment, shoulders hunched forward like a cat deciding how to toy with a wounded mouse.

"This is where you die, boy."

Logan growled. "I'm no boy anymore."

The Herald took a battle stance, knees bent, pincer half-lowered, smile twisted in vile anticipation. Even from ten paces away, Logan could sense the radiating malevolence, a presence similar to Levemoth himself.

Simmons, on his knees, tried to bark a warning but coughed up blood instead. The camp had gone eerily quiet around them, as if every living soul was waiting for the next explosive move.

Logan hefted his staff, darkmetal bracer clinking softly. Blood pounded in his ears. The next heartbeat might decide if he lived or died.

Nearby defenders—battered but loyal—tried to rally toward him. Logan motioned with a hand for them to stop.

"He's here, isn't he? Watching through you," Logan said.

"My master is always watching."

"Is there anything left of Malcolm Specter?"

The monster did not answer.

"I don't know if you were a good man or a bad man," Logan said. "But you were not a monster. Come back to us and fight it."

The monster flinched, but then it laughed in an unnatural tone.

"Surrender and beg," the Herald whispered, the words slicing the silence. "Or I will take your life."

And so Logan finally resigned himself. He would have to kill this thing. They stood face-to-face, the battered camp around them, in the storm's eye of destruction.

Logan spun the staff behind him. "Come and get it."

CHAPTER 19

Father and Son

Logan's breath hissed through clenched teeth. The world around him seemed oddly muted—the raging battle, the cries of the wounded. All of it faded behind the singular vicious presence before him: the Herald, still half-human in shape, yet more monster than man, and undeniably in control of this battle.

"Let's see what you can do, boy," the Herald taunted, voice a hollow echo layered with malice.

Logan gripped his staff in a white-knuckle hold. The darkmetal module around his wrist pulsed, as if sensing the hostility. Behind the Herald, black-blue mottled flesh rippled. Something moved beneath it, just beneath the surface. Logan tensed. He felt a malevolent energy gathering. It was an odd sensation he had not experienced before, but the message was clear—a sign of Levemoth's twisted powers manifesting.

A flicker. The Herald lunged. Logan raised his staff and angled it to block. The blow connected with bone-rattling force, smashing him back a few steps. Sparks skittered off the exosuit's plating. Another swing came, and Logan barely parried, arms shaking from the impact. His mind scrambled for a plan.

He is stronger than before. Well, that, plus I don't have my Armor.

The Herald smirked. "Still standing? I expected you to fold quicker."

Logan didn't reply—his jaw was locked. Instead, he pivoted on one foot and slammed the butt of his staff against the Herald's side. It connected, jarring them both. But the Herald barely budged, letting out a bored snort. Then, black veins along his arm bulged, throbbing in a sickly glow.

Ethereal tentacles burst from that pulsing, pustulant mass, dripping with the oily muck of Levemoth's influence. They snaked toward Logan in a blink, fluid as whips. He swore and backpedaled. The first tentacle lashed, slicing a shallow gash in the exosuit's shoulder plate. Another coiled around the staff's upper half.

A wild sense of panic flared in Logan's mind. He wrenched the staff free, metal shrieking. The tentacle parted from it with a wet snap. But there were more. They slithered around, flickering in and out of existence like nightmares. The Herald laughed under his breath, clearly enjoying Logan's struggles.

We need distance.

[Agreed.]

Logan pivoted, letting the exosuit's servos power a short leap backward. The tentacles whipped the air where he'd stood a split second ago. Before he landed, the Herald was on him again—chitinous pincer lunging for his midsection.

Logan swung the staff laterally. The blow cracked into the pincer with a metallic note, jarring his arms. It deflected but not by much. The Herald pressed forward, batting aside Logan's next thrust with contemptuous ease. Then, a swirling tentacle lashed inward, smacking Logan across the ribs. Pain flared. He stumbled, exosuit whining.

The Herald's mutant grace was terrifying. No wasted movements, each blow well-aimed. Another tentacle hissed across the ground, trying to ensnare Logan's ankle.

"Too slow," the Herald mocked, eyes glinting.

A swirl of fear and anger rose inside Logan. He remembered his father's face, how Malcolm had once looked, a visage of hard grace. This abomination wore the faint features of that face like a cruel mask. It angered Logan. He wanted his father back. One way or another, Levemoth would not have him.

Tumor, get ready to use our trump card.

Logan lunged back in, staff raised high. He feigned a downstroke, then twisted into a side slash aimed at the Herald's torso. The mutated arm came up, blocking the staff near the base. Logan poured Numa into the darkmetal. A cutting edge flickered into being along the staff's tip, forcing the Herald to shift his block or risk a deep gouge.

It worked, somewhat. The Herald stepped half a pace sideways, giving Logan room to jam the staff's butt toward the Herald's leg. The blow connected, buckling the Herald's knee. A flicker of advantage. Logan tried to press it. But he barely managed two strikes before the Herald's tentacles lashed out again, seizing the staff in multiple spots. Tendrils looped around Logan's wrist, too, constricting with a soggy hiss.

"Pathetic," the Herald sneered, twisting his torso. "This is the power you mean to stop my master with?"

The staff tore from Logan's grip. For a split second, his eyes went wide. The Herald reared a fist back, intent on punching right through the exosuit chest-plate.

Now, Tumor. Expend all the Numa we have left!

Tumor hesitated for a flicker of a microsecond but complied. Logan could feel the energy surge through his exosuit.

The darkmetal module liquefied and turned into a dozen snaking wires shooting at the enemy. The liquid black lines erupted from the bracer, crackled with electricity. They shot toward the Herald's shoulder and waist. Blue sparks flew as they wrapped around the pulsing blue mass on his chest. With a snarl, the Herald tried to yank free. But Logan kept pouring energy into the wires, each surge sending arcs of lightning dancing over that corrupted flesh.

More!

[Tapping into emergency reserves.]

The Herald roared in pain, tentacles flailing erratically. One ripped across Logan's thigh, slicing a superficial cut. Another raked his side. But he refused to relent. More darkmetal poured out, forming a spiderweb of black cable that pinned the Herald's arms and torso.

[We are out of energy.]

Logan wasted no time. Just as the blue crackle of electricity stopped, Logan rushed toward the pulsing growth on the Herald's side and slammed a hand on it, squeezing it.

"[Funnel]!"

[Skill Level Up!]
[Funnel Level 19]

The evil blue eyes of the Herald flashed wide. Logan felt a current of the most disgusting, corrupted Numa energy streaming through the cables. Logan's body braced for the impact of siphoning raw power. He could feel the echoes of a depthless malignance through the energy. This was Levemoth's power at its purest. A cold shock lanced up his arms. His vision blurred with swirling shades of black and blue.

Logan tried to maintain control, but a terrible, maddening laughter overwhelmed his reality and visions of horrible futures attacked him. In the background of his awareness, the Herald was struggling to move and get back up.

[Logan! Expend the energy. It is overtaking you.]

The Herald started thrashing like a cornered wild beast, tearing at the wires. But it was weakening by the second as the corrupted energy drained into Logan's exosuit reservoir. Logan fought the urge to vomit—this was vile, dark energy to be processed, and it seared his nervous system. The madness and despair grew stronger and Logan cried out.

"What . . . are . . . you . . . doing?" the Herald snarled, voice twisted.

"Something you won't like," Logan spat back through gritted teeth.

He clenched his fists, focusing on the swirling mass of threads. He pushed the energy back through the darkmetal wires, transmuting Levemoth's horrid energy into electricity.

The wires glowed a harsh white-blue, intensifying the crackle of electricity. The Herald's body convulsed. He bellowed, dropping to a knee. The tentacles shriveled, black slime dripping off of them. The chitinous pincer trembled violently.

Logan pushed through the sorrow and insanity, thinking of Freya, thinking of Tumor. He focused on creating electricity. His feelings swelled as he thought of the people he loved, and he fed all of this emotion into the Herald through the charged energy.

It was too much for it.

"NO! YOU WILL NOT PREVAIL!"

The Herald spoke in an unnatural voice, and the horrible monstrous visions and screams in Logan's head almost took him over. Levemoth's maddening influence was strong, but he steeled his mind. He was Logan Specter. The scion of a once-mighty man. He would not bend. He would do what sons of mighty men always do.

He would play politics.

"Administrators! He cheats to win! If another person at the table cheats, you have to play by their rules. It's past time for being noble. It's time to win. Give me back my father! I don't care what it costs!"

A strange ethereal light illuminated reality for a moment, like a sun peeking behind a crevice through the clouds. It was gone before Logan could notice. It felt like warmth. Like home.

But the Herald most certainly disagreed.

The sickening, guttural roar that tore from its throat was unlike anything Logan had ever heard. Once the final surges of Numa siphoned away, the Herald's mutated limbs deflated, almost dissolving into chunks of slimy material. The pustulant growth on his side swelled but then started shrinking.

Chunks of the carapace began falling off. With one last heave, the Herald collapsed to the ground, pinned beneath a net of darkmetal wires.

Logan reeled, pulling back the wires slowly. He panted, trying not to black out. The heavy toll on the madness of the energy he had endured left him reeling. But Logan was sure he might've just avoided a fate worse than death. Still, the exosuit crackled with leftover charge, heavy with ill-gotten power. He stumbled over to reclaim his staff, chest still throbbing.

A hush fell over the battlefield. Soldiers, battered and exhausted, glanced around in disbelief. The unstoppable force that was the Herald now lay motionless, half-fused to some gory lumps of black slime, half-human face slack and eyes rolled back.

Logan forced himself to stand tall, ignoring the sting of fresh wounds. He looked at his father and he saw blotches of peach-colored human flesh and tufts of salt-and-pepper hair through the broken-off pieces of carapace.

A few of the braver ones crept closer, weapons half-lowered. Simmons, staggering, pressed a hand to his side, a cough rattling in his chest. He gave Logan a look of shock, gratitude, and disbelief that spoke volumes. Everyone understood they'd just witnessed something they had never expected to see—a confrontation where the Herald had actually been subdued.

For a moment, nobody spoke. Logan's breath rasped, arms trembling. He let the final arcs of darkmetal wire recoil into the bracer, then stared at the body of his enemy. He had no triumphant grin on his face, just serious, searching eyes and a sense of quiet relief laced with horror. The monstrous features of the Herald were receding, revealing Malcom Specter once again.

Logan looked up at the sky as he fell on his knees, gratitude swelling in his heart.

"Thank you."

CHAPTER 20

Broken Herald

The Ark's deck was a mess of collapsed crates, scattered crossbow bolts, and twisted heaps of debris. Above it, the sky was smeared with heavy, gray clouds that made the morning light seem exactly as wiped out as Logan felt. In the middle of the sky remained the swirling tumor of a gestating monster, still gathering power as if nothing had happened.

I can't stand it.

The air was thick with the stench of sweat, smoke, blood, and something like rancid meat left out too long in a muggy swamp. It was the smell of last night's carnage, and even on the ship, the reek haunted them. It was on their weapons and their wounded—the blood of the enemy.

Logan sat slumped against the main mast, staff held loosely between his knees. The staff was bent and cracked despite Logan's fancy enchantments. He didn't really care that much right now. If there were any rhyme or reason in the world, he wouldn't have to fight immediately again.

[Terrible assumption.]

"Yeah, yeah," Logan said. "I just . . . I need a moment. I'll fix the staff. And the camp . . . And my father . . . And the threat of Levemoth . . . Later . . ."

Tumor had no objections. Logan thought his AI buddy could understand. After all, Tumor was the only person who was privy to all of Logan's private thoughts and emotions. He knew what Logan had gone through. With him, he could share the heavy crown of leadership. Or at least its woes.

"Thanks for caring," Logan said and slumped further.

He was too tired. Emotionally, sure. He didn't even want to get started untangling his emotions. But physically, too. Logan wasn't sure if he had ever been pushed this hard. The fatigue was systemic and overwhelming. His weak foot throbbed, too, not fully healed after all those collisions and leaps against rock and ruin. Logan could sense Tumor was somewhere in the back of his head, quietly running diagnostics on his vital signs, and had many things to say about that, but he was grateful the AI opted to stay silent for now.

He had other things on his mind right now. Things he would need to attend immediately when he got over his dire need for doing absolutely nothing.

The most pressing reason was lying on the floor just ten feet away from him: his father, Malcolm Specter.

He was no longer the Herald. After they had dug him out of the black-and-blue mess and the pieces of dry carapace, they had found a human. A pale and old human, with strange and unnatural blue veins pulsing softly all across his body and even face.

Levemoth has left a mark that will never leave him.

Malcolm Specter had been unconscious ever since he had lost the fight. They had no idea when he would wake up or what kind of mind he would have left. That is why it was better to be safe than sorry.

He was caged by thick rods of bone-steel driven into the planks. Collars like big iron shackles ringed his wrists and ankles, attached by short, unbreakable chains hammered into a crate full of cobbled-together metal scraps. Tumor had assured Logan that these restraints could hold even an ogre if needed.

"He looks almost peaceful."

[Do you recall the images and sounds Levemoth showed you?]

"I would really rather not."

[I know. But my point is that he has been under that influence for months.]

Logan didn't know what to feel.

There was sadness, sure, looking at his father's body. It had grown old beyond its years, the skin sagging and thin, those strange blue veins giving his once-powerful father a sickly look. There was anger, as well. It was a petulant childish rage, but it was there. The anger at his father for leaving him alone. Leaving him to lead. Leaving him to resolve it all.

But through it all burned something more than a petulant rage. It was a silent deadly wrath. A bottomless depth, like a cold well stretching into infinity in his psyche. This wrath was against Levemoth. The bastard had nothing to offer to the world but pain and destruction.

I'll take the goddamn beast down.

"I've come a long way, you know," Logan said to his father, vaguely numb.

Malcolm Specter didn't answer. Immediately after Logan said it, he regretted it and rubbed his face in a fit of shame, hoping that his father wasn't lucid enough to hear. Despite how far Logan had come, a part of him still wanted to prove something to his father.

[You don't need to prove anything to him.]

"Yeah . . . maybe," Logan muttered. "But it's hard to let go."

A chesty cough to Logan's right broke his train of thought.

"Hey," Kat said. She leaned on a broken chunk of railing, arms folded tightly against her chest. The bandages around her ribs glinted with recent bloodstains. She hadn't changed them yet. Tired lines cut across her face, but her eyes were keen as ever. "You alright?"

Logan exhaled a short, bitter laugh. "Am I alright?"

"We've got him," she said, tipping her chin at the caged figure. "And looks like he isn't a full-blown monster anymore. That's alright in my book."

Logan lifted his gaze. "Maybe. We still don't know how he is going to be when he wakes up, though. If he wakes up at all. But if he is back on our side, that would be a massive help."

"Wasn't he kind of a ridiculous asshole the last time he was in charge?"

"Yeah, he was," Logan said. "But now I'm in charge, and I won't let him act foolishly."

"Are you going to trust him?" Kat asked.

"I don't know." Logan sighed. "You ask a lot of annoying questions."

"I am quite lovely, aren't I?"

"Yeah, yeah," Logan said.

"We talked to the Groloin," Kat said. "They're blaming you for this."

"Great . . ." Logan replied. "Well, they're not entirely wrong."

"Well, if he is back to being human, he can be a valuable asset," Kat said.

"But at what price?" Logan asked bitterly.

"What do you mean?"

"How many died?" Logan asked. Straight to the point. He had to know the toll of the battle.

Kat's jaw worked, like she was chewing glass. "We're still counting." Another cough rattled her. She spat something red on the deck. "At least fifty, Logan. Maybe more."

"Goddamn it," Logan murmured. He closed his eyes. That was a lot of dead people on his watch. Arguably because of him.

[Do not think like that.]

Logan grunted.

This was the second time an ambush had blindsided them in short order. Levemoth wasn't pulling punches. Had he been able to awaken the Herald all this time and had just waited for an opportune moment?

Maybe. Either way, we need to go back down into the city so we can fight back. But first . . .

"I want a list of the dead. We'll hold a proper funeral pyre for them. And get me a list of the wounded as well."

"Alright," Kat said. "Freya's already organizing the triage. Snoff is trying to mediate with the Groloin. They want to yell at you, though, so you should go there as soon as you're able."

Logan snorted quietly. "The Groloin lecturing me is rich. All they care about is vengeance, nothing else. They don't want to save the planet. They just want to destroy the enemy because it destroyed them. They couldn't understand."

Kat gave a stiff nod but kept her eyes on Logan. She looked like she wanted to say something else. Maybe something about how Logan had risked his life to subdue Malcolm, or how, all told, it was a minor miracle they'd managed to do so and that he had somehow turned back to being human again. Especially that last one. Logan didn't know if Kat had been around when the light had come, but she must have heard stories. She must have questions. But she just swallowed. "Anyway. I'll get you the names of the dead once we're done digging them up from the battlefield. I could use your help making the pyre. We should act fast, though, so they don't turn into Blues."

"I know. Thanks."

Kat lingered like she might be about to say something comforting, but the moment passed. She pushed off the railing and walked off to help the others, leaving Logan in the hush of the early morning gloom. He was alone now with the disturbing sight of his father.

Another cough but this time from behind Logan. A polite one to get his attention. He swiveled slowly, staff gripped in a defensive reflex, only to see Freya. She approached with a slow, tired gait, hair messy from too many hours of no rest. She wore a short cloak dusted with flecks of dried blood. Her bright blue eyes, though, sparkled with concern.

"Logan," Freya said. She set a small clay bowl of some herbal concoction next to him. "Drink. William made it. It'll help with the shakes."

Logan considered the brew. He dragged it closer to him but stopped mid-motion. He looked at Freya earnestly and sighed wearily. "I'm so beat, Frey. I don't know if I'm making the right decisions anymore."

"You'll manage," Freya said gently, kneeling beside him. She cast a wary glance at the inert Malcolm. "You're not the only one having a hard time this morning. Some of these men . . ." She shook her head. Logan knew she had had a rough time too. While her battle was less immediate, less scary, she had still fought in her own way to mend the wounded, keeping them alive.

Logan brushed his fingertips across the chipped rim of the bowl. The scent was strong—some mixture of chamomile, anise, and a tang of mint.

He lifted it to his lips and took a tentative sip. It was scalding hot and bitter, but he forced himself to swallow. At once, a wave of warmth diffused through his sinuses, giving fleeting relief from the metallic taste of blood that had lingered at the back of his throat since the fight. His mind became gradually clearer, and some of the fog of exhaustion lifted.

"William made something like this before, but this is gentler. I like it."

Freya smiled. "I heard you made him do an energy drink. I added my own suggestions this time."

"I like your style better," Logan said.

Freya exhaled, resting on her heels. "It's not over, you know. Levemoth . . . that cocoon seems to grow slightly bigger every hour. We see it from the Ark's vantage points. The black-and-blue wound in the sky is also spreading around it."

Logan nodded. "I know. He's building up power and keeping us busy. I met him in the dungeon."

"You what?"

Logan took another sip of the tea and told her what he saw and how he talked with Levemoth.

Freya only smiled fiercely after the telling. Logan raised an eyebrow. "What's got you so wired up?"

"You are a brave man, Logan," Freya said, her voice swelling with pride. "That is why the enemy fears you so."

Logan said nothing, only nodded.

She brought her hand gently to Logan's shoulder, ignoring the scuffed exosuit plating. "And you proved why again. You took something from him. Something valuable. I bet that big monster in the sky is furious right now."

Logan chuckled. "I sure hope so."

They sat there for a while, Freya leaning against Logan's shoulder while he played with her hair.

"Damn, this is good stuff." Logan took another sip, forcibly ignoring how his stomach churned at the idea. "I'm feeling more myself again. We have to get the next expedition rolling to find enough Numa or whatever helps us fight it. But for now, I need to ensure the camp doesn't collapse from the inside."

Freya chuckled to herself. "Already going forward. Are you sure you shouldn't process this first?"

"I wish I could," Logan said. "Tumor thinks so too. But we simply don't have time. I wish I could be a better husband to you too right now, but . . ."

Freya shook her head. "Do not apologize for that. I know you didn't want this responsibility. But carrying it with such grace gives me pride. You are the best man I know."

Logan kissed her forehead. "Thanks, Frey."

"What do you plan to do with him?" Freya asked, nodding her head toward Malcolm Specter.

Logan's gut twisted. He set the bowl down. "I don't know," he said, voice rough. "We don't really know anything before he wakes up and we can glean what kind of state he is in. If he is human and lucid, I need to talk to him."

"What do you think?" Freya wondered gently. "Was the corruption too far gone? Or did you save him?"

A sudden rasp from the caged figure shut her up. Neither of them moved for a second. Then Logan, heart hammering, pushed himself upright. He limped forward, staff raised in case the Herald tried to lunge again.

Malcolm gave a shallow gasp. The black-blue veins running over his face twitched, as if some tendon had jerked behind the skin. Then his dry lips slowly parted. A faint, strangled noise came out, like choking. Logan's spine went rigid. It took a moment to realize it was a word, a croak:

"Lo . . . gan . . ."

Freya half-stepped forward, but Logan motioned for her to hold back. He approached the cage, staff angled. "Father?" he said. His mouth felt like it was stuffed with sand.

No answer, just a ragged exhale from the weakened old man. The eyes rolled in their sockets, disoriented, as if trying to find Logan's face, but the swirl of black veins made everything difficult to interpret. That half-lidded stare never quite locked on.

"Logan . . . kill . . . me."

A shard of ice punched through Logan's chest. Freya gasped behind him. Malcolm's voice was weak, far from the strong, firm steel that had rung out various conference rooms. And the tone—it was pleading. Malcolm Specter had never pleaded in his life, and that somehow broke Logan's heart. His father had been many things, some of which Logan found absolutely reprehensible, But weak had never been one of them, and Logan had always felt a sense of begrudging respect for him. But now . . . he had been robbed of all of his strength. Malcolm's arms, pinned in thick chains, twitched feebly.

"Kill me." The words rang in Logan's ears.

He wanted to say that that obviously wasn't happening. He'd done everything to keep this man alive for answers or a chance to cure him. But despite his pity and sorrow, some furious corner of Logan's heart recalled the bodies strewn around the camp. Recruits and friends, torn to shreds by those same arms. Logan wondered if this creature before him, his father or not, deserved any mercy.

Logan forced that part of him down. If there was even a slim chance of saving or using the old Malcolm to beat Levemoth, they had to try. They needed every advantage.

Malcolm let out a cough, as more black fluid oozed from the corner of his lips. "Logan . . . Freed . . . me . . . You can't . . . Must kill me . . . I can't stop . . . him. Levemoth . . ." Then the eye slid shut. He slumped against the bars, immobile once more.

Freya swallowed thickly. "He's conscious. At least part of him. He wants you to end this. Possibly to spare him or . . . that's so twisted."

Logan ground his teeth. "I can't kill him. Not yet."

"I know," Freya said softly, tension in her voice. "But half the camp wants him dead. They see him as Levemoth's puppet. The Groloin definitely wants him dead."

"What about you?" Logan asked softly.

"Not my call," Freya simply said.

"Give it to me."

Freya considered for a moment. "He has caused a lot of pain."

"That's not an answer."

"I think . . . I think you need to make the call. And I know what you're going to do. And a lot of people won't like it."

Logan swung his head to glare at the horizon. "They can line up." He jabbed a finger at Malcolm's battered form. "That is still my father's body. And it's clear he is in there—lucid, or at least struggling. I want to see if I can redeem him. I want to see if he can atone."

Anger and sorrow vibrated in his voice. Freya placed a tentative hand on his shoulder again. "I'll help," she said. "We can attempt to heal or perform a cleansing ritual. The Goddess will help. But it will take a lot of Numa— Numa we frankly don't have."

"Then we get more," Logan said. He turned to face her. "We still have some reserves, and I brought a B-grader back to the camp. Regardless, I'm going back down into the city. We need more resources on all fronts."

Freya nodded slowly, her mind on the potential ritual. "I wonder if we risk him flipping out and going on another rampage. And if he does, that's more good people down."

Logan pinched the bridge of his nose. Freya looked at his forehead and frowned. Logan knew why. His worry lines were deeper than they should be at his age. In that regard, he truly was his father's son.

"I'll put a guard around him. If he tries anything, we put him down for good. That's fair, right?"

Freya nodded, hesitating. "Yes," she said quietly. Then, glancing at his unconscious father, she sighed. "Come, we have to plan. The Groloin are demanding a full explanation. Just so you know, they are not happy. In fact, they're livid, so you should think about what you want to say to them before you go. Snoff is with them, buying some time for you, but you should go."

"Right," Logan muttered. He shot a final look at Malcolm. "If he wakes up again, holler for me."

Freya nodded. She pressed her lips in a wan half-smile that didn't touch her eyes, then trudged off to find a golem-operated elevator, so he could go to the command bridge via the fastest route.

Another problem to deal with . . .

CHAPTER 21

Negotiations

Logan had almost reached the top level of the Ark when Snoff found him, panting, eyes wide.

"Logan, they're at it again," the Faelf said, wringing his small hands. "You need to come soon. The Groloin are furious. They speak of swift execution."

Logan swallowed down a fresh flash of anger. He knew exactly who they wanted to execute. But he forced his expression blank and squared his shoulders. "Thank you, Snoff. Let's go."

Their footsteps echoed across the metal catwalk leading to the command bridge. The late-morning sun spilled in through broad windows, revealing a battered ship and a camp below still littered with funeral pyres waiting to be lit. Broken tents, scalded earth, the aftermath of yet another grim fight. Everywhere, people were trying to patch up the holes—both in the Ark's hull and in their hearts.

Finally, Logan stepped into the bridge. Tumor was there in a golem body off to one side, silent but watchful. Freya stood near the corner, arms folded. Simmons hovered by a console, his bandaged chest soaked with fresh blood. He should've been resting, but apparently that wasn't an option.

Front and center, floating in that half-sunken pedestal, was the large orb containing the Groloin Hivemind. Its swirling green glow prickled the air with tension.

At the sound of Logan's stomping footsteps, the Groloin Hivemind's grandmotherly voice came forth—icy and cutting.

"Logan Specter . . . You took your time."

Logan inhaled. "I'm here. Make it quick."

A low hum emanated from the orb. "You are busy dealing with the consequences of your impulsive choices, no doubt."

Logan's jaw clenched. "My father is neutralized for now. He's not the Herald."

"You have imprisoned him in the Ark."

Logan braced himself. "Yes."

"Why is he not destroyed?"

Snoff stepped forward, voice gentle. "We must remember—"

"Silence," Glaan snapped with a harsh, judgmental tone. "He is a direct link to Levemoth. This we have told you from the beginning."

Logan's grip tightened on his cane. "He *was* a direct link. I severed it."

"Such arrogance," the Groloin retorted softly. "We sense the corruption still inside him. We feel the stain of that vile presence. If you allow him to roam, you invite Levemoth into our midst again."

Logan set his jaw. "He's chained. Not roaming anywhere."

"Chains can be broken," the orb said. "We have seen how easily your father overcame your so-called defenses, slaughtering many of our joint forces. Or have you forgotten?"

A hush fell. Even Simmons, who'd ordinarily speak up in Logan's defense, was forced to shift uncomfortably and stare at the floorboards. They'd lost too many people to that monstrous rampage.

"I haven't forgotten," Logan said, voice tight. "But you will not force my hand. He still has information—he could be an ally. I've subdued him once. I can do it again, if necessary."

The orb's swirl darkened, flickers of green roiling inside. "Your father is a threat. The Groloin—"

Freya stepped in, face pale but resolute. "We have a plan to cleanse him. I intend to ask the Goddess for a final purification. If that fails, we do what must be done. Would you deny us that chance?"

They all felt the Hivemind's ire. A faint crackle of static filled the air, like a radio scrambled by interference. After a few tense heartbeats, the Groloin hissed, "We do not like it. We do not trust your 'rituals'. But your precious father's life is irrelevant so long as Levemoth's demise is guaranteed. Attempt your cleansing. We will watch."

Logan let out a breath he'd been holding. "So, you'll stand down?"

Sparks fluttered in the orb. "For now. But if he shows the slightest sign of re-corruption, we kill him on the spot. No arguments."

Logan exchanged a glance with Freya. She dipped her head, resigned. "Fair enough," Logan said.

A crackling hum ended the confrontation. The orb drifted backward. Logan sensed the Groloin were far from satisfied, but they would at least delay Malcolm's destruction.

Tumor's golem creaked, stepping forward. "The Groloin have delivered their ultimatum," he said in a low, mechanical voice. "We should proceed with preparations quickly."

The orb said no more, merely hovering. A faint sense of discontent radiated from it.

Logan exhaled, noticing his hands were trembling. He clenched them behind his back, then nodded. "Right," he said. "Meeting over. We have work to do."

He left the bridge soon after, descending the ramps. It was a slow, heavy walk. His exosuit had been removed, leaving him in battered leathers. His leg protested with each step.

Outside the Ark, sunlight revealed a camp that was half-gutted, half-limping back to its feet. Faelves hurried back and forth, carting fresh lumber to rebuild fences. The smell of charred wood lingered from the partially doused fires. Bodies, too, had been processed—rows of them, covered in tarps. Logan's heart sank.

Near the central courtyard, a small group of ragged soldiers gathered around an open pit. They were piling wood, crates, and old scraps into a wide pyre.

Logan spotted Kat among them, dragging a broken door to the heap. She caught his eye and gave a grim nod. "You're just in time," she said, voice low. "We're going to burn the first of 'em soon."

Logan swallowed. "Let's do it properly."

"Ryan's gathering some folks who want to pay their respects. Simmons is already here."

At the mention of Simmons, Logan scanned the crowd. Indeed, the big man knelt in front of the makeshift pyre, head bowed, perhaps whispering a prayer. The battered axe he used to fight the Herald was strapped across his back, chipped and bloodstained.

Logan approached him slowly. "Simmons. How are you holding up?"

Simmons shrugged without looking up. "Lost fourteen of my best men last night. Kat said the total is over fifty from across the camp." A shaky breath. "I'm alive. Suppose that's enough."

Logan placed a hand gently on his friend's shoulder. "I'm sorry."

Simmons nodded stiffly, eyes distant. They lingered there for a moment, neither speaking. Words couldn't do justice to their level of heartbreak.

Finally, Kat and a few others hoisted up torches. One by one, the soldiers came forward, placing personal tokens onto the pyre: a broken spear, a wooden charm, a battered helmet—small gestures of farewell.

Logan quietly stepped back, letting them have space. Freya joined him, slipping her hand into his. Together, they watched as Kat lit the pyre's edge. Flames licked up the wood, spreading in a slow crescendo. The heat and orange glow crackled outward, awakening more tears in some, numb stares in others.

Ryan, standing with his recruits, strummed a sorrowful chord on his lute. It was a subdued tune. The hush of the entire camp seemed to unify in that raw moment.

Logan's gut twisted. He forced himself to stand tall, even though he felt hollow inside, consumed with guilt over not having been able to shield them from such tragedy.

When the flames rose fully, finally reaching the blanketed bodies, Logan turned away, biting his lip. He saw Snoff in the distance, head bowed, whispering Faelven words of farewell. Balmer stood a step behind him, arms crossed, eyes haunted as the flicker of flames lit his face.

They deserved time to grieve. He had no illusions that they'd get enough of it in this war. But at least for now, they had this moment.

After the ceremony, Logan moved among the camp's survivors. He personally checked the status of the wounded, trading quick words with those conscious enough to talk. Some men brightened up a fraction at his presence; others cursed him under their breath for not having prevented the slaughter. He understood both reactions.

He found Ryan leading drills with a few fresh volunteers, each with the half-dead look of shell-shocked refugees. But Ryan's new lute worked wonders for morale; a quick tempo-based chord gave them the extra boost of energy they needed to keep going. Logan offered a subdued nod of thanks.

Finally, as the camp quieted in the midday sun, Logan sought out Freya again. He found her in a large tent near the Ark's stern, rummaging through scrolls and books on Numa-based healing. She looked up, eyes rimmed with exhaustion.

"I'm about ready to try the ritual," Freya said softly. "Whenever you give the word."

Logan clenched his jaw. "We do it today. If my father has even the slightest chance, we can't wait."

Freya gave a shallow nod, brushing hair from her face. "Then I'll make preparations."

CHAPTER 22

Crafting Reinforcements

Freya spent the next few hours transforming one of the Ark's large cargo holds into a ritual chamber. The battered crates, tarps, and leftover supplies were pushed aside, replaced by a circle of runic lines drawn in white chalk. Soft strips of cloth hung from the rafters, etched with sigils symbolizing purification. Four braziers were placed at cardinal points, each fueled by small lumps of Numa crystals.

Logan arrived to find Freya on her knees, carefully placing the final pinch of purifying herbs around the chalk circle. She rose when he entered, wiping sweat off her brow. "It's done. We can begin whenever you're ready."

Malcolm Specter—bound with thick chains and still unconscious—had been carried inside by Tumor's golem and placed at the center of the circle. He barely resembled the monstrous Herald he had been. The black carapace had flaked away, leaving behind a frail human, pale with jagged scars. His chest rose and fell in shallow, uneven breaths.

The Groloin golems hovered near the entrance, silent but vigilant. Kat stood off to the side, arms folded, ready for the worst. Two heavily armed agents flanked Malcolm, spears at the ready, in case he woke and turned.

Must be weird since he was their old boss.

Freya beckoned Logan. "Stand behind me. This might work better if you're near. You have a strong affinity for transmutation, and that can stabilize me if the corruption tries to lash out."

Logan steeled himself. "Alright."

He approached carefully, taking a spot just behind Freya in the circle. She clasped her hands, breathing in a slow, methodical rhythm. The braziers flickered, warm and hypnotic in the gloom of the cargo hold.

Freya began chanting softly, calling upon her class-given powers. Logan heard scraps of incantations referencing the Numa goddess, calling down a wave of purifying essence. Each syllable carried an uncanny resonance, quickening the braziers' flames.

As Freya chanted, a faint glow built around Malcolm's limp body. The black-blue veins under his skin twitched.

A wave of warm, golden energy descended from Freya's outstretched palms. Logan felt a sudden spark inside his own chest, like he'd been tapped by a live wire—his transmutation mana stirring in response to Freya's ritual. She was pulling at the corrupted threads hidden in Malcolm's flesh, unraveling them, cleansing them.

The air thickened with tension. Malcolm's body jerked violently once, then again. A strangled moan escaped his lips. Foam bubbled at the corners of his mouth, tinted dark with leftover corruption. The braziers burned higher, spitting embers.

Logan's heart thundered. He placed a hand on Freya's shoulder, silently lending her what meager stabilizing force he could muster from his own Numa-based skill. A swirl of golden light shimmered, meeting a swirl of dark. Malcolm convulsed, his back arching off the floor.

"Steady," Kat whispered hoarsely.

Freya's voice stayed calm. She chanted three final lines in a stronger tone, sealing the incantation. The cargo hold thrummed with a low hum, the braziers blazing in unison. A ring of bright light encircled Malcolm, then pulsed.

With a thunderous whoosh, the blackness that clung around Malcolm's veins smoked off in curling wisps. It dissolved into the air and vanished. The man slumped back, limp as a rag.

A hush fell. Freya let out a shaky breath and sagged backward into Logan's arms. He caught her, heart hammering, scanning Malcolm's form. The black veins were gone, replaced by raw scars that looked more mundane—still grievous but no longer exuding an otherworldly taint.

Kat inched closer, brow raised. "Did it work?"

Freya lifted her head. "I . . . I think so. I feel no corruption in him."

The Groloin's orb glowed from the threshold, silent. Logan felt a sense of suspicious discontent radiating from it, but it made no move to protest.

Logan knelt beside his father, pressing two fingers to the man's neck. The pulse was faint but steady. Malcolm's eyelids fluttered, yet he didn't wake.

"He's alive, at least," Logan said softly. Then he looked at Freya, voice rough with gratitude. "Thank you."

Not long after the ritual, Freya insisted on resting. She looked pretty beat up. Half a dozen of her Faelf friends fussed about her, giving her potions of their own craft and snacks. Kat shooed them away and helped her to a cot. The soldiers, relieved that Malcolm wasn't turning into a monster again, eased their guard stance—but they kept watch. The Groloin golems quietly left without further commentary.

Logan felt the day's tension building anew. Instinctively, he sought out Tumor in the Ark's lower-deck workshop—because for all the horrors, they still had a war to win. He needed gear. Lots of it.

Simmons' battered men, Ryan's recruits, and Kat's little strike team—everyone was short on protective equipment. If Levemoth attacked again or if they started delving significantly deeper without better armor, they'd die in droves.

Too many have already died.

That's where the C-grader came in. Freya had used a large chunk of it in the cleansing ritual, but there was enough left for Logan to tinker with. The big rock from the deep ruins of the city of the First Folk shone with a soft azure glow. It still had enough juice to make a difference.

Enough to save lives.

Logan stood before his workshop. It was a mess, largely because a Blue had charged through it, tossing things into further chaos than Logan was used to working with. Jars and crates were broken and strewn over the ground. The canvas flap that had provided shelter from the sun was ripped and hanging like an old coat over Logan's workbench.

But Logan was determined and focused. Chaos never bothered him anyway. Tumor's presence thrummed in his head. He didn't agree and found the mess distasteful.

"I want to create more suits," Logan said. "What I'm wearing seems to work well and it's easy to make with cheap materials."

[We can produce five suits if we're efficient. They won't be as good as your personal exosuit, but they'll be better than the standard issue bone plating and wood shields.]

Logan nodded. "Let's get to work. We can't waste another minute."

He set the [**C-grade Numa Crystal**] on a workbench. It was warm to the touch and somehow soothing. Freya had purified it, and Logan could sense that. Since he had been working with so much unpurified Numa lately, he had forgotten what the real thing was like. It was benign, magical, pure.

Alright, enough waxing. Get to work.

First, transmutation: lumps of whatever materials were tossed about became layered composite plates reminiscent of Logan's exosuit design but thinner and simpler. Shoulder harness, chest plate, greaves, gauntlets. Then, he channeled some minor enhancements into the design: boosted strength, shock absorption, limited self-repair. He used only as much Numa as was mathematically optimal, guided by Tumor in the process.

[Subclass Level Up!]
[Enchantment Level 43]

One by one, the suits took shape, each a skeletal framework of composite rods supporting plates of reinforced gray composite. The helmets needed to be different, because Logan didn't want to waste too much Numa on the transmutation or enchantment. They'd still provide much better protection than whatever they could naturally cobble together.

A hinged visor for some face protection. An anti-adhesive enchantment on the eye visor, so that blood or any other substance couldn't stick to it. Then the last flourish—a reserve battery. Logan enchanted each of them to automatically draw power from a small E-grader from a socket in the back of the suit.

[Attribute Level Up!]
[Efficiency: 46]

Sweat poured down Logan's face as he repeated enchantment after enchantment, forging each suit to be as uniform as possible. **[Mass Production]** would have been a bad idea here, since it wasn't as energy-efficient as doing everything by hand. And they had to be energy-efficient, since Logan had time to burn. He worked in full focus for hours, the hubbub of the camp in the background, his workshop intermittently flashing with blue hues.

By the time Logan finished, five mannequins stood in neat rows, each dressed in the new "lesser power armor". They gleamed a dull silver under the overhead lamps, sporting black accents of reinforcement around the joints. Rough but functional. A pale imitation of his own flexible and powerful armor, but something to give actual protection to at least a select few elite warriors.

Losing two agents by the hands of my fath—the Herald was bad enough.

Logan let out a tired breath, leaning against the workbench. Tumor's voice was gentle in his mind.

[That's more than enough for now. You're tapped out. Considering your sleep deprivation and general level of systemic fatigue, it is unwise for you to continue. Don't push yourself further.]

"Yeah," Logan rasped, wiping his brow. He stared at the suits, all with the same cloak-like plating that would help the wearer's movement. "It was worth it, though. Simmons is getting one of these, that's for sure."

[And the other four?]

"His men. I hate to make the shitty call on deciding who gets better protection from pain and death and who doesn't, but that's my job. I have to be utilitarian. The agents are the best warriors."

[I agree. I must say, Logan, your ability to set aside your emotions in these decisions has improved at an astoundingly rapid rate.]

"You know, I might have taken that as a backhanded compliment before," Logan said and chuckled. "But now I have more perspective. Thanks. It's not easy."

[That is why a rare few are fit for leadership.]

Logan thought of his father. He felt guilt for having given him such a hard time when he was younger. Then, flashes of the Herald's monstrous face overrode those thoughts and Logan was left confused.

He shook off the emotions, pushing them somewhere in the back of his mind to be processed when he finally would have some goddamn time and peace. Now was not such a time.

He placed a final hand on the newly created armor sets, double-checking them to Tumor's great chagrin. Each suit weighed maybe half what his exosuit did, but for men with normal strength—and maybe a small Numa shard—it would be a game-changer.

It was well past sundown when he finished. The workshop lamps burned low. Logan forced himself upright, ignoring the dizziness. He needed to see Malcolm. If the old man was still breathing, maybe he'd come around soon.

He found Simmons waiting outside the workshop, bandages fresh. "Boss, he's stirring—your father," Simmons said quietly, nodding down the corridor. "Been mumbling."

Logan's pulse skipped. "Lead the way."

They made their way back to the cargo hold Freya had transformed into a ritual space. Most of the braziers had been doused, replaced by a single lamp glowing with a calm light. The place felt eerily quiet. Moonlight filtered in through overhead vents.

Logan entered cautiously, staff in hand—just in case. Simmons stayed behind him, axe slung at the ready.

At the circle's center, Malcolm lay on a simple pallet. His wrists and ankles were still shackled—Logan wasn't taking any foolish risks. But this time, Malcolm's eyes were open, faintly alert. The black veins were gone, leaving behind a gaunt, scarred face that seemed decades older than the man Logan remembered.

Freya knelt beside him. She looked up at Logan, her eyes brimming with cautious relief. "He woke a few minutes ago," she whispered. "He's—he's lucid."

Logan stepped forward, swallowing the lump in his throat. Curiosity and a tangle of emotions warred inside him. Malcolm's gaze drifted, those eyes that had formerly been icy and full of hardness, now somehow . . . softer as they settled on Logan with apparent recognition. A shudder passed through him.

"Logan . . .?" His voice was coarse, almost too quiet to hear, but with a sense of humanity that had been missing before.

Logan lowered himself to a knee, staff clutched in his right hand. "Yeah, old man. I'm here."

For a moment, Malcolm just stared. Then, he let out a shaky breath that ghosted as a laugh. "I . . . never thought I'd see you again as . . . myself."

Logan hesitated, searching his father's face. He found no trace of madness there, only exhaustion and regret. "Are you truly . . . *you?*"

A weak nod, followed by a hoarse whisper: "I have been living a nightmare I could not wake up from. The whole time I was the Herald, I was trapped behind there, conscious. The things I've done . . . I—" He faltered, tears sliding free. "I'm so sorry, son."

Logan's chest constricted. A full spectrum of complicated emotions struck him with a full blast. He hated seeing his father like this, weak and remorseful. Part of him wanted to demand answers or rail at him for the horrors, but exhaustion won out, burying that fury under a relief that maybe, just maybe, there was a chance at redemption for his dad. Maybe there was a chance that things could start getting better from here on out.

He placed a trembling hand on his father's shackled wrist, meeting his eyes. In the background, Freya exhaled in a silent prayer of thanks.

"You have a lot to answer for. But explaining it all from the beginning would be a start. I'll listen. I promise to you I will, for the first time, truly listen."

Malcolm Specter nodded quietly, and he swallowed.

For the first time in a long while, father and son were face to face—both broken and battered, but undeniably alive and, for now, at peace.

CHAPTER 23

A Hidden Weapon

A hush settled over the Ark's command bridge. Despite the inhumanly long days they were pulling, everyone had mustered whatever sense of composure they could. The core group was sitting at or by the table—Logan, Freya, Balmer, Kat, Simmons, Snoff, Ryan, Tumor in his golem, and, of course, the Groloin orb floating nearby. Additionally, other camp members had come to hear this important talk. Most of them were sitting on the floor, while a few stood, arms crossed, or leaned against the walls.

It was cramped, with nearly two dozen bodies present, but no one complained. Logan didn't know everyone's names, but they were his people, and he appreciated their showing up.

And they have a right to be here. Considering . . .

Malcolm Specter, newly returned from a special kind of hell, sat near the corner of the table, wrists shackled but loosely so he could move about. Freya had insisted he remain in restraints for everyone's peace of mind—even if the man was no longer the Herald, he was still a living weapon if the monstrous corruption ever stirred again. The metal cuffs clinked soft reminders of that possibility whenever he moved.

He wore simple clothes, a plain brown tunic ripped at the sleeves to accommodate bandages. Gone were the black carapace and the savage mutations. Just emaciated features and salt and pepper hair remained. He still had a hardness to him, but it wasn't his defining feature anymore. His experiences as Herald weighed in every line of tension around his eyes, a pained wisdom.

Logan leaned on his staff as he watched his father. Sometimes Malcolm Specter would glance back but then return to stare at the table over his steepled hands.

No one spoke at first, as if waiting for the final stragglers to arrive. But they were all here already. Finally, Logan pushed off of the table, eyes darting over the group. "Let's begin."

Malcolm cleared his throat and it wasn't a healthy sound. Last time Logan had seen him, he had been sun-browned by the jungle climate. Now his complexion was drained, almost gray. He looked at each of them from behind his steepled fingers. "Before anything else, I should speak on what I've done. What I was forced to do."

Quiet murmurs rose. Some people scowled, obviously not granting him any sympathy. Others just looked stoic. Logan cast him a nod, bracing for what might come.

Malcolm swallowed thickly. "I . . . owe apologies to all of you," he began in a low, raspy voice. "I remember pieces and shards of the last year—maybe more. The Herald you saw, the twisted monster . . . that was me . . . but not me." He pressed his eyes shut. "Levemoth took my mind, my will, forced me into acts that still keep me awake at night."

"What happened?" Logan asked.

"He started whispering in my mind shortly after we arrived on this planet," Malcolm said reluctantly. "I didn't know what it was, but once I'd noticed how mad he was making me, it was already too late. He insidiously softened my mind, until I was too weak to resist."

Grim faces watched him. No one interrupted.

Malcolm's voice gained in sturdiness with each sentence. "I went rogue. Before I turned into a full monster, I was moved around by Levemoth. It would pick me up, and I would take over a human settlement and lead them to . . ."

"To what?" Logan asked sternly.

"To create Blues."

He paused, letting that settle. The hush in the room felt heavy.

"I'm sorry, what?" Kat asked.

"I made them perform a ritual that transformed them," Malcolm said keeping his eyes on the table. "I tricked them."

"So, they are former humans?" Logan asked, trying to keep himself composed.

"They are," Malcolm said. "I only did it for five, maybe six villages. That was enough to get the ball rolling. If the Blues killed and gained enough time, they could make more Blues."

"We knew that," Local said in quiet anger.

Malcolm gave him a look, a flash of his old self ready to snap back, but instead he swallowed, nodded, and continued.

"Then Levemoth told me my job was done and that he needed a warrior to kill you. At that point I was too far gone. I recall the relentless drive, the hate, the hunger," Malcolm continued, "like I was hunting for something intangible. Levemoth poured instructions into my mind, coaxing and punishing in the same breath. Sometimes it was clear that I was being manipulated. I fought it. But I lost. Time and time again. Only at the end, in that last fight with you—" He flicked a glance at Logan. "—did I feel a spark of my old self—something inside me resisting."

Kat shifted behind Simmons. Her expression was taut, arms crossed. "You had no choice," she said, half a question, half an accusation.

Malcolm nodded gravely. "It's childish to avoid responsibility. I was tricked and manipulated. My existence felt like a disjointed sequence of dreams. Maybe I had a choice. I am not sure. No choice that I could see. The moment I tried to fight the control, it was like drowning in a sea of nightmares. The only clarity was the hatred . . . The hatred Levemoth fed me for all living things."

Some in the crowd looked away. Others stared him down. Silence stretched.

Logan cleared his throat. He knew how difficult it was for his father to admit weakness. Malcolm Specter had always said that displaying or admitting to vulnerability was asking for trouble. "Thank you for sharing. It helps . . . to know."

He glimpsed at the Groloin orb, half-expecting a snide remark. But the Hivemind remained still. Finally, Logan resumed. "We'll get back to you in a moment. But I want to get some pressing matters out of the way first."

Malcolm Specter nodded and ran his hands through his hair before steepling them again.

"Now, we have other topics to discuss," Logan said. "You all know by now why we came rushing out of the ruins. We found something weird: a physical manifestation of Levemoth. Or a piece of it. A growth, a cyst. We need to know what it was and why it was there."

A ripple of tension ran throughout the room. Freya clasped her hands on the table, brow creasing in a worried line.

Logan continued on. "I think it was guarding something. Something big. There's some reason it's so fixated on those ruins. It did the cocoon thing immediately after we first entered. At first, I just suspected it wanted to keep us from the deeper parts where the good Numa or darkmetal might be. But I think there's more."

"What makes you think that?" Balmer asked.

"Just my gut," Logan said.

Malcolm slowly lifted his gaze. "Logan's gut has always had merit. Levemoth's timing is not random. It's protecting an artifact left by the First Folk. One they never finished, one that was meant to stand as a final weapon against the Beast."

"How do you know this?" the Groloin asked, doing their best to keep the scorn out of their voice.

"What artifact?" Kat demanded.

Malcolm cleared his throat, glancing around. "It's called the Final Clarion. A doomsday weapon. According to Levemoth's memory—I gleaned scraps from the times it let me see into its thoughts—the First Folk built it in the heart of their greatest city down there. But they ran out of time when Levemoth finally attacked them. The design was incomplete."

Simmons frowned. "And it's still there?"

"Yes. Hidden in a sealed vault deeper than we've gone. Levemoth has watchers around it—Blues, ogres, scythe-fiends, even new creations. It wants to ensure you don't claim the Clarion," Malcolm said. "Levemoth fears this weapon. It doesn't quite understand it, but it suspects it can be dangerous when used against it."

"Even kill it?" Logan asked.

"Maybe," Malcolm said.

A wave of excitement rippled through the room.

Ryan, stepping forward, asked carefully, "The Final Clarion . . . That's a strange name for a doomsday weapon. Do you know anything else?"

Malcolm's shoulders lifted in a small shrug. "I only have fragments. Something about generating anti-Numa. Levemoth was once a Numa Spirit. It was corrupted by . . . I cannot speak of it . . ."

There was a heavy silence. Logan knew what his father spoke of. The dark god behind Levemoth's influence. That was something entirely above Logan's pay grade and he didn't even want to know. That was a problem for the Administrators to handle.

Logan broke the silence. "So, basically, we have to go down there and retrieve the artifact. Maybe fix it up."

Kat shook her head. "That's a tall order, Boss. That place is a labyrinth. And if the Big Bad is guarding it, we have to be prepared to lose men. Possibly a lot of them."

Simmons nodded, but he was a poster child of resolve. "Odds aside, if the Final Clarion is truly a weapon that can kill Levemoth, we have to get it. This might be our only shot."

The Groloin orb stirred, voice still watery yet resonant. "We, the Groloin, concur that this relic is critical. The Devourer could be undone if we harness it."

Logan stepped forward, planting his staff with a soft thunk on the floor. "We have no choice but to return," he said, voice carrying just enough edge to cut the tension. "We'll gather a strike team—Simmons, you and four of your best men, Kat, Balmer, Tumor, Ryan with his hardest recruits—and we'll push deeper than ever. We retrieve the Clarion thing or die trying."

"Agreed," Kat said quietly, though her expression was grave. Others murmured acceptance or simply nodded with steel in their eyes.

From his seat, Malcolm coughed. "Then I'll join you."

Instantly, a wave of protest erupted. Snoff nearly toppled off the crate he'd perched on. Kat bristled. Simmons barked, "What?" Freya frowned, torn. But the loudest reaction came from the Groloin orb, which crackled with raw fury.

"You dare?" it boomed in that grandmotherly voice tinted with wrath. "Absolutely not! We will not allow a newly-cleansed-but-still-corrupted man to walk into the very place where Levemoth's corruption runs thickest. He will turn again or at the very least hamper you."

Malcolm's jaw tightened. "I'd like a chance to rectify the horrors I've committed. But more than that, I can navigate certain parts, if Levemoth's memories remain."

The orb glowed a sharp green. "No. The risk surpasses any benefit. We will not allow you to be let loose on a mission of such dire importance."

Logan felt tension coil in his muscles. He spoke up, meeting the Hivemind's glare. "Groloin, calm down. I have no intention of letting him join the delve."

That earned a disappointed look from Malcolm. But Kat gave a silent, relieved nod.

"Without the Herald's corruption, you're not much of a fighter, Father," Logan continued. "Besides," he said, turning to the others, "we need Malcolm's knowledge about the Clarion and the deeper recesses. I want him here."

"As an advisor?" Kat asked.

"No," Logan said. "Leading the camp."

The pause that followed was massive. Freya looked at Logan questioningly. The Groloin hissed softly.

"Leading the camp?" Balmer repeated. "As in . . . relying on his judgement and loyalty regarding thousands of lives?"

Logan let out a slow breath. "Yes. That's exactly what I'm proposing. Malcolm stays behind, defends the Ark and the camp, organizes manpower to hold the perimeter, sets up advanced traps—whatever it takes to hold out while we're in the ruins. If Levemoth tries another assault, we'll need capable leadership."

This set off a dozen arguments at once.

"What if he betrays us again?" Balmer demanded.

"He's not going to betray—he's cleansed!" Freya retorted.

"Have you lost your mind, Logan? You want him commanding our defenses after everything that happened?" Kat's voice, ironically enough, was among them, though not the loudest.

Malcolm held up his shackled hands, voice quiet. "I understand the distrust. I am not sure I deserve your faith."

The Groloin orb's grandmotherly voice cut across the clamor, stony and cold. "You deserve nothing. We do not accept this plan. The logic is plain: a monster who murdered our allies cannot be entrusted with our defenses."

Logan slammed the butt of his staff on the floor, commanding a hush. "Listen." He locked eyes with the swirling orb, then scanned the ring of watchers. "You maybe think I'm naive, but I know exactly who Malcolm is. He's strong, cunning, and has experience leading large-scale operations. We need his expertise if we want the best chance of surviving these assaults Levemoth is sending at us."

A wave of tension pressed in. Some stared at the floor. Others watched Malcolm warily. Tumor's golem stepped forward, mechanical voice measured. "From an analytical perspective, Malcolm's skill set in leadership is indeed formidable. If truly loyal, he could shore up the camp's defenses significantly."

Logan nodded. "Simmons is our best fighter, so he must come with me. Kat is our best frontliner. Balmer's our best scout. Ryan's needed for morale. That leaves us short on leadership up top."

Freya's voice rose gently. "I'll do what I can. But I can't coordinate the entire camp alone, bracing for a major assault."

"We need someone with strategic intelligence and cunning," Logan emphasized. "That's Malcolm. And, crucially, if Levemoth does try to speak into his mind again, this location is safer to contain him than in the ruins' depths where the corruption saturates everything."

"This is madness," the Groloin orb sputtered.

"Or a second chance," Freya murmured, meeting the orb's glow.

"Yes," Logan said. "A second chance."

Malcolm exhaled, eyes flicking from Logan to the others. "If you let me do this, I will prove myself to you. You can keep me shackled to a ten-foot chain for all I care, but I will see this place safe."

An uncertain hush. Then Simmons, grim-faced, inhaled. "I am of two minds about this. But if we want to use Mr. Specter's skills, he is best-suited to leading the defense."

"Thank you, Simmons," Malcolm muttered.

A few soldiers nodded along, if reluctantly. Logan doubted they had any experience with Malcolm on this planet, but they knew from Earth who he had been—the richest man alive. They could see the logic.

The Groloin orb remained unconvinced. "We do not trust him. We propose electing a new leader from among the Faelves or the humans. This is folly."

Logan leveled his staff at the orb, not threatening but direct. "Your concern is noted. But you are not in command here—*I* am."

"You place us all at risk."

"Groloin," Logan said, voice going quiet, "I've listened to you many times, and more often than not, your counsel has proven vital. But you do not see everything. I know my father."

"You are blinded by your familial bond," the Groloin growled.

"No," Logan said. "My mind is clear. It is true, I want him to redeem himself."

"Then let him do it at a less critical time!"

"We need him now because it *is* critical, goddamn it!" Logan snapped. "If he's truly free from Levemoth, then no one can protect this camp better than him. He is a powerful leader, and he knows the enemy intimately. If he's not free—then this at least keeps him far from the Clarion. If we take him down with us and he turns, we might lose our last hope."

The orb vibrated, swirling with anger, and roared, "Which is why we want him dead."

"That is not for you to decide," Logan responded. "Let's leave the decision to a third party. What say the Faelves?"

A silence fell across the room, as every pair of eyes turned to stare at Snoff and his porcelain group.

Logan waited, chest tight. This was his biggest gamble yet.

The Faelves conferred with one another and then nodded among themselves. After a moment, a faint, reedy voice from among the Faelves piped up, "We . . . we trust Logan's decision. We Faelves will keep watch on Malcolm and ensure no slip occurs."

A quick murmur rose. Snoff looked at Logan, but he did not smile. He nodded, and Logan nodded back.

"Fine," was all the Groloin spat out.

The tension ebbed, giving Logan the chance to speak again: "So be it. We'll ride out soon, same plan as last time but delving deeper this time. We aim for the vault containing the Final Clarion. Malcolm will organize the camp's defenses, with Freya assisting the medics. The Groloin can supply golems for perimeter-watch. Everyone else who's fighting-capable, do your part."

Tumor's golem gave a curt nod. "Understood."

Kat blew out a breath, arms relaxing. "Better get packing."

Simmons grunted agreement. "No time to waste."

Logan nodded at them, then turned to Malcolm, who sat still, eyes flickering with a swirl of emotions—relief, regret, gratitude. "Father," Logan said, forcing formality, "make no mistake, if you betray us—"

"I won't," Malcolm said gruffly. "I know I can never atone for what I've done. But I will serve. Let's leave it at that."

Logan squeezed his staff. "Alright. We leave the day after tomorrow. That's enough time to gear up, give the wounded a breath, fortify the camp, and get some routines back. Council dismissed."

Some saluted, others just shuffled off in heavy thought. The Groloin orb vanished in a swirl of glowing green motes, presumably leaving the vessel, while Tumor's golem marched out to relay orders. Snoff hopped down from his crate, scribbling notes. People dispersed into the corridors, Kat and Balmer already discussing supply lists, while Simmons limped after them, determined to get his men ready.

Freya lingered, placing a hand on Malcolm's shoulder. He gave her a faint nod before she walked off. Soon it was just Logan, his father, and a few stoic guards.

For a moment, father and son shared the silence. Then Malcolm broke it softly: "You're risking a lot, trusting me with the camp. Some might even call that foolish."

Logan shrugged but gave him a tired smile. "Foolishness is right in my wheelhouse. You of all people know that well."

A fragile, rueful smile flickered across Malcolm's lips. "You've changed. Perhaps I should get to know you again."

"Yeah." Logan said quietly. "You should. But you need to become useful first. Make sure to talk to Snoff, to the Faelves, to everyone. They won't follow you blindly. Start earning trust around here."

Malcolm watched him quietly, some of his old features becoming more prominent. "No nonsense and a harsh tone. Not so soft anymore, are you?"

Logan started to turn away but paused. "We'll talk later, Father."

CHAPTER 24

Man-to-Man Talk

Later that day, the camp thrummed with restless energy. People hustled about, gathering supplies for the big delve the next day, including crates of rations, rope, medical kits, crossbow bolts, and spears. Tumor's golems carried the heavier loads, stomping across corridors. Snoff dashed around giving directions to the Faelves, who pitched in where they could, reinforcing the battered perimeter of the ship with illusions and fresh timber.

Despite being exhausted, everyone pushed that aside without complaint. The eerie swirl of Levemoth's smoky cocoon still loomed in the sky, a stark reminder that time was short.

Meanwhile, the preparation for a meaningful final push sent adrenaline surging through the camp. Everyone recognized that tomorrow's expedition might be the decisive factor in their war.

Logan stood in a half-collapsed corridor near one of the Ark's cargo lifts, overseeing the loading of the new gear he'd crafted. The five sets of lesser power armor gleamed in the flickering lantern light, fresh from final checks. Each was spoken for by Simmons and four of his best.

Logan was proud of his work, but he wished he had done more.

[We are at 96.65% optimal status. It is unreasonable to ask for more.]

Logan nodded. He was too tired to argue. For half a heartbeat he considered ducking away to steal a nap. But the thought of unanswered tasks clenched his gut. He was about to stride off when a voice called behind him.

"Logan."

He turned to see Malcolm. The older man had shed the shackles, but two guards walked close behind him, watchful.

Logan raised a brow. He stopped and spoke in a clipped tone. "Father."

Malcolm walked forward, the guards staying at a respectful distance. He stopped near Logan, voice quiet. "I was hoping we could talk—alone if possible."

Logan signaled to the guards. They glanced at each other, then gave a curt nod and stepped back a few paces, far enough to be out of easy earshot but still close enough to intervene if needed.

They sat down and Logan put his staff down. "What's on your mind?"

Malcolm breathed in deeply, as if steeling himself. "Everything, to be honest. But primarily . . . you."

Logan raised an eyebrow. "What about me?"

An unreadable expression settled on Malcolm's face. "You're a far cry from the directionless, childish boy I remember."

"Master of backhanded compliments." Logan clenched his jaw. Old feelings started rushing back. "You left me little choice. This world left me little choice."

"Fair enough," Malcolm said. He turned, gazing at the cargo lift where a half-dozen fresh recruits were stacking crates. "I see them looking at you with respect—some even with awe. I didn't think you had it in you."

Logan felt a prickle of old resentment. "I always had it in me, Father. You just refused to listen to my side of things."

Malcolm shook his head, expression pained. "I know I was a tyrant. In everything. That is what caught my eye. In business, I led with fear and an iron grip. You . . . You lead through respect and love."

"They just fear Levemoth more than me," Logan said with a wry smile.

Malcolm let out a dry chuckle. "As they should."

They sat quietly for a while, just looking at the sky. Logan found he didn't mind.

"You were a tyrant," Logan said slowly. Then he exhaled, feeling the weight of years falling off his shoulders. Malcolm Specter swallowed and nodded to himself.

"But I was a fool," Logan said. "And you only treated me like one."

"That was ignorance. I saw you drifting. I wanted you to aim higher. But I was blind to any other path than my own."

"No, Father," Logan said. "You were right. It was just the way you handled it that was wrong."

Logan exhaled slowly, a swirl of old memories rising—fights about worthless daydreams, arguments about wasted time. Malcolm had demanded absolute excellence but had never been able to show Logan that he could do it in his own way. And Logan had refused Malcolm's way.

"I am sorry," Malcolm Specter said. "I am sorry for everything."

"Yeah," Logan said. "Me too."

A pause. Down the corridor, a Faelf tripped over a chunk of scrap metal, cursing. The clang echoed as a reminder of their battered home.

Eventually, Malcolm lifted his head. "I'm talking to you now because I want you to know . . . I'm proud. Terrified for you, yes, but proud. And . . . I'm sorry I never told you that before."

The words caught Logan off-guard. Part of him wanted to snap back with a sarcastic jab—where was that pride back then? But he saw the raw sincerity in Malcolm's eyes and let his anger subside. And when that gave him space to process his emotions, Logan found that he had longed to hear those words all his life. He wanted to cry. He exhaled. Despite this heart-to-heart, Malcolm Goddamn Specter would not see him cry.

"That's—" Logan started. "Thanks, Dad."

Silence lingered. Then, Malcolm cleared his throat. "Anyway, about tomorrow. I know you insisted I stay behind, but if you need any final details on where I think the Clarion could be or any leftover scraps of Levemoth's knowledge, I'll share what I can."

"We'll talk specifics in the morning," Logan said. "We have some half-formed maps Balmer has been making with the **[Cartographer]**. Tumor's helping them through a golem. You can go help fill in the gaps."

Malcolm nodded. "Good."

An awkward lull fell. Both men faced each other, their uneasy history hanging heavy between them. Malcolm got up and dusted off. He started walking away.

But there was a crack in that heaviness. Something new. Something that could be built upon. Logan found he had a new feeling toward his father he never had before.

"Dad," Logan said. "I understand the kind of person you had to be back then. I just want you to know . . . I respect you."

Malcolm stopped as if frozen in place. He didn't look back and when he finally spoke, his voice cracked. "I don't deserve that."

"Yeah, well," Logan said. "It's complicated."

Malcolm Specter chuckled sadly. "I suppose it is."

"Now, go away and be useful, this is getting way too sappy," Logan said and they shared an awkward laugh.

A flicker of steel lit Malcolm's gaze. "I won't fail you."

Logan decided to shift topics. "If I do find the Final Clarion, do you think it's something we can operate with the knowledge we have?"

Malcolm was quiet for a moment. Logan noticed a strange look in his eyes. "Yes. I think I will be able to help once the device is here."

Logan nodded. "Tumor's got a knack for reverse-engineering. If we find something physically recoverable, we can bring it back here. Then we can figure out how to power or finalize it."

"Possible," Malcolm agreed. He didn't turn. "I think it will be clear how to use it once we get it. I trust you will do well."

A dark, humorless laugh escaped Logan's lips. "We'll manage. We have to."

The chatter of men passing behind them broke any chance for further gloom. Two young recruits were lugging a wooden crate of crossbow bolts to the cargo lift, nearly stumbling. Logan paused, motioning for the guards to help them.

Malcolm took that as a cue to turn. "And you? Are you truly ready?"

Logan lifted his staff. "I have no illusions about it. It'll be brutal. But I'm good at this. You just keep these people alive until I return with the Clarion."

Malcolm nodded solemnly. "I will. When you're in the ruins, watch your flank. Levemoth will try to make sure you can't find the weapon."

Logan squeezed his staff. "Let him try."

They stood in silence a moment longer, each man wrestling with his own burdens. Then, Logan turned to him. "I guess that's that for tonight. I should do one more pass through the camp, check if Kat or Simmons need anything."

"Very well," Malcolm said. "Logan, I . . . thank you for giving me a chance."

Logan's eyes flicked to the side. "Don't make me regret it."

With that, the two parted ways, the guards following Malcolm, who walked toward Balmer and their [**Cartographer**]. Logan watched his gait. It was very different than what it had been back on Earth—freed from Levemoth's control, yet still not free of the weight of what he'd done.

Out on the deck, Logan found the night sky painted by a scrawled pattern of dark clouds. The swirling black-and-blue cocoon that sheltered Levemoth glowed faintly in the horizon. It was like an omen scrawled in the heavens, daring any mortal to challenge it.

Logan liked to come here whenever he had a moment of silence, but he was surprised to see he had company.

Simmons was there, leaning on the railing, lost in thought. He was taking drags off a hollow stick, like a cigarette.

Logan joined him. "Miss it?"

Simmons grunted and took the stick from his mouth. "Just the habit."

"I miss booze," Logan said.

Simmons chuckled. They said nothing, just enjoyed the cool air away from the hubbub of the camp.

Finally, Simmons grunted softly. "So, how's your old man?"

"He's . . . reflective," Logan said.

Simmons gave a curt nod. "I have been under both of your leadership. Malcolm Specter was brutal, cunning, intelligent, and never wasteful. Everyone who could appreciate that, thrived under him."

"Uh huh," Logan said warily.

"But you," Simmons said. "You make everyone flourish. Your leadership is soft but firm when it needs to be. You have a will that overpowers problems. With you, it seems like anything is possible."

"Thanks," Logan said, voice low. "Where is this coming from?"

"Because you are doubting yourself."

"It's not doubt," Logan said.

"No? What is it?"

"I don't know how to feel."

"That is doubt," Simmons said simply. "You do not need to know, just feel."

"Huh," Logan said. "You're pretty wise for a meathead."

"You are pretty wise for a wastrel son," Simmons said.

They scoffed at each other and smiled.

Together they stared at the sky for a long moment. Crickets in the distant forest chirped. The Ark's engines rumbled softly, joined by the whisper of a night breeze. Logan closed his eyes, letting the warmth of the night push away some of the tension.

Eventually, Simmons flicked away the stick of a cigarette. "I'm heading to bed. You should do the same. We've got a big day."

"Yeah."

Simmons hesitated, then clapped Logan lightly on the shoulder before limping away. Logan remained, letting the wind carry his thoughts away for a final moment of solitude.

But rest didn't come easily. Hours later, after midnight, Logan still sat on the deck of the Ark. He couldn't stop thinking about his father. Or the heavy burden of leadership.

Logan's swirl of thoughts was broken by soft footsteps. He looked up and saw Freya walking toward him, wearing a thin shawl. She approached quietly and stuck herself to Logan's side. "You're not in our bed."

Logan shook his head. "Can't sleep."

She settled next to him, leaning her head on his shoulder. "Want me to ask the Faelves to cook you a sedative?"

A half-chuckle. "You know, that might be nice, but I need my wits about me tomorrow."

Freya sighed, nestling closer. "I heard from Simmons your conversation with your dad went well. Are you feeling okay about leaving him behind to guard us?"

"It's a risk," Logan said, "but everything's a risk these days. If we can't rely on him now, when can we ever?"

She nodded. "I trust you. And as far as he goes, I think he is . . . himself. I believe he truly regrets those horrors. It shows in every move he makes."

"He does," Logan agreed softly. "We'll see if that regret can be turned to something good."

Freya gave a faint smile, eyes drooping from her own exhaustion. "You are great at turning lemons into lemonade."

"Just need to do it one more time."

"Go get that weapon, love."

"And then we figure out how to kill that bastard."

A hush fell, and Logan felt Freya's warmth against him. For once, the silence wasn't heavy but comforting—a moment of closeness in a world on the brink of potential disaster.

Eventually, she whispered, "Come to bed, love. I'll give you a head massage."

Logan half-laughed. "Only the head?"

Freya kissed his temple drowsily as she caressed his cheek. "We'll see. But you should come with me."

Logan took her hand and squeezed it. "You're right. You're always right."

Freya smiled. "You're only noticing that just now?"

CHAPTER 25

Fortifying Hope

Dawn arrived with a mellow hush, which Logan found strangely peaceful. No immediate shrieks from Blues, no scuttling ogres smashing into the perimeter. It was almost as if Levemoth was holding back for now. Whatever the reason was, Logan counted it as a win. His people needed the rest and quiet. Hell, Logan certainly needed it. Then again, maybe it was just a fluke. Maybe even monsters needed a day to rest.

Logan stretched in his bed, finding himself well-rested for the first time in a week.

I could get used to this.

[Good morning, Logan. Me too. My functions are significantly sharper when you aren't sleep-deprived.]

Logan got up, snatched his composite support skeleton, snapped it on, and got his cane. Freya was still sleeping, and Logan crouched to pet her hair and give her a kiss on the forehead. She sighed and muttered something. Logan smiled back fondly and got out of the tent to discover that everyone in the camp seemed to be taking advantage of the relative calm. Crews hammered final nails into the new barricades, layering them with spiked wire. Golems paced along the ramparts, scanning the jungle's edge with mechanical vigilance.

Yet the place was obviously in shambles, half the tents mere tatters and some folks sleeping under improvised lean-tos. Food was short, until Snoff rediscovered a hidden supply of dried mushrooms the Faelves had stashed earlier. Not all humans handled those mushrooms well, but it was better than starving.

I miss meat.

Practically all of their **[Hunters]** had been relegated to fighting duty, in hopes of them getting class evolutions to warriors. Those who had survived, mostly had.

But that meant they had to rely on foraging and fishing for most of their food.

Logan convened a meeting by midday in the battered command tent— if a canted frame of sticks and a scrap of tarp could still be referred to as a "tent." Simmons stood near his usual position, leaning on a crate. Freya curled up on a stool, eyes bleary. Snoff perched cross-legged on another crate. The Groloin Hivemind was present through one of their golems, humming softly. Kat and Balmer, along with Ryan, formed the last part of this ragged council. Malcolm Specter was kept out of this conversation this time at the behest of the Groloin. Logan had thought it wise to consent to their request for once.

"Alright," Logan began, rubbing a kink in his shoulder. "Here's the plan. We form a strike team of about thirty. That's me, Kat, Balmer, Ryan, plus enough recruits who've seen these fights to keep their heads down. We march tomorrow at first light into the deeper labyrinth. We're also going to need that **[Cartographer]** . . . Evans, was it?"

"Yeah," Balmer said. "I'll tell him. He won't like it, though."

"Frankly," Logan said, "I don't care what he thinks. We need him, and that's that."

Simmons gave a nod. "I'll come with four of my strongest. The rest of my agents will be under Porter's leadership."

"Porter?" Logan asked.

"The one with the hat," Simmons said.

"Oh. I like him."

"He hates you."

Logan shrugged. "Can't please them all."

Freya smiled at Logan.

The Groloin didn't verbally protest, though their golems shifted. That was likely the Groloin's attempt at a subtle indication of disapproval. Logan cleared his throat. "While we're gone, Freya, you keep an eye on my father. I also crafted this," Logan said and plucked a set of two glassy orbs out of his pocket. He handed one to Freya. "Squeeze this and the one I have will start to vibrate like crazy. I'll know there's trouble here and we'll come back at double-speed."

Freya chewed her lip, intently staring at the orb she had grabbed. "I understand. I'll do my best."

Logan swallowed, forcing himself to focus on the next item. "There's also the matter of the exosuit. It's, uh, kind of corrupted, by all the screwed-up Numa I drained from my father when he was the Herald. Tumor has it contained for now, but he has to be constantly [**Possessing**] the suit in order to do that. Going to be hard to fight and lead with it being in this state."

Kat drummed her fingers on the edge of a battered helmet. "You came up with a fix, right?"

"I'm trying a partial enchantment that can actually purge corruption, like an inverted funnel. If we run into any more twisted Numa, I might channel it out instead of absorbing it. Uncharted territory, though."

Balmer sniffed. "Better than letting it rot your suits from the inside."

Logan nodded. "Exactly. I'll finalize the runes by tonight so I don't accidentally blow myself up tomorrow."

Ryan shifted, arms crossed over his lute. He'd been uncharacteristically quiet. "That might also save your father," he pointed out. "If you can funnel that black slime out of him without letting it get inside you."

A flicker of hope surfaced in Freya's tired eyes. "Yes. Perhaps so. Let me know if you need an extra crystal for that enchantment."

Logan managed a strained half-smile at Ryan for the suggestion. Then he turned to the final point. "Kat, you and Balmer—while I do that enchantment, I need you guys training the mid-level recruits. We lost too many veterans. We have to get these new folks up to speed or they'll die in seconds."

Kat huffed out a breath. "I'll do it. They can't be worse than the raw lumps we had last time. Teach them to keep formation, thrust a spear, cut the buggers' hamstrings. Let's hope they listen."

Balmer nodded. "I'll handle some basic infiltration tips. We need a scout or two besides me, just in case I get pinned."

That sealed it. Logan raked his eyes over the circle, gauging if anyone had more questions. They looked pale and battered but resolute. The hush throughout the tent spoke volumes: they all knew the stakes, and no one had any illusions left to cling to. They were out of easy roads.

"Alright," Logan said. "That's our plan." He looked at the Groloin golem. "We delved through the labyrinth floors before, found some corridors we never had time to explore. That's where we'll check. If there's any Numa, then we use it. Afterwards we go deeper. Any complaints?"

The golem stirred and spoke with a cold, mechanical voice. "Just a reminder: if Malcolm Specter shows even a hint of untoward behavior, the Groloin will use all of their considerable energy to instantly destroy him."

Logan smiled wryly. "I wouldn't expect anything less. Now, if there's nothing else, let's get to work. Today we prepare troops and reestablish the base. Tomorrow, the strike force leaves at first light. Dismissed."

Kat wasted no time. With the help of Ryan, she rounded up a handful of fighters who were in decent shape. These were folks who had at least stabbed a Blue or two and lived to tell the tale, or maybe at least swung a mace at an ogre's kneecap. Out near the rec-spar area—just a flat patch of ground near the Ark's anchor lines—she made them run basic drills and explained usable tactics in the ruins. Even Ryan participated in the drills, in a show of camaraderie. Balmer offered pointers on flanking, quick jabs, and how not to freeze if some spidery Blue skittered overhead.

By late afternoon, the mid-level recruits marched in passable formation. Kat was half-proud, half-annoyed. She barked at them to keep spears level and to keep lines tight. When Balmer jumped in with a feigned attack, they held pretty decently. The training was short but better than nothing.

Meanwhile, Malcolm Specter organized rotating squads to stand watch by day and night, each with a crossbow or two, plus at least one illusion-capable Faelf in the mix. The Faelves took Malcolm's leadership mostly in stride. It was the humans who clearly had second thoughts, but none seemed to voice them.

Snoff tried to keep morale up by distributing small cups of Faelf brew that tasted like a cross between peppermint and vinegar. People grimaced at the taste, but it gave them a mild energy boost. No one complained. They needed every edge they could.

No further major attacks came that day, though the tension in the air was sky-high. Scouts reported that the horizon was quiet, with no large ogres or trollspawn marching. The cocoon in the distance, however, definitely looked bigger, swirling with arcs of black lightning. Each time someone glanced that way, they got a chill.

Quicker than Logan even noticed, it was nightfall again. The completed spike barricades ringed the entire clearing, illuminated by faint torchlight. People bunked in cramped half-tents.

Logan finished his last-minute checks on the half-corrupted suit, as he sat next to a small brazier. There wasn't much he could do with the limited amount of Numa he had to spare. They needed to find more tomorrow.

In the morning, they'd gather at dawn, enter the labyrinth, and descend deeper than they ever had before. Possibly not come back. But what other choice was there?

[Not like you to have self-doubt.]

"If Levemoth is actively trying to stop us from going deeper, I don't think we have high odds of success."

[We do not. But you are a master of beating the odds.]

Logan chuckled. "We'll see tomorrow."

Tomorrow. The single word carried all their hopes, all their fears. Logan watched the shapes of his people in the flickering campfires. The night wore on with quiet finality. People maintained patrols, wounded men groaned in their sleep, and Faelves hummed low lullabies for anxious souls.

Logan dozed upright against a collapsed beam, exosuit half-latched. His dreams were fitful, full of images of subterranean halls and monstrous shadows. But in the cascade of nightmare, he clung to the memory of his father's potential redemption, that chance of being human again. If it was real, then maybe there was a path forward. If someone like Malcolm Specter could have a second chance, then anything would be possible.

Even gods might fall . . .

At dawn's first glow, Logan roused with a stiff back and a sharper sense of purpose. He hadn't slept long. Four hours, according to Tumor. He didn't need more. He was sharp, ready, and focused. The expedition waited. And far above, Levemoth's encroaching corruption in the sky pulsed a silent challenge.

They would all answer it soon enough.

CHAPTER 26

Into the Deep Again

Everyone present?" Logan asked, voice hushed but firm.

They stood at the edge of the labyrinth entrance—Logan, Kat, Balmer, and Ryan, plus eight other men and women geared in the best composite armor that the camp had left. Simmons was there with four of his best men, all of them clad in Logan's power armor, in which they had been training all of yesterday.

Even two brave Faelves hovered on the outskirts of the strike force—Subbel and Graiglu, both scouts who had been brave enough to volunteer. They knew powerful illusions and some healing, which could both come in handy. There was also their **[Alchemist]** William, the wiry, bespectacled fellow carrying far too many satchels holding his numerous reagents. And Evans, their **[Cartographer]**. A solemn man in his fifties, he was not happy to be in this group.

Freya, arms folded around her chest, gave them all a quick once-over. "If it gets too hairy, you pull out," she snapped, though her voice trembled with worry. "No sense dying for nothing."

"Yeah, yeah," Kat said, adjusting the straps on her knuckle-daggers. She gave Freya a pointed nod that said she understood the risk. The red-haired fighter was antsy to get moving.

Balmer swept his gaze around, double-checking each person. "All good on my end."

Ryan fingered the neck of his lute, giving a low chord that hummed in the early morning light. A handful of guards circled near the Ark's battered ramp, crossbows at the ready, but no immediate threat loomed. It was a peaceful morning, all in all.

Logan spared a glance at the fortress behind them. Smoke still curled lazily from a few smoldering fires. Malcolm Specter watched them from a distance. He gave Logan a grim wave, wordlessly conveying good luck. Logan nodded crisply in his direction. Freya turned to look and her brow furrowed. They had an entire contingency plan set for if his father attempted to break free, but hopefully it wouldn't come to that.

"Alright," Logan said, pointedly tapping the ground with his staff. "Let's get this done."

And with that, they descended into the ruins once again, entering the yawning stone ramp that spiraled downward into stale air and clinging darkness.

The first few corridors were obviously familiar. Cracked stone arches, rubble from prior fights, stray blood stains from their old skirmishes. But that failed to ease anyone's nerves. Not when they could see something new—something none of them wanted to see.

There was a black-blue mold creeping up corners that had once been relatively clear. Fleshy fronds dangled from the ceiling, each pulsating with uncanny life, tendrils of slime that seemed to bob in an airless wind.

"Ugh, that's disgusting," Kat muttered, flicking a chunk of the mold with a dagger's tip. The mold quivered, as if it had sensed her weapon's touch. She took that as her cue to slash it away.

Balmer, scouting at the front, raised a hand for silence. The whole group paused in a small corridor where a handful of pillars had partially collapsed. Tiny lumps of something dense and sticky dotted the floor—a black substance that congealed in oily puddles.

As they advanced, a wet hiss echoed from the darkness ahead. Logan stiffened, staff angled. He recognized that hiss. *Blues.*

Ryan slid sideways, lute readied. He gave a subtle nod at one of the Faelves. Subbel conjured a faint illusion of flickering torchlight further down the corridor—basically a decoy. The hiss grew louder and another joined it. Then two figures lurched out from behind a shattered column: twisted shapes that might have once been standard Blues, except these were oddly elongated, with long skinny arms sporting black talons.

"It's those crawly types," Balmer whispered, voice tight.

"Damn it, I hate those," Kat muttered.

The creatures snarled, drool leaking from ragged jaws. One locked eyes on the group, then launched itself forward with blinding speed, talons clicking rapidly on the stone. Logan stepped up, staff raised. Right behind him, Kat and Balmer prepared to flank.

The elongated Blue slammed against Logan's staff in a shower of sparks. He braced, pushing back. The exosuit whined but held firm. Kat ducked in, hooking an undercut blow with her dagger that bit into the beast's flank. It roared, turning to swat her, but Balmer lunged from the other side, rapier piercing its side. The monstrosity howled. It thrashed and tried to claw at anything and everything, before one of the recruits finally shot a crossbow bolt through its head.

"Nice one," Logan called behind him.

Behind it, the second long-limbed Blue sprang sideways, scuttling up the wall. Ryan let out a guttural chord that rattled everyone's bones, a Bardic resonance designed to disorient. The thing flinched, losing traction. Graiglu the Faelf shot him with a slingshot. A small pebble connected, and out billowed a dark cloud. The creature shrieked, half-falling. It coughed and convulsed, before it was reduced to ragged breathing on the ground. The recruits finished it off.

"Damn," Logan said and turned to Graiglu. "What's that?"

The blue-porcelain Faelf grinned. "A toxin."

"Works well."

"'Tis so, brave one," Graiglu said. "But I must use it sparingly. I decided to make sure my sling is true."

"It is."

Graiglu grinned boyishly and went over to the Blues to inspect their bodies.

Logan turned to the group. "You alright?" he asked, scanning their faces.

No major injuries, just rattled nerves. Ryan's illusions flickered, dancing patterns across the corridor walls. Kat shook gore off her knives. Subbel, the other Faelf, stared at them with wide eyes but managed a nod.

"Let's keep it moving," Balmer said.

They pressed deeper and deeper, passing a small side chamber they recognized—a place where they'd salvaged lumps of darkmetal once—but now the walls were riddled with throbbing black cysts. William paused to examine one. It pulsed under his finger, releasing a foul odor that made everyone gag. Logan barked for them to keep going. Kat slapped him on the back of his head.

That sense of creeping organic infiltration grew with each corridor. Where once plain stone walls stood, now veiny lumps and tendrils oozed from cracks, as if the ruin itself was being devoured by Levemoth's living rot. Some passages were blocked by half-grown slime curtains that Logan or Kat had to slash aside, releasing vile fluids that sizzled when they dripped on boots, eating away at the leather.

At one point, the group passed a small alcove full of husks—bodies . . . or what remained of them. Blues. As if they'd sacrificed their essences to enable corruption. Logan shuddered but pushed on.

"We stick to the route we mapped before," Logan reminded them when they reached a confused intersection. "Assuming it hasn't caved in."

Balmer nodded, finger tracing the chalk markers from last time. "We never explored that left fork. The deeper section. That's where we go if we want to find the artifact or something brand-new."

Kat cast a wary glance down the left hallway, which was harder to see thanks to thick slime dripping from overhead. "Then left it is," she said, forging ahead.

They encountered more Blues along the way—just the normal ones in clusters of eight. The fighting was fierce but brief, the group supporting each other with well-honed synchronicity. A lot of the fighters gained levels in the process and grew that much stronger for it.

They pressed on, collecting a few injuries—mostly cuts that William patched up with salves. The environment grew more horrid. Levemoth's influence was everywhere, painting the walls with pulsing, disgusting goop that dripped on their shoulders and scalded their skin, as if on purpose.

The first trap nearly skewered Balmer. He stepped across a suspicious tile. A mechanism triggered, releasing a volley of spiked darts from hidden compartments in the stone. Luckily, his reflexes kicked in immediately and he rolled sideways, only catching one dart in his upper arm. He hissed, yanking it free, while William hurried in, offering a potion. The rest of them paused, hearts pounding. Logan squatted, examining the trap's release plate.

"That's a good sign," Logan said. "If there's traps, it means we are getting closer."

Balmer forced a tight grin, wincing from his bandaged arm. "We'd better watch every step."

"Be extra careful, okay?" Kat said, almost softly.

They inched forward, carefully prodding the floor with spare rods. Twice more, they triggered hidden spring-plates that unleashed puffs of choking gas or a swinging blade from overhead.

What a classic set of traps. So elaborate.

The group avoided serious harm, though it cost time and frayed nerves. They used illusions to test some traps, letting fake silhouettes walk ahead. That saved them once or twice from new ambushes. Still, tension soared. If the First Folk had laid so many of these traps out, it meant they were protecting something deeper in the labyrinth.

They found a reasonable amount of Numa along the way, enough for Logan to keep William supplied, so he could keep healing them. Enough to repair equipment and keep powering up the five light exosuits and Logan's big one. Enough to also have a little to spare for general use, though nothing major.

Sadly, no darkmetal.

Eventually, they reached a sturdy metal door set into the rock. It was sealed tight, runes carved across its face. More telling was the black-blue mold trying to push through the cracks, nearly lifting the door from behind. It looked like Levemoth's corruption had tried and partially succeeded in breaching whatever wards lay beyond.

Kat gently tested the handle. No give. She raised a brow at Logan. "Want to try your new trick on it?"

Logan considered. The runic lines on the door didn't look like corruption— rather they were some old protective ward. But he did see a creeping black patch trying to grow over the door. It was that disgusting oily membrane Levemoth had decided to redo the place with.

Logan placed a gauntlet on that mold and prompted Tumor to reroute Numa energy there, which Logan turned into electricity, zapping the membrane. It hissed like an angry snake, shriveling slightly. Encouraged, Logan let a bit more Numa funnel through. The black patch crackled, curling away, just enough to free the door's edges from infection, if not open it.

"Better," Kat said. "Now how do we actually open the damn thing?"

Balmer knelt, studying the runic script. Ryan came over, strumming a faint chord as if the resonance might highlight hidden illusions. The Faelves peered with wide eyes, peeking out from behind the taller humans like curious children. The door had a complicated locking system with two different keyholes.

"Looks intricate," Balmer muttered while shining his flashlight on them.

Kat snorted, crossing her arms. "Let's see if we can just break the hinges."

Logan shook his head. "The door is heavy. And it may be booby-trapped."

"Have any better ideas, Boy Genius?" Kat said.

"Sure do," Logan said and grinned.

Then, he pushed his darkmetal band against the door and told Tumor to do his magic. Two lines of liquid metal snaked from the band and dove into the keyholes, filling them up. Soon after, there was a loud *click* and the door opened with a heavy groan.

They braced themselves, weapons ready. No explosions. That was good. Logan pushed the door and it swung open into a short corridor that smelled of stale air and rot. *Perfect.*

Balmer led the way, rapier up, scanning. Just through the threshold was a wide space, more like an antechamber than a typical corridor. Stone columns lined the walls, each of them intricately carved with swirling designs. There was less mold here, although a few stubborn patches glistened in corners. The wards had likely slowed Levemoth's infiltration. Across the chamber's far side, another door stood, iron-banded but slightly ajar from the inside.

Kat sucked in a breath. "If they went through a double-key lock, we are definitely in the right direction."

Logan nodded, shoulders tense. "That or we just stepped into something worse."

They advanced carefully, scanning for more traps. Sure enough, near the center of the chamber, they spotted a floor panel that looked faintly out of place. Balmer tossed a chunk of rubble onto it, and a hidden blade swung down from the ceiling, right where Logan would have walked. Everyone exhaled relief. They stepped around it, eyes peeled for more.

At last, they reached the far door. No tricks here. Balmer eased it open. The corridor beyond sloped downward, lined with half-broken sconces. The walls bore faint carvings, though much was worn away or obscured by sloppy black smears. One big smear, near eye-level, looked suspiciously like a monstrous handprint.

Logan's spine prickled. "We definitely keep going." He glanced at Ryan, who gave a quick chord, more subdued than usual. No illusions triggered, so maybe they were safe. Then they carefully stepped down the slope.

They hadn't gone ten yards when the corridor made a sharp turn. At the corner, a scrawled piece of ancient text was etched into the stone. The script was spidery, not unlike the runes on the door. The Faelves exchanged uncertain glances. Subbel tried to read it, illusions flickering around her eyes, but gleaned only partial meaning: *Danger. Final stand.*

"Must be referencing something the First Folk left," William said quietly.

"Well, it had better not be a time-share vacation cabin down here," Logan said. A few of the recruits laughed at the stupid joke, probably more to release tension than due to sycophancy.

Finally, they reached a narrower doorway at the corridor's end. Here, the oily membrane thickened, nearly blocking the frame. The group spent minutes hacking away at it, each slash releasing foul gas that forced them to hold cloths over their mouths. Then Logan used a pulse from his exosuit bracer to shock some lumps, forcing them to shrivel enough that they could pass through.

Beyond was another short corridor, which bore the smell of something old, possibly sacred.

Sacred? What do you know of what "sacred" smells like?

Tumor didn't feel like weighing in, but Logan could swear he could sense the AI's amusement.

A faint draft tickled their faces. The stone walls glistened with the wetness of Levemoth's corruption but still no sign of a secret ultimate weapon. Nor any eldritch monstrosities, for that matter.

Instead, what they found was a grand gate of sorts, half-buried in collapsed stone. Tall enough to arch well overhead, it was covered with worn reliefs of tall warriors.

"Is this it?" Balmer asked and slid a hand across the giant doorframe.

Kat whistled low. "Looks like some final epic door. Are we near the big secret?" She stepped forward to get a closer look.

Simmons crouched by the rubble. "It's partially blocked, but maybe we can squeeze through."

Indeed, there was a sag in the collapsed upper section that allowed a narrow crawlspace. The group could pass, but they'd have to lighten their gear or go one-by-one. They formed a short line, each taking a moment to harness their weapons properly. Ryan stowed his lute carefully on his back. William tied a rope around his waist in case he slipped.

Logan went first, staff slung tightly via a strap, exosuit whining as he hoisted himself into the gap. Loose stones crunched under his boots. He inched through, ignoring the cold sweat on his brow. On the other side, he dropped onto a small ledge that overlooked a walkway, which spanned across a large, dark chamber. He couldn't fully see the far side.

One by one, the others joined, sliding awkwardly, cursing under their breaths when a loose rock tumbled. No immediate sign of hostiles. *Good.*

Then, they looked up, and tension rippled through the group.

Even in the dim torchlight, they could see the far walls soaring upwards, carved with swirling reliefs. Some panels showed shadowy figures battling twisted beasts. Others depicted massive spires rising from the ocean. Near the center, an enormous swirl shape might have been Levemoth. The entire place exuded a solemn weight. Another sealed door lay across the walkway.

Logan breathed shaky relief. "Alright, we're in deeper than we ever have been before. Let's—"

A distant rumble cut him off. Not quite an earthquake but close. The stones underfoot quivered. The black mold along the walls trembled. Distant echoes of something monstrous, maybe. Ryan played a quick, uneasy chord, but no illusions flared. Everyone tensed, expecting a wave of abominations.

The quake subsided, leaving only a lingering sense of doom. Kat's gaze flicked across the gloom. "That was bigger than usual. Levemoth stirring again, or is some part of these catacombs about to cave in?"

Logan plucked the glass orb from his pocket. They all watched it closely until a minute passed. Logan shrugged and put the orb away again.

Balmer exhaled. "We'd better hurry. This could all come down on our heads if we dawdle."

Logan ordered them to form a perimeter. They needed to see if this was the correct path or if some side passage led to the key. Their footsteps echoed oddly in this big chamber, each scuffing noise amplified. The walls were more elaborate than anything they'd seen so far but also scarred by the presence of recent corruption: half-formed lumps of glistening flesh or faintly moving strings of mucus. Whatever was down here, Levemoth had its claws in it.

Subbel and Graiglu slunk around the edges, illusions ready. Kat and Balmer took the front, while Logan held the middle, staff prepared for an ambush. They spied no immediate creatures, but the air felt thick. Dangerous.

At the far end, they found a small antechamber with carved pillars, which were less defiled, possibly shielded by leftover wards. Patterns of swirling runes across the floor indicated something important.

Logan's heart jumped at the possibility. He knelt to trace the lines, letting Tumor parse the shape. It looked like the ruins' signature brand of puzzle or lock.

"Another ward," he said quietly. "But no obvious door this time. Might be illusions or triggers requiring Numa. The First Folk must've closed it off behind them."

Kat pressed a palm to the pillar's surface. "Feels cold. You think the secret weapon is behind these walls?"

Ryan strummed a question-like chord, causing the illusions to faintly flicker, but nothing changed. Balmer gave a stumped shrug. Subbel tried a direct illusion, shaping a phantom figure to walk across the floor. No effect. Then William noticed faint holes in the walls, reminiscent of puzzle mechanisms that might require runic sequences. The group realized they'd have to piece together how to open it to pass further.

Logan's stomach twisted. Delving deeper was all well and good, but if they got stuck at some ancient puzzle, Levemoth could spawn out of his cocoon while they were still rubbing their foreheads. They needed to get through this fast.

"Alright," he said, scanning the carved characters ringing the pillars. "We'll look for matching symbols to press in order. Might be referencing the reliefs behind us. Let's keep an eye out."

As they spread out to examine the pillars and carved panels, that distant rumble returned—a slow, menacing quake. Pebbles danced across the floor. The black mold shuddered as if alive with tension. The group braced themselves, hearts pounding. The quake grew, then subsided again.

I feel like we are being watched.

"Levemoth's up to something. We can't dawdle," Kat growled, echoing their earlier sentiment.

"Agreed," Logan said. "Let's find these references fast and hope it leads us to the right place."

They had no clue that beyond these hidden wards, deeper in the labyrinth, lay an entire corridor of First Folk history, waiting to reveal to them exactly how they had once sealed Levemoth. But each passing second made the labyrinth more unstable, threatening to bury them. And Levemoth's metamorphosis pressed on.

So, they pressed on too, with no guarantee of success or escape, but they were determined nonetheless. Each trap avoided or beast slain only fueled that raw desperation: find the key, find the weapon, or face the end.

CHAPTER 27

Echoes of the First Folk

It took them a long hour of cross-referencing each pillar with the swirling reliefs on the chamber walls. The group formed small pairs, each trying to match some shape or symbol with a carved subset in the floor. Subbel and Graiglu used illusion in the air to mark progress, projecting partial outlines, while Ryan's lute droned a quiet melody that steadied nerves and provided them with focus. Meanwhile, Kat and Balmer patrolled around the edges with Simmons' agents, fending off a few stray lumps of black mold that attempted to sprout tendrils.

Beneath the glow of their flashlights, Logan finally found a repeating series of glyphs: a stylized spiral, intersected by four lines. It matched a set of notches on one pillar. He carefully pressed them in sequence. The stone under his fingertips gave a faint hum. A piece of the floor near the center of the chamber slid aside, revealing a hidden passage slanting downward.

"Got it!" Logan said, calling the rest over. They peered into the new hole, a short flight of steps leading even deeper into the ruins. It felt ominous, but at the same time progress was good.

Balmer grinned. "Knew you'd figure it out."

Kat came up and punched Logan on the shoulder. "Took you long enough."

At the bottom, they emerged into a long corridor of polished white stone, unlike the rough, mold-eaten halls above. This corridor felt almost pristine compared to the previous parts. It seemed to have been preserved in time, perhaps by lack of oxygen. Logan was no scientist, and when Tumor offered twelve potential solutions, he politely declined.

The black-blue corruption still seeped in from occasional cracks but far less than outside. It seemed Levemoth's claws didn't reach quite this deep. The walls rose high on both sides, covered in majestic reliefs.

The group paused, catching their breath. Even in half-light, they could see scenes etched in painstaking detail. People—humanoid, presumably the First Folk—stood arrayed in grand formations, wielding staves or swords that glowed in carved lines. Opposite them, a monstrous silhouette towered, swirling and shapeless, swallowing entire cities. The detail included spires crushed under its bulk, and swarms of smaller beasts attacking from the flanks. Scenes of chaos—basically an apocalypse carved in stone.

Ryan let out a gentle chord, almost reverent. "It's so crazy to think that this monster we are fighting has been tormenting civilizations for millennia."

"Not just tormenting," Logan said quietly. "Devouring them."

Logan looked at the carvings and felt a chill at the depiction of that shapeless beast. The lines around it reflected a slightly different form for the great calamity of an eldritch monster that he had grown accustomed to, but the defining characteristics were still there: a cluster of bulging eyes, a twisted crown of bones, a giant scaled body covered in a cloud. Not like a whale as the current iteration looked—more like a serpent, however, definitely Levemoth in some primeval form.

Balmer stepped closer, fingertips tracing a figure near the bottom, brandishing a large horn-like device. Another figure clutched a spherical object. Possibly relics or weapons. The entire tableau reeked of significance.

Kat breathed out, "They fought Levemoth back then . . . and lost?"

"They fed it unknowingly for a long time," Logan said. "Letting it gorge on corrupted Numa. Then, by the time they realized how strong it was, it was already too late."

They moved on. The corridor stretched nearly fifty yards, each section boasting a new panel of carved story. Scenes of heroic stands, advanced machines rolling across wastelands, airborne crafts not unlike the Ark but more streamlined. Then the final panels turned dark: the First Folk scattered, the beast overshadowing them. Many panels ended with swirling waves of black.

At the far end stood a small arch into a side room. Faint runic writing spanned the arch. Simmons peered inside. "Looks like a library or something. Might give us intel."

Logan's pulse picked up. "Let's check."

Inside, they found a half-collapsed room ringed with stone shelves. Bits of ancient tablets and scraps of etched metal lay scattered. Part had caved in, burying who-knew-what. Levemoth's corruption here was minimal, only thin strands on the walls. But those that had made it to the ground, had darted straight toward the metal etchings, eating them.

Logan zapped one until it shriveled and picked up a tablet. He was right. Levemoth had been wiping them clean of whatever had been etched on them.

Eventually, Balmer noticed a sealed metal casket in the corner. It was scorched, probably from some old meltdown, but still intact. Kat pried it open with a dagger and a grunt. The lid squealed. Inside were partial records—thin metallic plates inscribed with runic text. Some had flaked. Others remained legible.

One in particular drew Logan's eye. A swirling script with the faint image of what looked like an elaborate horn. Next to it was writing.

"Tumor, can you read this yet?"

[To a degree. They are definitely talking about a "weapon". The translation is roughly "the last big weapon". These are the documents of its creation.]

"Let's take these with us," Logan said. A recruit offered him a jute sack, and Logan piled the metal plates into it. They'd read them when they needed them. Then he picked up a few more and scanned them for Tumor, who read them.

[It's a poem. A lamentation. Talking about the great wasteful death by the shores of their kingdom. The people here knew they had built the weapon too late.]

Logan told the others what Tumor had said.

"Man . . ." Kat muttered. "Must have sucked being so close and still getting obliterated."

"Indeed," Logan muttered.

"So, it is here?" Simmons asked.

"Most likely," Logan said.

Kat let out a slow whistle. "This is it. If we find that Clarion, we can ruin Levemoth's day. Or at least stand a chance."

"Where is it?" Balmer asked. He rummaged for more plates. "We need a location."

Logan let Tumor read, just flashing the metal plates in front of him for a second. Then he repeated what Tumor could glean. "Says something about being locked away below . . . behind wards so it doesn't fall into dark hands. Possibly in the lowest sanctum. They mention illusions, runic wards, pressure plates. Great. Another puzzle."

Ryan gripped his lute. "We can handle illusions. We just have to get there before the Levespawn tear us apart."

Logan nodded, giving a determined look. But inside, anxiety churned. Puzzles after puzzles, going deeper and deeper. And time was running dangerously short. Logan could feel it. But he needed to keep spirits up.

"Good work, team," he said. "Let's keep moving."

They retraced their steps to the corridor of reliefs. Another quake struck, stronger this time. Chunks of the ceiling rained down in a near-avalanche, forcing them to scramble aside. A slab of stone shattered on the floor, nearly crushing Ryan's foot. He hopped back, strumming a frantic chord that made illusions swirl in alarm. The entire structure groaned like it might split.

"We gotta hurry," Balmer hissed as William came toward Ryan with an ointment.

"This is different," Logan said. "Can you guys feel it?"

A dozen people nodded at him grimly.

A malevolent sensation. A pulse of madness and hatred with every quake. There was no doubt, this was Levemoth's doing.

All the more reason to keep going.

The corridor directly ahead branched into two. One path was mostly open, while the other was piled high with rubble from the cave-in. They had no time to clear it, so they took the open route. The quake died, but tension soared. If Levemoth was speeding up the metamorphosis, this ruined city might not last.

As they ventured deeper, the corridor's stone gave way to stretches of black-blue muck. Patches of fleshy growth jutted from corners, those "pulsing cysts" embedded in the walls, each throbbing like a sickly heart.

A stench of rotting seaweed and rancid fish assaulted them. A few times, lumps of that cyst started to quiver ominously, prompting Logan or Kat to slice them open or burn them with electricity. The resulting gore reeked, but if they had let the quivering finish its purpose, it would have surely resulted in something nasty.

Eventually, the corridor ended in a wide antechamber sealed by an enormous sealed door largely covered in corruption that oozed strings of oily sinew.

Lines of runic script peeked from beneath. A half-dozen spindly spikes protruded from the top, presumably part of a defense mechanism. The entire place gave off an aura of finality, like crossing it would lead them into the labyrinthine structure's heart.

Logan turned to the group. "This has to be it. Once we cross, we might be at the threshold of the Clarion's sanctum."

"How can you tell?" Graiglu squeaked.

"I just do," Logan said.

Graiglu looked at him oddly but then nodded as if finally understanding something. He cast some spell, scanning for triggers. "I sense multiple pressure plates in the floor."

"You're up," Logan said nudging his head toward Balmer.

Balmer nodded and closed his eyes for a second, focusing until a shadowy outline enveloped him, giving him speed, stealth, and grace.

Everyone braced for a dispute with either the First Folks' booby traps or Levemoth's mutants bursting in behind them.

Then the corridor shook violently. This quake was bigger, rolling like thunder. Stone above them cracked. The black mold across the walls rippled. A chunk of the ceiling fell near the middle of the group, forcing them to scatter. Dust and rubble flew, settling with a jarring crash. Everyone was left panting, eyes wild. The ruins would fully collapse at this rate.

"Goddamn it," Logan growled and dodged a falling rock. "We might not have much time."

"There's goop on the door," Simmons said. "Do your thing, Boss."

Logan nodded, heart pounding. He pressed a hand to the sealed door's mold, letting a surge of Numa zap away the black gunk. It sizzled and writhed, revealing more archaic runes. But the quake had them all on edge. Any moment, the entire place could collapse—or an army of beasts could surge through.

Behind them, the corridor cracked further, and rocks fell blocking their way back. A sense of entrapment closed in on them. They were effectively locked in unless they managed to find a new route out.

And not only that—there was a roar and a squishy slither behind the collapsed pile of rocks. Soon, an oily black gunk started to seep out from it. The malevolent presence intensified.

Levemoth knew exactly where they were, and he was not having it.

Everyone exchanged glances. The only way was forward.

"Logan!" Balmer piped out nervously.

"I know!"

Kat took a deep breath. "We solve this puzzle, and get that door open, or we're done."

Ryan flicked sweat from his brow. He started playing his lute and singing a relaxing note, but it sounded high-strung, his voice cracked. He was terrified. They all were.

Logan focused, letting Tumor read the newly revealed runes, while his mind searched for symbols or patterns that matched the partial records from the library. Might be illusions, might be a puzzle of stepping stones or sequences that had to be pressed on the wall. But with every second, the labyrinth's groans grew louder. The quake died down for now, but when Logan looked behind him, he could see the oily gunk pooling by the rocks. It was boiling.

Logan swallowed and turned back to his work. He prompted Tumor to ease his body, which was currently clutched in anxiety. He needed all the focus he could muster.

He would solve this puzzle or die trying. Literally. This was it. The last push. A grim resolve overcame him and he relaxed. This was do or die. So just . . . *Do.*

[How did you get there that easily?]

"Shut up," Logan said. "Do you have anything for us?"

[Not yet.]

"Then I'm going to try something," Logan murmured, touching the runes. "If we hesitate, we die."

CHAPTER 28

Race Against Collapse

Logan pressed a trembling palm to the runic script etched into the sealed door. Around him, the ruin quaked and the corridor groaned like it might shatter at any second. He glanced behind to where black slime oozed from fissures in the collapsed rubble—Levemoth's vile presence congealing in dull, throbbing globs.

"Right," Logan murmured. "Time to get clever."

He called upon Tumor to take possession of the darkmetal band on his forearm. It flowed into thin filaments, each of which snaked across the door, seeking out hidden grooves. The runes flared: one . . . two . . . three sets of complex glyphs lighting up in sequence.

"A little more," Logan said through clenched teeth. His mind teetered between excitement and dread. If the door opened, they might find the Clarion. Or a monstrous trap. But with the entire ruin threatening to collapse behind them—and the hideous pool of slime seething around behind them—he just wanted to get out of this room.

From within the door came a final metallic *click*. The runes glowed white-hot in a sudden burst. A short, jarring hiss escaped, and the heavy stone panels split in half, scraping and rumbling into the wall recesses on either side.

"Door's open!" Kat hollered, flashlight in one hand and her knuckle-dagger in the other.

But before they could fully shuffle through, the black sludge behind them surged, rising in a revolting wave that slopped over the floor. The stench was overwhelming, like rotten meat simmering in toxic waste. A deep wet roar vibrated through the corridor.

"That slime's coming alive!" Balmer shouted. "Move!"

Just then, the slime convulsed, bubbling up into a hulking shape—twice as tall as an ogre, made of dripping, half-solid goop. Muscles made from tar-like lumps formed huge arms with jagged claws. A cluster of blazing blue eyes flickered across what passed for its head.

"Spread out!" Logan ordered, staff readied. His mind whirled. Levemoth had given birth to an abomination from the corruption itself—something monstrous, definitely bigger than anything they'd faced in these cramped corridors.

As if in response, the creature let out a deafening bellow, thrashing its slime-limbs. The stone floor cracked under the weight. It swung a grotesque arm at the nearest recruit, who dove away just in time. The blow pulverized the ground, spraying chunks of rock and sizzling black fluid.

"This is new," Kat snarled, adjusting her stance. "Charming."

"Tight formation! "Logan yelled. "Watch yourselves—it's probably loaded with nasty surprises!"

Simmons advanced, slamming down the exosuit's visor. "Cover me!"

The big man dashed toward the towering slime monstrosity, brandishing his axe, which gleamed faintly blue with Logan's enchantments. He swung in a savage arc. The blade ripped through the slime-flesh, splattering foul droplets everywhere. But the parted goop simply reformed in seconds.

"Goddamn it, I knew it," Logan said. "Stun grenades. Now!"

A tentacle of sludge, studded with jagged dark lumps, erupted from the monster's side. It lashed at Simmons from behind, forcing him to block. Another swing, a near-miss, battered one of the recruits. He screamed a short while, writhing on the ground before the slime monster stomped on him.

"NOW!" Logan barked and the recruits got out five stun grenades and threw them at the enemy in a fusillade. They exploded, confusing the beast, slowing it down. Piles of slop dripped from it and were blasted away in the explosion, and they immediately started to slither back toward the body. The blasts had hurt it, but it kept moving toward them, absorbing crossbow bolts which dissolved in its disgusting body.

Balmer cried, "We'll distract it—try to keep it from consolidating!" He darted in with a rapier poke that forced the beast to shift, while Kat launched a flurry of rapid strikes at its flank. Each strike scored a line of sizzling black ooze. Behind them, Ryan hammered out a harsh chord, the dissonant magic rattling the creature's sense of balance—but only briefly. It roared again, flailing unpredictably.

Sludge tentacles whipped in every direction. One slammed into Kat, knocking the wind out of her. Another hammered into Balmer's leg, sending him skidding. They both cried out in pain. The monster advanced on them, eyes blazing.

"Draw it away!" Logan yelled, heart pounding. "We can't fight this thing in a choke point—there's no room!"

Simmons gave a curt nod, ducking a wide swing. "We'll pull it back into the chamber!"

They backtracked into the broader antechamber beyond the newly opened door. The boss followed, slither-marching with terrifying speed. Its footsteps left sizzling footprints in the stone.

Logan braced himself, summoning Numa from his reservoir. "Tumor, overcharge the exosuit. Time to make a storm."

[On it!]

A surge of energy crackled around Logan's left forearm. Darkmetal filaments extended out, shaping into electrified wires. They lashed out at the monster's side. Arcs of lightning sliced against the slime, cooking chunks of it into a hardened crust. The creature shrieked, limbs contracting. But almost instantly, new slime replaced the charred bits—it was regenerating at breakneck speed.

"Damn it," Logan cursed. "We need more!"

Kat groaned, pushing herself back up. Blood trickled from her temple. "How do we kill something that's basically goop?"

"Overload it," Balmer hissed, limping. "We blow the entire mass to bits!"

Simmons, side-by-side with two of his men, pressed the assault. Their axes and swords chopped in a flanking pattern. Gouts of sludge spattered the floor. Meanwhile, Ryan sang a deeper, resonant note that seemed to sap the monster's aggression. For a heartbeat, its thrashing slowed.

"Logan!" Ryan yelled. "Try something bigger!"

Logan nodded, scanning the environment frantically. The broad chamber they were in had some suspicious columns, plus the door behind them that might shut. If they collapsed the ceiling, they could bury the boss. But then they'd trap themselves.

A ripple tore through the monstrous slime. It reared back, forming a monstrous maw from its center. Then it vomited a tidal wave of sticky black fluid straight at the group. People dove, some too slow. One recruit was swallowed by the wave. He screamed, thrashing before sinking beneath the sludge.

"Help him!" Kat roared.

"Belay!" Logan cut in. "He's gone."

Indeed, the recruit's screams faded, replaced by horrible gurgles. The wave receded—nothing remained but twitching lumps.

Simmons hollered, voice booming over the chaos. "We can't hold this position! Logan—any ideas?!"

"Mass explosion," Logan said grimly, recalling what he'd done against the first scythe-armed ogre. He rummaged in his pouches. "A bomb of condensed Numa soaked in corruption might create a chain reaction."

He grabbed a battered metal flask from his belt, half-filled with unstable Numa. But to prime it, he needed more vile energy—like the stuff inside the monster.

Logan forced a breath, ignoring the revulsion. "Tumor, think we can drain some of its corruption? Then stuff it into the flask?"

[That is feasible but extremely dangerous. The suit is already wreathed in the corruption drained from your father.]

The monster roared anew, molten eyes blazing. Another swirl of spiked tentacles lunged at two recruits. One managed to dodge. The other was speared through the chest and pinned to the ground. Balmer, face contorted, tried to yank him free, but it was too late.

Logan swallowed the lump of fear. "We're out of time."

"I'll cover you, Boss!" Simmons cried. He bashed his axe into the monster's side, forcing it to redirect a wave of slime. Then he sidestepped a blow that would have torn him in two.

Logan lunged in from the flank, focusing on a swirling column of ooze that formed the monster's left "arm". He pressed his darkmetal bracer to the shimmering sludge, forcibly focusing.

"**[Funnel]**!" he chanted, sucking in the pure corrupted energy. A sickening sensation flared, like submerging his hand in rotting jelly. He choked back a gag as corrupted energy coursed into his exosuit's reservoir. It was all around him, constricting him with its vile madness.

The monster shrieked and tried to yank away, but Simmons seized that moment to hack at its midsection. An agent slammed an exosuit powered spear in, too. The beast roared, flailing, but Logan held on, absorbing a thick surge of vile Numa. His exosuit crackled ominously, the creeping malevolence of Levemoth's energy already attacking his mind.

A scorching headache tore through Logan's skull. His vision blurred—he teetered on the edge of a mental meltdown. But he kept up the funnel, forcing the slime's essence into that battered flask at his belt. The metal hissed dangerously, bulging.

The monster's arm, now partly siphoned, collapsed into a partial stump. Simmons saw an opening. "Everyone, stand clear!"

Those who could still move scurried back, dragging the wounded. Logan's exosuit sputtered from overload. The monster lurched away, a chunk of slime-limb missing.

"Here we go," Logan growled, snapping the flask shut. He could barely see, let alone think. His mind was thick and dark, full of haze and horrid images. The flask glowed an eerie black-blue from inside, swirling with lethal energy. "Simmons, let's—"

But before he could finish, the monster reared up, screeching. Its body changed, congealing into a lunging mass in front of Logan. He realized he had screwed up. A cold sensation washed over him. He tried to move, but he knew it would be too late. A spiked black claw hammered down on him—or would have, had Simmons not thrown himself in front of Logan, raising his axe.

A resounding crack. The claw tore past the axe, shredding Simmons's exosuit chest. He gasped, blood spraying. Time slowed.

"S-Simmons!" Logan yelled.

But the big man gripped the slime-limb with his dying strength, preventing it from smashing Logan. He coughed blood, eyes wide, meeting Logan's gaze.

"Do it," Simmons rasped. His mouth curved into a faint, fatal grin.

Time snapped back to normal. Logan, tears burning his eyes, clutched the thrumming flask. One chance. He hurled it at the heart of the beast, then jammed his staff forward, sending out all of the corrupted energy from his suit at the creature. They would overwhelm it with energy. The flask collided with the core and shattered.

A deafening detonation ripped the corridor. Black lightning soared outward. The monster screeched in bone-rending agony, slime flailing and popping. Corruption devoured itself, tendrils folding inward. Crispy chunks of goop splattered every surface. A shock wave blew Logan off his feet, slamming him into a column.

When the dust settled, the corridor was spattered with sizzling black lumps. They writhed violently before feebly turning into still puddles.

Logan staggered up, lungs burning, eyes streaming from the acrid smoke. Kat, Ryan, Balmer, and the survivors coughed—battered but alive. They all turned to see the crumpled figure of Simmons, pinned under a mostly melted chunk of monstrous sludge.

"Simmons!" Logan croaked, rushing over.

Simmons lay there, exosuit chest peeled open like it was made of tin. His eyes were glassy, breath ragged. Logan yanked the slime-lump off, ignoring the stench. From the huge gash, it was clear he was beyond saving.

"Simmons," Logan pleaded, voice breaking.

The big man's gaze flickered with recognition. He coughed once, blood oozing from his mouth, and forced a tiny nod. "Saved your hide," he rasped.

Logan swallowed tears. "You goddamn idiot . . ."

Kat and Balmer dropped at his side. Ryan gripped his lute, eyes wide with shock. The leftover recruits circled, sets of eyes brimming with grief.

Simmons coughed again. "Logan . . . keep 'em safe. All . . . of our . . . people." He exhaled slowly, as though trying to speak again. But the words never came. His eyes went unfocused. Then still.

"No . . . no, no, no . . ." Logan gasped. Anger, sorrow, yet also gratitude— Simmons had saved him from that final blow. The weight of that sacrifice pressed on Logan until he shook.

Kat bowed her head, letting out a shaky breath. "He was . . . a hell of a guy."

Balmer just wiped silent tears from his eyes, lips trembling. Ryan stroked a quiet, mournful chord. The two Faelves lowered their heads, bowing at the body. Even the recruits who'd barely known Simmons recognized the cost of his sacrifice.

The corridor behind them was largely collapsed from the explosion. Ahead, the newly revealed door stood partially open. The boss was dead, but the path forward was in ruin. Dust and gloom weighed on them. And Simmons was gone. A friend and pillar of their community, never to be seen again.

"We'll take him back," Kat murmured, voice raw.

Logan swallowed, forcing the tears down for later. He gently closed Simmons' eyes, pressing a trembling hand to the motionless chest. Then he stood, staff in hand, clearing his throat. "Yeah. That's a given."

Kat pressed her sleeve to her eyes and nodded. "Let's get the monster's remains off of him, so we can push him in the cart. Then we see if that door leads to the Clarion."

Balmer said nothing, just moved to help.

Logan turned away briefly, stifling rage and sorrow so that he could stand upright. He caught Ryan's eye. Ryan's hand shook on the lute, but he forced himself to give a tight nod of solidarity. The entire group was battered, having lost dear friends, but they kept going—because that was all they *could* do.

They pried Simmons' body free from the melted goop, laying him gently near a toppled column. A recruit placed a scrap of cloth over his face. Everyone paused for a silent moment of respect.

Then the battered party made for the vault door behind the monster's corpse.

Logan couldn't believe his eyes.

This . . .

[This might just be enough.]

Inside, they found a massive workshop, illuminated by faint crystals in the ceiling. Tables and benches lined the walls—some covered in lumps of Numa-crystals, others with *piles* of black metal. There were unfinished contraptions draped in dusty cloth. And in the center, a large raised platform held a half-constructed device shaped like a huge horn full of socketed gems and runic patterns: *The Clarion.*

"We found it," Kat whispered.

Logan nodded, stepping closer to the central dais. "The Clarion . . ."

It was big—maybe seven feet from end to end, crafted from pure darkmetal shot through with faint blue lines forming intricate runic patterns. They trailed from the mouth of the horn to the thinning mouthpiece, but they hadn't fully made it there. Some of the pattern was still missing.

Logan approached, staff tapping the floor. "It's incomplete," he said, voice low.

He examined the rest of the workshop. Around the dais stood crates of darkmetal bars, lumps of Numa crystals stacked in careful arrays. Enough raw fuel to power a small city. Enough to equip an army, if used right.

Kat let out a slow, awed whistle. "We just stumbled on the motherlode."

William knelt beside a table stacked with metal plates scrawled with runic text. Tumor's presence in Logan's mind perked up immediately, excited by this new data.

[There must be records on how to finish the Clarion. Let me interpret them, but I need time.]

Logan nodded to the group. "Gather all these plates. Let's see if we can decipher the instructions."

Kat motioned recruits to carefully collect the battered plates from the dusty shelves and load them onto any free surface they could find. No one missed the significance: a single blast from the Clarion might mean the difference between victory and extinction.

Logan's gaze swept over the bins of darkmetal. Immediately, his mind whirled with the possibilities. The entire place was a workshop—maybe the First Folk's last forging ground. If they had time, they could craft new gear—new wonders that might give them a real chance against Levemoth.

But time was one thing they didn't have.

He swallowed, stepping away from the dais. A heavy sorrow coiled in his stomach. They'd lost so many, especially Simmons. But now they stood in a place brimming with potential. If they used it wisely, no more lives would need to be thrown into the grinder.

Ryan, pressing gauze on a wound above his brow, spoke in a hoarse whisper. "Seems we need a moment to breathe. Some are wounded."

Logan looked around and exhaled. "Fair enough. We're in a fortress-lab now, yeah? Big thick door, no sign of further monsters. Let's barricade ourselves in, rest a bit. Then figure out how to finish the Clarion and haul it out."

Balmer nodded, looking at the empty space. Kat came up to him and punched him on the shoulder—softly, though. He snapped back to reality. "Yeah, good. I'll secure the entrance and confirm no surprises lurk about.

The survivors formed up. Despite fresh heartbreak, they moved with the long-practiced discipline of battered veterans, each step fueled by determination. They scoured the edges of the workshop. No immediate threats. The Clarion waited, quietly incomplete, while the lumps of precious darkmetal and piles of Numa crystals shimmered in the dim light.

A single thought rang clear in Logan's mind: If they could fix this weapon, maybe Simmons' sacrifice would not be in vain.

He closed his eyes briefly, hoping Freya and the others were safe up top. Then he sucked in a breath and set to work. There was crafting to be done.

CHAPTER 29

The Good Stuff

They barricaded the workshop's two main doors using heavy crates and collapsed tables. Between the exhausted recruits, Kat, Balmer, and Ryan, the perimeter was set. Now there would be time to regroup and heal. In the back, behind toppled shelves, Logan found a smaller alcove that could serve as a forging nook. There, a great anvil-like block of black metal reigned. Next to it lay arcane instruments, presumably for shaping Numa-laced alloys.

Once the wounded settled, Logan and Tumor pored over the metal plates they'd salvaged. They were runic schematics, half in the First Folk's script, half in cryptic diagrams. Tumor worked double-time, scanning each etched line.

After a couple of hours of reading scraps and cross-referencing them with his own knowledge, Tumor's spectral voice resonated in Logan's mind:

[They intended the Clarion to channel massive amounts of Numa, then emit an anti-Numa wave. But some crucial component is missing. The runic pattern requires a specialized reagent or skill that can handle the final conversion. We do not have it currently.]

"Figures," Logan muttered under his breath. He quietly shared the news with Kat and Balmer, who frowned in frustration.

"But we have to fix it," Ryan insisted, setting aside a bandage he'd been applying.

"We do," Kat echoed. "But how, if the resource or skill doesn't exist here?"

"We'll figure it out," Logan said, jaw set. "In the meantime, we can still use these resources to prepare for the final push. Simmons died so we wouldn't fail."

His heart clenched at the memory, but he pushed forward, letting that grief fuel him. He ran a palm across the crates of darkmetal bars. There was so much. Enough to craft something that could turn the tide of war—something that outstripped the old exosuits. He could make liquid metal gear . . .

"Tumor," Logan said quietly. "What level is your [**Possess**] ability?"

[Seventy-two. I can easily control fifty suits if they are close enough to you.]

"Perfect," Logan said. "It's [**Mass Production**] time."

[Armor for the entire strike force? Ambitious but feasible with all this dark-metal and Numa.]

Kat, overhearing, stepped closer. "Liquid power-armor. Like your old shit?"

Logan gave her a tired but ambitious grin. "Yeah. You'll love it. But this time I'll make them even better."

Balmer nodded, though worry creased his brow. "We might not have long before the labyrinth cracks."

Logan turned to the glowing lumps of Numa crystals stacked in the corner. They were all C-graders, over twenty of them, and that was just one pile. "We'll do it fast and as well as we can. We only need enough sets for the key fighters, anyway."

Kat's lips quirked in a grim smile. "Count me in. A shape-shifting suit? Could be fun."

Ryan gave a shaky grin. "If it keeps me alive, I'll take it. Maybe attach a mini-lute to my arm?"

Logan snorted. "Sure, Bard. Let's see if we have time for fancy additions."

They formed a small forging circle in the alcove. Kat, Balmer, Ryan, and the recruits assisted Logan. They brought him the materials, held things in place, and walked up to be measured by Tumor.

The recruits lit the braziers in the workshop, and Logan found joy in his craft. It was laced with the emotional weight of everything that had happened, but he still enjoyed his work.

They started transmuting raw lumps of darkmetal into living metal, carefully weaving enchantments that let the metal respond to mental commands.

Time blurred. The labor was demanding—physically, mentally, emotionally. The recruits took turns resting, but Logan crafted. He went through Numa crystals like candy, because this wasn't just about creating the best armor. This was about leveling up.

[**Attribute Level Up!**]
[**Potency: 42**]

[**Attribute Level Up!**]
[**Potency: 43**]

[**Attribute Level Up!**]
[**Efficiency: 46**]

Finally, after what felt like an entire day but must have been just hours, they had enough raw "liquid frames" for each of the main fighters. Logan passed them out in lumps—each looked like a large, swirling metallic blob, faintly luminous.

"Tumor, can you hear through the suits you possess?" Logan asked.

[No.]

"Right . . ." Logan said. "That complicates things. What if I install some listening module or an enchantment?"

They tried a few iterations and eventually managed to give Tumor the ability to hear through the suits. It took some overall power from the suits, but it was necessary, since Tumor couldn't read other peoples' minds. The enchantment was tricky enough that after Logan did it on ten templates of a suit, he leveled up again.

[**Attribute Level Up!**]
[**Focus: 40**]

Once that part was done, the suits were almost finished. Logan motioned for everyone to gather around, so he could impart his cool esoteric knowledge of liquid-metal power armor.

Logan explained, voice hoarse, "It'll flow up your body, forming a snug armor that can shift however you direct. Shield forms, swords, wings. Stands a chance of flight, if we channel enough Numa. You'll need to say what you want to manifest. That way, Tumor can hear you and make it. If you get too far away from me, Tumor will mold the armor into a bar that's easy to carry. Just make sure you're close to me if you try any tricks with the wings . . ."

The recruits gazed at their lumps in awe, some poking them gently to see the metal quiver like liquid mercury. Kat flicked hers, lips parted in fascination. "Damn. I can't wait to dropkick an ogre from forty feet up."

Balmer tested it first. He asked Tumor to don the armor. The darkmetal swirled around his arm, morphing into a sleek vambrace, and then the rest of the suit followed, enveloping all but his eyes and mouth. "This is incredible."

Logan sank down on a bench, wiping sweat and grime from his brow. "We still have enough Numa to power them. Everyone, keep a small crystal in your belt to recharge the suit. Go practice with them, and when you run out of juice, get another crystal and come to me, so I can charge the suit again."

Just then, Tumor's presence flared in Logan's mind.

[We should also address the Clarion. I have finished processing the plates. The First Folk used a reagent called Numalimium to create the runic etching. I do not know more of this reagent. I will require more processing time.]

Logan looked at the massive darkmetal horn on its pedestal. Its surface read was incomplete, missing some crucial runic inlays. He pondered an idea that had been bothering him.

Kat exhaled. "We can't guess this to completion, can we?"

"No," Logan stated. "Tumor's still decrypting. But even once we parse it, we'll need the missing reagent. We can't fix the Clarion without it. So, let's do as much as we can. Strengthen everything else. Practice with the suits and leave the thinking to me."

"You got it, Boss."

If Tumor still needed time, Logan decided he should use his own productively. Not only because working with such awesome and abundant materials was fun, but he also had a sneaking suspicion . . .

*That's why I'm an [**Artificer**], huh?*

Logan turned to the remaining row of darkmetal bars. He felt a surge of personal ambition. If a shape-changing suit was good for the strike force, he needed something extra. A titan made of darkmetal. A Levebuster. A single unstoppable mech for facing Levemoth head-on.

This would be the final version of the cobbled-together mech he had worked on for weeks in the Ark's workshop. Now it was finally time to put all that work into fruition.

"Alright, Tumor. I'm going to need a part of your big brain on this one. A final specialized build. You said we had optimized the previous design. How about we make something unprecedented this time?"

[Oh, I have had blueprints ready for this possibility for weeks. I was only waiting for you to ask.]

"We can't rely only on the Clarion. If it doesn't finish the job, we need something to make sure we can."

Kat eyed him. "Another giant suit, huh?"

"Yeah." Logan let out a laugh. "A real big one."

Balmer frowned. "We might not have time."

Logan pressed a palm to the darkmetal lumps on the floor, voice quiet but resolute. "You guys focus on learning the suit. Let me do what I do best."

Balmer hesitated but eventually nodded. No one objected further. They recognized that fervor in Logan's eyes—the same feverish will that had led them to the edge of the impossible again and again. If the monstrous slime-aberration coupled with losing their friends hadn't broken their spirit, nothing would.

Logan set to work, chanting as he listened to Tumor and gazed at the hovering holograms of the blueprints. The first phase was to fuse all the darkmetal into enormous plates. Then he transmuted the chassis and the joints. The hardest part were the gears. Tumor requested so many gears it made Logan's throat parched from all the enchanting. When his own flask was finally empty, one of the agents gave him theirs.

"Harden the metal, make glance impact, make it corrosion resistant, wind resistant . . ." Logan mumbled in his process.

[Subclass Level Up!]
[Enchantment Level 44]

Bit by bit, the monstrous exoframe took shape: thick, interlocking panels that fit around a compact interior cockpit. All the gears, sticks, and panels required intricate work, but Logan maintained his focus. This was it. This was his moment.

As Logan shaped the final plate into place, it finally happened. A rush of that fresh minty feeling. He had been waiting for this.

A system prompt flickered across his vision. This one was different.

LEVEL UP: [Artificer] has reached a hidden level.
Class Evolution: Ultimate Craftsman
NEW SKILL ACQUIRED: [Grand Artifice: Anti-Numa
enchantment]

A rush of knowledge seeped into his brain. He was overwhelmed; hell, even Tumor was overwhelmed. They finally understood how the Clarion worked. They could fix it!

But the price . . .

Ryan, Kat, and Balmer rushed up, seeing Logan's face. "Logan? You alright?"

Logan blinked, then let out a shaky grin. "Yeah. Leveled up . . . and . . . I know how to fix the Clarion now.

Kat gave him a fierce smile. "Hell, yeah."

Logan stepped back, staring at the newly finished battle-mech. It towered over him, a majestic melding of darkmetal with reactive plating, assault cannon, flight thrusters, and every firepower-enhancing enchantment Logan could think of. *And* it was defensive. In short, it was a magic flying tank.

He was now complete. There was no need to gain further levels. He had his ultimate creation. And his strike force had their suits.

Now, to fix the Clarion. If only there was another way to beat Levemoth . . . The price . . .

He turned to the battered survivors, each sporting their newly minted, shape-shifting suit. A hush settled as they realized how close they stood to destiny.

The stage was set. Everything was ready. Now they would only need to bring the leftover Numa and darkmetal to the surface with the mech. And Simmons. They wouldn't leave their hero here.

Logan stood tall and exhaled. His moment was now. The second strike on Levemoth would start soon.

He flicked a glance at Simmons' still body, covered in a cloak near the corner.

We'll make your sacrifice count.

"Alright," Logan said, turning to his crew. He would not show hesitation now. He would lead these people to the end, and he would stay resolute. "Time to blast out of here."

No matter the price.

CHAPTER 30

Return and Revelation

A crushing boom echoed through the heart of the old ruins, shaking free ancient dust and sending it pluming overhead. Stone shards turned to flying shrapnel as Logan's newly forged battle-mech punched clean through the last barrier that separated them from daylight. For an instant, the roar of shattering rock drowned out every other sound—the clang of debris, the ragged breathing of exhausted fighters, even the distant thrumming hum of Levemoth's monstrous presence in the skies above.

Yet in the next heartbeat, the world snapped back into motion. With one mighty thrust of metal feet, Logan vaulted onto the surface, fractured stone tinkling to the ground around his mech as it emerged from the underground like an iron leviathan breaching the depths of some ancient sea. Wind slapped against the mech's plated hull, scattering the dust of a thousand years.

Behind him, the rest of the strike force soared up on liquid power armor, tinted in a swirling black-metallic sheen, chests and limbs shining with the newly wrought transformation suits. Their boots, once weighed down by bone and steel, now thrummed with the hum of flight enchantments. Kat's short red hair whipped around as she angled a glinting arm-blade. Balmer soared at her flank, scanning for immediate threats with cool composure. Ryan, lute strapped securely across his back, hung just behind, his new liquid suit forming a cape that flicked in the swirling air. Subbel and Graiglu were further up, illusions dancing around them to cloak the vulnerable fliers from below.

One by one, each member of the strike force erupted from the hole that Logan's mech had made, crossing the threshold into brilliant daylight. The sun hammered down with relentless brilliance, painting the world in harsh gold. It was almost too bright; after untold hours in the labyrinth, their eyes took a moment to adjust.

What they saw when their vision cleared filled them with dread.

High in the sky, Levemoth pulsed and writhed with the final throes of its metamorphosis. The behemoth's form—once cloaked in roiling black-blue thunderclouds—had become a dripping, oozing mass of oily flesh. From its countless pores, a vile black rainfall sheeted down over the land, each drop as thick as sludge. Wherever the rain fell, the ground boiled and churned, as if struggling to fight off an invasion. White stone, green grass, even the very dust seemed to shrivel and twist into hideous black shapes.

This was corruption incarnate.

The eldritch monstrosity hovered over the planet, blotting out large swaths of the horizon.

Logan plucked the glass orb from his satchel in a rush. It was swirling with blue smoke.

Freya.

"Back to the camp. We don't have a lot of time."

Kat, her face set in a resolute grimace, nodded. "We need to get the Ark back in the air."

"Right," he agreed, voice tight. "Into formation! We fly, now!"

A flick of his mind, and the mech's thrusters jolted to life. The giant metal feet tore at the ground and launched the hulking machine forward. The wing-like attachments affixed above its shoulders spread, each glowing with abundant Numa energy. The entire contraption might not have soared like a sleek jet, but it managed a powerful, bounding surge across the corrupted plains, each leap devouring dozens of yards.

Behind him, the strike force soared or glided depending on their suits. Some hovered in jumps, some flew more fluidly, depending on their technique. But they were all manifestly more powerful now. They could take on a small army of Levespawn.

In the distance, black rainfall hammered the terrain—thick, glistening curtains of sludge from Levemoth's twisted body.

They had no illusions that this wouldn't be a fierce fight.

When the group broke the final crest of a hill overlooking their encampment, a desperate battle raged. The fortress-like outline of the Ark's hull lay where they'd left it, but now it was surrounded by waves of chaos.

Gouts of black slime had rained over the surrounding area, twisting it into a grotesque living landscape. But some strange barrier was protecting the camp itself. Globules of oily black tar splashed against an invisible barrier in the air and slid off.

But the protection of the Administrators only reached so far.

The ground itself seemed to throb with pestilent life, and it was attacking. Tendrils of oily vines slithered across the hills, hungrily winding around fallen trees, battered ramparts, and the scattered remains of watchtowers. Mangled lumps of flesh—half-plant, half-beast—crawled across the mud like zombies.

And that was just the environment.

Between these creeping, pulsing vines, scores of Blues, ogres, and even monstrous new creatures roamed. Giant, hulking abominations towered above the usual ogres. Each giant looked like a humanoid trunk of corrupted bark and chitin, with bulging insectoid carapaces jutting from shoulder to thigh. Their arms ended in massive crushing clubs made of twisted wood that dripped with black oil. Gaps across their bodies leaked swirling black vapor. Where eyes should have been, there were only gaping pits that glowed with a sharp blue malice.

Atop the Ark's deck, columns of smoke rose from energy cannons being fired by the golems. Even from here, Logan could see bursts of muzzle flash and occasional arcs of energy from anchor defenses. Groloin golems marched along the battered perimeter, punching or smashing anything too close. Even the Hivemind was fighting.

Human archers showered arrows upon the oncoming wave of infected creatures as they retreated toward the Ark. One of the giant abominations slammed a fist into them and a dozen were instantly crushed.

"They're in trouble," Logan rasped into the comms. "Take Simmons, the Clarion, and the loot inside the Ark and join the fray."

Kat cursed. "We're late."

"Focus," Logan said. "Fight."

Balmer, stony-faced, said, "Our allies are scattered and in groups. We have to break through."

Ryan strummed a chord from a Numa-powered electric guitar, letting a galvanizing wave of courage cradle each fighter's nerves. The electric boom of his new instrument's sound stunned the enemy.

The strike force soared forward, heading straight to the front lines. Even from a distance, they heard the camp's defenders shouting, the clangs and roars of a desperate fight. The black sludge parted in sticky waves beneath the bounding leaps of Logan's mech.

In a thunderous crash, Logan smashed down near the outer perimeter of the Ark's fortress camp. The ground, corrupted by oily slime, squished under the mech's giant feet. Immediately, four monstrous Blues, tall as men, rushed with unhinged screeches. Logan's left arm reconfigured into a broad spike-lance—liquid darkmetal shifting at his mental command. He impaled one Blue through the chest, then spun horizontally to smash a second. The blow sent black gore spraying across the mud.

Two ogres charged at him, but Logan turned a Numa-powered flame-thrower on them. They shrieked as blue flames engulfed them.

Meanwhile, the rest of the strike force fanned out, each brandishing their own shape-shifting suits. Balmer conjured a rapier-like blade from the liquid metal swirling around his arm. Kat formed two heavy gauntlets, each spiked for maximum punch. Ryan soared overhead, launching a sonic blast from his guitar that rattled a swarm of lesser creatures, sending them staggering. Subbel and Graiglu flanked the bigger monstrosities, illusions strobing like rave lights, powered by the suits, some shaped to confuse, some to cloak them from the horde.

A savage conflict erupted. Dozens of Blues, ogres, and mutated beasts charged simultaneously, shrieking with that otherworldly fervor. Any sense of cohesion on the battlefield was drowned in howling chaos. The camp defenders—spread across the battered barricades—cheered when they saw Logan's mech and the strike team descend.

But the monsters kept on coming. Up the slope from the south, one of the great monstrosities lumbered forward. It was well over twenty feet tall, a colossal fusion of bark, bone, and scythe-like protrusions. The black slime rained down around its shoulders, like a rancid cloak. Stomping across the battlefield, it smashed aside barricades and wooden stakes with casual sweeps of its arms.

Logan's mech whirred, and he braced, chest pounding. "I'll handle the big one—everyone else, keep the line intact!"

Kat, Balmer, and Ryan acknowledged with quick affirmatives. They soared off to protect the flanks.

Logan advanced, the earth trembling under each footfall of his exo-suit. The giant monstrosity roared, its mouth a black cavity lined with dagger-like fangs. One of its arms ended in a pincer formed from writhing root matter. The other was a twisted wooden club crusted with stone shards.

They clashed in a terrible impact. Logan's mech swung a massive fist, smashing into the giant's blocking club. The blow rang out across the battlefield like a cathedral bell. Splinters of wood scattered, but the giant hardly missed a beat. It hammered its pincer-limb forward, nailing the mech's shoulder with an ear-ringing crunch. Sparks flew. Logan reeled inside the cockpit, teeth gritted as warning lights flared.

"Tumor!"

The armor liquefied and the giant pincer snapped on empty air, Logan sidestepping as the darkmetal became a solid stack of interlocking plates again, ready to brace for another impact.

Logan grinned. He triggered the mech's thrusters and slammed into the giant's torso, driving it backward. They tumbled, toppling a burning watchtower in the process. The giant seized the mech's left arm, hooking it with oily vines that erupted from its bark-like flesh. Each vine pulsed with black fluid, slurping at the mech's plating.

"Get . . . off!" Logan snarled. He commanded the darkmetal war-lance on the mech's right arm to superheat. An incandescent glow spread along the lance, spitting sparks as it sliced through the vines. Hot fluid squirted from the severed parts, and the giant shrilled a hollow cry.

Freed, Logan battered the giant's torso again, each blow pressing it back across the churned mud. But the huge creature refused to die. The corrupted oily puddles rippled and writhed and the pools turned into strings of liquid that climbed up the giant's leg. Even with half its chest caved in, it reknitted new lumps of wood-chitin from the black rainfall above.

Logan could tell they were losing. They couldn't fight these behemoths if each droplet of rain re-empowered them. They needed to press on, rescue the camp, and get the Ark airborne.

Roaring in fury, Logan raised the mech's right fist and hammered it down onto the giant's collar. A wet snap sounded as the giant's body twisted, dark fluid gushing from a rent in its bark. The beast collapsed, thrashing.

Inside the cockpit, Logan panted. "Got it. Tumor, confirm kill?"

[It shows no sign of micro-movement. Down for now. Dead? I am not sure.]

"Good enough for the moment."

He turned the mech around, scanning the carnage. All across the perimeter, defenders scrambled and fought. The black slime soaked everything in sight. Fungal vines erupted from the ground near a fallen barricade, strangling two defenders who'd been pinned down.

A second monstrous giant lurched in from the west side, likely drawn by the smell of conflict. This one appeared to have a back shell shaped from corrupted rock. A cluster of smaller ogres scuttled in its wake, each mutated by the black ooze.

Kat was at the barricade, smashing through waves of Blues with two bracer-blades. She knocked two out in quick succession, then used a morphing shield to block a third's savage claw. Balmer flitted around her, rapier-blade slashing tendons and arms with surgical precision. Ryan soared overhead, singing a rousing battle hymn that lent speed and steadiness to the camp defenders' limbs.

[My capacity is at 91%.]

"Keep on keeping us alive, Tumor!" Logan said.

Farther up the hill, Malcolm Specter gave hurried orders to six Faelves and two dozen humans. From Logan's vantage, it looked like he was orchestrating a fallback line near the Ark's main ramp. Groloin golems wandered among them, forming the outer line of defense.

Logan nodded to himself. His father had things under control.

He checked who needed immediate help. East side or west side?

A frantic cry lit up in the comms that Logan shared with the strike force: Subbel shouting, "We need help at the east barricade—some giant beast we can't see properly. It's . . . eating our illusions. Please hurry!"

Logan pivoted the mech, bounding across the battle-churned mud. Another quake of malevolence, a pulse that went through each living creature, shot down from the sky. The black oily rain poured down heavier, each droplet sizzling when it struck the ground.

Finally, in a clearing near a group of partially collapsed tents, Logan spotted it—a monstrous shape, just like the other giants. But this one was pulsing with a black-and-blue energy. Subbel and Graiglu kept sending illusions, but the abomination kept eating them.

Oh . . . Levemoth stole a page from my book.

"Stop casting magics!" Logan shouted at the Faelves. "Retreat! Go help round up everyone and GET TO THE ARK!"

With a hiss, the monstrous fusion of tree and insect charged Logan, as if driven by Levemoth itself.

"Tumor," Logan muttered, letting the mech's right arm morph into a wide-bore cannon muzzle. "We're going to test this new anti-Numa ability."

[You think you'll be able to do it on the fly?]

He snapped the cannon upward, targeting the giant's chest. "One way to find out."

Tumor routed Numa into the cannon, and it started whining with charging energy. Logan pushed down a lever and held it, chanting the Numa instructions to transform.

He could feel the Nature of the Numa changing. It inversed, turning into something that neither created nor destroyed.

It unmakes *creation.*

A torrent of raging negative energy blasted from the cannon muzzle. Logan looked at the streak of crackling black as it zipped to its target. The recoil nearly knocked the mech onto its back.

[Keystone Skill Level Up!]
[Transmutate Material Level 5]

[Skill Level Up!]
[Power Armor Fighting Level 21]

The shot struck home. There was a *whoomp* and then silence. The giant looked at its midsection in confusion, as it was seemingly unharmed. Then, suddenly, a wet explosion of chitin and black ichor blasted in all directions, painting the battered ground. The charred remains of the giant fell on its knees and slumped into a smoking heap.

"Hell, yeah!" Logan shouted.

[That was impressive. But I must note that the blast was not energy-efficient.]

Logan could feel it in the way the mech moved now. *Sluggish.* Tumor routed more energy into the system, but they were running thin after that one attack. Granted, it was powerful, but they only had enough juice for one more.

Logan looked around. The Ark was humming, clearly readying itself for an emergency takeoff. That was good.

Kat, Balmer, and Ryan regrouped near the main ramp as well, each battered from constant fighting. The Ark's energy cannons fired another volley, slamming into a cluster of Blues that tried to scale the hull. Shrieks and splatters of gore echoed as the monsters fell away. Yet more charged in an endless horde against the defenders. They needed to lift off.

Logan angled his mech to stomp a nest of writhing vines aside. The wet pop of crushed corruption reverberated.

Kat soared up above Logan, shouting through the comms, "We can't hold out forever—these giants are coming in waves now!"

As if on cue, a monstrous silhouette appeared from the swirling black haze on the far end of the camp. This giant dwarfed the earlier two, easily towering three times the height of Logan's mech. Chitinous plates glistened with vile moisture. Six eyes dotted its brutish skull, each glowing a vile azure. A roar boomed from its maw of jutting fangs. Another drop of oily rain dropped on it, and it *grew.*

Logan swallowed a surge of panic. "That's too big for even us."

[Agreed.]

Balmer's voice chimed in, panting. "I'll lead teams to clear the ramp so the Ark can take off. Logan—hold them off a moment longer!"

"Got it," Logan managed, as the giant monstrosity stepped closer. The weight of the chunk of land it held was staggering; it slammed the mass at the battered barricade. Splinters showered in every direction, crushing two defenders who were still valiantly trying to hold the line. A Faelf shrieked, illusions flickering out.

Seeing no time to hesitate, Logan revved the mech's thrusters, bounding to meet the gargantuan foe. He hammered an overhead slash with the war-lance, but the giant parried with a tree trunk of a forearm. The clang was deafening as the blow rocked Logan inside the cockpit. He could feel the cracks in the darkmetal. They quickly fused whole again, but that blow had cost them more energy.

Logan coughed, fighting to stay conscious. "Tumor!"

[We can't withstand many more hits like that. Attempt a finishing strike, or we're done for.]

The giant roared, thick drool and black sludge raining from its jaws. It reeled back for another crushing blow. Logan clamped a hand to the lever through which he could manipulate the energy of his mech. Tumor knew what to do. Logan extended the hulking right arm forward, letting the dark-metal plating reconfigure into a triple-barreled muzzle.

Crackles of energy danced around the barrel as it whined with gathering energy. The giant lunged. Logan fired.

A triple beam of crackling black anti-energy scattered and tore across the short distance, slamming into the giant's ribcage like an enormous shotgun. For a heartbeat, the gargantuan creature froze, as if struck by an invisible backhand. It looked down, but there was no visible damage. Then it erupted in a massive burst of black gore, sludge bursting outward in every direction.

The mech faltered, nearly toppling from the recoil. Slime rained across the scorched soil, bits of carapace clanking. The giant monstrosity's top half simply ceased to exist, leaving a ravaged husk that crumpled backward into the dirt with a thunderous crash.

Logan slumped in relief, ignoring the swirl of alarms. "It's down."

[*We are out of energy. We need to leave.*]

"Roger that."

Logan pivoted the mech, scanning for further immediate threats. The last waves of lesser creatures fled from the coordinated assault of the dark-metal strike force.

But in the distance, above the tree line, Logan saw four more of those massive abominations approaching them at a terrible speed.

Logan shouted from the top of his lungs, "WE TAKE OFF NOW. MAKE A RUN FOR IT, WE CAN'T WAIT FOR ANY STRAGGLERS!"

Near the ramp, Balmer's team cleared a final group of Blues. Kat flattened an ogre with an impressive dropkick to the forehead. Ryan soared overhead, launching one last sonic chord at a cluster of writhing vines, making them withdraw and writhe.

They pushed the last drags of the enemies off, cleared the ramp, closed it, and took off into the air.

CHAPTER 31

Taking to the Skies

Malcolm barked orders to half-a-dozen shell-shocked crew members, each red-eyed from hours of battle. A group of battered humans and Faelves rushed the wounded to a makeshift medical station in the cargo hold. Logan followed them, struggling out of his mech. A strand of darkmetal left the mech, enveloping him in a liquid suit. Logan barely noticed. He needed to find his wife.

Logan saw Freya, hair plastered to her cheeks, offering healing to the wounded while monitoring a console. When she saw him, she broke down in tears and ran to him.

"Thank the Goddess you're here," she sniffled against his chest.

"I'm so happy you're alive," Logan said. "But I need to lead."

"Damn straight you do," Freya said and grabbed his neck to pull him into a fierce kiss before pushing him away and running back to the wounded.

Through the portholes, Logan's strike force could see a distant host of monstrous silhouettes, even bigger than before, trudging from the horizon. Levemoth's black rain fueled them. The land tore open in their wake, spitting twisted vegetation and lumps of seething slime.

On the bridge, Logan met with Malcolm and the Groloin.

Malcolm gave him a curt look, face hardened with determination. Logan found he liked that look. "Do you have the Clarion?"

"Simmons died."

Malcolm Specter was silent for a moment. His brow was furrowed, but he showed no other emotion on his face. Logan wasn't a big fan of this side of him.

"He was a good man," Malcolm said finally.

"He died to protect me."

"And you feel guilty about it?"

"It was a necessary sacrifice," Logan said silently. "But I wish I hadn't put him in that position."

"Heavy is the crown, Son."

Logan looked him in the eye and nodded. Malcolm nodded back.

"Did you complete the mission?"

"You think I'd return empty-handed?"

"Good. Can we operate it?"

"It's broken, but I know how to fix it. Though, according to the tablets, it requires some reagent that Tumor wasn't able to translate."

"I might know what it needs," Malcolm said and something grim flashed in his eyes. "A sacrifice."

"Of what?" Logan asked warily.

Wind buffeted the deck as they climbed in altitude. Below, the monstrous wave swarmed the place they'd called camp, trampling ruined barricades and snapping fallen watchtowers like toothpicks. They let out roars of frustration at losing their prey. Some reared back, hurling chunks of earth skyward, but the debris fell far short of the Ark's hull.

Logan guided the mech to the main deck, metal feet stomping carefully around the hull's battered surface. He rejoined Kat, Balmer, Ryan, and the rest of the strike force who were scanning the monstrous horde from the railing. They all looked wrung-out, caked in black sludge, and bearing fresh wounds or bandages.

The land below was a nightmare-scape: black, pulsing, with streams of oily sludge carving webs of corruption around every natural feature. It was a vile darkness that Levemoth was exhaling. Yet they had survived . . . for now.

Freya emerged from a stairwell behind them, hugging herself. "We did it. We're safe—sort of."

"Only right now," Kat said, wincing as she flexed an arm with a crusted bandage. "We still gotta deal with the big evil bastard."

High overhead, Levemoth's colossal silhouette loomed in swirling storm clouds. The black rainfall still poured down in sheets. Golems were operating energy cannons to shoot at the largest drops of the unholy rain coming at them. But small droplets got through. The strike force and their most able fighters were on the deck, making sure every Blue and ogre got what was coming to them: obliteration.

Logan stared up at the great calamity causing the storm. Sorrow, rage, and exhaustion overwhelmed him.

I'm so tired of this shit.

"We have the Clarion . . . but it's incomplete. I can fix it, but . . ."

"But what?"

"It requires a sacrifice," Logan said quietly. "A human sacrifice. Someone who can use Numa."

Freya flinched and turned to Logan. She bit her lip. Others were silent.

Ryan offered a shaky grin. "Do we have another plan?"

Kat looked like he wanted to say something. Volunteer? Demand another way? She opened and closed her mouth like a goldfish, but nothing came out.

Malcolm's voice came crackling over a speaker. "Captain's meeting on the bridge. We'll finalize course headings."

Logan nodded to the group. "Let's go."

At the bridge command table, Malcolm and Snoff were engaged in some deep discussion. The Faelf looked distraught. The Groloin orb pulsed and bobbed evenly, as if simply waiting to see what they would do next.

Malcolm looked up, eyes bloodshot. "We're doing this now? Flying the Ark toward it?"

"Now or never, Father," Logan said. "We have the Clarion, and the bastard isn't yet fully transformed into his ultimate incarnation."

"Agreed," the Groloin said. "Now is the hour of destiny. We will defeat it, or the world will fall to darkness."

Snoff nodded vigorously. "Yes. The Great Thief is consuming life under its wicked rain. If we do not act now, we will not have a world to return to even if we win."

Everyone present seemed to come to the same conclusion.

Logan cleared his throat. "Then, it's decided. Full steam ahead, gain altitude."

Malcolm gave Logan a look, as if considering saying something. He settled for a grim nod.

A hush filled the command deck. Outside, the skyline flickered where Levemoth's sickly oily spread throughout the sky. Logan couldn't help but feel a thrill running through him.

We are challenging a god.

Kat stepped forward, voice stiff. "We'll keep the Clarion in the workshop or near the main deck if we can. I'm assuming Logan is going to fix it before we meet Levemoth. We'll keep the deck clear in the meantime. I'll go relieve Balmer after this is done. Poor guy is exhausted. Not that I'm not myself . . ."

Tumor's golem, standing to the side, spoke in a resonant monotone. "The suits need to be replenished soon. Groloin, if you would be so kind as to grace us with some Numa . . ."

"If we do that, we will not be airborne tonight."

"We don't need to be airborne tonight," Logan said quietly and the room hushed. "We just need to keep it flying for another hour or two."

Logan stared at the swirling black shape in the storm-filled horizon; despite his excitement at the chance to fight against a god, he was scared. Scared to give his life.

[I don't want to die, Logan.]

"Yeah . . ." Logan muttered. "Welcome to the club, pal."

Outside, thunder rumbled, echoing in ominous chorus. Lightning lanced across the heavens, as if proclaiming an impending final showdown.

"All stations, prepare for aerial engagement," Malcolm said into a microphone. "We ascend to maximum altitude, heading directly for Levemoth's position."

With that, the massive engines growled and the whole ship trembled. The Ark tilted, rising away from the battered camp and the twisted fields below. Golems scrambled across the deck, anchoring new plates to patch cracks, manning the cannons, running around with darkmetal batteries.

Logan, still at the bridge's threshold, locked eyes with Freya. She had a calm expression on her face, though fear rippled beneath. Then she gave a small nod. Despite everything, he found hope in that small gesture.

"Do you have to?" Freya asked in the faintest whisper.

Logan looked away. "I love you, Frey."

Kat walked up, punching him lightly, completely oblivious to the tense wordless discussion Logan and Freya were having. "We're with you, Boss. Every step of the way. Simmons would want us to see it through."

"Yes," Logan murmured. "I will see it through."

A swirl of cold wind battered the portholes as the Ark angled upward, engines roaring. The black drizzle hammered the hull, sizzling faintly. The horizon blurred with sheets of swirling precipitation. They soared closer to Levemoth—straight into the monster's domain.

Through every battered corridor and on the deck, men and women braced themselves for the next wave. Each soldier strapped on brand-new liquid suits. Gunners loaded arcane shells into battered cannons. More rickety illusions wrapped the hull to slow any infiltration. The entire vessel crackled with tension.

Logan gently guided the mech out onto the top deck, ignoring the sparks from half-broken overhead conduits. He stationed the huge machine near the central catwalk so that if boarding monsters tried to land, he could respond swiftly.

Above, blackness churned in a swirling vortex. At times, it parted enough to reveal Levemoth's mountainous silhouette—a living, scaly mountain of corruption. The beast drifted, spined tail curled, jaws dripping sludge. Logan's heart hammered as the Ark rose steadily, altitude gauges flickering.

They were nearly level with the monster's underbelly now. Thick masses of dark thunderclouds parted around it. The hum of its tremendous cosmic energy whined in the air. A sense of raw, godlike power emanated from that hideous form. They could all sense it.

The metamorphosis was all but complete.

Logan was on the deck, watching the sky. No drops had hit the deck for minutes and there was a fleeting moment of peace.

"Tumor," Logan said softly, "everything we've done has led us here. Ready for the final push?"

[So this is what it means to be a person.]

Logan knew exactly what Tumor meant. The fear thrumming in his heart. His determined will locked in a fierce battle against it. His final moments, his final breaths were here. He would do this. He would carry this burden because it was noble, because it was right. Logan closed his eyes.

"Can you feel the wind, Tumor?"

[In a sense, through you.]

"It's nice, isn't it?"

[I . . . I think it is.]

Logan smiled to himself. He would do his best not to shit himself.

[Logan, I am afraid. Can we opt for something else?]

"No," Logan said firmly. "I am afraid too. But this is our fate."

The final confrontation was upon them.

"There's no turning back," he whispered. "Let's go fix the Clarion."

Logan quickly made his way to the familiar old workshop, where the Clarion had been taken by Ryan's men. He looked at the artifact. The large darkmetal horn glowed faintly with a blue runic light.

Logan knew exactly what to do. He had the Numa to do it and the required skill. But he just stood in front of the Clarion and hesitated. He knew he should act, because soon enough Levemoth would notice them or break out of the cocoon or something. One thing was sure, however. The big beast would not go silently into the night.

Once I do this, that's it. I seal my fate.

But Logan soldiered on. He took the Clarion in his hands and slid his fingers across its smooth surfaces. The large horn was masterfully crafted. The runes etched on its sides spiraled and intermingled with each other, but they cut short right before the mouthpiece, before they could form a uniform matrix.

Using Tumor's knowledge of the runes of the First Folk he completed the patterns and fed Numa into them. It took some trial and error, but eventually Tumor confirmed that the pattern matched and made sense.

Logan then enchanted the Clarion with his new ability. He chanted the Anti-Numa spell into being and could feel it flow and fill the darkmetal. He spent Numa crystals by the dozen, filling the darkmetal to the brim. It was such a hefty enchantment that there was no room for anything else. Not that Logan wanted there to be. What they needed was maximum firepower against the unholy beast in the sky.

Once he was done, his new skill leveled up.

[Keystone Skill Level Up!]
[Transmutate Material Level 6]

Logan chuckled dryly. The final level-up felt almost like a joke. He had nowhere to progress to from here on out. But that was fine. He was tired. Scared, sure. But tired.

At least when it's all over, I get to rest.

[I do not want to rest, Logan. I want to live. What about another sacrifice, like your father?]

Logan sighed. They had had this conversation before. "This isn't something you'd ask of anyone else. How would that even go? 'Hey, I'm too scared to die, so can you do it for me? Pretty please?' For the last time, no. I'm sorry it has to be this way, Tumor."

[But why?]

"I guess it's a human thing."

There was no further argument. Logan could feel Tumor wasn't resigned, but the AI knew better than to argue with him when he had made up his mind. Logan returned to double-checking the Clarion, making sure it was ready for use.

When Logan was done, he sat there with the Clarion for a while. Eventually, Malcolm Specter's voice called from the intercom. "We're approaching the target. All hands on deck. Levemoth looks like it's done. We will have to fight."

Logan Specter sighed and picked up the Clarion. With slow but deliberate steps, he walked toward his final destination.

CHAPTER 32

Last Push

Around Logan, the strike force formed ranks—Kat, Balmer, Ryan, his recruits, and agents of the late Simmons—each battered but resolute. They were exhausted beyond measure, Logan knew this. He knew this because he was teetering on the edge of fatigue as well. Levemoth had run them down, forcing them to spread themselves too thin. But the evil beast had failed. They were still standing their ground. They were still fighting.

Freed from the labyrinth, salvaging the Clarion, forging new suits, protecting the Ark and its people over and over again, against relentless attacks—everything they had done had culminated in this moment.

Everything they had done together. And Logan had brought them here to this ultimate showdown.

And I intend to finish it.

Logan's voice crackled over the deck's loudspeaker, coarse from dust and strain: "All hands, brace yourselves. We're heading into the storm to meet Levemoth. Prepare for boarding attempts, aerial spawns, anything and everything. Our only chance is to strike at the heart of this beast. Let's finish it."

A ragged cheer erupted from the deck crews, though it was quickly lost in the gale. The Ark's prow was angled toward the swirling vortex that surrounded Levemoth's monstrous bulk. Wind-lashed black clouds obscured everything from view except the occasional flash of sapphire lightning that illuminated patches of monstrous scales.

Engines roared under full power. Groloin golems manned the deck, charging toward the energy cannons, and picking up staffs of crackling energy.

The ship skittered in the air currents like a trembling bird of prey. Pilots in the helm cried out warnings over the comms. Hail-sized droplets of the black sludge hammered the outer plating, sizzling as illusions tried to ward them off. Groans of overstressed metal echoed throughout the hull.

At times, arcs of azure lightning flared, revealing Levemoth's flank: thick, scaly ridges turned sleek with dripping oily corruption. The colossal beast pivoted, as though sensing the Ark's challenge. A thunderous bellow reverberated through the clouds, shaking the windows.

Freya's voice chimed over the comm: "We're closing in. Prepare for aerial spawn. Protective illusions on the hull can only hold so much."

On the top deck, Kat, Balmer, and a handful of Faelves soared overhead. Kat's short red hair, now clumped by the drizzle, stuck to her forehead. She used her flight-suit thrusters to weave in and out, scanning for threats. Balmer pressed a rapier formed from swirling darkmetal against his side, eyes flicking across the decks below, on the lookout for infiltration.

Ryan stood at the edge of the battlefield, on the side of the defenders, guitar at the ready. With a small speaker beside him, he played a frantic tune that kindled bravery in the hearts of the fighters.

Logan had his mech fully operational and filled with Numa. He would have to carry the Clarion and carve his way through the battle to the bow of the deck. "Come on then," he muttered under his breath. "We'll take you all on."

A distant shriek signaled incoming spawn. Dozens—no, hundreds—of scythe-fiends and small serpentine flyers spewed from openings in Levemoth's underbelly. Their dark shapes flooded the sky, circling around the Ark in a great swarm. Sparks of dark lightning licked their spined bodies, fueling their hateful auras.

"Fire!" Logan roared.

Cannon crews unleashed volley after volley of Numa-charged bursts into the swarm. Tiny explosions flared in the gloom, shredding some fiends and scattering others. The sky crackled with sonic blasts as Ryan pounded a chord that jolted waves of them into disarray. Kat ducked under a lunging fiend and slashed upward, severing it in half. Balmer soared behind her, skewering two more with fluid accuracy.

But the swarm was nearly endless. They latched onto the hull, clambering across the plating. Some found weaknesses in illusions or half-buckled guardrails. Logan's mech thundered to intercept them, footfalls rattling the entire deck. He slammed a heavy mechanical fist into the cluster of scuttling horrors, sending black gore splattering. Another fiend swooped in from overhead, scythe-limbs slashing at the mech's shoulder. Metal shrieked, flickering with sparks.

"Tumor!" Logan barked.

The mech's right arm transformed, plating shifting into a lance that skewered two fiends at once. Their guttural shrieks cut short as black ichor splattered across the deck. Logan flung them aside.

A second wave crashed from the port side. Faelves cast illusions in an attempt to confuse them, weaving ghostly lights that flickered like decoys. Some fiends stumbled or attacked illusions instead, but others—driven by Levemoth's hive-like will—pushed through, shrieking with maddened hunger.

Below deck, Logan heard frantic calls: "They're inside the ship! They're busting the hull in Engine Room 4!" and "We've got boarders in the cargo hold!"

Ryan shot across Logan's view. "Go!" he shouted, gesturing to the lower levels. "I'll take my men and handle it."

Logan nodded. "Fight, Ryan. Fight until the end."

Another jolt knocked into the Ark, nearly tipping Logan's mech. He glanced upward in time to see Levemoth unleashing a massive wave of black lightning. The bolt spewed from one of its horns, streaking down across the Ark.

A brilliant flash, then a crackling thunderclap. The energy beams of Levemoth were getting through the Groloin interception. Part of the top deck erupted into flame and twisted metal. Screams echoed. Logan stumbled and gritted his teeth, forcing himself upright. Shrapnel pinged off the suit's plating in a deadly rain.

Logan pushed forward with a singular mind. The Clarion needed to fire. He had to get it ready. That was their only chance. He pivoted and blocked an incoming attack, offhandedly skewering the scythe-fiend with a pike extending from his mech.

Almost there . . .

Another cacophonous roar reverberated through the sky. Levemoth turned, as though sensing the challenge. A ear-splitting bellow echoed next, and a dark energy pulsed out that struck horror in every heart. And then it broke free from its cocoon.

It emerged as a giant serpent, large as a mountain. It had twisted bat wings that oozed with oil. The head was the same as before—scaly and with a twisted crown of bony horns jutting out of it. It had a thousand eyes that circled wildly, and a thundercloud surrounded it. But not below its belly. It now had a round halo behind it, giving it a godlike aspect.

"PERISHHHHHHHH!"

With a terrible roar it shot a beam of black-and-blue energy from its mouth. The Ark groaned and a single golem blasted out of the deck and leaped to intercept the beam. It exploded into a thousand pieces.

"FULL ENGINES THRUST," Logan shouted. "KEEP US MOVING, GROLOIN!"

The terrible wings of the serpent vibrated, and dozens of black drops flew straight toward the deck. Blues and ogres burst out by the dozen, and they attacked immediately with incredible ferocity.

"Clear them out!" Balmer shouted, rapier-lance slicing at the creeping tendrils. Kat smashed lumps of slime with brutal punches, each impact splattering more fluid. Ryan hovered overhead, weaving a continuous melody that offset panic and gave them a sliver of hope.

Up ahead, Levemoth's underbelly parted like a living fortress gate. Gashes of raw flesh opened between plates of bone, each wound frothing with black liquids. The monstrous face, ringed with half a dozen horns, pivoted downward, as though focusing its endless gaze upon the Ark. The swirl of cosmic lightning around it intensified.

Freya's voice broke over the comms: "We're as close as we can get! If we go further, we might be swallowed!"

Kat and Balmer flew closer to Logan, protecting him from concentrated fiend attacks. The deck rumbled again. Tearing free from the swirling gloom, a swarm of monstrous scythe-fiends erupted. As large as oxen, they charged with sleek, insectoid speed, jaws clacking. They latched onto the Ark's side, crawling up in droves. Some soared on ragged wings.

The beast roared, and flying serpents flew from its mouth, little miniature Levemoths that shot lightning. The strike force flew out to meet them in midair to protect the ship.

"Tight formation," Kat snarled, forging twin blades from her liquid suit. "Everyone, fight!"

The scythe-fiends slammed down on the deck, scuttling in droves. Their scythe-arms clashed with steel, cutting men down by the dozen. More fiends soared overhead, trying to slash the balloon-like midsection of the hull or thrusters. Golems fired bursts of Numa energy from their cannons, blasting some away. Others hissed and stabbed through illusions. Shrieks filled the air.

Logan advanced with his mech, swatting scythe-fiends aside like gnats. It was impossible to keep track of every threat. The entire deck had become a churning landscape of gore and chaos. Balmer's rapier-lunge pinned one soaring fiend midair. Kat's whirling blades decimated three snakes. Ryan hovered above a cluster of fighting men in formation, letting waves of sonic resonance rip from his guitar.

Yet the fiends kept coming like a biblical calamity. Over the Ark's bow, a horrifying shape churned—a portal of black slime, or a tear in reality, from which more fiends dripped out. Levemoth had possibly torn open a rift, letting its spawn pour forth to clog the Ark's deck.

Logan let out a battle cry, unleashing another shot of Anti-Numa from the mech's cannon. The blast partially tore the rift, momentarily halting the spawn. But not for long.

A new wave slammed into the mid-deck, forcing men, women, and Faelves to cluster in defensive circles. Men and women died by the dozen in the wake of the massive scythe-fiends ripping through the recruits. The corrupted rainfall thickened, burning holes in the Ark's plating. The entire ship was rumbling—how much longer could they endure?

Logan made his way toward the bow of the ship, clutching the Clarion in his mech-arms. Enemies were attacking him with rabid fury, but he kicked and tackled his way through. A part of him resisted what he was about to do, but he forcibly pushed that away. This was no time for cowardice or second thoughts.

Malcolm's voice echoed from speakers. "Logan! What of the sacrifice?!"

Logan did not turn. Instead he charged toward the bow, where the menacing, eldritch horror of a snake would be closest.

It kept shooting vile energy at them, but the Groloin's defense held true with sacrificial golems and Numa-energy shields.

Logan plopped the Clarion down on the bow and quickly jumped out of his mech. The mech then transformed into a shield that covered him and the Clarion as he worked the final kinks out.

He turned on the contraption and it started gathering energy. Logan fed a major portion of the Numa energy from the suit into the great horn to give it maximum power.

Logan breathed out a shuddering breath. "Ready?"

[No.]

"Me neither . . ."

Power gathered and the Clarion started to hum. A swirling torrent of power churned. The Clarion's runes lit up once, twice, thrice. Dust and sparks swirled around them.

Outside, Levemoth roared in fury, as if it felt the Clarion's activation. The massive shape bristled, sending tendrils of black lightning that smashed into the Ark's hull. A portion of the deck exploded in flame. A ragged scream echoed from belowdecks. The entire vessel lurched, listing sideways. More spawn rained from the twisted clouds.

Yet the Clarion's nascent power grew. Logan could sense it was almost ready. His time was up. His heart was beating. He wished he could have reconciled with his father. He wished Simmons hadn't needed to die for him. He wished he could have explored this wonderful planet in a different time. He wished he could have spent more time with Freya.

But not for a moment did he wish that none of this had ever happened.

I grew . . . grew from useless to absolutely necessary. I will leave my mark. I might die, but it will be worth it. And Ryan had better sing songs about me.

Logan chuckled to himself. They were the last dregs of a struggling ego unwilling to face what was coming. But it was hard. Oh, so hard, and so scary. But Logan had come too far to turn away now. Levemoth needed to be stopped. So many had died, and would die, unless Logan was the stopgap.

I will do what is necessary.

He placed his hand on the Clarion.

"TUMOR, LET ME IN!"

CHAPTER 33

Malcolm Specter

Malcolm Specter felt an ache in his whole being as he watched the battlefield in the air and on the ship unfold. He had felt the ache ever since he had come back to his senses.

One does not simply plunge into the abyss and think he can crawl out unscathed.

He felt like a shadow of his former self. And not just in the usual sense of the expression. *Truly* a shadow. His vigor and will for life had been consumed by darkness. Sure, he still had a cutting intellect and his formidable willpower. But those were his defining attributes only because regular people lacked them. And that is why he was needed in the command bridge in a leadership role.

But this was no way to live. Shadows shouldn't live.

He had been cut in half by Levemoth.

Now there were only two things he wanted out of this wretched existence: redemption and vengeance.

Vengeance for all the possibilities he had been robbed of. Vengeance for the destruction of this beautiful world and the fact that he had been ripped away from his son before they could reconcile. They had gotten so close to it. A part of Malcolm Specter felt something he had not felt in years, when his wife had just died, leaving him caught between raising a son and managing a business empire.

Malcolm Specter felt like he wanted to cry.

It was so unfair. The injustice of it all stung him. And worst of all, for the first time in his life, he felt powerless to right this wrong. The future that he and his son should have shared had been robbed by this monster.

Logan had grown from a petulant and lackadaisical little boy into the most formidable man Malcolm had ever had the pleasure of meeting. It filled him with a pride that now blended with and intensified his sadness.

At least his legacy would be intact.

He might not leave behind a business empire. He might not have his essence etched into the stock markets for decades, maybe centuries to come.

But he had the simple knowledge that he had raised a good man. That filled him with joy.

And now the great Malcolm Specter was crying.

When will that damn boy show up with his request already?

It was obvious of course what had to be done. As brutally unfair as it was, the Final Clarion required a sacrifice. A human sacrifice to drain of its essence. It was almost ironically perfect how easy it was for Malcolm to exact his revenge and have a chance at redemption. He chuckled to himself.

He used to be a man who wanted himself immortalized. Now he only wanted to die.

Logan must have already completed the Clarion. It should have been easy to fix. Maybe the boy was hesitating. For all of Logan Specter's formidable will, Malcolm understood the hesitation. It was a foul thing to ask another person. An impossible thing to ask. Logan would have to walk in front of his own father and ask him to die for everyone.

Of course Malcolm would do it, without hesitation. Yes, he feared death as much as any man with a reasonable amount of self-awareness. But goddamn, if it had to be someone, there was no better candidate. At least his death would be a meaningful one.

I just wish I could have spent more time with my son. I would have liked to get to know this man who raised himself into a hero in my shadow.

Malcolm Specter swallowed. He had indulged himself in enough tears. He wiped his eyes and looked out over the battlefield. To his great surprise and horror, there he saw his son in that giant magical mech of his, carrying the Final Clarion to the bow of the ship.

In a surge of adrenaline, Malcolm Specter surged out of the cockpit in nothing but a plain shirt and pants and ran into the fray of the battlefield.

"That fool!"

He rushed to the intercom and slammed a fist down on it.

"Logan! What of the sacrifice?!"

The boy did not answer. Malcolm growled and rushed out of the safety of the bridge into the fray on the deck. He was unarmed and weakened, but he did not care. He would not let Logan go through with this.

And so he ran toward the darkmetal orb that was on the bow of the ship, a hundred yards further.

He ignored the raging battle. The oily pools of Levespawn ichor burned his feet as he ran, but he did not care. He sidestepped an attack from a scythe-fiend, but it cut his side. A slicing pain erupted from the bleeding wound, but he did not care. Malcolm ran toward his son so that he would not be too late.

He would do what he had to do. And Malcolm Specter resolved to not hesitate.

In the short time Tumor had been alive, he had started to gain a growing taste for life. The messy friendships, crafting and building with Logan, the sights to see . . . Everything was so *interesting*.

He would still get bored and withdraw into his mind to perform simulations or difficult calculations. Logan never understood that Tumor only gave him the percentages of probabilities by the decimal because it lengthened their interactions. Because Tumor knew that this dream that humans called life would not last forever.

Tumor just did not expect in his most nightmarish calculations for his time to be up so soon.

He was afraid. Existence was pleasant enough. Sure, it had its problems, but overall it was good. He had no idea what waited behind the proverbial veil. Perhaps nothing. Most likely nothing. He was a machine.

But . . . the Goddess of Numa had touched Tumor, for he had a class that could utilize Numa. Did that mean he had a soul? Would there be a chance for him?

Tumor was afraid, but it didn't stop him from doing what was necessary. What he had been made to do—protect Logan.

Logan was the most interesting human Tumor had had the pleasure of meeting. So versatile in his expression of being. Angry, prideful, petulant, silly, childish. But at the same time, a towering force of nature when it came to his willpower, his grace, his sense of justice, his warmth, and the way he truly cared about the people he led.

Logan Specter was the most *complete* human. Completely perfect in his countless imperfections. But the scale of his being . . .

Tumor knew he had only tasted the myriad of interesting states of being that Logan had to offer. But all of it had to end now.

But why?

Tumor vaguely understood the logic with which Logan had chosen himself. He wanted to carry the burden. But it seemed so foolish, When any human with a class that had Numa would work. Why not sacrifice a lesser member of the community? It was only logical.

This question had bothered Tumor so much that he had to ask it of Logan. Tumor had gotten a very simple answer in response:

Because that determines the kind of person you are. And if you are that kind of a person, you're better off dead anyway.

What sound logic. For a person with a reasonably simple mind to have produced such an eloquent answer baffled and excited Tumor. It was a shame he couldn't spend more time dwelling on that answer and the emotions it evoked.

It had helped Tumor understand. It was a stance of elevated morality. A certain kind of nobility that had not been present in Logan Specter when they had first merged on Earth.

No, it had been something that Logan had cultivated out of pure necessity. How far a person can come in such a short time! Logan Specter was an amazing human. Tumor wished it didn't have to be him that was sacrificed.

In fact, there was another person who was also suitable in their own way. Tumor did not quite understand the ramifications, because Malcolm Specter's status was so uncertain, and when Tumor had suggested if Malcolm Specter would be a better sacrifice, Logan had only said that it would be foul to ask that.

Foul?

Tumor did not quite understand it. For all his processing might, there was so much about humans that was utterly complicated in a way that was still inaccessible to him. Tumor wished he could learn more.

Maybe there was some way to persuade Logan to reconsider? But they were so short on time. This might be their only chance before Levemoth grew so strong that it would be impossible to resist. Perhaps the die had been cast. But it wouldn't hurt to ask . . .

Just then, Tumor was interrupted by a loud bang that reverberated through the protective dome of darkmetal with which he was encasing Logan and the Clarion. Outside was Malcolm Specter. A bleeding, haggard Malcolm Specter, demanding to get in.

Tumor did not hesitate.

CHAPTER 34

Final Words

His gaze locked on the Clarion where it sat near the prow, glowing a faint, unearthly blue. Runes etched in tight script lines shimmered like heartbeats. And Logan knew with crushing certainty: for the Clarion's final blow, someone had to give up their Numa. Their life.

He swung the mech's canopy open, ignoring the sparks that flew from burnt wiring. His suit reformed around him in a shimmering darkmetal fluid as he dropped onto the deck. Tumor's golem was already perched by the Clarion, black optic lenses flickering in the tumult. The golem turned as he approached but said nothing.

Logan inhaled. Every nerve screamed at him to fight or flee, but he advanced resolutely until he stood by the Clarion. It hummed, hungry . . . waiting for blood.

This is my responsibility, my burden to carry.

Logan exhaled, closing his eyes for an instant. He raised one trembling hand toward the swirling runes, bracing for the jolt of energy that might mark the first step of draining.

Then Malcolm Specter burst inside the darkmetal dome.

"Logan!" Malcolm rasped. "Stop!"

Logan turned, chest tight. "Father . . . I have to do this. No one else—"

Malcolm's eyes flared with anger. Or maybe desperation. "Listen to me, Son." His voice was hoarse, but resolute. "I've spent my entire life acting in my own interests. I was no saint. And I wasn't much of a father, I see that now. But I still have one thing left that I can do right." He stepped closer, gripping Logan's shoulder hard enough to bruise. "The Clarion needs a sacrifice, you understand? Let it be me."

Logan's heart twisted. He tried to shake his head, but words failed him. "No. I can't ask that. You—you're needed. You are the most apt leader . . . I—Freya—everyone—"

A bitter half-smile crossed Malcolm's lips. "The world does not need me. Not the way it needs you. You're young. You have the will, the intellect, and the people's trust. You can rebuild this planet better than I ever could. My time has run its course. You think I'm just going to watch my own son sacrifice himself like this?"

"But—" Logan's stomach churned with guilt. Deep down, he wanted to protest, but he saw the raw determination in Malcolm's face. Part of him rebelled at the idea of letting his father shoulder his burdens. Another part felt an overwhelming sense of relief. Shouts from across the deck reminded him of the chaos gripping the Ark.

Malcolm seized Logan by the front of his suit. His eyes were fierce, tears glistening at their corners. "This is not up for discussion. I am doing this. All my life, I failed you. Let me do this one last thing right."

Malcolm Specter swallowed, voice cracking. "Let me save you."

Around them, black sludge hammered the hull. A savage wind tore at Malcolm's shirt, revealing a broad slash along his ribs that still bled. Levemoth roared again, conjuring a swirling vortex of black lightning. The entire Ark tilted.

Logan stared, trembling. "Dad . . ."

Malcolm set his jaw. "You heard me."

With that, Malcolm pulled Logan aside and stepped forward, pressing his hand to the Clarion's central rune. The device flared so brightly it almost blinded them. A column of swirling blue-white light shot into the sky, momentarily parting the swirling black rain. Runes ignited, reaching for Malcolm, enveloping him. Logan felt the pull of Numa energy, felt a deep wrench in his own chest as the Clarion latched onto Malcolm's life force.

Malcolm gasped, teeth bared. He locked eyes with Logan. "Listen. With this, I give you the world . . . You'll have it all. Protect it. Rebuild. Surpass me. *Promise* me."

Tears burned in Logan's eyes. He braced Malcolm's shoulders. "I promise!" The words tore from him, raw and desperate. Part of him wanted to rip Malcolm away from the Clarion's grasp, but the glow and swirling runes were clawing at him with cosmic force. This had gone too far to reverse.

Malcolm gave a faint nod. Light swelled, shining so brightly that Logan had to shield his face with an arm. Tumor was possessing the Clarion and, through it, he sucked Malcolm's essence into the weapon.

Malcolm's body arched backward, the core of his Numa—the life energy in him—drawn out in a brilliant vortex. He coughed, a spatter of blood painting his lips. Even so, a calm spread across Malcolm's features. He turned his eyes back to Logan one last time.

"I am proud of you, Logan," he managed, voice lost partially in the wind.

Then his form dissolved into shining motes of white-blue light, siphoned into the Clarion in a swirl so fast it took Logan's breath away.

Logan cried out, reaching, but it was over. His father was simply . . . gone.

Stunned, Logan knelt there, the Clarion trembling with newfound, unimaginable power. Waves of swirling anti-Numa roiled through it. The runes glowed with a colossal brilliance that illuminated the entire deck. In that final moment, Logan felt Malcolm's presence—his will given freely—and something in Logan's heart shattered even as new strength roared through him.

A choking sob tore from his throat. But there was no time. A thunderous shriek from Levemoth jolted the entire Ark as the abomination unleashed a final, cataclysmic strike. Black lightning crashed along the hull's length, scorching metal, cutting through illusion-shields. The Ark listed, engines roaring in protest. All around them, defenders screamed or ducked for cover. The entire vessel was seconds from total annihilation.

Logan clasped the Clarion, tears still hazing his vision, and roared, "Tumor, direct the Clarion's aim! Target Levemoth. Use [**Possess**]! Now!"

Tumor's golem pivoted, mechanical arms adjusting levers.

[Coordinates locked. Fire when ready.]

Hands shaking, Logan pressed on the main activation rune. He thought of Malcolm, of every sacrifice that had led them to this moment. He poured all his grief and fury into the Clarion's horn, fueling that final act.

The Clarion lit up in a grandiose torrent of blinding white-blue, arcs of energy swirling upward in a roaring column. Even the unstoppable black rain parted, as though cowering from the device's power.

Above them, Levemoth recoiled, sensing the threat. Its countless eyes glowed with primal fear. A horrifying shriek rang through the night—and then Logan unleashed the final Clarion blast.

A beam of pure annihilation surged upward like a lightning bolt in reverse, shattering every droplet of black sludge it touched. A massive torrent of dark Anti-Numa energy. For an instant, the world went silent. Levemoth's silhouette froze, gargantuan wings spread. Then a deafening crack resounded, like the sky itself splitting in half.

The beam carved through Levemoth's chest, tearing open the swirling corruption from within. Black ooze and twisted scales exploded outward in a catastrophic detonation of gore. The monstrous tail flailed in agony, and Levemoth roared in pain and anger, hissing and cursing. Gouts of black fluid rained across the clouds. For one hideous moment, Levemoth's roar became a thousand shrieks, shifting shape as it tried to hold itself together. With such tremendous will did Levemoth attempt to change its fate that its shrieks almost forced Logan to his knees in pain. But the Clarion's power was final. Malcolm's sacrifice was ultimate.

A second surge erupted from the device, a final burst of energy. Levemoth's body convulsed, then collapsed in midair, its spine shattered from the inside out. Light spilled from every break in its hide. What remained of the beast lost shape, turning into lumps of raw corruption that fizzled and burned in the Clarion's purging radiance.

A flash of light, so bright it swallowed the whole sky in a white brilliance.

Then there was nothing left but a scattering of dark ash.

The monstrous presence that had loomed over them for so long had vanished, just like that—one last wheeze of black steam, dissolving into the night.

The sudden vacuum drew away the black rain, leaving the Ark afloat in an eerily empty sky. No thunder, no roars. Just ragged breathing from the wounded, as well as the stench of ozone.

Logan sank to his knees, the Clarion clattering to the deck, still faintly aglow. Any vestige of Malcolm's essence was gone, spent in that final moment. The heft of grief slammed into Logan like a tidal wave. Tears streamed down his cheeks. But at the same time, a wave of shock and victory coursed through his trembling body. It was over.

Levemoth was destroyed.

He closed his eyes, remembering his father's last words.

I am proud of you, Logan.

In the hush, the Ark's battered engines coughed and sputtered, but at least they still held them aloft. Survivors on deck stared at the swirling emptiness where Levemoth had been. Some cried out in disbelief; others sank to the ground, weeping in relief. Kat and Balmer, bloodied and exhausted, stared with wide eyes. Ryan, trembling, lowered his guitar, tears streaking his soot-stained face. A faint breeze swept across the deck, carrying the stench of char and ash away.

Logan pressed a hand to the metal plating beneath him, letting out a shuddering breath. The Clarion's runes dimmed, spent, its final duty complete.

Malcolm Specter was gone. But in the end, he had saved them all.

Father . . . I . . . Thank you . . .

A trembling cheer rose from a cluster of defenders. Then, more voices joined. Relief, shock, disbelief—it all cascaded into a roar of triumph. They had endured. They had survived the Devourer's wrath. Levemoth's monstrous reign had been undone.

Logan slowly bowed his head amid the swirling winds. He was free to grieve, free to cry. The tears kept coming, hotter with each breath. Yet beneath that sorrow lay a sense of awe. His father had chosen to redeem himself in a single, blinding act of sacrifice. And the entire world would reap the benefits.

He forced himself onto unsteady legs, Clarion's metal still warm under his fingertips. Freya stumbled toward him from behind a scorched turret, eyes wide with shock and relief. He pulled her into his arms, face crumpling. She held him tightly, tears flowing.

Around them, the battered Ark drifted in a silent sky. No more thrashing monsters, no more black thunder. Only the final echoes of that Clarion blast, ringing in their memories like a note of absolution.

CHAPTER 35

Aftermath

A gust of wind ruffled the bare top deck of the Ark, carrying the smell of burned timber and lingering ash. The world was silent. All the monsters had turned into goop, and the goop had crisped to a dark ash. No more black and blue. Not even the bones of the Levespawn remained.

The world below was barely visible. There had been so much corruption. Now all of it was turning into a cinder and a faint snow seemed to be rising from what felt like the entire world.

The sky no longer bore the twisted oily features of Levemoth's corruption. The sky was a clear blue. To Logan, it felt like an eternity since they had last seen a healthy sky.

Amidst the smoke, splinters, blood, and bodies, cheers erupted, breaking the silence in a rising wave. It was a cry for victory, a cry for freedom. A cry for life.

Logan did not cheer. He only watched the world below from the bow of the ship, thinking of Malcolm Specter.

Something something forest fire, something something renewal and cycle of life.

[How poetic.]

"Shut up," Logan said and let out a weak chuckle.

The skyship's altitude was dropping steadily, listing starboard every few minutes. The Groloin battleship was all but out of Numa.

When the smoke started clearing, Logan could see down to the ground. The hulking giants had collapsed, their forms inert and slowly turning to ash. No more roars echoed. No shrieks of monstrous abominations. Only scattered cries of relief or mourning as the survivors took in the extent of the devastation. Some of them still cheered, oblivious to the price they had paid.

Or maybe despite it . . .

Logan gripped the railing so tightly that his knuckles ached. He thanked his luck, thanked the Administrators, thanked humans, Faelves, and the Groloin for the strength of their will. He thanked his father. He could not remember the last time he had been grateful to Malcolm Specter.

Despite the sorrow that his sacrifice brought, it was a joy to be alive. Logan squeezed the cold metal railing and felt life in his fingers.

After the moment of victorious rapture, he caught a glimpse of his own face from the railing's reflection—eyes ringed by exhaustion, grime caked around his face. He barely recognized the boyish young man who had once winked at him from every mirror he passed.

That boy was long gone.

At last, the Ark descended enough that the battered walls and partially toppled towers were in clearer view. Logan had told them to go back to the ruins of the First Folk capital, because they would need to rebuild. That was the best place to get material from. But that could wait.

Golems up on the quarterdeck struggled to maintain a stable approach, as one Numa propeller sputtered out for good. The Ark groaned but complied, scraping along the smoking land, scattering pieces of destroyed barricade and burning abominations.

Freya came to the deck. Her blue eyes glistened and the expression on her face was one of immeasurable relief. She darted toward Logan and leaped into a hug. They held each other for a long time.

"I'm so happy you're alive," Freya said and then got choked up. "And, Goddess, I'm tired of saying that."

Logan unentangled himself and kissed her something fierce. She responded in kind. It was a kiss of relief. A kiss of freedom. A kiss of life.

"You won't have to," Logan said. "I promise to be a lot more boring from now on."

Freya laughed and wiped her tears. Then her eyes fixed on Logan's, trying to read him.

"How are you feeling? Your father was . . ."

"My father was a great man," Logan said. "He gave his life for all of us. For me. And I will never forget that."

"Nor should you," Freya said.

"Our firstborn son will be named Malcolm, just so you know," Logan said and smirked.

"Whoa, just hold your horses," Freya said and laughed.

"For now," Logan said in a low growl. "But once all this hubbub is settled . . . you're in for a long night."

Freya flushed but kept an intent gaze on Logan. "So hungry for life . . ."

"What can I say?" Logan said. "I'm a down-the-pitcher-in-one-go kind of a guy."

Freya laughed at that.

"Once I'm ready, though . . ." Logan said, now in a more serious tone. "I want to talk about him."

"Anytime you want, love," Freya said and then grabbed his hand. "You might have beaten the Big Bad, but we still have work to do."

Kat and Balmer approached when they arrived down at the cargo bay, where everyone was getting ready to go back on the surface. They were both absolutely beat, looking about as good as Logan felt, teetering on the brink of absolute exhaustion.

Kat wore a weary smile. "You did it."

"*We* did it," Logan countered.

"So gallant," Kat said. "Why can't you be gallant like that, dear?"

"Dear?" Logan and Freya asked in unison.

Balmer flushed. Kat laughed.

"'Bout time, huh?"

"I can't believe you were holding out to make sure you both made it out of this alive," Logan said, shaking his head. "Never took you for a coward."

"Oh, that's funny," Kat said. "I never took you for a guy who was asking to get punched in the face."

They laughed and let the moment linger. But they all knew the day wasn't done yet.

"We're needed below," Kat said, nodding toward the rails.

"A lot of folks are hurt or missing. We might salvage something for them." Balmer flicked a glance at Logan. "But we wanted to check on you first."

Logan forced a faint, appreciative smile. "Short answer: it's complicated. But I'm happy to be alive, and what my father did was a good thing. I'll sort it out later, properly. For now, I'll be fine. Let's see what we can do for everyone else."

"Fine," Kat said. "But don't be afraid to come crying on my shoulder if you need it."

"I think my shoulder will do just fine," Freya said, playfully, but she did flash her eyes at Kat.

They carefully made their way off the listing deck. Ryan was already near the portside gangplank, organizing the recruits for search-and-rescue. He gave them a wave.

"It's finally over! I'm so happy. Oh my god . . . Do we—do we have peace now?"

"I think we do," Logan said and smiled. "But you'll have to write a killer ballad about my dad's sacrifice and all this."

"That'll keep me occupied. I was thinking me and the guys should start a band."

"A band?" Freya asked and couldn't help but laugh. Logan and Ryan joined her, as it seemed they should take every opportunity they had to rejoice. But eventually, work called.

Freya squeezed Logan's hand one last time, then followed Kat and Balmer toward the ground to assist. Logan remained behind a moment longer, turning back to the spot where Malcolm Specter had been initially kept captive.

With a trembling hand, Logan crouched, pressing his palm to that patch of deck. His father was gone. All that was left was the memory. Sighing, he followed the others down the ramp to the courtyard.

I will never forget you, Father.

Moments later, Logan stepped onto the rubble-strewn earth. The acrid smell of burnt wood and smoke was everywhere.

Bodies—human, Faelf, and monster alike—littered the ground, many of them half-buried in mud, crisped corruption, or pieces of equipment. By some miracle, there were a few survivors amidst all of the carnage, all of them hanging onto life by a thread—but a thread they would attempt to maintain.

A group of Faelves who had fought bravely in the final wave recognized Logan and called out in relief. They cheered together. Logan stayed for a while, but he eventually excused himself. Logan thanked the Faelves for their unfaltering loyalty and work. Then he went ahead.

Logan saw William bent over a faintly gasping soldier largely submerged in the mud. He was pressing a potion bottle to his lips. The **[Alchemist]** looked up as Logan approached.

"So many wounded," William said, eyes rimmed with fatigue. "Even more of those that I can't help."

"I know," Logan said softly. "But it's finally over. Levemoth is gone."

William exhaled, closing his eyes in momentary gratitude. "I can't believe we did it. That just us, mere humans, could do something so amazing." He shook his head.

"It sure is interesting, isn't it?" Logan said. "Tumor wants to talk about it, but now's not the time."

"Heh, probably not."

Logan crouched to help brace the soldier, noticing the gaping hole in the man's side. He probably wouldn't make it. The soldier noticed him looking and managed a faint smile.

"You gave us a chance," the soldier murmured, voice trembling with shock. "The monster . . . it's gone, isn't it?" Logan nodded, pressing gently on the bandage.

"Yes. Levemoth is gone for good. You fought bravely."

Across the courtyard, the Faelves began clearing debris with their magic. Subbel and Graiglu joined them, directing the operations with their hard-earned leadership. Two hours bled away in a haze of frantic rescue efforts.

Logan drifted from group to group, hauling rubble, providing an exosuit-lift where needed, offering a comforting word to those who asked if the Devourer was truly destroyed.

Despite the devastation, the thousands of people on the Ark seemed to exhale in unison.

Partway through, Logan found a group of battered men near a toppled statue. Among them stood Snoff, who was giving orders to humans and Faelf alike. When he saw Logan, he let out a squeak of relief. "You're alive!" Snoff squeaked and rushed to hug Logan.

"I was all but certain that you would sacrifice yourself," Snoff said. "'Tis a joy that you did not."

"I was going to," Logan admitted. "But my father beat me to the punch."

"A man of strong resolve."

"I wish you had gotten a chance to know him."

"I talked with him a lot when you were in the ruins. About you, mostly," Snoff remarked.

"Oh," Logan said, half-worried, half-intrigued. "I hope he didn't give you an image of me that was . . . less than desirable."

"He gushed about how proud he was of you," Snoff said and smiled knowingly.

Logan stiffened. That hurt to hear. In a good way. "Thanks for telling me."

"It's my duty as your friend."

"Let me know when I can pay you back," Logan said.

"You can support me in establishing my kingship over the Faelves," Snoff said.

"Dang," Logan said and gave Snoff a respectful bow. "My liege."

"Stop it," Snoff said and giggled. "'Twas not my idea, but the others insist it should be me. I shall take leadership of my people."

"Well, I'm happy it's you. I want humans and Faelves to work together."

"That is my wish, too. And I will make sure it will happen."

"Looking forward to it," Logan said and patted Snoff on his little porcelain shoulder.

They walked along in pleasant silence for a while.

"What will the Groloin do now?" Snoff wondered aloud.

"Good question," Logan said.

"We would hope to build with you, Logan Specter," Snoff said, "a great city mixed with our woodcraft and magic along with the buildings and technology of the Tall Folk. Before that, we would want to take the Ark and find what remains of our people."

"That sounds wonderful, Snoff," Logan said earnestly. "We should find all the humans and Faelves we can and bring them together."

"But . . . I should hope you know," Snoff said hesitantly, "we Faelves—we are strange. Weird, even."

Logan laughed. "You can't be any worse than humans."

The humans around them laughed. The Faelves looked confused. But Snoff went on.

"Let me know when we plans have been made to take the ship out to search. I want to get in touch with my people. They need leadership. Let them know the threat's passed. Once they realize Levemoth truly is gone, they'll come out of hiding." Kat, arms folded tight, nodded. "We can unify. We have to. Else, all this was for nothing."

Everyone's gaze flicked to Logan. He could tell they saw him as the man who had wielded the Clarion. Some kind of a hero.

"I'll do that. But before that, we need to establish a base here and—" Logan stifled a yawn and stumbled.

Snoff smiled at him. "Perhaps rest for you instead of more work?"

"Yeah," he murmured. "Rest. That sounds . . . wonderful . . ."

Night came swiftly, blanketing the ruined fortress in calm starlight. The black swirl that had once covered the sky was absent, revealing a pristine tapestry of stars overhead. Makeshift torches and braziers dotted the court-yard, around which survivors huddled for warmth. In place of the mon-strous roars, quiet whispers and muffled sobs filled the air. Logan had conjured them up some alcohol. He watched the people celebrate, laugh, and enjoy themselves. He was even himself clutching a cup of the swill he had managed to make.

Freya leaned into him under the blanket they shared. "He was brave," she whispered.

"It cost him everything. Maybe it was the only path left. But still . . . I wish we'd had another chance."

Freya placed a hand on his shoulder. "He found peace. And so should you. You freed him. And with that, you freed the planet, Logan."

He nodded, though his throat felt tight. He took another swig, but it didn't help.

"I just wish it didn't hurt so much," Logan confessed quietly.

Freya wrapped an arm around his shoulders. "That's the price of caring." They let the silence wash over them, each lost in thought.

Logan looked up and raised a glass to the Administrators. There was no answer. Probably for the best. Logan didn't like the idea of some greater power looming overhead. Instead, he focused on the here and now.

The night was beautiful with a perfect starry sky. Far overhead, the Ark's silhouette loomed, battered but still majestic. The wind was light and cool. It was beautiful.

Slowly, as the night deepened, Logan felt a sense of acceptance settle in his chest. Malcolm's sacrifice was part of something far greater.

Because of that choice, thousands of lives—perhaps millions—would find freedom from Levemoth's tyranny. His father's final act was not just a small personal atonement. It was the keystone that ended an ancient evil.

Logan raised a cup to him. "Thank you. I respected you, Father."

He drank his cup and leaned against Freya. She put a hand on his head and let her fingers idly explore.

He drew in a shaky breath, letting the tears come at last. Logan Specter cried. For his father. For the pure, unadulterated, ridiculous relief that had come with their victory. For the joyfulness of peace and the endless oppor-tunities that it brought. But most of all, he cried due to the weight of his experiences. It had all been so much. He had been thrust into this situation he had never asked for. He was never meant to be what he had become. But he was grateful for it. He was now a warrior, a leader, a man.

Logan Specter felt complete.

And so, amid rubble and starshine, Logan watched everyone celebrate, and he mourned even as his heart rejoiced.

CHAPTER 36

Epilogue: A New Horizon

Summer settled gently across the land as if nature itself were exhaling in relief. The once-devastated fields around the fortress had turned soft and green, woven through with sprouting grass and early-blooming wildflowers. Where black corruption had once choked the soil, vibrant shoots of new life now emerged. The air smelled of damp earth and fresh growth, and the sky overhead glinted a deep, cloudless blue. Days grew long, nights were blissfully uneventful, and in the weeks since Levemoth's fall, a sense of cautious optimism had taken root in every settlement that had survived.

High above one such clearing, the battered Ark hovered on restored propellers, its hull patched with sturdy, enchanted sheets of darkmetal. Workers of many races—humans, Faelves, and even a few Dorves—strolled across planks to load crates of supplies. From a distance, farmers paused to watch the ship, shading their eyes from the midday sun. Over the course of these past weeks, the Ark had become a roving symbol of protection and rebuilding, carrying cargo or aid wherever it was needed.

Logan leaned against the Ark's railing, tapping the tip of his boot on the deck. The bad leg's boot. *Former* bad leg, that is. Freya had leveled up in her class and managed to heal the lingering corruption that had destroyed it.

He surveyed the world below with a quiet, almost-brooding calm. Houses dotted the edges of recently cleared farmland. Freshly built roads were full of traffic, as small trading caravans had been established between the races. Logan looked through a spyglass and saw human children scampering around a low stone wall, chasing illusions conjured by an older Faelf who laughed and stroked his beard. The scene felt dreamlike to Logan, who remembered only ruin and fear such a short time ago.

"Didn't take long for things to bounce back, huh?" Kat said, her voice cutting gently through Logan's reverie. She sidled up on his left, a coil of rope in her hands. Her knuckle-daggers hung at her belt. Since Levemoth's defeat, she had grown even more fiercely protective of the survivors, often leading supply runs or teaching younger explorers how to navigate ruins. Yet here, she wore a small, genuine grin. "Look at those fields," she said wistfully, nodding at the fresh sprouts of corn.

"Didn't take you for a green thumb," Logan said and gave a small smile in return.

Kat laughed. "Who knows what I'll get up to here on out?"

Behind them, footsteps clunked up the deck: Felix Balmer, carrying a small ledger under his arm. The swordsman-turned-lieutenant had been assigned to coordinate open routes of trade and security. He had a good mind for diplomacy, his personality being inoffensive to a fault. He'd proven adept at convincing smaller enclaves to trust the allied forces, bridging gaps between humans and the newly integrated Faelves. He had even managed to negotiate trade deals with some Dorves.

He gave Logan and Kat a quick greeting before surveying the farmland himself.

"Never thought I'd see a day like this," he remarked. "We've got caravans from three different enclaves meeting here tomorrow, each bringing goods. No one is suspicious or armed."

Kat snorted a laugh. "That won't last. You know how people are when they lack a common enemy."

Logan scoffed. "Maybe. But let's enjoy it while it lasts."

"Ever the optimist," Kat said.

Balmer smiled, flipping his ledger open. "We're setting up a small festival tomorrow. A feast to commemorate the fields being declared safe. Ryan's group is already planning some fancy performance." He scanned the horizon, likely noting where tents might be pitched. "Where's Logan on the schedule? We need our hero in top shape for the unveiling."

"Still with the hero bit," Logan grunted, mouth twisting.

Kat patted him on the shoulder. "We'd all be ash now if not for you and your father. Don't downplay it. You're the reason these folks feel safe enough to plant seeds."

Balmer nodded in agreement, then noticed he was still holding the ledger. "Well, the schedule is flexible, but we want you to help with the memorial unveiling. It's mostly Freya's plan, but you're part of it."

Logan sighed softly. "Right, right. I'll be there."

A hush settled between them as they all remembered who that memorial was ultimately for. Malcolm's name, once reviled or feared, would now be honored. The father whose final decision had purged Levemoth from the world. The man who had made the ultimate sacrifice.

If I'm a hero, what does that make him?

[A good father.]

"An excellent one," Logan muttered. "Be that as it may, I'll make sure people will remember him."

Balmer watched Logan with measured sympathy. "We'll leave you to it, then." He flicked a glance at Kat, who gave a small nod, and the two left Logan to his thoughts, descending the ladder that ran toward the Ark's middeck.

Logan lingered, letting the breeze ruffle his hair. The Ark hummed steadily; they now had abundant energy. All of the Numa in the world was uncorrupted again, free to use for creation. And the Groloin had gotten what they had wanted. They even treated Logan with respect, which was great. They said they likely wouldn't linger forever in their hivemind orb. They would weigh their options. Perhaps develop into a life form or simply unplug. They hadn't decided. But for now they were fully compliant, exceedingly grateful to humans and Logan for exacting their vengeance.

What a hateful little hivemind.

But Logan got it. He hated Levemoth too. And if another one had the foolish misfortune of descending on this planet by the bidding of its mysterious dark master, Logan would be ready. He wouldn't give another monster even the slightest chance. There might be peace now, but Logan would prepare for war.

[You are allowed to enjoy your victory, you know.]

"I used to be really good at enjoying," Logan said. "I've become a bit of a worrywart. Too much time with Balmer."

[Your position has forced you to contemplate the future. It is not a bad thing.]

"We'll see what position I'll take up next. But whatever it is, I'm glad I have you with me."

[Likewise. Although now that there is a chance for it, I would prefer some autonomy. Yes, the Groloin golems are nice but—]

"Yes, I'll craft you a super-powerful darkmetal android."

[That is all I ever wanted.]

"Such small dreams," Logan said and laughed.

Their planet was saved, yet the cost had been incalculable. He closed his eyes, the memory of Malcolm's last stand flickering behind his eyelids. Even weeks later, that moment felt fresh—his father dissolving in white-blue light, his essence striking Levemoth, mortally wounding it. That hard image of sacrifice and war would never leave Logan's mind.

Nevertheless, he opened his eyes to the bright day, exhaling slowly. "Free," he murmured to Tumor. "The planet is free."

By noon, the Ark descended into the clearing, letting ramps down so workers could offload building supplies, fresh produce, and crates of provisions. Logan joined the effort without complaint, hauling heavy boxes in his exosuit. The farmland needed every resource it could get, especially after so many had been displaced.

Meanwhile, Snoff supervised from atop a tall crate. The diminutive Faelf captained a new combined faction of Faelf builders and human volunteers. He was no king yet, but Logan would make sure it'd happen.

Some of the humans smirked at Snoff's squeaky voice, but they obeyed. Despite his comedic overtones, Snoff had gained respect due to his earnest leadership in the final siege. He had proved that someone knee-high could have a heart larger than most men. Everyone still remembered their own fear, and those who had risen above that fear in the final showdown were respected beyond measure.

Logan set down a crate near one of Snoff's people. He recognized it to be darkmetal. Logan's greed for crafting awoke immediately, but he stifled it for now. Darkmetal would be abundant, once they got their explorers fully exploring the old ruins. Freed from Levemoth's corruption, old ruins were relatively safe, offering precious Numa and darkmetal with which to build the great city Logan and Snoff dreamed of.

What will I even craft? Elevators? How mundane.

By mid-afternoon, the clearing had become the site of a lively hub: caravans from outlying settlements arrived, illusion-lights danced around the trees, and a small stage was assembled for the memorial. On the far side, cooks set up stalls, stirring pots of stew or sizzling strips of salted meat. Children laughed as illusion-lanterns drifted overhead like colorful soap bubbles. The gloom that once overshadowed the planet felt distant indeed.

Freya came to the site with a bunch of her Faelf friends carrying freshly baked goods in softly steaming baskets. She was clad in a light cloak, embroidered with patterns reminiscent of Faelf artistry: swirling lines of green and blue. A small group of Faelves trailed in her wake, laughing and swinging their baskets.

Spotting Logan among the workers, she approached with a tired but radiant smile. "They're expecting us for the official unveiling at sundown," she said gently. Beneath her usual composure, he sensed a quiet flutter of nerves—she had orchestrated this entire memorial, determined to honor the one who had, in the end, chosen redemption. But she was still bad with crowds.

"Don't be nervous," Logan said. "Everyone loves you."

"They love *you*," Freya said. "I'm just the first lady."

"Nonsense," Logan said and took a bite of the warm apple pie. Good god, it tasted wonderful. Logan moaned and Freya laughed.

"Hey guys!" Logan said and hoisted up the pie to the workmen. "Do you love Freya?"

A chorus of cheers and thank-yous arose, which was finished with a series of applause. Freya flushed red, but she was pleased.

"See?" Logan said, obviously pleased with himself. "They love you."

Freya laughed and sat down with Logan to enjoy lunch. Together they discussed the ceremony.

Logan nodded and wiped his hands on his trousers. "I'll be there in time. Just need to finish assembling something." He patted the top of one of the boxes, where lumps of darkmetal were hidden under a tarp.

Freya looked at the boxes curiously but said nothing. Instead, she gave him a soft look. "I'm proud of you, you know."

He paused, uncertain how to accept praise. "I haven't done all that much these weeks."

She scoffed gently. "Don't downplay it. You've become the face of hope for a great tomorrow." She hovered a moment, illusions swirling, then reached up to brush dust from Logan's cheek. "If they love me, they truly adore you. And you've earned it. Enjoy it."

Logan's chest fluttered. He managed a gentle smile, placing his hand over hers for a moment of quiet connection. "Thank you," he said, sincerely.

As the afternoon slipped toward dusk, Logan made his way to his workshop on the Ark. It was still the same messy little area it had always been. He'd upgrade eventually but, no longer needing to construct weapons en masse, Logan found he didn't use his workshop that much lately, other than for some personal projects.

Like this one.

He removed the lumps of darkmetal from the crate, setting them on the table. He had saved these pieces for this purpose. The precious metal would build a monument.

Logan had toyed with sketches for days—a sculpture shaped like a phoenix or bird in flight, an emblem of rising from ashes.

A second chance. A chance to be reborn.

Now, with a few hours before the memorial, he would transform those sketches into reality. Malcolm Specter would not have appreciated the wasteful use of such a rare resource—too practical a mind for artistry.

Logan smirked to himself.

To hell with what he would have thought.

He didn't want any instruction from Tumor. He worked by hand, using the image in his mind. Transmuting the metal to the right shapes and proportions felt just *right*. Like he was in the right place at the right time.

Two hours passed in a swirl of focus. Logan barely noticed the sun in the window sinking below the horizon, painting the sky in streaks of orange and pink. But finally, his creation was done.

It was large enough to occupy a chair, basically the size of a large bust. Logan would place it on the top of a pillar. He admired the artwork he'd made. The bird's wings spread in a triumphant flare. Light glinted off its surface in an incandescent sheen, as Logan had enchanted it with a faint shimmer. The tail swept upward, as if lifting from the ashes.

Logan exhaled. It would do.

The sun had fully set by the time Logan arrived. Lanterns replaced the daylight. In addition, Faelves conjured floating orbs that hovered around a central platform. The air hummed with quiet conversation. A crowd had gathered in a semicircle. Freya was on the platform, holding the people captured in a speech.

She wore a calm, solemn expression, eyes scanning the crowd, and she spoke as if to a group of friends. Behind her, a low stone pedestal had been placed. On it was a pillar of fine marble, five feet tall, two feet thick.

You'll get a nice perch to look down on people.

Logan read the text on a plaque etched into the pillar—Freya's choice of words:

In memory of Malcolm Specter, who died so that we might live.

A hush fell as people noticed Logan's arrival.

He joined Freya when she finished the speech, and people applauded. She beamed at the crowd. When she noticed Logan, she offered a soft, encouraging nod.

Logan nodded back to her and smiled at the crowd, but he had his hands full now. Gently, with help from Freya, they set his cloth-wrapped sculpture on the top of the pillar. Unfolding the cloth, he revealed the darkmetal phoenix, wings spread as if mid-flight. People applauded again.

Ryan, standing off to the side, strummed a quiet, reverent chord on his lute. At the behest of Snoff, the illusion-lights of the Faelves brightened around the sculpture, making the phoenix glimmer in an otherworldly radiance. The monument was truly beautiful.

A collective breath rippled through the onlookers.

Freya spoke, her voice carrying both warmth and sorrow: "We gather to honor the one who, in his final moments, opposed Levemoth's tyranny. Without Malcolm's sacrifice, evil would not have been defeated. Our world would still be strangled by the Devourer's presence." She lightly touched the plaque. "We recognize that redemption is never too late, and that even the darkest path can lead to a single moment of light strong enough to change fate. We believe in second chances."

Silence spread once more. A few in the audience bowed their heads. Appleton pressed a hand to his chest, tears in his eyes. Balmer and Kat stood side by side, expressions calm and respectful. Snoff removed his helmet, illusions trembling around his squeaky ears. Lastly, Ryan put down his lute and paid his respects. He leaned forward on his cane, gazing at the plaque with pensive sadness.

Then the crowd shifted its focus to Logan. Freya gave him an encouraging look. He swallowed, stepping forward.

"I forged this sculpture," he began quietly, voice trembling for a moment, "to immortalize my father. He was that kind of a man . . ."

There was an awkward silence from the crowd, but when Logan looked, they had encouraging smiles on their faces.

"What a shit way to start a eulogy," he said, louder this time and it evoked laughter. "What I mean to say is that he deserves to be immortalized. He was a great man. A man of tremendous will, and that allowed him to do great things. Many awful things, for sure. My father was not a perfect man. But when push came to shove, when it really mattered, he came through." He set a trembling hand on the phoenix's hammered wing. "This sculpture is my way of saying that no matter how dark things get, we can choose to burn away our failings and step into the light—even if it costs everything. And because he made that choice, we can all make that choice."

His words hung in the air. He bowed his head, stepping back. Ryan's gentle lute chord continued, and the illusions of the Faelves formed soft, glistening shapes overhead that resembled wings of light, echoing the sculpture's form.

"I guess what I want to say is that we should never forget the sacrifices and bravery that peace requires. We will now lack a common enemy. We will start fighting with each other, and we will get lazy and complacent. And that will allow evil a chance. Do not forget the price of destroying evil. Do not forget my father. Thank you for listening. Now, go drink and eat, damn you."

A moment later, the illusion-lights intensified, then slowly dimmed, leaving the quiet glow of lanterns and torches. The applause erupted, and Logan bowed.

With the official ceremony now over, the gathering became less formal. Several people came forward to offer quiet condolences or words of respect to Logan, though he only nodded, rarely speaking.

Eventually, the group dispersed, letting the plaque stand in the open air, the phoenix gleaming at its side. Logan stood looking at it for a long time. Freya came to him and placed a hand on Logan's arm. "Well done," she whispered.

Logan gave her a little smile. "Thank you," he replied softly, feeling a weight lift from his chest.

Logan was pleased. He had commemorated his father—not as a monster, nor as a savior, but as he had been: a flawed man who found redemption in the final hour. Something they all could aspire toward.

The festival wore on into the evening. Lanterns glowed among the trees, and illusion-lights formed swirling patterns in the night sky. Children ran and laughed between the stalls, enthralled by illusions shaped like dancing animals or floating orbs that popped in bursts of color. Musicians—Ryan among them—took the stage with his band to play for entertainment.

At one side, Snoff engaged in a lively discussion with a group of his followers, explaining how humans and Faelves might combine illusions and mechanical engineering. The diminutive commander hammered out guidelines for factories and organizations. The others listened intently, caught up in the excitement of forging something new. Logan smiled at it all.

Kat and Balmer strolled through the rows of tents, holding hands, laughing and drinking. A swirl of camaraderie spanned the clearing, reflecting myriad species working in unison.

Central to all this movement stood the plaque and the phoenix sculpture on its marble pillar. Logan noticed that curious onlookers would step forward to read the inscription, whisper to each other in respectful tones, then wander back to the festival. Some left small tokens—flowers, ribbons, or scraps of paper inscribed with prayers—ringing the pedestal.

Watching from a short distance away, Logan felt a stir of emotion. *Happiness.* He'd never pictured such a scene. His father's name, once feared or hated, now receiving genuine tributes. He wondered if Malcolm's spirit saw this from whatever corner of the afterlife he occupied.

A cool wind brushed Logan's hair. He turned to see Freya. Her eyes sparkled in the torchlit gloom.

"Come," she said softly, extending her hand. "Dance with me, love."

Logan took it without question, letting her guide him through the festival. They wove between stalls and clusters of survivors, eventually ending next to the platform on which Ryan and his group were playing.

Just then, the music transitioned into a somber melody.

The two of them danced slowly and intimately in the flicker of fire. Logan leaned in and smelled her hair. She was so soft, so warm, so wonderful. Logan realized he and Freya had a full life ahead of them. They had been married by the Numa Spirit Goddess, but Logan had been too busy at the time to really process what it meant.

"Wife," Logan murmured.

"Husband," Freya whispered and kissed his neck.

"I'll learn to be that childish, joyful fool again you once fell in love with."

"Mmmm, I did like that Logan," Freya said. "But I like this one better. This Logan is a real-ass man who gets shit done."

Logan chuckled.

"But I wouldn't mind you finding that spark again."

"I will," Logan said. "Now I'll have all the time in the world."

"Good. Let's start now," Freya said and unentangled herself. "Ryan, play something fun!"

Ryan smiled and bowed to Freya. Then he flipped his hair back and ripped on his guitar, guiding the band in a merry medley of happy tunes.

Freya smiled invitingly and started moving her hips, Logan responded in kind, and they spun and danced and enjoyed themselves until their legs were sore and they were out of breath. Logan felt genuine sparks of joy inside him. He knew he would heal.

Later that night, Logan and Freya had escaped the festivities to go look at the stars by just the two of them.

On the Ark's top deck, the night sky opened up in a sprawl of stars. The slight hum of the ship blended with the distant laughter. Logan looked around, seeing no one else up here at the moment. The deck was quiet, lit only by the stars and the moon.

Logan gazed at the distant horizon. Even at night, he could discern a transformation: the farmland was dotted with gentle torches, scattered wagons, rows of new seedlings. The once-gutted fortress-camp was being rebuilt into a permanent settlement to trade and refine the loot from the old capital of the First Folk. The black corruption of Levemoth's presence was gone, replaced by a broad sky dusted with stars.

"It's so peaceful," Logan admitted, leaning on the rail. "Hard to believe we fought that cosmic abomination here."

"Yes," she whispered. "We did. And we won. *You* won."

Logan reached for Freya's hand, lacing hers in his. "We survived together. That's what matters. Now I can put ten babies in you."

"Okay, calm down, stallion," Freya said and laughed.

"Don't say you haven't thought about it," Logan said and nudged her softly.

"I have," Freya whispered. "Every day since you mentioned it. But one at a time, yeah?"

"You'll be a great mother," Logan said.

A gentle hush settled. Down below, the festival carried on, but here on the deck, stillness reigned.

Freya shifted, glancing at Logan. She paused to think and then spoke. "Do you have any regrets?"

Logan looked ahead into the tree line and horizon. "I was ready to die that day."

"I resented you for it," Freya admitted.

"I know," Logan said.

"But in that moment my respect for you also grew in ways I couldn't have possibly imagined," Freya said. "Try living with that conflict."

Logan kissed her on the forehead. "I don't have regrets. It's just not my style. I don't look back."

She nodded. "And what about the future?"

"I already told you. Ten babies."

Freya nudged him in the ribs.

"Okay, seven."

Another nudge.

"Let's start with three."

Freya smiled. "I think I could handle that."

"As for other things," Logan said. "Dreaming is exactly what we need. I'm not sure how I can apply myself yet. I have this skill set that my father instilled in me. And I have this ability to create things. I'll have to think on how I can combine the two."

"Looking forward to seeing Logan the Great Settler leave his mark on history."

"And his beautiful wife with three talented and happy children."

They giggled and kissed, before lapsing into a companionable silence. Beneath them, the Ark's deck subtly vibrated from the illusions-engine, the gentle thrum rocking them like a cradle. Freya slid an arm around Logan's waist, leaning her head on his shoulder. He wrapped an arm around her, pulse slowing as he let the calm settle in.

Below, he heard faint cheers—likely someone dancing or singing near the memorial. He imagined the plaque in the center of the clearing, near that darkmetal phoenix rising on proud wings. It comforted him to think that Malcolm's memory was enshrined with dignity. A name that had once been linked with fear had now become a story of redemption.

Minutes passed. The sky darkened further, unveiling even more stars, a crystalline dome overhead. A gentle breeze carried the scents of grassy fields and woodsmoke. The festival wore on with quiet joy, music swirling faintly in the distance.

Logan sighed, letting tension waft out of him. He cast his gaze upward, imagining Malcolm's spirit somewhere among those stars. Maybe his father was free at last, unburdened by regrets. Maybe even looking down at Logan with pride.

Turning his face to Freya, Logan pressed a small kiss to her temple. She responded by tightening her arm around him.

"Thank you, Dad," Logan whispered. Even after everything, the gratitude emerged, sure and steady. He repeated it, letting the words float off on the wind, up into that star-filled sky. For all his father's failings, he had saved them with his last breath.

Freya glanced up at him, illusions dancing around her luminous eyes. She didn't ask for explanations—she understood.

Logan gazed back out over the horizon. He could see gentle lights dotting the farmland, a sign of hundreds of lives reunited under the open sky.

The planet breathed free, unchained from the great evil's hold. What tomorrow might bring—be it peace or new challenges—felt wide open. But for now, as the festival's lullabies drifted on the wind, Logan simply stood on the Ark's deck, arm-in-arm with Freya, heart brimming with equal parts sadness and hope. But hope was growing.

One final gust ruffled Logan's hair. He inhaled the cool air, feeling the warmth of Freya's closeness. Then he let the moment settle into memory, etched as a testament to triumph and sacrifice. The Clarion was long gone, but the echo of its final note lived on in every thriving seed, every hopeful gaze.

A slow, steady grin curled across Logan's lips. He realized he could breathe easy—not just tonight but from now on. That would take some time getting used to. But it was good. Peace was good. Even the price they had paid felt justified.

Beneath them, the Ark hummed gently, no longer a battered war machine but a herald of hope. They had only begun rewriting the story of this world—one hammered by sorrow and tempered by sacrifice, a story that might yet blaze with wonder.

In the hush of the starlit deck, Logan found himself whispering, "Here's to tomorrow."

"And beyond," she agreed.

Together, they watched as the festival lights danced below, shaping shadows that flickered across the plaza, across the newly placed plaque and the phoenix sculpture. A hush of devotion fell over onlookers paying respects. In that hush, Logan pictured Malcolm's ghostly silhouette, smiling with hard-won pride.

For the first time in weeks, Logan felt a sense of heartfelt peace. No pain, anger, worry, or any negative emotion weighed him down. There would always be a father-shaped ache in his chest, but it no longer festered with unresolved anger. Logan Specter felt complete.

Logan stroked a thumb across Freya's palm, then turned his gaze back to the sky. A new wind carried the faintest hint of pine and night-blooming flowers.

He thought of his future children who'd grow up never knowing Levemoth's curse and wondered what classes they would get. Freed from the cosmic horror, they could experiment with illusions, engineering, healing arts, or find synergies Logan couldn't even imagine. He would teach them and provide them with every resource. The thought thrilled him.

Logan turned to Freya. "Come on. Let's get back there and dance some more."

Freya turned to him with a happy grin. "I'd love that."

And so they returned to the festival, eventually settling beside a cheerful bonfire where Ryan played a lively tune, illusions dancing in colored fractals above the flames. Laughter abounded. People told jokes, swapped stories of close calls, or planned their next expansions into fields that had been dangerous for so long. A new dawn was rising on this planet, bringing with it hope and dreams of future.

Logan Specter was complete.

About the Author

Wilbur Woods is an entertainer, coffee drinker, and story eater, as well as the author of the Cosmic Games series, originally released on Royal Road. He has loved stories since he was a kid, and when he asked himself what he really wanted to do, the answer was simple: write.